The
CHAI
FACTOR

The CHAI FACTOR

FARAH HERON

HARPER**AVENUE**

The Chai Factor
Copyright © 2019 by Farah Heron.
All rights reserved.

Published by Harper Avenue, an imprint of HarperCollins Publishers Ltd

First edition

HarperCollins books may be purchased for educational, business,
or sales promotional use through our Special Markets Department.

HarperCollins Publishers Ltd
Bay Adelaide Centre, East Tower
22 Adelaide Street West, 41st Floor
Toronto, Ontario, Canada
M5H 4E3

www.harpercollins.ca

Interior book design by Lola Landekic

Library and Archives Canada Cataloguing in Publication
information is available upon request.

ISBN 978-1-4434-5764-4

Printed and bound in the United States

LSC/H 9 8 7 6 5 4 3 2 1

For Khalil and Anissa. The light within you is
bright enough to illuminate the darkness in the world.
Also, please clean your rooms.

The
CHAI
FACTOR

CHAPTER ONE

IF THERE WERE a Sufi saint who protected single women travellers, Amira Khan was sure she had royally pissed her off at some point in a previous life.

The last time Amira travelled alone, she'd been unceremoniously escorted out of the security clearance area of the Toronto airport, blocked from boarding her flight to Philadelphia. Nothing like that could happen now—this was a train, and there was no border crossing between the small city where she went to grad school and Toronto. No border meant no overzealous guards accusing her of terrorism because of her last name and fondness for Arabic calligraphy. But as her train appeared to be stuck in some place called Port Hope, and as a creepy man wearing silver pants appeared to be studying her, Amira clearly couldn't quite trust any deity to help her reach her destination unscathed.

She peeked at the creep. It wasn't his silvery-grey pants or his black shirt opened a button too far that was making the hair on her neck stand on end, but rather the man's intense focus. Amira sank in her seat, hoping to hide from him. She hated travelling alone. She'd left her grad school campus early partly because of overly forward members of the male species—only to now get stuck on an almost-empty train car with one.

Finally, the doors slid open for new passengers. Good. More people meant more protection should things get hairy with the locomotive libertine. She turned to look. Only one boarded and, holy hell, did he stand out. A tall man with an orangey-red beard, he had facial hair that was accessorized with a plaid flannel shirt and black suspenders, resulting in a look that some might call hipster, but Amira could only describe it as garden-gnome chic.

Sauntering down the aisle, he bobbed his head to whatever was playing through his earbuds—she guessed either Southern rock or "new" country. Yup. Either a hipster or a hick. She hoped that, whatever he was, he would keep on walking past the three empty seats in her section, as she was not in the mood for small talk. His long legs strolled by and settled into the window seat diagonal to Mr. Silver Pants. Good. Maybe with the lumberjack watching him, the libertine would stop drooling so openly.

The doors shut, but the train stood still, holding at the Port Hope station. She checked the time. By her estimation, they had been waiting in Port Hope for fifteen minutes now. This wasn't how her day was supposed to progress.

Amira had made the decision to come home early on impulse, after desperately trying to write her final project report in her dorm room while the undergrads in the common room loudly played something called Fizz, Buzz, Woof, which, from what she could tell, was a drinking game based on long division. At thirty years old, dorm living wasn't ideal, but it was all she could afford. And she didn't really blame the undergrads. She was once young and stupid herself. Arguably stupider.

But thankfully, she was almost done grad school. She had worked so hard, and the final home stretch felt so good. Her report was due to her adviser in two weeks, and she had one more meeting on campus a week later. After two crazy-hard years of work, she would be granted her master of engineering in June. She would then return to her consultant job at one of the city's biggest engineering firms, and those new letters after her name would hopefully mean a promotion within two years. Everything was falling into place. What could possibly go wrong at this point?

"Attention, passengers," the loudspeaker on the train crackled, "due to mechanical problems, all passengers are asked to disembark at this time. A replacement train is en route and will arrive shortly. We apologize for the inconvenience."

Amira groaned. Of course. Life always snuck in to kick her in the ass whenever she grew too smug.

The Port Hope train station was tiny. And old. And hot. Not much more than a small one-room heritage building with arched windows and a wide roof overhang. And with the hundred or so people from the train inside and outside the tiny stone building, it was now very crowded. Amira wedged herself in the corner of the room and tried to blend in.

"This is very bad luck, isn't it?" a thin voice behind her said. She turned. Crap. Silver Pants had found her. His facial expression did not improve with the closer vantage point. And he smelled overwhelmingly of too much cologne.

"Hmm . . ." She turned away, looking out the window, hoping he would take the hint.

"Are you from India?" he asked.

Amira's jaw clenched as she turned back to him. His brown skin was just a hair lighter than her own, and while his English seemed fluent, his accent sounded like he could have arrived only yesterday from somewhere on the Indian subcontinent.

"No," she answered.

"Pakistan then? Bangladesh?"

"I'm Indian-Canadian," she deadpanned.

He stepped closer. In the crowded station, it was barely noticeable that he had invaded her personal space, but Amira still tensed. Her eyes looked for an escape as his pants skimmed the full skirt of her dress. She needed to get out of this place.

What the hell had she been thinking when she dressed this morning? It would be near impossible to bolt or to kick the man in his iridescent pants wearing this dress and high-heeled ankle boots. She'd dressed up for her trip home—celebrating, in a way, her transition back into real life. And in her real life as an engineering consultant, tailored suits, or blouses and skirts, were Amira's armour, not the sweats and hoodies of grad school.

But now, she wished she had her sweats back. Or at least jeans.

"You like Hindi songs?" the creep asked. "I sing in a Bollywood music group in Toronto."

He stepped half a pace closer, his hand inching towards the hem of her dress. Leaning into her neck, he spoke softly. "I heard Canadian girls don't wear underwear . . ."

She froze, bile rising to her throat.

"There you are, babe," a loud, husky voice next to her said. "Couldn't find you on the train."

She turned to see the red-bearded man standing in her personal space. Up close, the garden gnome was bigger than he had seemed on the train. Bigger and more . . . everything. Hairier. Stronger-looking. And actually very handsome. His voice was deep, and although it was friendly, his eyes were intense, almost angry. And really bright green.

Amira clutched her bag. With a wall on one side of her, Brawny paper-towel dude on the other, and Mr. Sexual Harassment in front of her, she had nowhere to escape. One step forward and she would be pressed against Silver Pants, and one step sideways would put the garden gnome on her ass . . .

She bristled, taking a half step backwards and hitting the heel of her boot on the stone wall. The last thing she needed was these two boneheads competing over her.

"This your boyfriend?" Silver Pants asked.

Why wasn't her mouth working? In an hour, she would no doubt have a biting comeback on her lips that would've sent both guys packing, but in this moment, she was frozen.

"Yes," the garden gnome responded, placing his hand on her shoulder. It was warm and solid through the thick fabric of her denim jacket, but she still stiffened. She glared at the gnome, but he held firmly on to her, his bright-green eyes glaring back.

Despite the stereotypes of engineers being socially clueless, Amira liked to think she understood human nature pretty well. Especially male human nature. As a woman in a STEM field, she was usually surrounded by more testosterone than at a NASCAR rally. So, she *did* understand what was happening here. The lumberjack clearly had seen Amira's panicked expression when the creep approached her. He was acting chivalrous. He decided the poor, single woman in the train station was in danger, and it was up to him to sweep in to her rescue like some sort of garden-gnome superhero. And while Amira's logical brain told her to be grateful for the save, her anger did what it always did and silenced her logic. So, she couldn't find it within herself to feel any kind thoughts for her saviour. There were countless other things he could have done instead of pretending to be her boyfriend. He could have told the other guy to fuck off. He could have alerted the train staff about the harassment. He could have done any number of things that didn't involve touching her and claiming her as his own.

Predictably, though, the lumberjack's strategy worked. Despite his gnome-like attire, there was no denying he was a big man. A burly man. A man who could probably crush the creep with nothing but the heavy hand still perched on her shoulder. A small wave of terror passed over Silver Pants's face as he took two steps back. He eyed Amira suspiciously. The hand on her shoulder tightened.

"My apologies," Silver Pants said, inching away, before retreating to lick his wounds. Yuck.

CHAPTER TWO

THE MOMENT HER harasser was out of sight, Amira wormed free of the garden gnome's grip and glared at him.

"I don't need to be rescued," she said through gritted teeth. The last thing she wanted was more attention.

"Sure looked like you did." He grinned as he rocked back on his heels. "That guy was a snake. He would *not* have left you alone."

Amira stood taller to face down her noble saviour. It didn't do much good—the lumberjack had at least six inches on her. She bit her lip, keenly aware of two things: One, she was alone in the middle of nowhere and surrounded by strangers. And two, things might have gotten ugly fast if Paul Bunyan here hadn't intervened. Did he expect her to fawn over him now?

Paul Bunyan smiled again. Dude needed an axe or a wheelbarrow to really pull off this look, but she had to admit he did have a warm smile. "Duncan Galahad," he drawled as he shot his hand out, expecting her to shake it.

She didn't. Instead, she raised one eyebrow. "Galahad?" Her unwanted rescuer's name was Galahad?

"Yup, it's my real name. Originally, my great-granddaddy was called Gallagher, but the ship from Ireland apparently had five other Gallaghers on it, so he wrote "Galahad" on the ship's register. He didn't like being one of many. Big fan of Arthurian legend."

Amira crossed her arms. She should have stayed in her dorm. If she wanted to be surrounded by clueless men with false chivalry, there were plenty of awkward engineering students there to unnecessarily white-knight for her. They may not be as brawny as this guy, but . . . Amira shuddered.

This tiny one-room building felt hotter every second with the heat generated by dozens of annoyed train passengers. The soaring beamed ceilings and wood floors would have been charming in any other circumstance, but today only served to echo the irate voices and heavy footsteps. She looked out the window at the empty rails. Where was the replacement train?

"You okay?" Duncan asked.

She gifted him with her best scowl. The one that made interns cower in fear when she worked at the consulting firm. "You didn't have to tell him you're my boyfriend."

He snorted. "Yeah, I did. I know the type. He'd keep bugging you if I just told him to leave you alone. Guys like that have no respect for women, but they do respect man-code. Only way to keep him off you is to let him think you are someone else's property."

"I'm not a prize for men to fight over! I don't belong to anyone," she snapped.

"Okay, Princess Jasmine." He laughed.

"So, I'm Princess Jasmine because I'm brown?"

"No. Because of what you said. You sound like Princess Jasmine from *Aladdin*. Remember? When all the princes showed up to the palace . . . You've seen *Aladdin*, right?" He shook his head, like he couldn't imagine a grown woman not knowing everything about every Disney movie. "And anyway, I heard you tell him you were Indian. Agrabah is actually based on Iraq, not India."

Amira's mouth fell open. A big, burly lumberjack man-splaining princess movies was a new one.

"I live with my niece, she's into princesses," he explained with a wide grin that would probably charm the pants off every Disney nerd in a ten-metre radius.

Amira stared at the man a moment before shaking her head with disbelief. "Look, I don't need some mouth-breathing neck-beard who just emerged from the lumberyard to save me with grand gestures."

He snorted. "Mouth-breathing? I'll have you know my sinuses are perfectly clear." He inhaled sharply to prove his point.

Amira tried not to, but she laughed. This guy was funny. "Glad to hear it. Anyway, I am not a damsel in distress and would prefer to be alone."

He smiled faintly as he bowed with a flourish. "Of course, milady. It was kindly meant. I wish you well." He turned on his heel, and Amira watched Duncan Galahad's broad, flannel-clad back disappear into the crowd.

Finally alone, Amira pulled out her phone and called Reena, her best friend.

"What's up, Meer?"

She leaned back on the window. "What do you want to hear about first, Ree? The broken-down train? The guy who tried to put his hand up my skirt and was drenched in more dollar-store body spray than your prom date? Or maybe the unwanted rescuer named Galahad who's like a cross between a brave knight and Paul Bunyan?"

Reena laughed. "What the hell happened? I thought you were taking the bus down? Where are you?"

"Port Hope. I splurged on a train ticket, but there were technical problems. I thought the train would be more civilized. It isn't."

"Oh god, Amira. Are you stuck there?"

"No. Apparently, a new train is on its way. I should've splurged for first class."

"First class doesn't actually mean classier people."

"No, but it does mean open bar."

Reena was Amira's oldest and closest friend, and life was going to get a whole lot better once Amira was back to living in the same city as Reena. They had known each other since grade two, when tiny wide-eyed Reena nervously walked into Amira's classroom as the new transfer student. Amira had been ecstatic to have another brown girl in her class. And when Reena showed up that Friday night as the new girl in Jamatkhana, the Ismaili Muslim place of worship, Amira had found a soulmate. No one knew her like Reena did. She could always be counted on for support, but she never held back from calling Amira out on her shit. Reena had siblings, but Amira had been an only child until she was nineteen, and Reena had filled the sibling gap in her life.

She told her friend about the events of the last few hours, downplaying the situation with Silver Pants and embellishing her description of the garden gnome and his chivalrous bow. Reena had a lot going on lately and deserved a laugh.

"Green eyes and a red beard? Is the lumberjack hot?" Reena asked.

Amira thought about Duncan's strong forearms and broad back. "Picture an overgrown garden gnome with a regular gym habit."

"Brave Sir Galahad saved you from the evil villain. It's utterly romantic. The perfect meet-cute."

Amira bit her tongue. Reena was hopelessly addicted to romantic comedies and spent altogether too much time preoccupied with Amira's non-existent love life. Amira was certain it was to deflect attention away from Reena's own dating woes.

"Brave Sir Lumberjack isn't my type," Amira said. "He may not be an ass like Mr. Silver Pants, but . . . anyway, I'm not on this train to pick up men."

"It's too bad nothing happened with the guys at school. Your program was only 20 percent women. That kind of ratio should have worked in your favour."

Amira sighed. Around the time she started grad school, she gave up on choosing men solely based on, well, superficial compatibility, and had been open to finding a mature, lasting relationship. Maybe an engineer, like her. Educated. Maybe another Muslim. Maybe Indian. Someone who would watch Bollywood movies with her after the hockey game. Not that Amira watched all that much Bollywood anymore, or hockey, for that matter, but she would like the option. What better place to find an Indian than an engineering school?

But the five years off between undergrad and grad school had spoiled her appetite for dating her classmates, as living in a dorm full of brilliant, young engineering students as the "older woman" got stale fast. After the third try-hard player asked her to "teach him the ways of her sensual arts," she learned to stay in her room most of the time. Her grandmother's house, where she was returning to in Toronto, was blissfully free of men. Only her mother, grandmother, and eleven-year-old sister, Zahra, lived there.

"I have standards, Reena. Just because the men at school weren't up to snuff doesn't mean I have to nab myself a lumberjack. I'd prefer to find an Indian boyfriend."

"But didn't you say the Indian guy was a sleaze?"

"*That* Indian guy was a sleaze. You know as well as I do they're not all like Mr. Silver Pants. Let me finish school first, then I'll have all summer to find a nice man."

"Awesome. Summer project. I'll start narrowing my shortlist for you."

"Later, Reena. Three weeks."

"When you going back to work?"

"Not entirely sure yet. Apparently I have a new boss—Raymond emailed me about him. I'll call later and let them know my availability."

"Attention, passengers," the loudspeaker in the station blared. "The replacement train to Toronto is approaching. Please make your way to the platform for boarding."

"Got to go, Reena. I'll text you when I'm in town."

"Okay, I'll come over when you're home. I'm glad you're back, Meer."

"Me too. See ya."

Amira tossed her phone in her bag as a loud screech echoed through the tiny room and straight into her bones. She looked out the window to see the train rolling in. Only another hour to Toronto. Nothing else could possibly go wrong.

The new train was smaller than the one they left, and she was among the last to climb the metal stairs onto the car, so it was no surprise that many seats were already taken—she would have to sit with someone this time. And . . . of course . . . there was Mr. Silver Pants, smiling and motioning for her to sit with him. She didn't make eye contact and kept walking to the next set of empty seats.

Which, of course, was a quad of seats with only one person occupying it. And, of course, that person was Sir Garden Gnome himself. She sat heavily into the window seat directly across from him. At least from this vantage, she couldn't see the creep.

But she could see the lumberjack. Clearly. He smirked at her, the corners of his eyes wrinkled in mirth. "Milady."

"Shut up," she said under her breath.

He heard her, though. Expression still amused, he lightly ran his fingers over his beard. "So, you're not interested in polite chit-chat on the train, then, Princess?"

"I'd prefer you didn't call me that."

"Well, I didn't catch your name, so I'll have to use my own imagination."

Amira gave him a pointed look. "I've no doubt you'll think of several choice names for me. I've heard them all often enough, so don't think I'll care two hoots what you call me."

Duncan laughed, his head falling back in his seat as one leg crossed over the other, ankle meeting knee. "You're a prickly porcupine, aren't you, Princess? Teaches me to never try to help a damsel in distress."

Amira winced. Duncan was right. Questionable methodology aside, this guy *had* helped her. He saved a complete stranger from some serious harassment. She had always been adamant that bystanders have a duty to step in if they see someone being mistreated, and here she was being horrible to him for doing just that. She had let her anger at the world turn her into a bitch yet again. "I apologize for being rude earlier," she said, trying to sound sincere, "and thank you for intervening with that man."

He smiled. "It's the least I could do. Honestly, I wanted to punch the guy out, but in this day and age, a white man beating up a visible minority doesn't always go well."

"Usually worse for the minority."

"Yeah, you're probably right. Maybe we should start over. I'm Duncan." He put his hand out to shake again. This time, Amira took it and her long, slender fingers were enveloped by his wide knuckles.

She smiled. "Greetings, brave Sir Galahad. I am honoured to be the recipient of your chivalrous deeds."

He chuckled. "It is *my* honour to serve you, milady. And now, if you will excuse me,"—he gestured to the iPhone in his hand—"I have three songs to learn before tonight." He put his earbuds in and smiled, sinking in his seat and resting his head on the glass of the train window.

Fine with her—she had work to do. She pulled her iPad out of her bag. May as well get some of these journal articles read.

But hard as she tried, Amira couldn't seem to find her concentration. The train was noisy, and the couple behind her were arguing. Loudly. Amira couldn't help but overhear their squabble, and it only reignited her irritation.

Thankfully, they got up from their seats at the next stop. She scowled at the male half of the couple as they made their way down the aisle.

"What was that about, Princess?" Duncan removed his earbuds and narrowed his gaze inquisitively.

"That couple. Their argument was driving me nuts."

"You were eavesdropping?"

"They were right behind me! I couldn't help but hear. The man was pissed off that the woman invited her boss and his husband for dinner. Clearly he didn't approve of his wife working for a gay man."

"He give any other reason for not wanting the guy over?"

"Of course *you* would defend the homophobe."

"No. I wouldn't. I know you think I'm a redneck bumpkin, but believe me, I've got no problem with homosexuality. Just the opposite. But I try not to judge strangers without knowing the whole story."

Amira crossed her arms on her chest. The nerve of this man, calling her judgmental. After everything she'd been through in the last few years, she had every right to judge. She was about to tell Duncan that when he leaned over and looked down the narrow aisle.

"Actually, Princess, judge all you want. Just noticed the guy's wearing a Nickelback T-shirt."

She snort-laughed before lifting her iPad in front of her face, hopefully hiding her appreciation of his joke from him.

And the train rolled on.

This time, Duncan's music prevented Amira from concentrating on the report she should've been reading, as the sound carried even with his earbuds in. What was he listening to, anyway? Why did he have to learn songs for tonight? Was he some sort of musician? She could see it. He had that lumber-sexual look going that many musicians sported these days. Amira had once had a bit of an irrational attraction to long-haired, flamboyant musicians. She'd dated several who were convinced they were just about to hit it big, before she finally got tired of boyfriends who loved their guitars more than her. But despite her soft spot for people who made music, with Duncan, it only made him more irritating.

Was that Motown he was listening to? Sounded like it.

The man in front of her was an enigma. He might look like he just rolled off his tractor to fetch his banjo, but he knew there was a difference between Iraq and India, which is more than some of the small-town students she went to school with realized. He claimed to have no problem with gay men. And he rushed to the rescue of a brown woman being harassed by a brown man, instead of seeing it as some sort of intra-community issue that wasn't his concern. Plus, referencing Disney movies and listening to old Motown while on a train to the city? She snuck another look at him. Those eyes really were striking. Muddy green in this light, now that the sun was hiding behind clouds. But earlier, in the train station, reflected in the sun streaming through the window, they shimmered like emeralds in the desert.

Good lord, the man's eyes were inspiring poetry in her. Amira shook her head at how ridiculous she'd become. Clearly she needed more in her life than formulas and algorithms.

Duncan noticed her watching him. He nodded, a ghost of a smile evident behind his beard.

"Good book?" he asked.

"It's a research paper. Really dry. You learn your songs?"

"Almost. You know, I still didn't catch your name . . ."

Amira smiled again. "That's because I didn't give it to you." Any smart woman knew not to be forthcoming with personal information unless it was absolutely necessary.

He laughed. "Well, unless you want me to call you Princess Jasmine again, maybe it's better we don't chat too much. Don't worry, though, I'll still sit with you so that sleaze will think we're together."

She sat up straighter, frowning. "Well, you can stand down, sir. Don't do me any favours."

"It's no favour, Princess. I'm not entirely a selfless knight. You make me look good. Now, are you going to keep staring at me the rest of the way downtown? Because you're making it hard for me to concentrate on learning these songs."

Amira made a split-second decision right there and then. Nice eyes or not, she did not like this Duncan Galahad. Not one bit.

"Whatever," she said, turning off her iPad and looking out the window.

The rest of the train ride was blissfully silent. Amira read a bit, texted with Reena a bit, and did her best to ignore the impressive physique filling her entire field of vision whenever she looked in front of her. Who designed these seats, anyway? Who wants to look at someone's face while travelling? Thankfully, Duncan gazed out the window at the urban landscape rolling by, earbuds in, learning his Motown songs while tapping out beats on his leg.

When the train reached Toronto, he tipped an imaginary hat at her and left without a word. Fine. She was glad she would never see him again. And a quick peek before she slid out of her seat confirmed that Mr. Silver Pants had left, too. Even better. Maybe today was finally looking up.

CHAPTER THREE

AMIRA'S PHONE RANG the second she stepped off the train. She fumbled to find it, dropping her backpack and nearly sending her laptop flying. "Hello," she answered, out of breath.

"Hi, is this Amira Khan?" The voice was unfamiliar.

"Yes."

"My name's Christopher Petersen, and I'm doing an article for *Maple* magazine about the uptick in Islamophobia north of the border. I was wondering if you'd answer some questions about the incident last year when you were prevented entry into the US?"

Fuck. Still? Vultures needed to leave her alone. It had been well over a year now.

Her jaw clenched. "No."

"Pardon me?"

"No, I will *not* answer any questions. I've done several interviews on this topic and I'd like to put it behind me. And I do not give permission for you to use my name in the article either. I would prefer you didn't write it at all, but I'm sure a Muslim's opinion on that has no merit for you."

"Really?"

"Yes, really."

"I would think you'd want to raise awareness, to speak out against what happened to you on behalf of your community."

"I don't represent my community."

"I'm not sure if you've heard, but a woman was assaulted on the subway yesterday coming home from work. Her hijab was torn off. These incidents are becoming more common, even in liberal enclaves. I found some archived articles you wrote before your incident, and I was hoping you would clarify—"

"No. Mr. Petersen, I would not. And the media talking about this all the time isn't helping. People who disagree with you politically think hate is okay, because *you* are turning it into a political issue instead of a human one."

"Can I quote you on that?"

"No. Don't call me again." She hung up. Jaw still clenched, Amira dropped her phone in her bag and organized herself before heading off the platform. She couldn't think about that right now.

The giant maze of hallways and escalators of Toronto's Union Station was a nightmare to navigate on the best of days, but in the early hours of the evening rush, it was a sea of people as well. Amira was in no mood to fight the crowd, so she found a Starbucks and ordered an iced macchiato. She would wait out the crush before she had to brave the subway system.

She dug through her bag to find her phone again so she could call her mentor at work, Raymond, to let him know she was back in town.

"Hi, Raymond."

"Amira! Nice to hear from you. How are your courses going?"

"Pretty good. I've only got the report for my project left. I'm back in town. I decided to finish it here in Toronto."

"Wonderful news. And welcome home."

"Listen, Raymond, you said there's a new manager in our division? I'd like to speak to him about coming back to work."

"Jim Prescott. He transferred from the London office four months ago. He's overseeing manufacturing and automation. Are you still planning to come back after school's done?"

"That's the idea. I'll call him to set up a meeting about my return."

"Jim's great. You'll love working for him. How's the report going?"

"To be honest, I wish I were further ahead. I switched projects halfway through so I'm playing catch-up."

Amira's master's program was project based, meaning instead of a final thesis, her degree was dependent on the completion of a lab project demonstrating the practical applications of her knowledge. Her project had originally been about utilizing intelligent modelling techniques in computer-integrated manufacturing, but for the sake of her mental health, she abandoned it and found a new project. She just hadn't felt like she was cutting it there. It had been a competitive placement, and the other students working with that professor were at the top of their class. After one too many anxiety attacks when she was convinced she knew absolutely nothing about engineering, she asked her adviser for a transfer. Needless to say, it had been a stressful couple of months.

Despite what she told Raymond, her failure to start the written portion of her project wasn't a timing issue. In reality, her confidence had been so shattered after the mess of starting the project over that she wasn't able to sink into the complex part of her analysis while working in the lab. Amira worked very hard at school—but it had never come easy for her. Her algorithms and complex codes always seemed to take longer than her classmates', and solutions didn't materialize spontaneously like they seemed to for others. Abandoning her initial project only seemed to fuel her feelings of inadequacy about her abilities. Her classmates managed to thrive in their projects. Why couldn't she make it work? But admitting that inadequacy was digging deeper than she wanted to right now with Raymond. To be honest, she hadn't really discussed those feelings with anyone.

"I'm sure it will be fine, Amira. If you'd like, I can take a look at your report before you submit it. An extra set of eyes may help put your mind at ease."

"Raymond, that would be amazing. Thank you so much."

"It's no problem. I'm happy to help you. I'll email you Jim's contact information so you can set up a meeting. Anyway, I have a late visit to the Regent plant project. We'll talk soon."

Amira disconnected with a smile. Raymond was a senior engineer and team lead at Hyde Industrial, the consulting agency she had worked at for four years before grad school. After a few years of friendship, Amira had asked Raymond to be her professional mentor. She wasn't usually one to ask for help with her career, but Raymond was so generous with his time and advice. Amira's own father was also an industrial engineer and was highly respected in the field. But like most Indian fathers, he collected Amira's achievements like priceless gems, polishing and presenting them to his friends as proudly as if they were his own. Amira loved her father, and his support and encouragement meant the world to her, but she needed a bit of distance between him and her career. She didn't want to disappoint him and wasn't sure she wanted him knowing how much she struggled. Raymond's guidance meant she didn't have to rely on her father, or upset him.

Feeling better, Amira dialled her mother's number. She hadn't told her mum yet that she'd left school early, since it had been too late last night when she decided. Amira's mother was a pediatric nurse in a hospital and tended to work early shifts. Amira knew better than to call her late at night.

"What do you mean, you came home early? You still have two more weeks of school!" her mother said after Amira told her she was in Toronto.

"It was a last-minute decision. It's way too noisy in the dorm, and I can't focus on my work. I don't have classes anymore, just this project report."

"What about all your things?"

"I have to go back to meet with my academic adviser after the paper is in. Reena's taking the day off to drive me, and we'll pack up my dorm room then. I don't have much there."

"I wish you'd told us, Amira. Nanima has let out the rooms in the basement."

"What?"

"The basement apartment. She's rented it."

"But I live in the basement apartment!"

Amira, her mother, and her little sister, Zahra, had lived in her grandmother's house for eight years now, since her parents divorced and sold the house where she grew up. Zahra

had been three at the time, and Mum and Dad had thankfully figured out that having a second child almost twenty
years after their first hadn't saved the marriage as intended.
And even though she missed seeing her father regularly, she
had still been glad when they split. They were both amazing
people who brought out the absolute worst in each other.

"I know," her mother said. "But there are two other bedrooms in the basement, and she rented them out. Like Airbnb,
for a little extra money. You know she's on a fixed income.
And it's only until you're home from school."

"Mum, I'm home now. I'll be there in an hour."

"We didn't know that. I'm sorry, I can't tell them to leave
now. They've paid for two weeks. It's not our house, honey."

"But . . ." Amira stopped herself. There really was no point
in arguing—it was a privilege to be able to live in that house.
Mum paid Nanima rent, but nowhere near market value.
And no one asked Amira to contribute. She paid for grad
school with the money she saved by living there rent free for
years while working full time. Housing in decent neighbour-
hoods in the city was scarce and pricey, and even with her
nursing salary, her mother wouldn't have been able to afford
a decent place close to the hospital without Nanima's help.
And Nanima had been toying with the idea of renting out her
extra rooms for some time now. Amira couldn't expect those
rooms to stay empty forever.

This wasn't good. She had just left the dorm because she
didn't want to live with people.

"Who'd she rent to, anyway?"

"I don't know. I was out last night when they moved
in, and I worked early today. It's someone Nanima knows

through her cooking committee. Did you hear she's been made chairperson? She's at Jamatkhana cooking with those women every day, it feels like."

"Who are they doing all that cooking for?"

"Catering for events in the community. Weddings, funerals, that sort of thing. And they make food for the less fortunate. It's admirable service, but all of them together so much . . . I'm sure they gossip more than they stuff samosas. Anyway, it'll be fine, honey. You can work on your paper in your room."

Amira didn't see how this could possibly be fine.

"Okay, Mum, I'll figure something out. I think I'll get some work in at the library instead of coming home now. Unless you want me watch Zahra tonight. Are you still at work?"

"No. I'm home for the rest of the day. Try and get here before bedtime, though. Your sister will be happy to see you."

Amira's shoulders slumped forward as she rubbed the back of her neck. This was just her luck. Strangers. Living in her basement. Getting in the way of her school work. She slowly returned her phone to her bag. Maybe it would be okay? These were people Nanima knew from Jamatkhana, not some frat boys from the beer hall. They probably wouldn't even be home during the day, and Amira could just eat dinner upstairs and spend her evenings there with her mum and sister if they were around at night. At least she had her own bathroom. And a door that locked.

There was no point stressing about it now, so she grabbed her bags and headed to the subway to go to the library. The massive central reference library was the perfect place to lose a couple of hours in research, and if there were strangers in her home, she imagined she would be spending a lot of her waking hours in the Toronto library system. May as well get used to it now.

After a few productive hours of work, Amira made her way home a little after nine o'clock. Her grandmother's house wasn't big: a raised bungalow with three bedrooms upstairs and three downstairs. On the lower level, where she lived, there was a small kitchen and a combination family room/dining room with a bathroom and two bedrooms off it. Her bedroom was at the back, set apart from the other rooms and with its own bathroom, but the common areas would be shared with whoever rented those two rooms. To avoid meeting those strangers right away, and to catch her sister before she went to bed, Amira went in the front door to the upper level of the house.

The heady aroma of Indian spices and strong chai wafted out the moment she unlocked the door. Ah . . . the smell of home. Amira relaxed immediately as she entered the comfortable clutter of her grandmother's house.

"Amira, *beta*, you're here!" Nanima said from her usual seat on the sofa where she was watching a Gujarati soap opera. "Your mum told me you were coming today. Did you eat dinner? What can I heat up for you?"

Although quite healthy and vivacious, Amira's grandmother wasn't all that different than the majority of seventy-something Indian women—short, wide hipped, and always looking to feed everyone in her immediate vicinity. Amira leaned down to kiss her cheek and smiled. "I'm fine. I had a sandwich in the library. I'm surprised to see you. No Jamatkhana tonight?"

"Nah, it was a long day. I had a meeting with my committee in the morning but was late because I had to take Zahra to school. There was a mix-up with your mother and her shift. Then the committee meeting ran long because Shirin insisted we all taste this new recipe for *nankhatai* she made. Tasted the same as her old recipe. I mean, it's just a cookie—not spaceship science."

"Rocket science."

Nanima waved her hand in a *whatever* motion. "Will you come to Jamatkhana with me on Friday? You have old friends there who would love to see you."

Amira held back a scoff. Maybe rubberneckers there who'd love to see her. Although her grandmother was religious, Amira herself wasn't all that observant and rarely went to prayers. The last time she agreed to go to the prayer hall with Nanima, three people she barely knew asked her about the articles in the paper surrounding her "incident." Since then, she'd made peace with the fact that she only attended on Eid and special occasions. Still, it didn't stop Nanima from asking Amira to come along whenever she was in town. But Nanima never insisted and never made Amira feel guilty about skipping the rituals associated with her religion.

"I'll probably be busy with my final project. Where's Mum?"

"Reading that wizard book with Zahra. Putter?"

Amira smiled as she made her way to her sister's room and peeked in. Zahra was in the bottom bunk of her bed, her face illuminated by the phone in her hand. She looked up.

"Amira! You're home!" Zahra launched herself at her sister. Amira laughed, hugging her close and burying her nose in her baby sister's curls.

"Hey, Squish, glad I got you before bedtime." She manoeuvred Zahra back to her bed and sat next to her, grinning. "Where's Mum?"

Zahra leaned close, speaking quietly. "On her phone. I think Mum has a boyfriend."

Amira laughed. She had suspected her mother was seeing someone based on the cagey answers she had been giving recently whenever Amira asked what she was up to. She wasn't surprised Zahra had figured it out, too.

"Speaking of phones," Amira said, "you're not supposed to have yours in bed." She held out her hand and Zahra dutifully handed the smartphone over. It was Amira's old phone—she gave it to her sister when she bought a new one last year. There was no phone plan attached to it, but Zahra used it to send selfies to her friends over Wi-Fi nonstop. Eleven-year-old Zahra was a better millennial than Amira was.

Amira turned the phone off and put it in her pocket. "How're things here?"

"Good. I finally convinced Mum to read Harry Potter, so we're taking turns reading chapters to each other."

Amira glanced at her mother's closed bedroom door. "It's getting pretty late. Maybe you should leave it for tomorrow?" She spent a few minutes catching up before kissing her sister good night. Her mother still hadn't emerged from her bedroom. Must be serious. She made a mental note to grill her on this "boyfriend" later.

"Nanima, what's this about you renting out the extra basement bedrooms?" she asked her grandmother as she made her way back to the living room to grab her bags.

"Sameer and his friends. They have a competition in Toronto. Do you want some chai? It's fresh."

Crap. *Men* moved in? "I'd love some. Who's Sameer?"

"You know Sameer, beta? He used to live here." Nanima got up and went towards the kitchen. "There's a picture somewhere of you holding him when he was a baby. Neelam's son? From Ottawa?"

Amira had no idea who Nanima was talking about. Her blank stare must have betrayed her as her grandmother let out an exasperated *tsk*. She handed Amira a mug of hot chai and headed towards the basement door.

"Come, I'll take you down to meet him. Neelam is Shirin's daughter. Her son, Sameer, and some of his friends have a competition and they needed a place to practise in Toronto. I volunteer with Shirin on the food committee. You know her, beta."

Amira followed her grandmother as they made their way down the narrow stairs to the basement.

"Competition?" she asked.

"I think a haircutting thing? He said something about barbers, but then he said it was a singing contest. Do barbers sing?"

She froze on the stairs. Was this really happening? Had her Indian, Muslim grandmother just rented out her basement to a barbershop quartet?

"Three of them moved in yesterday," Nanima continued, "but they said the fourth was coming today on a train."

As she continued to the bottom of the stairs and stood in the small basement kitchen, Amira had a sudden thought. *No.* It was impossible. There was no way the slimy, creepy

Mr. Silver Pants from the train was the fourth guy in the quartet. This couldn't be his Bollywood singing group. Voices around the corner came towards her. She tensed, dropping her bags.

"I'll get the rest of my bags out of the car, Sam," a deep voice said.

A sound escaped Amira's lips. She didn't need to see the man; she *knew* that voice. It wasn't the creep from the train; although to her, he was a close second on the list of men she had hoped never to see again.

Duncan Galahad had moved into her house.

CHAPTER FOUR

DUNCAN GALAHAD AND those striking eyes were in Amira's kitchen. Her mouth went slack. *No.*

"Good lord, it's Princess Jasmine." He took two steps backwards, almost crashing into the slight man behind him.

Amira shut her mouth and willed her racing heart to return to normal. What had she done to deserve this?

"Jasmine?" Nanima questioned. "This is *Amira*, my granddaughter."

Recovering, the garden gnome's smirk returned. "So, you have a name."

"You two know each other?" the other man asked. Amira eyed the stranger in the room. He was younger than Duncan, probably early twenties, with hair that had been teased straight up as if escaping his clean-shaven brown face. He also wore plaid flannel, but on him, it looked decidedly more hipster chic and less mountain man. This was Sameer, she assumed.

Amira folded her arms over her chest. "We were on the train together."

"Why'd you call her Princess Jasmine, because she's brown?" Sameer asked. It was kind of an accusing question, but Sameer didn't sound annoyed or angry. Was it possible someone got along well with the garden gnome?

Duncan lowered his eyebrows. "No. Long story. It's because the princess here is no one's property." He turned and smiled tightly at her. "Glad to meet you, *Amira*. Looks like we're going to be roomies for the next few weeks. We're here for a barbershop quartet competition. I gather you're in the far room at the end of the hallway?"

She had been right. They *were* a barbershop quartet. This was easily the most ridiculous moment of her life.

"Amira is just back from university," Nanima gushed. "She's doing her master's in engineering. She has school work, so you boys don't disturb her. You're okay, right, beta?"

Amira nodded, heart still pounding and face straining hard to convey that this living arrangement was no big deal. "Yeah, Nanima, I'm fine. You go back upstairs, I'll just unpack."

"Okay. See you tomorrow. Good night." Nanima left with a warm smile.

"I'm just going to—" Amira stopped. She didn't have to explain herself to these two. She didn't even have to talk to them. They were invading her home, not the other way around. She picked up her things and walked silently to her thankfully empty bedroom.

She paced the room a bit, seething about the mess she found herself in. Amira wasn't usually one to give any weight to new-age, superstitious drivel, but she couldn't think of any reason why this could be happening to her other than she had angered the universe somehow. Hell, maybe there *was* a pissed-off Sufi saint out to get her. Wouldn't be a surprise, really. Pissing *people* off was Amira's talent; surely she could do it with saints, too.

How was she going to get her project done with the garden gnome and his barbershop quartet living and *rehearsing* here? She grabbed her phone and texted Reena.

Amira

Sir Lumberjack and his merry barbershop quartet are living in my grandmother's basement.

Reena

Hang on, I'm going to throw my phone in the Don River. Pretty sure I'll never get a better text than that. May as well give it up.

Amira

I'm serious. They're here.

Reena

What the hell? Should I still come over?

Amira

No. Meet me at the Sparrow in 15.

The Sparrow was a local haunt about a ten-minute walk from both Amira's house and Reena's apartment. They'd been hanging out there for years whenever both were in town. It was the kind of place with brewed coffee at all hours and decent beer on tap. And a killer Sunday brunch. Amira rushed out of the house after changing into jeans, afraid to run into the garden gnome again. How was she going to survive two weeks of avoiding him and his ridiculous quartet?

She was sitting at a table in the back, nursing a bourbon on the rocks when she saw Reena approach. Amira stood and gave her friend a tight hug before sinking back in her seat. Seeing her best friend in the whole world warmed her core more than the amber whiskey ever could. She'd missed Reena. So much.

Reena Manji was a little thing, barely five feet tall, with dark, shoulder-length curls and darker eyes. Despite recently turning thirty like Amira, she was routinely carded when buying drinks and could probably get away with paying the high-school student fare on the subway. Even though they had been living over two hours away from each other for the last few years, they talked or texted almost daily, so Amira knew Reena needed this bit of best-friend therapy, too. Reena's life was a wreck lately, with parents who managed to be both distant and way too involved in her life. Plus, a younger sister living with her whom Reena had no choice but to support and who had always treated her terribly. If any other person was going through the crap that Reena was dealing with, Amira would feel bad about meeting with her to complain about her own problems. But this was Reena. Reena's support was always unconditional.

After ordering a hard cider, Reena skipped any small talk and got to the point. "What in god's name was that text about, Amira? What lumberjack is in your home?"

"Nanima has rented the two extra basement bedrooms to some barbershop quartet she knows. And because my life is an exercise in cosmic torment, the annoying guy from the train is in the group. The garden gnome."

"A barbershop quartet."

"Yes."

Reena blinked repeatedly. "How does your nanima know a barbershop quartet?"

"Believe it or not, from Jamatkhana. One of the guys is the son or grandson of a friend of hers, I think. Sameer something. Really tall hair."

"Sameer from Ottawa?"

"You know him?"

Reena smiled. "No, but I know of him. He's a friend of a friend on Facebook. You know, it's high time you rejoined the twenty-first century and waded back into social media."

Amira had deleted all her social media accounts almost a year ago after burning out from dealing with people who confused opinions with facts. She didn't miss the inane updates from people she cared little about and was glad not to be up to speed on gossip these days. She frowned. "He doesn't seem very friendly. Didn't say a word to me when Nanima introduced us."

"Saira told me a rumour about him, but I can't be sure it's true. Neelam's son, right?"

Saira was Reena's sister. "I think so. I still haven't figured out who Neelam is."

"Shirin's daughter."

Amira shrugged. "Honestly, Reena? I find myself unable to care who these people are right now." She swirled her drink in her hand, letting the melting ice cubes crash against each other. She took a small sip before shaking her head. "How am I going to get any work done with four surly guys living down there? And there're only two empty bedrooms. It's going to be a tight squeeze." She rubbed her hand over her face. This day was so surreal. She considered pinching herself to see if it was a dream, but there was no way even her subconscious could come up with this insanity.

"You're sure there's four of them?"

"I'm assuming. It's a quartet. I've only seen Duncan and Sameer, though."

Reena giggled.

"What's so funny?"

"I think you may have misjudged your lumberjack. Don't think he's a garden gnome at all. I think he's a garden . . . bear."

"What?"

"The rumour I heard about Sameer is that he recently came out to his mother, and he's coming to Toronto with his boyfriend."

Amira blinked. She hadn't seen that one coming. Her own parents weren't particularly traditional, or devout, for that matter, enjoying Jamatkhana on Fridays and wine bars on Saturdays. But Amira knew what was outside her little bubble of secularity. Their sect was a comparatively forward-thinking branch of Islam, and many within their community were socially accepting, but not all. And gossip in the community was rampant. She could count the number of gay people who had come out drama-free on one finger. And even though her friend Sofie was out and proud, Amira hated the way members of the community continued to lower their voices and whisper when talking about her or her girlfriend, Jackie.

But Duncan Galahad was gay, too? She remembered his reaction to the man on the train—he did say he was the furthest thing from a homophobe; and she supposed a gay man would fit that bill, but *really*? Amira wasn't one to generalize with stereotypes, so it wasn't his masculine gait or his manly arms that made her think he was straight, but rather the possessive way he had held on to her shoulder at the train station, the way he seemed to look right into her when they spoke. Amira shivered. Gay?

She drained her glass of bourbon.

Reena grinned. "He could be bisexual. Or pan, or—"

"Who, Sameer? Or the garden gnome?"

"The garden gnome. Sameer *is* gay, at least that's what I heard he told his mother. But the other one may be into women, too?"

"Reena, what's your point?"

Amira was very familiar with the knowing smile on Reena's face. "No point, really," she said.

"If you're implying I have any interest in the bearded wonder, drop it. First of all, you just told me he's in a relationship, so why would I go there? And second, he's a white-knighting asshat and not my type, remember? And third, probably the most important point: I am working on my project and not looking for a man right now!"

"Yeah, but I'm sure you weren't expecting your knight in shining armour to be a musician. Or to be living in your house." Reena laughed.

God. Amira needed new friends. People who didn't know her deepest secrets and storied history. Best to change the subject now, before Reena went deeper down that grungy back alley of memory. "I can't believe my grandmother rented her basement to a gay couple," Amira said.

"It's a quartet. There may be two gay couples. Anyway, I doubt Nanima knows Sameer's orientation. Neelam asked Sameer not to tell anyone in his family. His grandmother is your grandmother's friend."

"Well, obviously news got out if you know."

Reena's nose wrinkled. "Yeah, I know. I told Saira not to spread gossip, but you know my sister. Juicy dirt before conscientiousness."

"But now you're spreading it, too!"

"You have to live with him, so you should know the truth. Besides, you said you're looking for an Indian boyfriend. I'd hate for you to make a move on Sameer before finding out he's sleeping with your lumberjack."

"I'm not going to make a move on any of them! I just want a quiet place to finish my work!"

Reena giggled again. "All right, all right, sorry, Meer. No boyfriend, just school work. But you have to admit, this *is* funny. A gay, Muslim, lumberjack barbershop quartet living in your basement. You couldn't make this up if you tried. Anyway, I'd offer up my place for you to study in if they're too noisy, but you know Saira's home all day. I think a barbershop quartet would be less disruptive than my sister blending kale smoothies every two minutes."

Amira stilled. "Did she eat anything today?"

The smile on Reena's face instantly evaporated. "Not really. Three blueberries and half a bunch of Swiss chard. I swear, her skin's starting to turn green."

"That's messed up, Ree. She can't live on that."

Reena looked at the table, her fingers drawing stripes on the beaded condensation on her pint glass. "I know." She frowned. "I made *kuku paka* yesterday since she used to love it when we were growing up. And all she did was complain about the smell of chicken all night. She didn't eat a bit."

"What's kuku paka?" Amira asked. Reena's family was Gujarati Indian via East Africa, just like Amira's father. But Amira's mother was directly from Gujarat, India. Reena was obsessed with anything food related and was a fabulous cook, but Amira wasn't that familiar with the East African dishes she made, since at home, Mum or Nanima always did the cooking.

"Chicken in coconut sauce. Anyway, all she ate was the spinach I made to go with it."

Amira gentled her voice, knowing to tread lightly here. "She needs help, Reena. Did you mention that doctor to her?" Amira had done some research and found an Indo-Canadian therapist in Toronto who worked on a sliding scale. No way in hell Reena's parents would pay for Saira to see a therapist, so Reena would have to cover the cost herself with her meagre finance clerk salary. Amira knew she was nowhere near qualified to diagnose Saira with anything, but having known the woman for as long as she had known Reena, she couldn't ignore that something was up with her.

"No. Not yet. I will, though. I know she won't take it well. She's getting nasty."

"What'd she do now?" Amira asked. She loved Reena to bits, but she would never understand how her otherwise strong friend continued to put up with the abuse her sister had been throwing her way since childhood. It had undoubtedly been worse since Saira moved in. Amira was so happy to be back in town, where she could support her friend better.

Reena bit her lip, looking down. "She threw Bob out the window. He's dead."

Amira froze in place. "She didn't. Dead like . . . forever dead?"

Reena nodded.

"I'm sorry, Ree. God, how could she . . ."

"It's just a sourdough starter. I can start another one—"

"No, Ree, that's not the point. The rest of us may have thought you were whack-a-doo for the attention you paid to a blob of dough, but everyone knew Bob was important to you. You started that sourdough and took care of him for two years. I can't help but think Saira's obsession with health food has something to do with your baking and cooking hobby, but as your sister, she should respect what's important to you, not throw it out the window."

"I know, but she's going through a lot. She lost her job, and then her fiancé . . ."

"What happened with her fiancé, anyway? What was the guy's name . . . Jordan?"

"Joran. He was Dutch. Assuming he still is. She caught him in bed with his cousin or something. Anyway, Saira's been through a lot lately. I'm trying to cut her some slack."

"She moved into your apartment, insisted you buy organic kombucha crap for her, and now she throws away your sourdough starter? I don't care if she caught her man with all his cousins and aunties, she can be having a rough time and still treat her sister like a human being! She's always treated you horribly, Ree. This is nothing new."

39

Reena frowned. This wasn't the first time they'd had this conversation, and Amira felt sure it wouldn't be the last. But beating her best friend over the head with the truth hadn't helped before. It would be awhile before Reena would be ready to stand up to her sister and the rest of her family. If she was ever ready at all.

The subject needed to change. Amira smiled warmly at her friend. "Thanks for the offer of your place, though, but, we'll see. Maybe the Merry Men rehearse somewhere else? Or maybe they're quiet. How loud could a barbershop quartet be, anyway?"

"Yeah. Who knows, they may be Canada's first miming barbershop quartet." Reena grinned. "Should be interesting at your place, though. How are things coming along on your paper?"

"I've barely started. I have tons of notes from the work I did with my project supervisor, but I need to do loads of research on the applications of my findings. And I need to write it up into a readable state. Switching from computer integration to vibration and noise control meant so much more work."

"Damn. Maybe you should have stayed put."

"No. It's fine. I'll get it done."

After they chatted a bit longer, Amira said goodbye to Reena and walked home. The brisk spring chill was refreshing, and after talking it out with Reena, Amira was feeling better about the upcoming weeks. It felt so good to be home again that she wasn't going to let a handful of whimsically singing hipster men steal her optimism.

CHAPTER FIVE

THE HOUSE WAS quiet when she let herself in the side door and made her way down to the basement kitchen. It was late, but Amira was used to chai and a snack before bed. She wasn't sure how stocked the basement kitchen was, but chai fixings were a given—even by Indian standards, Amira's family took their chai very seriously. She moved quietly—she didn't want to attract the attention of the minstrels—as she filled a pot with water and put it on the stove. Peeking in the cupboards, she found loose tea, but only premixed chai spices. She preferred freshly ground spices in her chai but didn't want to wake anyone by sneaking upstairs to raid her grandmother's spice cupboard. She'd have to settle, for now.

"Making tea or coffee?"

Startled, she dropped the tea tin on the counter before turning around. Sameer. "Masala chai. Want some?"

"Okay."

She poured a bit more water in the pot and left it to boil. Turning to face him, Amira tried to think of a non-threatening, supportive thing to say without letting on that she had been listening to gossip about him.

Maybe she could compliment his . . . she looked at his head . . . hair? He frowned, running his hand through it, making a mess of the towering style. She bit her lip.

This was why she usually avoided the grapevine. She hated that she knew his secrets—secrets he didn't want known. She smiled, hoping her expression didn't betray her discomfort.

"I'm sorry, by the way," he said, not meeting her eyes.

"Sorry? Why?"

"We kind of invaded your home. Your grandmother told us you were away."

"Yeah, it was a last-minute decision to come home. Wasn't your fault."

He looked down at his feet.

"You okay?" Amira asked.

"Yeah, fine," he said sharply. "I just . . . you know what? I'll skip the tea. It might keep me up. I'm just . . . I'm going to bed."

He ran his fingers through his hair one last time before leaving.

Amira shrugged. Clearly something major was under that man's skin. Probably worried she would discover he was gay and tell his family. Or maybe he was having relationship problems? Trouble in paradise with the garden gnome? It was possible he was just anti-social. Amira's chai was boiling by that point, so she added milk to the pot, stirring it absent-mindedly while thinking about this predicament.

It was probably a good idea to speak to Sameer about how often the quartet would be rehearsing and how noisy they would be. But after that interaction, it was obvious he didn't want to make friends. Figures. She had only met half of this quartet so far and neither of them seemed to care two straws for her. Not much of a shock there; first impressions were not her strong point. But finishing her report would be even more stressful if there was an engineer-versus-singer feud in the basement. She pulled down a mug for her chai.

"That tea for the taking, Princess? Smells amazing." It was Duncan who startled her this time.

She spun to face him. "You keep calling me Princess and I'll call you by my secret name for you."

He grinned as he leaned back on the counter behind him, crossing his arms in front of his chest. "Oh, this'll be good. What do you call me in your head?"

"Lumberjack."

A furrow appeared between his brows. "That's not very original. Big, bearded guy in flannel? Heard it lots of times. I expected more from you."

"Also . . ."

One eyebrow raised. "Also, what?"

She reddened. "Garden gnome."

His head tilted way back in laughter, and his beard almost glowed under the pot lights. The laugh was loud, reverberating deeply through the small room.

Amira huffed as she fetched a second mug from the shelf. "Sugar?" she asked, once he stopped laughing.

"Just one."

She poured his chai, added one teaspoon of sugar, and handed it to him before fixing hers with half a teaspoon.

Duncan crossed his legs, grey socks barely peeking out under his jeans. He had removed the suspenders and unbuttoned the top of his plaid shirt, revealing a grey waffle-knit undershirt. He looked enormous in her small kitchen. The man took up space. Physical, even metaphysical, space. Like the energy of the whole house needed to reassemble itself due to his presence. Somehow, she had spent a large portion of her day with this odd man and she felt like she'd had to reassemble herself to fit him into her life. And he would continue to be in her life for two more weeks.

She exhaled. They needed to find a way to get along; she didn't want the stress of household tension to ruin her focus. And since Sameer didn't seem to want to fraternize with her—probably for good reason—Duncan was the only one who could answer her questions about their group.

"So, can I ask you something?" she said after gently blowing on her chai.

"Sure, what's up?"

"Um, this group of yours, it's a barbershop quartet?"

"Yeah, we're entered into the Ontario regionals. There was an online voting process to get this far, and if we win, we go to Vegas for the finals."

Amira had no idea barbershop quartet competitions were a thing. Actually, she didn't know barbershop quartets were still a thing, other than on *The Simpsons*.

"And you sing . . . ?" she asked.

"I'm the baritone. A barbershop group has four parts: a tenor, a lead, a baritone, and a bass."

"No. I mean, what type of music?"

"Oh, the guys like to pick the songs. I'd be happy with more classic rock arrangements, but Barrington's into Motown."

"Barrington?"

"He's the bass. Low notes. Sameer and Travis take turns

singing lead or tenor. Tenor's the highest notes, above lead. As the baritone, I sing above the bass and, sometimes, above the lead, too. The four pitches harmonize together to create an overtone unique to barbershop."

This was fascinating but not the information she needed from him. Duncan finished his musical theory lesson and sipped his chai. "Hey, you make a fine cuppa! My grandma would be proud, if she were alive. Now, that woman knew her tea. She would evangelize on the teachings of W.E. Gladstone while sipping: If you're cold, tea will warm you; if you're hot, it will cool you. If you're sad, it will cheer you; if you're excited, it will calm you the fuck down. Grams had a bit of a potty mouth."

Amira blinked. Was this man real? "Okay. Um, so you'll be rehearsing here? Or do you have a rehearsal space somewhere?"

He snorted. "Your family gave us a steal on the rent here, and we still could barely afford it. We don't have another place. We'll be rehearsing here, Princess. Often."

"Don't call me that."

"Sorry. *Amira.* I sincerely hope we don't bother you too much, but it's why we're here. To work on arrangements and find our groove. We need to be perfect. I don't know about the other guys, but I intend to win this thing."

Amira clenched her jaw. "I need to finish my report. It's due in two weeks. I came here for quiet."

He stood straighter. "Well, you can go to a library. We can't exactly take our song and dance routine on the road, can we?"

"Yes, but this is my house!"

He leaned forward, looming almost a head taller than her. "We're paying rent. We have every right to be here. We were told the basement would be empty and we could make as much noise as we needed to. Maybe you should just go back to your fancy engineering school."

Amira clutched her chai tightly, knuckles whitening. She really, really did not like this man. Or this situation she was in. "Where the hell are the rest of you, anyway? Isn't this supposed to be a quartet? I've only seen two. And how are four of you going to cram into only two rooms?"

He smirked. "Don't worry, we'll manage our sleeping arrangements just fine. Two rooms are plenty."

Did that mean he and Sameer *were* a couple? Amira still couldn't picture it. "Barrington and Travis went to see another barbershop group perform downtown," he continued. "Scoping out the competition. Sameer stayed behind because he had to pick me up from the train station and then visit his grandmother."

"Shirin," Amira said.

"What?"

"His grandmother is Shirin. She's friends with my grandmother. Don't you know your friends at all?"

"Why the hell would I know what his grandmother's name is? Look, are we done? I'd like to unpack my things."

She grimaced. "Yes. Go. Please."

He put his empty cup heavily in the sink and walked away without turning around.

Stupid garden gnome.

CHAPTER SIX

AMIRA WOKE TO find a meeting had been scheduled with Jim Prescott, her new manager at Hyde Industrial, for that morning. His assistant had emailed that Jim was eager to meet her and hammer out a return-to-work plan. A good sign. She made plans with Raymond for lunch afterwards to catch up.

She showered and dressed carefully, trying her best to groom herself to look appropriate for re-entering the corporate world. She was out of practice at taming her wild hair and walking in heels, but she was glad to step into her professional persona again, even for just one morning. Comfort was fine, but Amira was looking forward to her power suits. She needed the fierce confidence her blazers and pencil skirts gave her, even when she had to pair them with steel-toe shoes at work sites and factories.

Walking towards the basement kitchen, she heard unfamiliar voices speaking. Male voices.

"I know we were thinking about 'A Kind of Magic,' but isn't 'The Show Must Go On' a better Queen song? Is it too depressing? I mean, we're hardly . . . oh, hello." The speaker smiled when he noticed Amira. He had a voice that could almost be described as singsongy. Duncan and another unfamiliar man were standing next to him. These newcomers, she assumed, completed the missing half of the barbershop quartet. Sameer was nowhere to be seen.

Duncan let out a low, appreciative whistle. "Ooh, look at the princess today. The devil really *does* wear Prada."

Amira raised one eyebrow at him. She checked out his outfit—jeans and plaid flannel, of course. "You wouldn't know Prada from Wrangler if your life depended on it."

He didn't skewer her with a smart comeback; he only stared at her, green eyes intense.

Finally, he shook his head slowly and laughed. "Meet our other guys, Travis and Barrington. This is our incomparable host, Amira. Don't call her princess, her highness doesn't like that."

She glared briefly at Duncan again before turning to the two newcomers. Travis was the one who had said hello earlier. A handsome white man of average height, he had tanned freckled skin, floppy brown hair, and pale blue eyes. His wide smile beamed at Amira as he shook her hand.

"Thrilled to finally meet you. I was telling Barrington how much I love this house. So rare to see intact mid-century features these days. Swirled ceilings and a wet bar in a basement! Most people prefer contemporary design nowadays, but where's the personality in that, right?"

"Thanks?"

Clearly Travis was the quartet's resident friendly guy. She was glad they had at least one.

Travis reached out and touched the ends of Amira's hair. She had left it down this morning, taking advantage of the fact that, even though she was going in to work, she would not be visiting a factory today. "I love your hair," he said, running his fingers through the ends. "It's very healthy. You have to let me give you a blowout one of these days."

A little forward, but he seemed non-threatening. And she had to agree with his assessment—her hair was her best feature. Long, midnight black, and wavy, it was probably way more work than it was worth. Not to mention that tying it up while in factories or shoving it under hard hats was a pain. But her hair was her security blanket.

She'd had men tell her they'd fantasized about her hair before, but blow-drying it didn't usually factor into it. "Um . . . okay . . ." She hesitated.

"Of the four of us, Travis is the closest thing to an actual barber," Barrington explained, a friendly smile on his face, too.

"I'm a hairstylist in Ottawa," Travis said.

"And I work in a tech start-up. Plus, I'm a part-time grad student," Barrington added with a grin. His voice was even lower than Duncan's. "Apparently, you're also in grad school?" Barrington was easy on the eyes, too. A large black man, he was taller, broader, and a hell of a lot friendlier-looking than Duncan Galahad.

So, if Sameer and Duncan were together, were these two a couple? It was a bit more believable as both seemed to have received the "be friendly to strangers" memo. And as much as she didn't believe it earlier, she was starting to understand Sameer and Duncan's relationship. Duncan could smirk while Sameer scowled. A match made in grouchy heaven.

Should she flat-out ask them their relationship statuses? Amira had never been great at deciphering sexual orientation, so she usually didn't bother trying. But if these four were going to be living here with her, it would be nice to know who belonged to whom.

"Degree?" Barrington asked.

She smiled. "MEng. You?"

"MBET."

She had a friend who'd done that degree. She smiled. "MBET! I—"

"WTF!" Travis interrupted quite loudly.

They all turned to Travis's giggling face. "I felt left out—I wanted to speak in letters, too."

Duncan snorted. "Why do teenagers and grad students always speak in acronyms? It's like they think they are above us commoners and our complete words." He shot a glare at Amira.

Determined not to let the red beard get under her skin, she turned back to Barrington. "MBET is like an MBA with more of a technology focus, right?"

He nodded. "Yup. And entrepreneurship. I have one year left."

"I have only one report left, then I'm done."

"Congratulations. Can I pour you a coffee?" Barrington held out the stainless-steel coffee carafe.

Amira checked the time on the microwave. "Thanks, but I need to run. I have a meeting downtown. It's been a pleasure, gents." She left with a wave for the two nice members of their group and resisted the urge to glare at Duncan on her way out.

Hyde Industrial Consulting was located in an impressive, glass-fronted low-rise near the waterfront downtown. The location was a bit of a pain to get to, being a decent distance off the subway line, but Amira was happy to take a streetcar from Union Station and walk the half block to the building. Entering through the revolving door, she was overcome with a warm feeling of familiar comfort mingling with excitement for the future.

Despite her issues in school, Amira loved working as an engineer. As a consultant, she'd had the opportunity to work on so many projects, most in the manufacturing sector. She loved meeting new clients, taking on new challenges, and using her expertise to solve complex problems. And with her new advanced degree? Amira was going to get better assignments and prove herself capable of a senior role. This was just the beginning.

"Oh my god! It's Amira!" Shelley, an old friend at Hyde, was unexpectedly at reception. At first, Amira had maintained contact with Shelley through social media after leaving, but since she'd gone silent online, Amira had lost touch with her old lunch buddy.

"Shelley! What are you doing at reception?" Amira smiled as she bent down to hug her friend over the counter.

"Regular chick is sick. She's always sick. We didn't have the time to get a temp this morning, so, of course, 'that HR girl' is the one *voluntold* to cover for her." Shelley spoke the words *that HR girl* in an exaggerated English accent.

Amira chuckled. "I have a meeting with Jim Prescott to discuss coming back."

Shelley smiled. "Yay! I'll tell him you're here." After she made the call, Shelley grinned. "I'm glad you'll be back. We need more women around here. Things are so . . . disheartening lately."

"Really?" That sentiment was unusual for Shelley. She was the sunny optimist at work.

"Yeah"—she glanced over her shoulder towards the offices—"you'll do fine, though. I was just telling Dave that things will be better when Amira's back."

Amira's heart swelled. It felt good to be appreciated. "It will take me awhile to get used to this place again."

"Nah, it's like riding a bike. Hey, you know what? I'll put you back on the Hyde employee distribution list. Nothing like an employee newsletter to make you feel like part of the team."

Amira laughed. Jim didn't make her wait long; he soon appeared in reception, hand outstretched.

"You must be Elmira. Pleasure to meet you. I have heard much about you," Jim said with a distinctive English accent.

"Amira. Thank you, sir."

"Come, let's meet in my office."

Jim Prescott was an older man—Amira guessed late fifties—with dark hair, a large waistline, and short legs. He walked slowly and deliberately, in stark contrast to her former boss, Jennifer, who always seemed to be four steps ahead of everyone in the room. Jim seemed friendly enough, though, and as Amira knew from experience, engineers didn't always look like you expected them to.

He led her to the same glass-walled office Jennifer had used. A large fern still stood in the corner, although it looked bigger than the last time Amira had seen it. Nothing else was the same, though. Jim apparently wasn't as partial to family pictures and inspirational quotes as Jennifer had been.

Jim lowered himself into the slick leather office chair behind the glass-topped desk and gestured for Amira to sit.

He smiled, lifting a beige manila folder from the corner of the desk and opening it. "My assistant pulled your personnel file." He flipped through the loose papers inside for a few moments as Amira perched on her chair. "So," he finally said, "I see you've been away for a while. Maternity leave?"

"No. I've been in grad school. I've almost completed my master's."

"Have you? Good girl. I apologize, but girls your age are always running off to have babies. And you were told you could return to Hyde after your schooling?"

"Yes. Jennifer Chen granted me a leave of absence for school and guaranteed I could return to my position when finished."

He lifted up a cream sheet of paper, topped with Hyde Industrial's distinctive green and blue logo. "Ah yes. Here it is." He read the letter. "Hmm . . . a two-year unpaid sabbatical to complete your education. They certainly do things differently here in Canada, don't they?"

Amira squeezed her lips shut. She was starting to wonder if this Jim Prescott was as supportive as Raymond believed him to be. "And you're ready to return now?" he asked.

"Yes, sir. I'm just completing my final project report. I have one more meeting with my academic adviser and then I am available to return."

"Excellent, excellent. Congratulations. I am pleased to hear that. How long had you been at Hyde prior to deciding to leave?" He began leafing through the papers in her file again.

"Four years, sir."

"Ah, here is your most recent performance review." He scanned the pages. "Two years old, though, but impressive nonetheless. Is it your plan to stay with the firm long term?"

"Yes. I'd hoped advancing my education would help leverage my career to a senior consultant position in a few years."

He looked up from the file. She had trouble reading him. He could have been anywhere from surprised to pleased or even disgusted. Proper English upper-class manners, she figured. "Oh, is that so?" He smiled again. She was starting to wonder if that smile could be trusted. "May I be frank with you, Mrs. Khan?"

"Ms." Crap. She shouldn't have said that, but Mrs. Khan just made her think of her mother.

"Pardon me?"

Amira sighed. "It's Ms. I am not married."

"Oh, you're not married? Pretty little thing like you, won't be long, I think. Miss Khan, I will be honest with you. I think you may face an uphill battle here if you expect a senior position in the near future. It is a competitive marketplace, and I am not sure about my predecessors, but I don't believe people should advance in the field based on anything other than ability. Not because of some letters behind one's name, or to fulfill any . . . perceived requirement. You must also keep in mind that senior roles are very challenging at Hyde. Lead consultants are expected to work demanding schedules, with little time for domestic obligations. And as you have been away for so long, I see little evidence of your ability to meet our expectations."

Domestic obligations? What the hell? And was he really implying it would have been better for her to stay at work and impress him instead of getting her master's degree? And she couldn't even begin to approach that *perceived requirement* comment. She smiled tightly, but her blood was starting to heat.

"A good first step," he continued, "would be to partner with some of our longer-standing consultants upon your return to help you reintegrate yourself into Hyde. Have you remained in contact with anyone during your sabbatical?"

"Yes, Raymond Chu. He's my mentor."

"Yes, Ray. Generous of him. He's an impressive chap. Doing a wonderful job on the Regent plant project. The project manager took him out for a steak dinner last night to thank him." He chuckled. "I understand they enjoyed most of a bottle of scotch together. Anyway, young lady, I'm not saying it's impossible for you to move ahead at Hyde, but I wouldn't want you to think you have an advantage because of anything other than results. I run a meritocracy here."

"Of course, I understand that, sir."

"Excellent, excellent . . ." He returned the loose papers to the file folder and placed it on the corner of his desk. "Well," he said, turning to look at the calendar pinned on the corkboard behind him. "How about we say May fifteenth for your return date? That's four weeks away. I'll have you shadow Ray on the Regent plant project at first." He stood. "If we're settled, then, I have another meeting to get to."

Amira stood, feeling dizzy. She was glad her legs held her weight. "Thank you for meeting me, Mr. Prescott. I appreciate your time."

That smile again. Positively reptilian. "Of course, my dear," he said, holding out his hand. She had to shake it but wasn't the least bit surprised when it was cold as ice. "It was a pleasure to meet you. I wish you well on the completion of your studies. Now if you'll excuse me . . ."

Amira walked out of his office. Her friendly smile was painted on her face. Her legs were moving exactly as they should, one step in front of the other, hips swaying just a bit. She casually swept her hair behind her shoulder. She walked as if every molecule in her body wasn't vibrating with anger. As if nothing was wrong at all. She approached Shelley to say goodbye.

"It was great seeing you, Shelley," Amira said, straining to keep her voice light and cheerful.

"Yes," Shelley answered, standing and grabbing her purse. "Wish I could chat, Amira, but I have a meeting. I need to stop agreeing to cover the reception desk. Dave, our admin, has tons of receptionist experience, but they always ask me. As if I don't have enough to do." She rolled her eyes. "Let's do lunch some weekend before you're back. I'll catch you up on the scoop here."

"Uh, sure. That sounds good," Amira said, pulling out her phone and opening her calendar. She went through the motions of arranging a lunch date, but Amira wasn't really paying attention. Her nerve endings were still vibrating with anger, but she managed to mask it.

"You good, Amira? You look a little shaken."

Okay, maybe her cloaking shields weren't at full strength. "Yeah, I'm fine. Great seeing you, looking forward to our lunch."

"Great, me too. Bye, hon." Shelley disappeared down the hallway.

Amira left through the big revolving door and made her way to the same café where she and Raymond had met for weekly lunches for years. The meeting with Jim went shorter than expected, so she had time to kill. After ordering a latte, she found a seat at the back. The coffee smelled strong and acidic. She wasn't sure she would be able to stomach it.

Amira was no naive ingenue—she understood what Jim had been implying. He assumed she thought she would get preferential treatment at Hyde, even the promotion she wanted, just because she could tick off so many "diversity" boxes. Did he think she planned to exploit her skin colour? Maybe her religion? Unlikely. This was Toronto, one of the most multicultural cities in the world. Hyde Industrial had no shortage of minorities of any kind. But what they did have a shortage of, at least at the consultant level, was women.

Sexism in her chosen field wasn't new to Amira. She was used to the off-colour remarks and classmates who preferred not to work with her on projects—or worse, assumed she didn't know what she was doing. But Amira had first sought the position at Hyde because of their progressive hiring practices. Because of the female senior engineers in the firm. Sexism rearing its ugly head in what was supposed to be the progressive nirvana of Hyde Industrial was disappointing.

Amira had barely touched her coffee by the time Raymond arrived shortly after twelve. He took the seat across from her at her table.

"Great to see you, Amira. Just saw Jim, he tells me you'll be back in a month?"

"Yeah, May fifteenth."

"Looking forward to it. We going to start our weekly lunch dates again?"

"Sure," Amira said.

"You don't sound too excited to come back. Where's my chatty friend?" Raymond asked.

"Raymond, you said Jim's great. Do you like working for him?"

"Yeah. I miss Jennifer but I don't really have complaints about Jim."

"Where did Jennifer go?"

"She transferred to the Singapore office. There's been a lot of international lateral moves at Hyde lately. Restructuring. New blood, new perspectives."

Amira frowned. "Do you find Jim to be at all, you know . . . sexist?"

"Sexist?"

"Yes. He said some things to me. Implied he thought I expected to get promotions because of my gender."

"What? You don't expect that, do you?"

"No, of course not. I just . . . I got the sense he was telling me he'd never give a senior position to a woman."

"Did he say that?"

"Not really. He said I couldn't expect to get a position for any reason except merit. And he implied a successful lead consultant wouldn't have time for domestic obligations. And would be expected to go to steak houses with clients."

He laughed. "Why would that eliminate you? Men and women share domestic duties these days. And he's right—I'm rarely home to put the boys to sleep. Plus, you eat steak, right? Just not pork."

"Yeah—"

"I've found him to be progressive. He hired a female engineer just last week. But I will say one thing about Jim:

he's big on action. He wants visible results. He's much more customer focused than Jennifer."

"He seemed sexist to me. He also called me a pretty young thing."

Raymond laughed again. "He's old school, that's for sure. But seriously, Amira, I'm sure you misinterpreted it. You've been out of the office environment for a while, but take it from me, I've been working with the guy for four months now. You'll get used to him."

Maybe Raymond had a point. She *was* out of practice at deciphering office politics. Amira sipped her coffee, thinking. "So, what did Jim mean when he said this would be an uphill climb for me?"

Raymond paused, seemingly deep in thought. "What happened with that immigration issue you were dealing with last year? Did it get sorted out?"

Jesus Christ, so Jim *was* racist? "It wasn't an *immigration issue*. I was detained at the border for no reason. Does Jim have an issue with immigrants?"

"What? Of course not. He's an immigrant himself, isn't he? I was just wondering if he read any of those articles about you. I know Jennifer saw them—she was pretty angry on your behalf. But Jim's not the type to approve of his staff gaining . . . infamy. Like I said, he's very client focused, and distracting clients from the consultant's abilities would be frowned upon."

Amira grimaced. "It was a year ago, and I wasn't working at Hyde then. I've moved on, and thankfully the media has, too." She strategically left out the bit about getting a call from a reporter only yesterday. She never imagined that she would lose promotion opportunities thanks to her super-fun racial profiling holiday, but then again, she didn't expect that she would be going back to work reporting to a *Mad Men*–era engineer.

"Good, hopefully it never comes up," Raymond said. "He doesn't know. I'm sure he would have said something when I was just talking to him about you."

"Okay, so it's not for my gender, race, religion, or my unfortunate history with the Toronto airport customs officials. Why did Jim say it would be an uphill climb?"

Raymond paused again. He really seemed to be putting a lot of thought into Amira's problem here. She was lucky to have an ally like Raymond at work. "We're friends, so I'll be honest with you, Amira. The buzz around the office is there's a new senior position opening up soon. A whole new division that will be under Jim's umbrella. Maybe he was warning you away from applying until he's seen evidence of your ability."

"I'm not expecting to get a brand-new senior position! And I told him as much, in our meeting. I know I've been gone for a while. All I said was I was hoping for a promotion within a few years. But if there is no chance of ever moving ahead, then what's the point of me staying at Hyde?"

Amira cringed as the words left her mouth. The thought of leaving Hyde was terrifying, and not just because she loved it there. They really were the forward-thinking firm. Her colleagues, Raymond, Jennifer, and so many others, accepted her. They understood her and treated her like a peer, not some cute little engineer wannabe like some of her classmates treated her.

"I have an idea," Raymond said. "How about you get a letter of reference from a professor? Jim loves reference letters."

"From who?"

"Wasn't one of your professors the guy who wrote that text on sustainable manufacturing?"

Amira's shoulders slumped. "My first project supervisor. Not likely he'd give me a good reference. I told you about him, remember?"

"Right. The guy who made jokes about girls not getting math."

"Yeah."

Raymond paused a moment, then smiled. "Your academic adviser is Alison Kennedy. Get her to give you a reference letter. A glowing one. I happen to know that Jim admires her research on linear sensor systems. He mentioned her when I told him I did my master's there."

"You think a reference letter from Professor Kennedy will mean he'd one day promote me?"

"It will put you in the front of his mind. He got a note complimenting my work from a client a couple months ago, and he was talking about it for weeks. Jim has no idea how amazing you are, so let's show him. It can't hurt either way."

That was true. It couldn't hurt. And if her project was really well done and accepted with little or no revision required, Professor Kennedy would likely give her a glowing letter of recommendation. "You still willing to look over my final report?" she asked Raymond.

He grinned. "Of course I am."

Raymond was amazing. With his help, she had the potential to produce a kick-ass project and leave Professor Kennedy with no choice but to sing her praises in any letter Amira asked her to write.

She could do this. She *would* do this. She was going to show this old-school prat exactly who this pretty little thing was.

Amira smiled widely. Game on, Jim Prescott.

CHAPTER SEVEN

AMIRA WENT STRAIGHT to the library after meeting with Raymond, taking off her blazer and getting to work. Now more than ever, her focus was not on just finishing the damn report but making it the absolute best it could be. She went through countless research sites and found new sources that dug deeper into the topic of noise and vibration reduction. She found every book in the enormous reference library that so much as mentioned noise dampeners and their applications in manufacturing. She texted several classmates and emailed her project supervisor to ask his opinion on which journals to dig up. Eventually, when all the letters and numbers on all the screens and pages were starting to bleed into each other, Amira called her mother to see what was happening for dinner. Mum had worked an early shift and told Amira she was just about to put a frozen lasagna in the oven. It wasn't hard to convince her to skip the frozen dinner and meet Amira at their favourite Middle Eastern sandwich shop instead. She wanted a chance to really catch up with her mother and sister, and the thought of mediocre frozen pasta wasn't appealing after her trying day.

Sitting at a grease-stained table in the tiny shop, Amira unwrapped her spicy beef shawarma, grinning at Mum and Zahra.

"I needed this," she said, licking the juice dripping down her hand after her first heavenly bite.

"Tough day?" Mum asked, passing Zahra a bottle of mango juice.

"Yeah. Just work stuff. Been a lot of changes at Hyde since I left. It's going to take some getting used to. I don't want to talk about it now, though." She took another delectable bite. God, it was so good to be back home. The food in this city was second to none.

"How are your dance classes going? You have a summer recital, don't you?" Amira asked Zahra after they'd made a dent in their sandwiches.

Zahra had been going to a Bollywood-style contemporary dance school for years. In the last few months, she had also started lessons in Indian classical Kathak dancing, something that their mother had studied as a child back home in India.

"Yeah, the Bollywood Beat one is in July. Are you coming? I have a duet and a group dance. My classical recital is in September."

"Of course I'm coming. How's the Kathak going? You still like it?"

Mum smiled with pride at Zahra. "She's doing wonderfully. If you were on Facebook, you'd see the video I posted of her last rehearsal."

"You enjoying it, Squish?"

Zahra bit her lip, then smiled. "Yeah, the dance is harder, but I like it. I don't like the dance school as much as Bollywood Beat, though. But my teacher is nice."

"It's better now, right, sweetie?" Mum asked, a reassuring lilt to her voice.

Amira tilted her head. Zahra was usually quite positive, and she was obsessed with all things dance related, so hearing anything other than unrestrained enthusiasm about the dance school was a surprise. "What's the problem with the school?"

"It's better now, but the kids there have all known each other, for, like . . . forever. I'm new."

"But, Zahra, you make friends so easily. You don't like those other kids?"

Zahra looked out the window. "Some of the girls were mean to me at the beginning. They got in trouble, so they stopped."

"Did you know about this?" Amira asked her mum.

"Yes, of course. We dealt with it, but we're going to keep an eye and take stronger steps if it happens again."

"What happened?"

Zahra looked at her mother, unsure if she should say anything, but Mum nodded gently, urging her younger daughter on. "One of the girls, Priya, said I shouldn't do Kathak dance since I'm not Hindu."

Amira sat up straight. "That's ridiculous! Did she say anything else?"

"Another one said I wasn't really a Muslim because I don't wear a hijab. Then she said Muslims can't be trusted and only cause problems, so I shouldn't be at the school. Anyway, Miss Kavita got really angry and talked to us all about racism and stuff. Priya and Ruchi had to say sorry and I think they got in trouble. They don't say that stuff anymore."

Amira closed her fist around her bottle of mango juice. "But they aren't really being friendly either, are they, Squish?"

"No. It's okay." Zahra took a slow bite of her pita.

"It's not okay." Amira looked at her mother. How could Mum keep her at the school?

"Zahra was singled out when she first got there because of her talent," Mum said. "The teacher was very impressed at how quickly she picked it up. It seems the other girls resented the attention."

"Miss Kavita says I have natural rhythm since I've been dancing Bollywood style forever. She said I can have a solo in the recital, but I'd need individual lessons for that."

Mum shook her head. "We barely have time for the lessons you already take, Zahra. Your school work would suffer. Not to mention the cost . . ."

"I can do individual instead of group. I know it's more expensive, but we can ask Dad to—"

"No, Zahra. We've talked about this."

"You want to take individual classes so you don't have to be with those girls?" Amira asked.

"No, it's fine. They don't bother me anymore. I just want the solo in the recital."

Amira looked carefully at her sister. Zahra was an extraordinary girl—smart, resilient, friendly, and usually the most exuberant, enthusiastic person in the room. Amira could read between the lines. Even though Zahra said it was okay, it wasn't.

Zahra was getting older, and with that came the realization that there were many places where she would be seen first and foremost by her religion or the colour of her skin, and as a person after the fact. Amira had heard it all growing up. Not really fully Indian because she's Muslim or because her dad's family left India in the 1800s. Not a real Canadian because she's brown. Hell, even within their own community, they were judged. Zahra was the girl from that scandal-prone family with the divorced parents and the weird, single sister who was all over the news. And now, with so many people seeing Muslims as the world's villains, just being herself was about to get very difficult for Zahra. Amira was not sure her family could keep sheltering her forever.

"I'm sorry, Zahra. I'm really sorry that those kids were mean to you. They should not have said anything about your religion. That was wrong."

"I know, Amira. They were just jealous. Mum said people are mean to Muslims right now because they don't know any"—she looked at her mum—"but Shayla is Muslim and in the class, too, so they *do* know Muslims. I think they're just mean."

They ate quietly for a while. Zahra was probably right; these were probably just mean girls, jealous of the attention the new girl was getting.

"Mum, can I get baklava?" Zahra asked.

Mum smiled, pulling out a ten-dollar bill from her wallet and handing it to Zahra. "Get three."

Once Zahra was out of earshot, Amira gave her mother a pointed look. "Why can't we just put her in the individual class? Can't be that expensive."

Mum snorted. "More than double the price."

"Is money that tight?"

"No, of course not. It just seems wasteful. The school itself costs so much more than Bollywood Beat, but Kavita is the best classical instructor in the city. Anyway, it's fine. Zahra will have to learn to work with difficult people."

"But Hindu nationalists? I can't believe this would happen in Toronto."

"They aren't Hindu nationalists, Amira. They're eleven-year-old girls."

"Their parents might be. I wrote an article about this a few years ago. The sentiments are spreading outside of the fringes, both in India and—"

Zahra returned to the table, so Amira swallowed the rest of her rant. These were not topics she spoke about with her sister around. Mum was likely right, anyway; they were probably not sprouting far-right ideology, at least not intentionally. The world was full of these mean girls. If you're a bit different, they use it as ammunition against you. The problem wasn't that Zahra was Muslim, but they used her religion as a rock to whip at her because of jealousy. Amira hated that they had found such an easy target on her sister's chest.

She wished she could do something. She half-wanted to storm into that school and insist that the trouble kids were transferred out of Zahra's class, or even better, kicked out of the school once and for all. A couple of years ago, that's exactly what she would have done. But now, she knew that it wouldn't really help in the long run. All those articles she wrote for online blogs and magazines, as well as her university paper, plus all those tweets and Facebook posts, all for the purpose of raising awareness about intolerance—but she hadn't helped anything. She hadn't changed any minds; the world wasn't any better. Fighting all these tiny battles was having no effect on the war. But it was killing her. She made a decision a while ago to stop engaging, for her own survival.

While eating their dessert, the three made plans for amusement park visits and shopping trips over the summer, but Amira's mood was already soured. Once home, she headed down the stairs to the basement, rubbing her temples to stave off the headache forming. Between the meetings with Jim and Raymond, working in the library all afternoon, and then that unsettling conversation with Zahra and her mother, she was physically and emotionally drained. Clearly, life was going to be an exercise in emotional torture until her project was signed, sealed, and delivered to Professor Kennedy. But she had no choice but to keep at it and not let anything else distract her.

Not even the bearded garden gnome standing in the kitchen and peering into the tea tin with a wrinkled brow.

"There you are, Princess," he said. "How'd you make that tea last night? There are no tea bags . . . and this tea doesn't smell like what you made. I saw you do something funny with a pot."

"I'm not here to make your chai."

"I know that, I just want you to tell me what you did. It was really good. Hell, you tell me what you did, and I'll make *you* some tea. You look beat. Long day?"

"Yeah, that's an understatement." She kicked off her shoes and pulled out a pot from the cupboard. A good cup of chai would be amazing right now, but she couldn't trust an inexperienced chai maker to brew it to her specifications.

Amira silently carried out her chai routine, making a mental note to swipe some of her grandmother's fresh spices from upstairs for next time. She filled the pot with enough water for two cups and added two heaping spoons of the strong black loose tea and a bit of the chai spice blend. She let it boil for three minutes before adding a generous splash of milk and bringing it back to a rolling boil. She then strained the brew directly into two mugs.

Duncan watched her silently through the process, maybe realizing Amira was in no mood for friendly small talk. Or what was more likely when the two of them were involved, aggravating banter. And for some reason, being watched by a burly lumberjack type while making chai didn't annoy Amira. Honestly, after what she had gone through today, Duncan Galahad was probably the least of her annoyances now. She added one teaspoon of sugar to his mug.

"Thanks," he said once she handed it to him. The smile he gave her was unlike any she had seen on him before. Genuine, honest, and a bit concerned.

"You're welcome." Amira nodded to him and took her mug to her room.

. . . .

AMIRA WOKE EARLY the following morning, eager to get back to work. And thankfully, it seemed working was possible while living with a barbershop quartet. There were no interruptions. No male voices, no clapping hands, singing, stomping feet, beat boxing, yodelling, spoken word, or anything else she half-expected to hear from a weirdo barbershop quartet. Maybe this would be okay?

She didn't know much about a cappella. Her experience with musical groups was all amplifiers, keyboards, and electric guitars, so she hadn't appreciated how silent they would be with no instruments. If this is how they "rehearsed," she could work with these guys around, no problem. But as she was opening the second academic paper, downloaded from yesterday, she heard it. Snapping fingers. Then clapping. Then a deep, guttural, throaty sound to a steady rhythm, before a clear, crisp voice started singing.

Oh god. "Stand by Me"? Really? This was the most original song the guys could come up with? Amira tried to ignore the singing and continued working. And it worked, for about thirty seconds. Until the chorus started.

Loud, powerful, and resonant. Whoever was singing the chorus, he had the best singing voice.

They continued through the next verse. At least three of them, maybe all four, harmonized together. She couldn't deny these guys sounded good. Really good. But that was beside the point. They were distracting.

But as Duncan said, they had the right to be there. They had the right to practise. She moved to the far side of her room.

But their voices carried. Starting and stopping, trying out different arrangements, discussing, arguing, clapping, and preventing Amira from being able to concentrate. She grasped her phone and looked through her backpack for her headphones but couldn't find them. She finally connected her phone directly to her speakers. Queuing up the Bollywood playlist Zahra made for her, she played it at a volume high enough to drown out the boys. She preferred silence when she studied, but she wasn't above a touch of noise warfare. She read for two more minutes before a loud pounding shook her door in its frame. She stormed over to open it. Duncan, of course.

"Can you put your volume down, you're making it hard to practise."

"You guys are making it impossible for me to study. Can't you sing quietly?"

His nostrils flared. "No."

"Just that? No?"

"Yes, just no. It's useless to practise quietly. We need to practise it the way we'll be performing it. Loud!"

She squeezed her lips together before turning and unplugging her computer. "Fine! I'll go upstairs."

"You do that, Princess," he drawled, clearly pleased he'd won.

"Don't call me that!" She turned back to her door and slammed it shut, wishing she had yanked that idiotic red beard right off his face. She paced the room, gathering the things she needed to work upstairs. That man made her absolutely insane.

Storming past the boys, who were standing around the family room, she tramped up the stairs and settled in the dining room. She sprawled her books around her and tried to focus, but she could still hear them below her. Belting out at top volume, sounding even better than earlier. They changed something—new key maybe? She liked this variation more. She tilted her head. It would sound even better if the bass would stop humming during the chorus so that the best voice could sing alone, pure, clean, and unaccompanied. That would sound awesome.

"Those boys are good, aren't they?" Nanima strolled into the dining room, a mug of chai in her hands, and sat across from Amira.

"They are. But distracting. I'm having trouble focusing on my work."

"Why don't you wear ear . . . bits?"

Amira couldn't help but chuckle. "It's ear*buds*, Nanima. Or headphones. Anyway, I don't like music while studying."

"I don't understand this band, though. Why are these young men singing old-man music?"

"I don't get it either, but apparently barbershop quartets are trendy again. They're a strange bunch, that's for sure. Are you home tonight or do you need me to watch Zahra?"

"No, I'm home. I think your mum said she is going out after work. Come up for dinner, I'm making korma."

Nanima took a sip of her tea, then tilted her head as the singing started up again. "I heard some of those boys are, you know, different. Fruit."

"Huh?"

"You know, poofs."

Amira raised a brow. "Seriously, Nanima? *Poofs?* She knew her grandmother wasn't exactly the most forward-thinking elderly Indian woman out there, but Amira loved her too much to challenge her less-than-sensitive comments, most of the time. Deep down, she knew Nanima was loving and accepting, even if she didn't always seem that way.

Nanima nodded. "I heard they all are, except for Sameer, of course. I don't know how much I like renting to those people, but I promised Shirin before I met them. She says Sameer needs to be around Ismaili Muslims more. He needs better influences. I am glad you are down there with him. You're such a good girl."

Nanima obviously hadn't discovered her friend's grand-son was a poof just like the rest of them, but unless he was careful, she *would* find out. Amira's gut tightened. She still didn't think Sameer liked her very much—Duncan probably told him she was a spoiled brat, but she really felt for the guy. Having to hide his true self from his family and from his community had to be torturous. She wasn't going to out him—no one deserved that—but she hoped one day he would be able to be honest with his family.

But right now, she needed to change the subject away from the boys downstairs. "Where's Mum going later?"

"To a play with friends from the hospital. I'm glad she's getting out. Farida works too hard. I want her to come with me to Shirin's daughter's anniversary party next weekend. There is a nice man I met at Jamatkhana who just moved here from Winnipeg." Nanima leaned in and whispered, "Divorced, like her. He'll be at the party. But your mum only wants to go out with work friends. You know your mother . . . I can't tell her what to do."

Amira smiled to herself, remembering Zahra's suspicion that Mum had a new relationship. Was that who was taking Mum to the theatre? If there was a relationship, it seemed Nanima hadn't figured it out yet. "Mum is almost fifty. She doesn't need her mother telling her what to do."

Nanima smiled. "Then what is a mother for? Can I pour you some chai, beta?"

Amira was about to agree to the chai when the guys started a new rendition of the chorus of "Stand by Me." This time louder. And clearer. The singer sang alone, with no accompaniment from the others. She had been right. It did sound better.

But someone down there obviously didn't agree. Voices raised in a heated debate before they even finished the chorus. How were these guys supposed to win a group competition if they couldn't make it through a song without snapping at each other? She heard a door slam.

Amira rubbed her face before shutting down her computer.

"You know what, Nanima? I'm not going to get any work done here. Can I borrow your car to go to the library?"

"Of course," Nanima said.

Amira needed to retreat and regroup. She had been home with these guys for less than twenty-four hours and she was already pulled into their drama.

CHAPTER EIGHT

RETURNING LATE FROM the library, Amira had dinner with Nanima and Zahra before heading downstairs. She could hear the guys' voices and found the four of them crowded around the small television in the family room watching baseball.

"Amira!" Travis grinned. "Come join us. These jocks are so engrossed in this game, I swear I could strip naked and sing 'God Save the Queen' on the coffee table and they wouldn't notice. I can't do sports . . . I wouldn't know a baseball bat from a fruit bat."

Duncan, Sameer, and Barrington seemed to be taking the game seriously. None of them so much as glanced at Amira as she sat on the couch with Travis.

"Did you get your work done?" he asked.

She shrugged. "Some. I wish the library was closer, though. I borrowed my grandmother's car today but I won't be able to do that every day. Your rehearsal earlier sounded great."

He waved his hand dismissively. "We were terrible, but I guess it's to be expected. It'll take us awhile to really gel as a group. Rome wasn't built in a day." Travis's last sentence was belted out in song, which elicited loud shushing from Sameer. Travis's mouth upturned with mischief as he sang the next line of the Morcheeba song.

Amira chuckled, fascinated to learn two things about Travis. One, although he had a lovely voice, his was not the best voice in the group she had identified earlier. And two, Travis appeared to annoy Sameer as much as Amira annoyed him. Duncan seemed to be the only one who didn't irritate Sameer. They were definitely a couple. "Haven't you all been singing together for a while?" she asked.

"Technically, but not all in the same room. We just formed this group. We don't even have a name yet. We registered for the competition with a place-holder name, but we can change it."

"What's your temporary name?"

"Sam I Am What I Am . . . Sameer's choice, of course." He glanced at his co–lead singer, eyes narrowed. "He doesn't want to keep the name, though. Honestly, I'm not sure this whole experiment will work. Sameer's been in a mood since he went to his grandmother's last night. I'm half-expecting him to call it all off and send us packing . . ."

"No one's packing to go anywhere," Duncan shot out, eyes not budging from the screen.

Experiment? Definitely a story there . . . but Amira didn't want to know it. Staying out of the boy-band drama in her family room was the best survival strategy she could think of to get through this. She smiled at Travis.

"You know what? I'm going to make some chai and see if I can get some papers read before bed. Have a good night."

"Good night, Amira. Oh, and"—he glanced at Sameer and Duncan—"I'm sorry if we were disruptive earlier. Some of us need to learn not to swing our testicles around to see what they'll hit, and some of us need to learn to ask for help when we need it."

She snorted. Travis was a funny guy. In other circumstances, he would be exactly the kind of person she would love as a friend, but not now. School work now. Not getting sucked in further with this band of merry men.

After another hour of work in her room, Amira called Reena and filled her in on the boy drama in the basement.

"For someone who wants to stay out of it, you're certainly taking an interest in this singing group."

"How can I not? They are literally just outside my door."

"Who do you think that Travis guy meant was swinging his nuts around?"

"Duncan, I'm assuming. An 'asserting his masculinity' thing."

"Humph. Men." She paused. "I'm trying to picture them. All the guys are hot, right?"

"Yeah, but they're all gay!"

"You don't know that for sure, do you?"

Heated male voices erupted in the family room, followed by heavy footsteps heading up and out the door. "They're arguing again," Amira said.

"Maybe they're a new and modern polyamorous family?" Reena suggested.

"If so, I think Mum and Dad may be splitting up."

"Which ones do you think are Mum and Dad?"

Amira laughed. "No clue . . ."

"You know, Meer," Reena said between giggles, "I'm going to have to come over for a visit. I want to meet these Boyz II Men wannabes."

An hour later, when the place was once again silent, Amira padded out to the kitchen to make a hot turmeric milk. She couldn't sleep, and this old Indian home remedy always did the trick for her. As she put the cup in the microwave, she cringed at the sound of footsteps behind her. It was probably Duncan. She braced herself for another argument as she turned around. It was Sameer.

"Can't sleep," he mumbled, not making eye contact. His hair was mussed and he wore plaid pyjama pants and a white T-shirt. Amira looked closely at the man for the first time. There was no denying that Sameer was good-looking, with fresh features and a youthful gaze. She also couldn't miss the faint frown lines and the dark circles under his eyes.

"You like *haldi doodh*? Turmeric milk? It always helps me sleep," she offered.

His face softened. "My mum used to make me that when I was little. Haven't had it in years."

Amira smiled as she silently prepared a cup for him. Some milk, a half spoonful of turmeric, a pinch of ground cardamom, and a squirt of honey. As it warmed in the microwave, Duncan joined them and pulled a beer out of the fridge. He nodded to Sameer.

"You okay, Sam?" he asked.

Sameer ran his fingers through his hair. "Yeah . . . no. I don't know. Was this a mistake?"

"That's for you to decide. You have the most at stake," Duncan said.

This little chat was getting serious. Amira smiled awkwardly and started to inch out of the room.

"Amira, wait," Sameer said. "Can . . . can we speak to you for a second? Just a few minutes."

The microwave chimed. Amira took the hot milk out and stirred it before handing it to Sameer. What could they possibly want to talk to her about?

"We need to ask you a huge favour . . ." Duncan said. Amira's brows shot up. How huge? He smirked. "Don't worry, Princess. You'll be fine. I'm your knight in shining armour, remember?"

"Just give us a minute to explain," Sameer added, his expression pleading.

"Fine. Let's go sit in the family room."

She settled into the old armchair, watching the two men carefully. Duncan was sprawled comfortably on the couch, legs out in front of him and crossed at the ankles. He leaned back and rested one hand behind his head. In contrast, Sameer perched tensely next to him.

"So . . . what's this favour?" Amira asked, clutching her mug to her chest.

Duncan glanced at Sameer, obviously wanting him to start. Sameer took a deep breath.

"Okay. Um, here's the thing. When we agreed to stay here, we were told that even though we weren't renting the whole basement, just the two bedrooms and shared use of the common areas, there wouldn't be anyone else here. But you are here, and well . . . you are . . . you know . . . you, and you have the right to be here. This is your home, not ours. And we don't really know you . . ."

The kid was clearly upset. And he clearly had trouble making any semblance of sense when he was upset. Amira had hoped that the obvious tension in the basement would be enough to make his band of minstrels leave her house, but Sameer's nervous posture and runaway mouth melted her resolve, just a tiny bit. She felt for the guy.

"And we thought we'd have privacy down here," he continued, staring directly at his own knees. "I didn't want to stay here at first, I didn't want to be living with, you know, friends of the family, but we couldn't afford anything else, and I told your grandmother we needed our own space, and, you know, not be expected to socialize, go up for chai and samosas every day, but then—"

"Sameer," Duncan interrupted. "You're rambling."

Sameer lifted his eyebrows as he looked at Amira. Poor kid. He looked like a lost puppy. She decided to throw him a bone.

"Relax, Sameer. What is it you need from me?" she asked.

He shifted in his seat. "I don't know you, but I hope I can trust that you . . . can you keep anything you see down here to yourself?"

Amira tensed. What kind of stuff were they expecting she would see? Was the barbershop quartet scene some sort of kinky, exhibitionist community? Had Travis been serious about singing "God Save the Queen" in the buff?

"You can put your eyeballs back in your head, Princess. Sameer just doesn't want you to tell anyone he's gay," Duncan said.

Sameer looked at Duncan, relieved he said the word for him.

"Is that all?" she asked. Of course she wouldn't tell anyone, not if he didn't want her to.

He frowned. "My grandmother doesn't know, and she keeps asking me why I don't have a girlfriend. In Ottawa, it's just me and my mom, and she's been okay with it, but when I told her I was coming here, she made me promise not to let the Toronto family know. I just don't want gossip to spread."

Amira cringed. "I'm sorry, Sameer, I think it already has. I heard gossip you were gay from a friend here."

"Fuck." His shoulders crumpled in on themselves. He sat quietly for a few seconds before looking at Duncan. "Maybe we should go back . . . I hate feeling like everyone's watching me."

Duncan's nostrils flared. "We can't go back, Sam. The only way to make this work is if we rehearse together. Running off to Ottawa means the end of our chances."

"But gossip is already spreading; my grandmother will find out . . ."

Amira looked at Sameer carefully. Poor kid had one of the most expressive pair of eyes she had ever seen. He wore his heart on his sleeve, and something about him kicked her protective instinct into high gear. If they left Toronto, Amira could get the quiet place to work she wanted, but then these four boys would have to give up on their dream of winning the competition. As bizarre as it seemed to her, this barbershop quartet competition obviously meant a lot to Sameer, and to Duncan. Not that she cared two bits about what Duncan wanted, but she had started to develop a soft spot for her grandmother's friend's grandson in the last ten minutes. She had an urge to keep him safe. He could be the little brother she always wanted. In fact, if he weren't gay, he would be a perfect . . .

That's it. Amira half-expected a light bulb to appear atop her head. There was a way to solve all his problems. But it would be a big sacrifice from her. Unless . . . unless she could barter with the barbershop quartet.

"I have an idea," she said with a smile. "I propose a truce. You guys keep quiet every morning for me to work. Say, till about noon. You wake up later than me, anyway. If I want to keep working after that, maybe one of you can take me to the library since I don't have a car."

Sameer looked hurt. "You'll only keep my secret if we stop rehearsing in the morning?"

"No," she reassured him. "I'll keep your secret no matter what, honestly. But if you agree to my terms, I have a way to make sure no one gossips about you. At least not the kind of gossip you're afraid of."

Duncan was obviously quicker on the draw than Sameer, as his face slowly transformed into a wide grin. "You're good, Princess. I think that might work."

"What?" Sameer asked, looking back and forth between Amira and Duncan.

Amira smiled. "No one will think you're gay, because I am offering to be your beard."

"My beard?" Sameer asked, brows knitting together.

Duncan grinned as he ran his fingers over the red strands on his face. "Yeah, and she's not talking about my fine specimen here. Princess Jasmine is willing to be your fake girlfriend while we're in town."

She shot a sneer at Duncan. "Don't call me that."

Sameer looked at Amira with wonder. "You'd do that? I don't know . . ."

"I think it's a great idea," Duncan said. "If your family thinks you're dating the hot Indian chick in the basement, the rumour mill will change course and your grandmother will stop nagging you to settle down. Then we can stay here, focus on the quartet, and win the competition. You two can break up when we go back home."

Duncan thought she was hot?

Sameer didn't look convinced. "So, we'd go on dates?"

Amira wrinkled her brow. She hadn't really thought this idea through. Actual dates could get awkward—and she really didn't have time for dating right now.

"We probably wouldn't have to," she said, thinking aloud. "It would work if all of us just hung out together, but we'd let people think Sameer and I are together, instead of you two."

Duncan nearly spat beer out his mouth. "I'm not with Sameer!"

"What? You two aren't a couple?" Had she read this wrong?

Duncan exploded in laughter, his loud cackle filling the room. "No. I'm as straight as a fly rod, Princess."

A what?

Sameer also laughed, his face brightening as his frown lines finally eased. "Duncan and I only met in person the other day. We're not dating! We met on a barbershop quartet forum."

There were barbershop quartet forums? "But . . . you're sharing a room, aren't you?"

"No," Sameer said, still laughing. "Travis and I are sharing a room. We've been together for a year and a half. Barrington and Duncan are sharing the other room."

"I'm sleeping on the floor," Duncan added. "On an air mattress. Barry is engaged to a woman in Waterloo."

"I'm confused," Amira said.

Duncan blinked away his tears of amusement. "I don't know why you never asked us, but here are our details. Sameer and Travis are from Ottawa and are, quite honestly, made for each other. Barrington hails from Waterloo, where he left behind the beautiful Marcia, who has him whipped stiffer than a cheese soufflé. I'm from Omemee, a small town about forty-five minutes north of Port Hope, where you and I met. Barry and I have known each other for a while through music, but we only met Sameer and Travis in person once we got here. We've all been really close online for about six months."

"It doesn't matter who sleeps with who, anyway," Sameer said. He paused, a small smile still on his face. This was the first time she saw a real smile on him, and she was struck at how much it transformed him. After a few seconds, he nodded. "I'll have to discuss it with Travis, but you know what? I think this might work."

Duncan smiled widely as he patted Sameer on the back. "Congratulations, buddy. Like me, you now have a beard."

CHAPTER NINE

"SO, THE LUMBERJACK is not gay, then," Reena asked.

"So he says. Half the quartet plays for one team, the other half for another." Amira swirled her spoon through her bowl of fragrant Thai curry soup, letting the spicy aroma of chili and lemon grass soothe her stress away. It was Friday—a few days after she had made the deal with Sameer and Duncan, exchanging silent mornings for her services as a fake girlfriend. And even though her "relationship" with Sameer hadn't seemed to have taken off yet, the boys kept up their end of the bargain faithfully, staying out of sight and sound before noon each day. She assumed they stayed in their rooms, but she didn't hear them at all. She got a solid five hours of work done each day before they started singing, and her stress was reduced from full-on tactical assault to mere irritation. To reward herself, she had taken the subway downtown for some afternoon window shopping and a Thai dinner with Reena.

"You'll keep this to yourself, right?" Amira asked.

"Of course I will. I have to say, you've found an odd way to keep the place quiet, though. Most people don't start a new relationship, even a fake one, because they want alone time. What's going to happen when Nanima and Shirin start planning your wedding?"

Amira groaned as she absently watched her friend take pictures of their dinner with her phone. What would she tell her family after Sameer told his grandmother about their budding new romance? She hated lying, but for this to work, her family also had to believe she was dating Sameer. Maybe if they kept to one, maybe two dates, both families would realize this wasn't serious. "It won't come to that. Nanima loves weddings, but I think even she wouldn't go bridal sari shopping after less than two weeks of dating."

"Maybe not, but we're talking about dating her best friend's grandson. She may be too excited about combining the families. This could get out of hand, Amira," Reena teased in a knowing tone as she put her phone away.

"It won't."

"Can I be the maid of honour at your fake beard wedding? I'd love a turquoise colour scheme. It really is my colour."

"Shut up."

"The hairstylist boyfriend will have to be the best man."

Amira rolled her eyes. It wouldn't come to that. No one was marrying anyone. No one was even dating anyone, except of course Sameer and Travis.

"My mum went bridal sari shopping for me last week," Reena said with complete nonchalance before slurping noodles from her spoon.

"What? You're not even dating anyone!" Amira stilled. "You're *not* dating anyone, are you?"

Reena snort-laughed. "No! You know I've put a moratorium on men right now. But my mother found me another eligible bachelor. She jumped the gun and started looking at salwar kameez before I'd even met the man. Mum's not taking me turning thirty and still being single too well."

Amira cringed. That was one area she would always be grateful for when it came to her family—her parents never laid on that Indian pressure to be married at a young age. It helped that her family was a bit unconventional themselves, but no one batted an eyelash when Amira announced she was going to grad school instead of settling down. No one said she was getting too old to be single, and she was a good ten years older than her mother had been when she married and gave birth to Amira.

"Did you at least meet the man?" Amira asked.

"Yup. Mum invited him to brunch. Kinda-sweet old guy. At least forty-five. A divorcee from Winnipeg. Dude's wife left him out of the blue a few years ago." She paused. "I won't be marrying him."

Amira laughed so hard, soup nearly came out her nose. "Oh my god, Nanima is trying to set my mother up with that guy!"

Reena giggled. "A successful single man with most of his hair? He's a hot commodity." She shook her head. "Seriously wonder about the quality of the potential husbands my mother finds for me. Clearly I am supposed to be lowering my expectations in my golden years."

Amira laughed again. "I'm also in my golden years but I'm fake-dating a man five years younger than me!"

Reena smiled. "They know I'm not cut out to be a cougar. When are you and Sameer going public with your courtship?"

"No idea. I've barely spoken to him since we made the deal."

"But you're getting on well with the other guys?"

She shrugged. "Don't know. I've been in my room most of the time."

Reena squeezed her lips together a moment, as if reluctant to say something. "You know what, Amira?" she finally said. "I kind of miss the old you."

Amira scoffed. *Old her*. What the hell was that supposed to mean?

Reena continued. "You used to drag me everywhere, even going back to high-school days. Concerts, festivals, lectures, book clubs. And you knew everyone. You made new friends all the time. I get that we've grown up but . . . you always had a huge personality. Lately, you've just . . . I don't know. Folded into yourself. And you snarl at anyone who tries to unfold you."

Amira looked down at her half-empty bowl. This wasn't a new complaint. She knew she was different. The combination of grad school and being away from her hometown had altered her.

She closed her eyes briefly. That wasn't it. She knew damn well why she had changed. It all started that stupid day at the airport. "I know."

"I don't want to upset you, Amira. I still adore you, it's just . . . you'll miss out on great connections if you never let people in. I know trusting people is hard, but—" She flashed a sad smile. "I get it. I hate the world right now, too. I'm definitely not the one to talk about never leaving her comfort zone. But you need more in your life than me, your family, and work."

Reena was sort of right. Yes, the world was a complete Dumpster fire, and staying in her own little bubble was certainly easier on her mental health. But it wasn't that trusting new people was hard; it was more like she just didn't care to do the work of building that trust anymore. But that sounded slightly misanthropic, so she smiled reassuringly at Reena. "But you're the best, Ree. Why would I need more? We're going to have an awesome summer. Once school's done—"

Amira's phone rang. She glanced at it—unknown number. Tensing, she instinctively feared it was another reporter. But on a Friday night?

She reluctantly answered. "Hello?"

"Hi, um, Amira, this is Sameer."

"Oh, hey. Did I give you my number?"

"No. I got it from your grandmother. Anyway, I was wondering . . . the guys and I were thinking, we're going to this beer festival downtown later, since there's a barbershop booked, so we're going to check out the competition and Travis thought I should ask you—"

"Are you asking me out, Sameer?" Amira asked. Reena erupted in giggles.

He blew out a puff of air. "I'm trying to. How am I doing?"

"Not too bad. Your fumbling is kind of charming. I do have two questions, though. First, can I bring my friend Reena? She'll be discreet. You're bringing a quartet on our first date, after all."

"Uh, sure, I guess. What's your other question?"

"What time and where?"

"It's at the Liverpool Brewpub, downtown somewhere. Eight o'clock."

"I know where that is. We'll meet you there."

After disconnecting the call, she smiled at Reena. "Does this work for getting out of my comfort zone? A beer festival with the quartet. I hope you don't mind being a fifth . . ." She paused. "Sixth wheel tonight? They're going to the Liverpool Brewpub."

Reena grinned. "It's fabulous. I need to meet your boy band."

It was a clear, warm evening so they decided to walk to the brewpub. The sun was setting over the horizon, bathing the sky in a rosy, almost otherworldly glow. There was nothing Amira loved more than Toronto in the spring. She was born and raised in the city, and she loved that her home was the kind of place with a Peruvian coffee house next to an Afghan kebab shop, next to a Jewish deli wafting with the scent of bagels from a wood-burning oven.

The weather, the lively streets, and Reena's company were doing great things for her mood. Grad school was almost done and her project report was well on its way. Even the issues at work seemed minimal right now. Raymond would have Amira's back and stand up for her, if needed, just like he always did.

And she was weirdly looking forward to spending time with most of her new roommates. Reluctantly, she agreed, at least to herself, that Reena was right. She did need more in her life than work and family, and maybe it was time to slip back into her social-butterfly old self. Fortuitously, there was a group of 75 percent friendly guys right in her basement who wanted to spend time with her. This could be fun, even if she had to ignore the flannel-clad 25 percent.

As they approached the entry to the brewpub, Travis's voice made her smile even wider. "Amira, you look gorgeous. I'm so glad you came." She turned to see her four roommates walking towards her. Travis pulled her in for a hug. After Amira introduced Reena to the quartet, they went into the pub.

Liverpool Brewpub was a large new building, half microbrewery, half restaurant, by the waterfront downtown. Entering, Amira took in the high, beamed ceilings and wood-panelled walls that contrasted so well with the glossy slate floor and minimalist table settings. A seamless blend of urban and rustic that really appealed to her. They found a table near the stage. Soon after arranging themselves, Reena leaned in close.

"Duncan *is* hot. Gorgeous eyes."

"Reena. No. Don't get any ideas."

"He was staring at you in line."

"He wasn't. He doesn't like me."

"You told me he was rude and annoying. He seems perfectly charming to me."

"Give him time . . ."

"Shall we order nachos for the table?" Duncan said loudly, eyeing a menu. "Sweet! They've got pulled-pork nachos."

"No pork," Amira said.

Duncan looked up. "Right. Muslims. Two orders, then? One regular and one with pulled pork for us heathens. Or, wait—" He looked at Amira and cringed. "Sorry, you probably don't want pork at the table. Two regulars, then, hold the bacon—"

Sameer laughed. "I don't have an issue if you guys eat pork. I just won't."

"Fine with me, too," Reena added.

They sorted out what to order—one order of pulled-pork nachos, one order of barbecue chicken nachos, hold the bacon, one pitcher of beer, and one of cider.

"So," Barrington said after they finished ordering, "you guys don't eat pork but you do drink?"

Reena laughed. "Yeah, I know. A bit hypocritical. Amira and I aren't very religious."

"To be honest," Amira added, "the pork thing is really more habit than anything else. I never ate pork growing up, so it seems strange to do it now." Her nose wrinkled. "Smells weird."

Duncan pushed his chair out as if he was about to stand. "I'll get the girl to change ours. I don't want to—"

Sameer laughed. "Honestly, it's fine. Travis eats bacon at home all the time. The sight or smell doesn't offend us, we just don't eat it."

Duncan moved his chair back in, but still looked concerned. The waitress came with their drinks.

"You two live together?" Reena asked, motioning between Sameer and Travis.

Travis nodded, smiling with pride. "Yup. For about six months. We have this tiny loft. I love it."

"It's not a loft. It's a glorified bachelor apartment," Sameer said.

Travis waved his hand at Sameer. "It's fabulous. The location is amazing. Smack-dab in the middle of downtown Ottawa. Walking distance to the gay village and to my work. And the upstairs neighbour loves it when we sing. She turns off her TV and always claps when we're done. I'm never leaving that place."

Amira laughed. "You guys always sound great when I hear you." Duncan frowned at her, so she turned away from him. "Have you decided what songs you're singing for the competition?"

"We've got two solidified," Barrington said. "Still arguing on a third. We're doing 'Stand by Me' and 'Jolene.'"

Sameer laughed. "We're doing 'Jolene' so long as Travis stops screwing it up by singing *Justine* instead of *Jolene*."

"Justine? Why?" Reena asked.

Travis smiled. "My sister's name is Justine. In high school, a boyfriend dumped me for her, so I used to sing it to get under her skin."

Amira laughed. "Holy shit, really? Did it last between them?"

He scoffed. "Of course not. You think anyone can be happy after walking away from this?" He waved his hand towards himself with flair. "He came crawling back a month later. I wasn't about to go there again. But that song will always be for Justine. I'm going to sing it at her wedding one day." He sang a few bars of the song, substituting *Justine* for *Jolene* and flawlessly mimicking Dolly Parton's country twang. Barrington grinned and joined in, his low voice contrasting with Travis's high notes.

Reena laughed, clapping when they were done. "You and your sister close?" she asked Travis.

Sameer answered for him. "Too close. They even work together. But Justine's great. All of Travis's family is great.

"Amira mentioned you're a hairstylist?"

Travis nodded. "Justine and I work at a salon in the ByWard Market in Ottawa. A really funky place, it's amazing. If you ever want a trim, you should come by the house. I miss having my hands in hair all day." He smiled as he tenderly ran his fingers through the back of Sameer's hair. Sameer's eyes half-closed for a second and the tips of his ears turned pink. "Sameer just finished pharmacy school and will be searching for a job when we get back," Travis continued, his hand still on the back of Sameer's head.

"And you?" Reena asked Duncan. "What's your day job?"

"I'm actually a singer," he said. "And a substitute teacher."

Amira nearly dropped the beer in her hand. "You're a teacher?" She hadn't expected that. Lumberjack, carpenter, maybe even some other skilled trade, but not a teacher.

"Yeah. High-school music and sometimes history. I used to work at a local school, but it closed. Been looking for something permanent for a while, but good teaching posts are sparse where I live. Substituting lets me work when I want, so I can keep playing music."

Amira could not picture it. Smirking, sarcastic Duncan teaching kids? She worried about future generations of musicians if their teachers were like the garden gnome.

"Where do you play?" Reena asked.

"Here and there. I sing with a few local bands that do mostly bar gigs around home, and I teach private guitar lessons."

"Duncan's amazing," Barrington chimed in. "He's got a YouTube channel where he does metal classics on the ukulele. We're lucky to have him."

Amira turned to look at the man in question. His hair had been neatly trimmed and artfully messed in the front. Probably Travis's doing—travelling with a hairstylist was handy. He wore no flannel today, instead a dark grey button-up topped with a black cardigan. How he managed to wear suspenders one day and a cardigan the next and not give off any whiff of nursing-home fugitive was a mystery to Amira. Must be the vibrancy of the beard, which almost glowed in the low light of the restaurant. His green eyes looked darker while still sparkling with the reflection from the overhead lights, like murky green pools reflecting the moon.

Damn it. What was it about this man that made her think in trite poetry?

Still, she couldn't help but wonder what the rest of his face looked like under that beard. Suddenly, one of his eyebrows raised a fraction of an inch as the ghost of a smile flitted across his mouth. He noticed her staring at him. She turned away quickly. The food arrived then, a thankful distraction from that awkward moment.

"You know," Reena said, piling nachos on a plate, "in high school, Amira was a bit of a groupie for guys in rock bands. What's the music version of a puck-bunny?"

Amira pinched her friend's leg under the table. Unfazed, Reena continued. "These days, she's not really into music, though."

"I enjoy my silence," Amira said, glaring at her friend. "And I don't have time for anything but school right now. Thank god I'm almost done."

"Then what?" Sameer asked.

"I go back to work at the same consulting firm where I worked before grad school. They gave me a leave of absence."

"What kind of engineering do you do?" Barrington asked.

"Industrial. I work as a consultant in the manufacturing sector."

Barrington's proud smile split his face. "Wow. That's hardcore; you must be brilliant. That's what your master's degree is in?"

"Believe me, I'm far from brilliant, just determined."

"What's your final paper about?" Sameer asked, picking jalapenos off his nachos and putting them on Travis's plate.

"Vibration and noise control in manufacturing," she said.

Duncan rolled his eyes. "Noise control? Why am I not surprised . . ." He shook his head.

For her own mental health, Amira decided to ignore the garden gnome. "My program had a lab project component. For my project, I used finite element modelling to develop new algorithms to analyze how different noise-dampening materials work in practical applications. My report will discuss the most recent research in the area and review possible applications in the field."

"Fascinating," Barrington said. "I can't say I know much about engineering, but I do know sound dampening. That's the stuff lining the walls in a recording studio, right?"

"Yup. Although my work deals with plant noise, not music. In a recording studio, the dampening is as much for keeping the good sounds in as the bad sounds out."

"The concepts are the same, though, right?" Travis added. "You could totally use your findings in the music industry. I mean, musicians are all about maximizing vibrations and sounds, while you're about minimizing. Same principles, though."

Duncan snorted loudly. "Minimizing sounds? Minimizing enjoyment, I say."

Amira ignored the lumberjack and continued. "I suppose. I haven't worked in sound reduction before; I don't know much about careers there. My consulting work was mostly on computer integration in manufacturing. I'm hoping the advanced degree will help me transition to a senior consultant position in that area within the next two years."

"You have it all planned out, eh, Princess?" Duncan asked. "Have you scheduled time for marriage and kids yet?" He almost snarled with derision.

What the hell was this guy's problem? One minute he's all concerned and chivalrous about the pork, and now rude comments? Amira opened her mouth, hoping something sharp and biting would find its way out, when Reena elbowed her, presumably a pre-emptive strike to shut her up.

"How old are you guys? If you don't mind me asking," Reena said. "I'm thirty, like Amira."

"Wow, I would never have guessed," Travis said. "You two both look so young! I'm twenty-eight, same as Barrington. Sameer is twenty-five, and Duncan, our wise elder, is thirty-two."

"Nice! I know you two are together"—Reena waved her hand towards Sameer and Travis—"but Duncan and Barrington are single, right?" The cider was most definitely going to Reena's head. Amira pinched her friend again, hoping it would put a stop to this interrogation.

Although . . . it was interesting to learn Duncan was thirty-two. He definitely carried himself like the wise elder in the group, despite his current immature sulking. She saw his mouth tighten to a straight line. His maturity seemed to match Zahra's tonight.

Did that pout have something to do with his single status? Maybe this was a sore spot for him?

"I'm getting married in the winter," Barrington said. "But Duncan's still looking for perfection. Of course, he'll never find it, since I'm marrying it."

"Perfection is highly overrated. I like less determination. A more easygoing personality," Duncan said.

Barrington laughed. "That is so not true. You like them complicated and fastidious."

Duncan scowled again, before looking straight at Amira. "Nah, what would a meticulous planner do with me? You know, Princess, spending so much time with noise dampeners may dampen your ability to enjoy life."

That's it. Amira was done turning the other cheek. She pointed her finger at Duncan. "Look, gnome boy, if you think I'm going to show some new disdain for my life by seeing it through your eyes, you're sorely mistaken. We are all aware that you have nothing but contempt for my life choices, so why don't you take that Yukon Cornelius beard and shove it up your—"

Reena pinched Amira this time. Hard. She winced and glared at her so-called friend.

The lights in the restaurant suddenly dimmed. "Group's coming on," Sameer said.

Travis turned to Amira and Reena. "This is Fourth Fret. They're huge in the barbershop community out here. Our toughest competition."

Fourth Fret consisted of four singers: two attractive men and two attractive women, all with dark hair and looking to be in their early to mid-twenties. The men wore slim black suits, white shirts, and skinny black ties, and the women wore white blouses and black velvet skirts. Even before they opened their mouths, Amira wasn't impressed. They looked so . . . cookie cutter. The same. They were different races, but they still looked like siblings. She liked the eclectic look of Duncan's group better. Or, rather, Sameer's group.

But from the moment the guy on the far right pulled out a pitch pipe to find their first note, Amira was transfixed.

She knew so little about barbershop music, but these guys were spectacular. They didn't just sing, they entertained. Unexpectedly, they started with a Taylor Swift song, and after they shook it all off, they seamlessly transitioned to "Bohemian Rhapsody." They snapped their fingers, danced, and were so expressive, their bland cookie-cutter looks were all but forgotten. In between songs, they told jokes and interacted with the crowd. In a word, they were amazing.

Amira eyed her companions. Sam I Am What I Am had the vocal talent, but did they have that certain unknown factor? The "spark" to beat Fourth Fret? Sameer with his rambling and scowls, Barrington with his pleasant professionalism, and Duncan with his smirks and underhanded comments. Not to mention all the infighting whenever they rehearsed. She could only picture Travis engaging with the audience like this, but if they were going to compete with these guys, they would all have to be on.

After the quartet sang their final number ("The Longest Time" by Billy Joel) and left the stage, the table was silent. Amira wondered if they were thinking the same thing as her.

"Those guys were . . . good," Reena said, diplomatically.

"They were awesome," Barrington groaned. "We have a lot of work to do."

"But we'll do it," Travis said. "We can sing those guys into a corner, we have the chops."

"But we're nowhere near that calibre." Sameer fidgeted with the cardboard coaster on the table.

"We will be, Sameer." Travis looked at him. "We'll get there."

Amira looked at Duncan, conspicuously silent during this pep talk. Of the four of them, he was the only one who worked professionally in the music industry. No doubt his opinions on their chances were different from the others.

He noticed her looking at him again, but this time he didn't smirk, or scowl. He nodded, smiling sadly, as if he understood what she was thinking. They needed so much more than singing chops to win, and they were far from ready.

But what she didn't get yet was why this was so important to them. Duncan said he intended to win this thing as if his life depended on it. All of them had put their personal and professional lives on hold and tucked themselves away in her grandmother's basement to rehearse for a barbershop quartet competition. Why? It seemed so silly. Certainly silly compared to her current goals. But these guys seemed even more stressed than she was.

And a tightening constriction in her stomach told her that their stress was rubbing off on her, which perplexed her to no end. Why did she care what happened to these four singing misfits?

· · · ·

THE NEXT DAY, Amira kept to her routine and worked all morning. But by afternoon, yesterday's late night caught up with her and she couldn't convince herself to keep working, so she wandered upstairs to see if anyone wanted to do something.

Her mother was in the kitchen, standing by the microwave and looking into her phone. Amira watched her for a second before interrupting. Mum was looking amazing these days. She used to wear her hair long, and usually pulled back into a ponytail, but she'd recently had it cut into a more structured shoulder-length style that brought out her natural waves. And although she'd always been small and slim, her mum looked stronger these days. Less stressed and overworked, more vibrant, and as a result, even more beautiful than ever.

"Hi, Mum, you're not working today?"

She turned and smiled at Amira, slipping her phone into the pocket of her jeans. "No. I'm taking Zahra to a dance class later. Do you want some biryani?"

"Sure." Amira pulled down a bowl from the cabinet. "Where is she now?"

Her mum spooned the chicken biryani from a plastic container into Amira's bowl and put it in the microwave. "She's at Bollywood Beat but she has an emergency Kathak lesson in an hour."

Amira laughed. "Emergency? I don't think I want to know what constitutes a dance emergency. I was hoping you, Zahra, or Nanima were free this afternoon to go to a movie or something."

Her mum took her own bowl to the dining table and sat down, putting her phone on the table in front of her. She shook her head. "No one is ever free in this house. Your grandmother is at a funeral."

"Anyone I know?"

"Probably not. At her age, funerals are social events."

Amira laughed. After the microwave chimed, she brought her bowl to sit with her mother. "Nanima says you work too much lately."

Her mum's mouth tightened. "I know, she said that to me, too. But I'm not working any more than I always did. *She's* the one out of the house all the time. The woman is in her seventies and out six days a week, and she says *I* work too hard?"

"She's always had a busy life."

Her mum sighed. "I know. I'm happy she's healthy and vibrant at her age, but I can do without the judgment. She's annoyed that I have a social life one minute, then tells me I don't get out enough the next." Mum took a bit of her rice, furrowing her brow in disdain.

Amira didn't know what to say. She agreed that Nanima was a touch too judgmental, but she'd never heard her mother complain about Nanima judging her, instead of others.

"Anyway, enough about that," Mum said. "Are you available to watch Zahra tomorrow morning? I'm on the early shift."

"I'm home, but I need to be working on my project."

"I'll tell her to stay out of your hair. She has homework, too. I don't want to ask your grandmother. I'm much too dependent on her."

"Did Nanima say that?"

Mum didn't answer for a while, only ate quietly. Amira could see the tension in her mother's shoulders. It suddenly occurred to her that she hadn't seen her mother and grandmother in the same room even once since she'd come home. Of course, with everyone in the family busy, and Amira's head in academic journals most of the time, it was no wonder. She couldn't expect everyone to be around at the same time.

She'd always assumed her mother and grandmother had a good relationship. They'd have to have been close for Mum to move back here after the divorce. But thinking back, she didn't remember them ever doing anything social together. Not cooking together, not shopping or going to movies together. Certainly not the relationship Amira had with her mother. Or the relationship Amira had with her grandmother, for that matter. True, Mum always worked hard, but Mum made time for Amira and Zahra consistently, rarely for her own mother.

It was funny how coming back after being gone so long illuminated a family dynamic she hadn't noticed before.

"No, of course not. It's fine," Mum finally said. "Just some old ghosts that have come back to haunt me. I'm honestly grateful for my mother's help with Zahra. And yours, too, Amira." She reached over and squeezed Amira's hand for a second. "I'm glad you're back in the city . . . but I hope you don't think you need to keep living here with us because of me. If you can help with Zahra when you're here, that's great, but your own future should come first."

Mum stood, talking her empty bowl to the kitchen. She clearly didn't want to talk about these ghosts, and Amira was fine with that right now. Mum would be leaving to ferry Zahra from one dance class to another very shortly, and this sounded like a big conversation. She wondered if it had anything to do with this mystery man. Mum still hadn't mentioned him.

"Mum, let's do dinner, soon. Just me and you. Maybe after this report's done and I have time to breathe. We need to catch up properly."

Mum turned back and smiled. "I'd love that, sweetie. Focus on your paper now, and we'll find time when you're done. And be honest with me—if the responsibilities here are getting in the way of your work, let us know. We can manage Zahra on our own. Education always comes first."

After finishing her rice alone, Amira went downstairs. She still didn't feel like getting back to her report. Maybe one of the guys was around to chat with.

But the basement was empty. Quiet. Eight people living in this small house, and no one around the rare time Amira wanted company. She made a pot of chai and sat on the sofa. She was about to call Reena when the side door opened and heavy footsteps came down the stairs. Amira sat up straighter and smoothed her hair. When the footsteps finally reached her, it was only Barrington and Duncan, not the whole group.

"I just had, easily, the best burger I've had in my life," Barrington said, falling heavily into the armchair. "They used grilled cheese sandwiches as buns."

Duncan chuckled as he sat on the other end of the couch. "I can't get over the food you guys have in this city. Going to have to start running again or I won't be able to do those dance moves you're insisting on, Barry." He paused. "On second thought, maybe it's a good thing. It would mean the audience wouldn't be tortured by my spastic twerking."

Amira had been aiming to ignore the garden gnome but she snort-laughed at that. And made a mental note to sneakily watch one of their rehearsals.

"You guys aren't practising today?" she asked.

"We should be," Barrington said. "After seeing what Fourth Fret can do, we should be working double time. But Travis and Sameer had plans for brunch with a friend who lives here now. Anyway, I need to call my beautiful lady. See you later." He stood, smiled, and left the room.

That left Amira alone with Duncan. She was aching for company, but alone time with the garden gnome wasn't what she had in mind. She considered the politest way to escape, since she didn't want a rehash of last night's snarkfest.

"He's so whipped," Duncan said, lounging comfortably two feet away. "He talks to her every night before going to sleep. As his roommate, I have to state how glad I am they haven't discovered phone sex yet."

"It's sweet, though. They must miss each other." Amira placed her empty mug on the coffee table.

"Maybe. I'm glad I have no relationship getting in my way right now. Between Barry calling his girl every two minutes, and Sam and Travis's bickering, it's a wonder we get any practising in at all. Not to mention the constant sour moods."

"So, that's why no girl back home in . . . Om . . . where was it? It's not your futile search for perfection?"

"Omemee. And no. Perfection or not, my life wouldn't suit a relationship right now. No steady job, I work week to week. What about you, Princess? No prince to show you his magic carpet?"

Amira frowned. Was that sexual innuendo? She honestly had no idea. "No. Only grad school in my world right now."

He sat quietly next to her, clearly deep in thought. This conversation had to be a record—the longest they'd gone without snarking at each other since the day they met. Amira didn't want to poke the bear, so to speak, so she said nothing lest she set him off again.

He sighed audibly and scrubbed his hands over his face. "Ugh. I should have brought my guitar," he mumbled with hands over his face.

"What?"

He removed his hands. "My guitar. At the last minute, I decided not to bring it since I took the train because my brother needed my truck. I thought we'd be rehearsing non-stop, and this is a cappella, no instruments. But now I'm antsy. Longest I've gone without a guitar, ever. My fingers are itching . . ."

"I have a guitar," Amira said.

He leaned towards her, a grin spreading on his face. "You do?"

"Yeah, hang on . . ." She took her mug to the kitchen before fetching her rarely used guitar from under her bed and bringing it to him. "I don't think it's been out of its case in years. My dad got it for me on my seventeenth birth-day. He didn't buy me lessons, though. I learned a bit with books, but that eventually fizzled." She handed him the hard plastic case.

He unlatched it and whistled. "She's a beaut. I expected a cheap entry-level instrument, not this."

Amira smiled at the sight of her old mahogany Fender acoustic/electric. Even if she didn't know how to play the thing, she loved the look of it. "I know. My dad was going through a bit of absentee-father guilt. He's away for work a lot, so we didn't see much of him back then. He'd have bought me the moon if I'd wanted it."

He took the instrument in his hands and began strum-ming. It was fascinating how his whole stance changed once he had a guitar in his arms. Parts of him relaxed, while others held firm on the wood body. It looked as if a lost limb had been returned to him.

He smiled warmly. "It's out of tune." He fiddled with the tuning pegs until he was happy with the tones the strings produced.

Then he looked at the strings, smiled again, and started playing. He plucked individual strings as his hand snaked across the frets at a ridiculously fast speed. It was a complicated arrangement of a simple melody that Amira immediately recognized, a song she wouldn't have expected him to play.

"'Enjoy the Silence,'" she said. "Depeche Mode."

"Yeah." He grinned at her, continuing to play the melody. "Song's been stuck in my head since last night, when you said you enjoy silence."

She loved that song, although it wasn't one she'd heard or thought about in years. He started singing, his clear, deep voice resonating through the small room. That voice . . . it was the one she'd identified while listening to the boys rehearsing from her room. His was the best voice in their quartet. She watched him singing. His finger work on the strings was impressive enough, but what was remarkable was the way Duncan's entire air changed as the song came out of him. It wasn't just sound waves created by the vibrations in his throat or the guitar string vibrations resonating through the hollow wood body—it was more than that. As an engineer, Amira found it fascinating how the individual mechanisms that created music became so much more than their individual outputs. With Duncan, the effect was even more pronounced. The music wasn't just coming out of him, it *was* him. When he reached the chorus, her skin erupted in goosebumps.

When he finished the last verse, he continued finger picking the melody, then slowed down until a final strumming of all the strings with flourish. He looked at Amira, green eyes twinkling with shy pleasure. "It's a nice instrument."

She couldn't resist that look of bliss on his face. "Feel free to use it whenever you'd like, while you're here . . . it's great that it's getting some love."

Still smiling, he ran his fingers over the neck with affection. "Needs new strings. I'll pick some up tomorrow. Thanks a lot, Amira. This will really ease my nerves."

"No problem," she said, getting up. "There's more chai in the kitchen if you want."

She escaped to her room. Watching him play was strangely disconcerting, and she didn't understand why it made her uncomfortable. She needed to put some distance between herself and Duncan. Plus, he called her Amira instead of Princess. It felt odd.

But at least she'd discovered one thing—she and Duncan Galahad *could* coexist.

CHAPTER TEN

THERE WAS NO way in hell Amira could coexist with Duncan Galahad and his merry minstrels. She was sure she had been suffering from turmeric-milk-induced delusions when she came up with this deranged bearding-for-silence scheme. Despite a few successful days, the quartet had already reneged on their end of the bargain. It was barely ten o'clock Sunday morning, and after only two hours of silent work, Amira heard the heavy footsteps start. Zahra, who was sitting on Amira's bed watching a movie, managed to hear it through her headphones and looked up.

Then doors started slamming.

Followed by the tense hushed voices.

And then tenser voices that couldn't figure out how to be hushed anymore.

"Now I'm the one being unreasonable?" That was Travis's distinctive speech, only without its usual lightness.

"What's going on?" Zahra asked.

Amira stood and opened her door, ready to go out there and tell them to cut the noise. "Sounds like the co-leads are having trouble coexisting again." Some more muffled mumbling followed, and then Travis's angered voice again.

"Who exactly are you afraid will see us in the Village, anyway?"

"Fuck, guys, I thought we were going over choreography this morning?" That voice was Barrington, sounding more annoyed than she had ever heard him. Amira didn't even know he swore.

"Jesus, people, keep your voices down. We're not supposed to make noise before twelve." That was Sameer.

"Oh, lest we upset your precious beard?" Travis said. "I think you enjoy rubbing this in my face, don't you? Can't upset Amira, she's the right gender *and* religion to save us all. You know what? Screw this. I need air."

Heavy footsteps again, loud cursing, and Duncan telling them all off in embellished language she would prefer her sister didn't hear. Then the opening and slamming of the side door.

Shit. A wave of nausea passed through her.

"What are they talking about, Amira?" Zahra asked.

"Nothing. Pretend you didn't hear that."

Apparently, Travis *was* upset about this bearding arrangement, after all. Amira's chest tightened. She needed air, too. She needed to get out of this damn house. She gathered up her books and laptop.

"Come on, Zahra. Let's go to the library. I'll get you a donut first."

Duncan stopped them at the bottom of the stairs. "Where are you going?" he asked.

"Library."

"Did you . . ." He rubbed his upper arm. "Did you hear their fight?"

"Look, Duncan, I'm sorry people are upset, but I'm at a critical point in my report and I don't want to lose my train of thought."

He blew out a puff of air. "I'll drive you. Sam?" he called out. "Borrowing your car to take the girls to the library."

The ride was tense. Painfully awkward. Duncan was weirdly quiet, squeezing the steering wheel while focusing squarely on the road ahead. Good—Amira had no interest in discussing the fight between Sameer and Travis, especially in front of her sister. Zahra was uncharacteristically quiet, too, clearly weirded out after hearing the guys scream at each other.

Amira wished she could forget what she'd heard Travis say. This bearding idea was a whim—she hadn't really considered how it would make Travis feel. Affable, enthusiastic, affectionate Travis, probably the nicest guy in their quartet, was upset because of *her* idea. He didn't deserve to be cast aside because of Sameer's family's expectations. He didn't deserve to be Sameer's secret.

She hated that Sameer was hiding Travis, but Amira got it. She was Indian. She was Muslim. She knew that the so-called traditional values that many held on to, combined with over-involved families, meant Sameer had almost no choice when it came to upholding his family's expectations, even if those expectations dripped with intolerance. She knew how soul sucking it was to be the subject of the hushed voices of judging aunties. Hell, she'd lived it since that day at the airport. Probably before that. She'd lived it since her parents' divorce. Since then, her family had been skirting the fringes of their community. In fact, she couldn't remember ever feeling that they completely fit in. Among them, but not one of them. She looked back at her sister. Now Zahra was living it, too.

She peeked at Duncan. His jaw was clenched as he focused on the road in front of him. He was obviously bothered by Sameer and Travis's fight, too. Amira closed her eyes, trying to calm herself. She was actually shaking. Nothing like the hollow ache of guilt to trigger her anxiety. She needed to chill or she'd never get any work done today. She silently repeated a prayer for strength.

"I'll pick you up, too. Three o'clock work for you?" Duncan said, pulling into the parking lot of the plaza that held a small library, a drugstore, and a donut shop.

"Yeah, fine. Thanks." She reached into her purse and pulled out a five-dollar bill and handed it to Zahra. "Get whatever you want, then meet me in the library."

Zahra took the money and silently left the car. Amira turned to look at Duncan before getting out, her hand on the door handle.

"I would appreciate it if you guys would refrain from swearing at the top of your lungs when my sister is downstairs. She is only eleven years old," she said quietly. She opened the door.

"I'm sorry. You're right."

She nodded as she started to get out of the car.

"Wait, Amira."

She sat back down.

"Travis liked the beard idea, you know."

"What?"

"When Sam and I first told Travis about it, he agreed it would work. Of course, I don't know what he told Sam privately."

Amira's shoulders slumped. "I know."

"You shouldn't feel bad about Travis being upset."

She stepped out of the car. "Look, the only thing I'm feeling right now is stressed. This is my master's degree, Duncan. I've got a fifty-page report due in a week, and I'm not even done the first draft yet. If you guys upheld your end of the bargain and kept it quiet at home, I'd be writing right now." She picked up her backpack.

He frowned. "Well, I'm so sorry, *Your Majesty*. God forbid the princess should care about anything but Her Highness's own precious concerns. I guess us common singers are too far beneath your more worthwhile pursuits." He wagged a finger at her. "Remember, *Amira*, you made this deal with us. It was your idea."

Teeth clenched, she narrowed her eyes at him. "Well, getting tangled in your web of nonsense was not part of the deal. Be here at three." She slammed the door.

Goddamn Duncan Galahad. Amira was so completely and utterly done with him. She couldn't believe this after their conversation yesterday. When she had loaned him her guitar, they had been civil to each other. Maybe even more than civil—she had wondered if there was a possibility of a friendship there.

No. Not anymore. The guy was an ass, not a friend.

Why she had ever thought she could trust four men to be considerate to her, to treat her like a human being whose own needs were just as important as theirs, was beyond her.

Amira unpacked her computer, hands still shaking. She had completely lost her temper there, and as the fiery rage abated to a smoulder, she started to feel bad about it. She had gotten into a heap-load of trouble in the past because of her explosive temper, which always emerged in a fireball of fury whenever she felt threatened. There was a reason her high-school classmates called her Wrath of Khan. Her temper was what got her into trouble at the airport that day when she realized she was being racially profiled. Her temper was probably the reason she was single.

Duncan had hit a sore spot. True, part of it was the fact that this all happened while Zahra could hear them, but it was also men assuming their concerns were more impor-tant than hers. Men assuming she cared about what was going on in their lives simply because they were men.

But, of course, *she did care*. She felt terrible for Travis, and she wanted things to work out between him and Sameer. And . . . *ugh* . . . this project was so important and she needed to stay focused on it. She opened the file on her computer and got to work.

It shouldn't have been a shock that Duncan was nowhere to be seen at three o'clock when she and Zahra walked out the library doors. Of course he stood them up. Abandoned at the library. Fists clenched, Amira turned to Zahra.

"Want to walk home or take the bus?" It was only a half-hour walk, but Amira was exhausted.

"Bus. I'm tired," Zahra said.

Her phone rang. She checked the screen. It wasn't Duncan, but Nanima. She answered it.

"Beta, make sure you come home for dinner today, I'm making your favourite masala shrimp."

"Yeah, I'll be there. Zahra and I are catching the bus home from the library now. Duncan was supposed to pick us up but he was a no-show."

"Oh no . . . I can come get you, I'm just leaving Shirin's now. Which library?"

When her grandmother pulled up five minutes later, Amira got in the car, realizing the ridiculousness of being thirty years old and getting picked up by your grandmother after doing homework at the library with your sister. But, of course, if Duncan had bothered to get his ass to the library like he said he would, this wouldn't have happened.

"Did you girls get a lot of work done today?" Nanima asked as she pulled out of the parking lot.

"I finished my homework, then took out three books and a movie," Zahra said.

"I'm stuck on a point in my project," Amira said, sinking into her seat. "I'll be so glad when all this is over."

Nanima smiled knowingly as she turned onto the main road. "Yes, I'm sure you're looking forward to your free time, especially now."

"What do you mean?"

"Maybe you'll want to visit Ottawa? Shirin told me you went on a date with Sameer."

Crap. News of their "relationship" had started to spread. Amira inhaled deeply. "It was just one date," she said. She hated lying to her grandmother, but as angry as she was at the boys, she couldn't out Sameer.

"Is this what they were all talking about before?" Zahra asked.

"No. I told you to forget what you heard."

"What were they talking about?" Nanima asked.

"Nothing. They were arguing about their group. Music stuff."

Nanima giggled. "You two are getting close, aren't you?"

"Nanima, it's nothing. We just went to see another group perform."

"The best love stories have to start somewhere, beta. This is good. Shirin is so happy, she doesn't mind if the relationship is unconventional."

Amira could bet Shirin didn't know the half of how *unconventional* this relationship was.

"It's okay, though, you two are so modern," Nanima continued. "It's no problem these days. In ten years, no one will care that you are so much older than him."

In ten years? "Don't get ahead of yourself. One date is not serious."

"So, you *are* dating Sameer?" Zahra asked.

Amira put her hand to her forehead.

"You are going to go out again, right?" Nanima asked. "It would be so lovely! You know . . ." She switched to speaking in Gujarati and lowered her voice, maybe hoping the language change would make Zahra tune them out. "Neelam never married Sameer's father. And she raised him alone, separate from the family. All Shirin wants is for Sameer to be happy and have a normal life. She said some of his friends in Ottawa are very . . . strange. He needs to settle down with a good Muslim girl. And he would be good for you, too. Such a polite, sweet boy. Sameer is a pharmacist, you know. Not like those heavy metal boys you used to go with."

Amira closed her eyes. Reena had been right. One date and Nanima was ready to buy saris and rent a hall. She needed to call this off before someone hired the mehndi artist. But how?

They reached the house and Amira went straight downstairs alone, telling Nanima she would be up in two hours for dinner. She found the family room empty, despite seeing Sameer's car outside. Good. She didn't want to have anything to do with the barbershop quartet now, so she headed straight to her room before any of them could emerge from their respective man caves. But, of course, living with four roommates makes alone time impossible. The knock on her door came after less than ten minutes of silence.

Sameer's dejected face greeted Amira when she opened it.

"Can we talk?" he asked.

"Sure." She motioned him in.

He paused in the doorway, eyes skirting to her unmade bed.

"It's fine. You can be in my room." When he still hesitated, she had to chuckle at her situation. Seriously? Her grandmother was practically interviewing DJs for their wedding, and he wouldn't even enter her bedroom? Even Amira's fake boyfriends were repelled by her. "We're dating, remember? Come in."

He slowly walked in and sat on the edge of the bed. "I'm sorry," he said.

"You say that a lot."

"I know," he said, swallowing. "To a lot of people. I can't seem to stop disappointing everyone lately." He looked at his fingers.

Amira crawled onto the bed and sat in the middle, wrapping her arms around her bent knees. "You and Travis still fighting?"

He nodded, turning to look at her. "It's almost our default state lately. I don't blame him. This trip was supposed to change everything. This isn't how any of it was supposed to go."

"How was it supposed to go?"

His eyes unfocused as his face slackened. "We were supposed to be amazing," he whispered.

Amira watched his forlorn expression. She smiled softly. "How did you guys start this group, anyway?"

A tiny, wistful smile emerged. "Travis and I met in a men's choir in Ottawa. For fun, we started doing some a cappella stuff together, and we met Barrington and Duncan online after we posted some videos on a barbershop website. The four of us connected immediately. We used to sing on Skype all the time. Have you seen our audition video? For the competition?"

"No."

"Here, look." He pulled his phone out of his pocket and searched for the clip. Once he'd found it, he handed her the phone.

She started the video. Against a bright-blue backdrop, Travis stood alone, a solemn look on his face. He started singing slowly, a soft soulful rendition of an old David Bowie song.

Sameer joined Travis after a few lines, his face a little more optimistic, his louder voice joining with Travis's sombre tones as the tempo picked up a bit.

The screen then split, with Travis and Sameer moving upwards as a box appeared on the lower-left corner: Barrington against a yellow backdrop. The tempo picked up again, and the three of them sang a few lines together, Barrington's deep bass harmonizing with Travis and Sameer's higher tones. Their faces were happy by this point, and the low accompaniment made the overall sound so much richer. Before long, a final box appeared in the lower-right corner with Duncan, against a green background. His smile was the widest she had ever seen on him, and his green eyes were twinkling with joy. Their sound now seemed complete: four distinct voices, harmonized together.

They sang exuberantly, feeding off each other. Grinning, laughing, snapping their fingers, and bopping to the music. Their voices together melded—each could be heard but the sound together was so much more than the sum of their individual abilities. It was doubly impressive because only Sameer and Travis were in the same room when this was filmed.

As the song slowed, Barrington and Duncan's little squares moved off-screen so it was only Sameer and Travis again, singing while looking into each other's faces.

The final high note was held as Sameer and Travis gazed tenderly at each other while lowering their foreheads to meet.

Amira swallowed, her skin pebbled with goosebumps. "You guys sound amazing. You could totally beat those other singers. That was Bowie's 'Modern Love,' right?"

He nodded, a small smile appearing on his face. "Travis said that me hitting the submit button on this video was the bravest thing he'd ever seen me do. I took a step past the point of no return. Even though my family's not really into barbershop, this video is out there. If any of them see it, they'll know."

And now he had taken two giant steps backwards by "dating" Amira.

"You haven't deleted the video," she said, handing him his phone. "That's something."

"I know," he said. He raked his fingers through his hair, mussing up his gravity-defying style. He looked at his sticky, gel-covered hand and chuckled sadly before wiping it on his jeans. "Travis is going to kill me. I can't even keep my hair the way it's supposed to be."

"Sameer, you're too hard on yourself."

He shook his head. "I deserve it. This trip was supposed to be my grand coming out. I was going to introduce them all to Travis, even though my mum told me not to. But when I got here, I just couldn't do it. I'm a coward. And now . . . I've wrapped you up in my nonsense, when all you wanted to do was peacefully finish school. I'm sorry."

Amira winced. "Duncan told you what I said in the car?"

"Yeah. I don't blame you for getting angry. It's not your fault."

"Yes, but he was being nice. He didn't have to take us to the library. I shouldn't have screamed at him. I overreacted. I have a bit of a temper, and your baritone brings out the worst of it."

Sameer laughed. "Duncan's a good guy, Amira. The best. He's like the glue that holds us together."

She frowned. "Am I going to have to apologize to the garden gnome?"

He laughed again, louder. "Does he know you call him that?"

"Yes."

Still laughing, Sameer fell back on the bed, his head landing near Amira's knees. "It's *so* perfect for him. You two are hilarious to watch. I don't think anyone ruffles his feathers as much as you do."

When he finally stopped laughing, Sameer rested his left hand on his heart as he stared at the plaster swirls in the ceiling.

"Sameer?"

He looked at her. "Hmm?"

"I know I don't know you that well yet, but . . . I'm proud of you. I think you're braver than you realize."

He closed his eyes. "I don't know. I hope I will be one day."

CHAPTER ELEVEN

AMIRA FELT HER project beginning to stall again. After the impromptu therapy session with Sameer, her thoughts had turned to navel-gazing and wondering if she would ever find a relationship as affectionate as Sameer and Travis's. It didn't seem likely. The temper that hammered Duncan in the car eliminated the possibility of the kind of sweet partnership she saw on that video clip. Not that Travis and Sameer's partnership was all that sweet lately but it would be if they didn't have the ridiculous family intolerance to deal with. They were good guys—great guys. She still smiled when she remembered their expressions at the end of the song. Those two should be angst free, frolicking hand in hand anywhere they wanted to be, not holed up in Nanima's basement with a heart-load of pain and an ill-tempered pseudo-girlfriend.

But pipe-dreaming for fairy-tale love was useless in the modern world, so Amira pushed aside those thoughts and focused all her attention on her report. She worked diligently until dinner, then went upstairs to join her family—her whole family, because apparently it was a Sunday night miracle.

Mum, Nanima, and Zahra were all sitting at the table when Amira walked into the dining room.

"Wow. We're all here?" Amira asked, taking her seat.

"Why wouldn't we all be here?" Nanima asked, spooning some shrimp curry onto Amira's plate. Mum passed a plate of flaky parathas to Amira. She took one.

"We haven't all been together since I got back, that's all. How was work, Mum?"

While enjoying Nanima's superb shrimp curry, spinach, paratha, and salad, Mum told animated stories about her day, including a hilarious tale about catching a patient, who had failed to tie the back of his hospital gown, stealing another nurse's lunch from the staff room. Mum seemed in a great mood—nothing at all like yesterday. Nanima laughed at Mum's stories, and Zahra spoke with enthusiasm about an upcoming dance performance in a Hindu temple.

It all seemed so normal. Lovely, even. Maybe she was wrong about Mum and Nanima's relationship being strained. They seemed fine—a completely normal mother-daughter dynamic, and being with them was a balm to Amira's stress right now. She needed this time with the fierce females in her family, to remind her that she could be as fierce as them. Mum, a successful career woman and single mother, steady, intelligent, and driven. And Nanima, always loving, and always going above and beyond when her family needed her. These women were her inspiration. When she thought about what Sameer was going through with his family and his relationship with Travis, how could she feel anything but gratitude for the family she had?

"So, you said you were having issues with your research? I hope Zahra didn't get in your way," Mum said.

Zahra rolled her eyes. "I was good. I was doing my own homework."

Amira laughed. "She was good. Very quiet. I'll be okay." She didn't want to mention the issues with the quartet and the fight with Duncan, lest Nanima bring up her date with Sameer again. "I just wasn't in the right frame of mind to work earlier."

Nanima smiled knowingly and even tried to wink at Amira. "Maybe you had another picture in your frame?"

She raised a brow at her grandmother. What did that even mean?

Mum took another paratha from the plate. "If you're having trouble with your school work, you should call your father. I was speaking to him the other day, and he mentioned he'd be happy to help with your paper. This is his area of expertise, after all."

"You were talking to Dad?"

"Don't act surprised, I do still have a minor child with the man. And I've known him forever, it feels like. Do you think you'll have time to visit him this summer? He's offered to buy you a ticket if you'll take Zahra down in August. I'm not comfortable with her flying alone these days."

Amira shook her head slowly. She hadn't flown out of the country since the incident last year. She wasn't exactly afraid; she just wasn't all that keen on the idea of facing the border guards again, especially with the giant black mark no doubt attached to her name in the database. She squeezed her lips together. Okay, maybe she was a little bit afraid.

"It's fine, Amira," Mum said gently. "They said it's no problem to travel again. I don't want her going alone."

Either did Amira. She reluctantly agreed. She'd go, but only to be there to watch out for Zahra. Besides, it wasn't really what happened at the airport but the aftermath that haunted her. And she could avoid the aftermath if she kept her mouth shut. "I'll call him after my report is in to figure out a date." She forced a smile. "I'm on track. I don't think I'll need Dad's help."

She wasn't exaggerating. Right before dinner, she'd had a bit of an epiphany about her analysis, with a clearer idea on how to get it down on paper. "I'll tell you one thing— the glass of champagne when it's done will taste so good. Actually, forget glass. I'll deserve a bottle."

Mum grinned, holding up her glass of water. "Hear, hear, Amira. I'm so proud of what you've accomplished. I'll be right there celebrating with you."

Amira clinked her water glass with Mum's, and then Zahra's, since an eleven-year-old wouldn't let a toast happen without insisting on joining in. She then held her glass out to Nanima, but Nanima didn't seem thrilled to toast her granddaughter. Her arms were folded in front of her, a sour look on her face.

"You should celebrate by saying shukkar to Allah, not drinking," Nanima said.

Amira snorted. "Believe me, Nanima, I'll be thanking God a lot, too."

"Let the girl celebrate," Mum said. "I know you don't approve of drinking, but Amira's a grown woman. She's earned the right to live her life the way she wants."

"Drinking alcohol is against Islam," Nanima said.

Amira raised a brow at her grandmother. She was long past any guilt for the way she chose to observe her faith. And with everything else going on, she had no time for regrets, anyway. But she had been under the impression that there was an unspoken truce in the household between those who chose to consume alcohol and those who didn't. It had been years since Nanima had made comments like these.

"Don't you start on that again," Mum said to Nanima. "We are all allowed to practise our faith however we feel comfortable, so long as we're not hurting anyone." Mum smiled a touch too widely and turned to Zahra. "Did you find the next book in that ballet school series at the library?"

After dinner, Amira headed back down to the thankfully empty basement and got right back to work. She stayed up much too late, and woke early Monday morning. With only a quick break for chai and toast, she worked well past her appointed quiet morning hours, and it paid off. Amazingly, wonderfully, unexpectedly, she finished the first draft of the body of her report at three o'clock Monday afternoon. After giving thanks at least ninety-nine times, she immediately emailed it to Raymond, then she called Reena.

"Ree, we have to celebrate."

"You're done your report."

"Close. Done the body of the first draft. Conclusion, then a few rounds of editing, and this baby is toast. You can call me master."

"Amazing. So, where should we celebrate?"

"You know what, Reena? I think I want to let loose. Can we celebrate at your place?"

"Sure, if you don't mind Saira schooling us on the calorie count of bourbon versus Irish whiskey."

"Better than avoiding Sir Galahad and his merry minstrels."

"Ah, your hairy nemesis! You see him after you told him off yesterday?"

"No. I've been locked in my room, typing. I didn't even notice when they started singing today. I guess I'm getting used to their sick Motown beats."

"Awesome. I'm so happy you're mostly done. A celebration is definitely in order. I have an afternoon meeting, so not sure I can step out to the liquor store, and there's only kale chips at home to snack on. God, I could go for some fried Indian munchies. You have anything on hand?"

"I could use some fresh air. I'll take a walk up to the store and get some snacks and bourbon. Should I come around six?"

"Sure. See you then."

. . . .

AT FIVE THIRTY, Amira was packing up a tote bag with booze and fixings for papri chaat when her phone rang.

"I'm sorry, Amira. I can't do tonight. Saira's in the hospital," Reena said.

Amira sat heavily on a chair. "What happened? Is she okay?"

"She passed out at the gym and they called an ambulance. She's dehydrated. They're giving her an IV."

Amira winced. "Oh my god. I'm sorry. Should I come to the hospital?"

"No, she'll be fine. She's just shaken up." Reena's voice was monotone. Almost robotic, which is how she always sounded after her sister lost it on her. "The ER doctor hinted she might be underweight, but she assured him she was just going through some stuff right now. When the doctor left, she laid into me."

Amira lowered her forehead into her hand. She wished she could do something to help her friend, but she felt stuck. "You want me to come to the hospital anyway? For you?"

"No, it's fine. I'm sure we'll be here for hours. Rain check? We can celebrate tomorrow?"

"Reena, are you positive? You don't really want to be alone with her for hours, do you?"

Reena was quiet for a few seconds before she murmured, "No, I don't."

"I'm on my way, Ree."

Amira stashed her tote bag in the fridge and ran upstairs to ask Nanima if she could borrow her car, since she knew Mum was at work. Thankfully, her grandmother was home with Zahra. She found her in the kitchen making dinner while Zahra sat at the dining table doing homework. Nanima agreed readily and said she would pray for Saira.

When she got to the hospital, the emergency room nurse recited all manner of rules and regulations about the number of guests emergency patients were allowed at a time. Thankfully, this was Mum's hospital. Amira texted her, and Mum immediately appeared in the ER and took her to find Reena and Saira.

The room they found them in was one of those clinical ward rooms—the kind that somehow looked stark and crowded at the same time. Reena was in an old chair, shoulders slumped and eyes focused away from her sister. Saira was sitting up in bed, her phone in her hand. A bottle of one of those meal-replacement shakes was on the table next to her. Amira would bet that Saira hadn't let a single drop touch her lips.

Reena smiled sadly when she noticed them. Saira gave a glassy stare before painting on a fake smile. "Amira and Farida Aunty! What a surprise!" Amira stepped forward to hug Reena as Mum went to Saira.

Amira finally took a good look at her best friend's sister. She had changed in the months since she had last seen her. Hair longer. Less makeup. Stronger cheekbones. Visible shoulder bones under her workout tank top.

Reena clearly hadn't been exaggerating when she said Saira had lost a significant amount of weight.

"Hi, Saira. Reena and I had plans tonight, but she said you weren't feeling well. I thought I'd come by and say hello," Amira said.

"Yes, well, family comes before friends. I heard you were back in town, Amira. I understand you're still living in your grandmother's basement?"

"What did the doctor say?" Mum asked, inching the milkshake closer to Saira's hand.

"This hospital is the worst. The doctor barely spoke to me and shoved that crap at me," she said, pointing at the shake. "I'm not drinking it. Hey, Amira, maybe you can run out to Active Juice and grab me one of their goddess smoothies? Reena wouldn't go. She said she didn't want to leave her parking spot and pay again. She could have walked, though."

"Saira," Reena said gently, "the doctor wanted you to drink *that* shake. You can't send me to get another one."

"Are your parents here?" Mum asked Reena.

"They're on their way," Reena answered.

"We will be out of here soon," Saira said. "I don't know why Reena called our parents. It's no big deal. The stupid gym didn't have the air conditioning on. It's a gym, for god's sake, people are going to get hot and sweaty . . ."

Amira and her mother sat with Saira for about ten more minutes, listening to Saira blame her hospital admission on everything from the treadmill she was on, to the quality of the smoothies at the gym snack bar, to the fabric of her workout pants. She even managed to find a way to blame her older brother, who lived in Ottawa. Reena sat quietly, listening to her sister rant, with shoulders curved inwards and her normally happy mouth in a straight line.

"Oh, Farida. Amira. *You* are here," a voice from the doorway said. Amira turned to see Reena's mother. Reena's father stood expressionless behind her.

Mum stood, frowning. "I work here. Amira is here to support Reena and Saira. Did you see the doctor?"

Reena's mother came into the room, barely looking at Amira or her mother. "Saira just has the flu; it is not necessary for it to be broadcast to the whole community."

"Mum," Reena said, "Amira and her mother are not going to tell anyone that Saira's not well."

"I'm absolutely fine," Saira snapped. "Just hot. They didn't have the right kind of protein bars at the gym snack bar. I'm going to complain to the manager. And Reena didn't buy the bars I like. I mean, they are not *that* expensive—"

Amira's mother furrowed her brow. "You didn't eat anything before you went to the gym? Saira, you need fuel before working out. When I spoke to you last Eid, I told you—"

"That isn't your business," Reena's mother said, nose turned up haughtily.

Amira's mum shared a glance with Reena and Amira. "I want to help Saira. I told you about that doctor—"

"We don't need help. We don't need outsiders talking about us. Especially you. And Saira does not need a therapist— maybe you should look at your own broken family before you throw stones at ours." It was rather impressive how Reena's mother could make a statement like that with her daughter lying in a hospital bed, clearly in crisis. Amira had honestly never liked the woman.

Amira's mum smiled, but obviously didn't mean it. "It was kindly meant. I will see you at home, Amira." She turned on her heel and walked out.

Reena turned to Amira and mouthed, "Sorry." The apology wasn't necessary, but appreciated. Amira had heard that kind of crap about her family before, but not for a long time.

When her parents had divorced, there had been gossip about them. A lot of it. Amira never really figured out what was going on since she was a self-absorbed twenty-something at the time, but she could see that her mother, who had never seemed to fit in all that well, became even more of a pariah to certain people. Not everyone—her mum did have true friends within the Ismaili community, but to some, Mum was an outcast, and Amira didn't really understand why.

"You'd better go, too," Reena whispered beside her.

She leaned in and hugged her friend. "Okay," she said softly, "call me if you need anything."

Amira knew Reena had tried to talk to her parents about Saira's deteriorating coping skills and weird eating habits before, but they had been furious at the suggestion that anything was wrong. Now that Saira was in the hospital, she hoped they would be open to the possibility of getting Saira real help, but Amira didn't hold her breath. Their stigma against mental health issues was too strong.

She wished she could bring Reena home with her now, as she knew her best friend had a long and emotionally painful night in store with her family. But there was nothing that Amira could do. She felt utterly helpless.

She drove home thinking of Reena and her parents, and also of her own mother. It felt like such a contrast: the amazing woman who toasted Amira's accomplishments and stood up to her own mother yesterday was essentially told she was without worth today. Not that Amira cared much about what Reena's mother thought, but it suddenly struck her that Mum had put up with that sort of shit for years from people like Reena's mother, and still she wanted to help Saira. Amira wouldn't have done that. Did that make Mum a pushover? How could she put up with it? Forget how—why?

CHAPTER TWELVE

ONCE HOME, AMIRA came in the side door of the house and sat at the top of the stairs to think.

"Princess has been relegated to the top of the tower, waiting for her prince?" asked a voice from the bottom of the stairs.

"I'm not in the mood, Duncan." She stood and slowly took her heavy limbs down the stairs and went straight to the living room to sink into the sofa.

"What's wrong?" he asked, eyeing her curiously.

"Reena and I were supposed to be celebrating tonight, but I just came back from the hospital. Her sister, Saira, is in emerg."

He sat on the armchair opposite her, concern in his face. "What happened?"

"She passed out at the gym. I doubt she's had a full meal in weeks."

"Shoot. That's tough."

"I know. And it doesn't help that Reena's parents are bonkers . . . they claim only white people get mental illness, and Saira's just upset because she caught her fiancé in bed with his cousin or something."

"Clearly there's a lot more to this story. Sounds like a country song."

Amira chuckled sadly. "Saira needs help. My mum tried to talk to Reena's parents; she's a nurse, but they won't listen to her. They think Mum can't possibly know anything because she's just an uncouth Indian."

Duncan's nose wrinkled. "But aren't they Indian, too?"

Amira nodded. "Yup. Although they are further diaspora. They're Indian from Tanzania, while Mum's from India. Reena's parents seem to think being further removed from India makes them classier, or something."

"Really? That's crazy! Is that a common belief?"

"Oh, hell no. My dad is East African—from Kenya, actually, and he didn't have an issue marrying an Indian. Reena's parents are just a special brand of self-hating minority. We're too Indian for them. And too liberal, probably." Amira shook her head, curling her legs under her. "To be honest, they just don't like Mum, so they probably use the India thing as low-hanging fruit. My family, Mum especially, is a bit of an oddity in our community. She didn't really hang out with other mothers. I guess because she was younger than them— she was only nineteen when she got married and had me. And now Mum's divorced. And she's not very traditional. She's just as likely to have Fleetwood Mac playing in her car as Lata Mangeshkar."

"Who?"

"An old Bollywood singer. I'm sure there's more to it, but no one talks about it." Amira tucked her feet tighter under her legs. "I remember when I was little, we'd go to these big parties and Mum would spend the whole time playing with kids instead of talking with adults. I used to think it was because she was so young herself, or because she was training to work in pediatrics back then, but I later realized it was because my friends' parents wouldn't include her in their conversations. And Dad was always away, so she was always alone."

Amira smiled awkwardly. She wasn't sure why she was telling Duncan such personal things about Mum. That run-in with Reena's mother brought up old memories that had been buried for a long time. "I don't think it's like that anymore. My mother's not hugely religious, but she does go to our mosque pretty regularly with my grandmother and seems to have a busy social life. So things are fine for her now. What about you? Your parents traditional or black sheep?"

He laughed, his low rumble strangely comforting to Amira's mood. "Funny you should say *sheep*; my mother grew up on a sheep farm."

Amira sat up. "Really? Are your parents farmers?"

"Nah, not anymore. They have a hobby farm, though. My mom's an RPN—that's a practical nurse. She works in a doctor's office in the next big town over. And my dad worked at the utilities company, but he took an early retirement, so he tends to the property and animals. My brother still works at the utilities company."

"Hey, both our mums are nurses! My mum's an RN at a hospital. So similar." Amira smiled. She'd never have thought that she would care about having something in common with the garden gnome, but somehow it felt nice that they weren't as different as she'd thought. After the last couple of hours, she needed to know she was on the same page with someone at least.

But Duncan didn't look pleased. His brow was furrowed and his mouth a tight line. He clearly had misgivings about his mother's similarity to hers. Maybe because she was only an RPN instead of an RN? Changing the subject seemed wise. "What animals do they have?"

"Bunch of chickens, two goats, and a monster rabbit. Oh, and a sheepdog mix. They're all really for Maddie, my niece. She's ten. My parents spoil her."

"Didn't you tell me you live with your niece? Your brother's daughter?"

"Yup. He has custody of her. I live with him to help out."

"Where's her mother?"

His focus wandered to the floor.

"Sorry," she said, "I'm being nosy. Forget I asked."

"No, it's fine. Shayna is probably here somewhere. In Toronto, I mean. Hopefully in a shelter. Maybe on the streets. I hope not in jail."

"Oh, no, I'm sorry."

"Yeah. She's from Omemee, too. We all grew up together. Ryan was with Shay since high school. She was always a party girl, and all the warning signs were there."

"Alcoholic?"

"Yup. And everything else she could get her hands on. Not a lot to do in tiny towns, lots of people turn to chemical entertainment. Shay cleaned up for a bit, even gave up everything when she was pregnant. She wasn't so good about abstaining while breastfeeding, though."

"Oh god . . ."

"Thankfully, Maddie's fine," he said, voice laced with affection. "She's my real princess. Ryan hasn't seen or heard from Shay for three years now, so that's good, but I'm afraid if she came back with hollow promises, he'd take her right back." His head shook slowly. "Such a weakness for that woman."

Amira wasn't sure what to say. Duncan obviously cared a lot for his brother and adored his niece. There was a human side to Duncan Galahad, and the fact that he let Amira see it was disconcerting. And also touching.

"That's something else we have in common," Amira said to break the silence. "We both live with young girls."

Duncan smiled. "I haven't gotten to know Zahra too well. What's your sister like?"

"She's amazing." Amira smiled fondly. "She's my favourite person in the world, and not just because she's my sister. Zahra is full of personality and unfiltered enthusiasm. She dives headfirst into everything with exuberance." Amira paused. "It's a tough time to be a Muslim girl, and we've tried to shelter her from what's going on in the world. But Zahra's tough, too. She's going to shine. She has my mother's strength."

"And her sister's," Duncan said. Was that a compliment? Amira's brows shot up, but Duncan was still talking. "Maddie's the opposite, unfortunately. She hasn't seen her mother in three years, and only rarely before that. Her crappy home life has affected her. She's a bit anxious and really wants to please people, and she worries when she doesn't know how. But I think she'll be okay. She's really coming into her own lately and has grown a lot more confident. I'm really trying to be there for her when she needs me. To be a good influence, you know?"

The garden gnome a good influence? Amira wanted to scoff. But maybe he was right. Duncan was many things, but she couldn't deny that he was loyal and supportive, and he obviously loved his niece. "How's your brother with her?"

He shrugged. "I can't deny that Ryan's had it tough, too, but he fought his demons. He does the best he can. He's sacrificed so much for Maddie. And my parents play a big role in her life, too." He was silent awhile, thinking. "It sounds like your sister and my niece should get together. They'd probably complement each other."

This little chat with Duncan was going well, but little-girl play dates and high tea were out of the question. Hang out with Duncan *and* his family? Go out for high tea and tween spa days? No.

Amira smiled blandly and stretched her legs in front of her. It was wise to end this interaction on a high note. Bonding over their nurse mothers and the girls in their lives was surely about to go sour. No doubt he had scathing comments about her life choices waiting beneath the surface.

It was time to politely extract herself. She didn't need this bond with Duncan Galahad to grow any deeper.

CHAPTER THIRTEEN

JUST AS AMIRA'S feet hit the carpet, Duncan ran his hand over his face, then smiled with apparent effort. "Anyway, enough of this family drama. What were you supposed to be celebrating?" he asked.

She'd forgotten she was meant to be letting loose with Reena tonight, not scrutinizing family turmoil with her roommate. Amira smiled proudly. "I finished the first draft of the main body of my report. Only the conclusion and editing left."

He whistled low. "That's great. Congratulations. Where were you ladies heading to celebrate?"

"Oh, just Reena's apartment. I wanted to get drunk, and I don't do that in public."

He raised his eyebrows. "I've seen you drink in public. At that brewpub."

"That was just one beer. I wanted to drink more tonight."

"Wild when lit, are you?"

She scoffed. "No. Wild isn't usually a problem."

"Then why're you scared to drink in public?"

Amira bit her lip. This conversation was getting personal. Talking about her parents or her friend's parents was one thing, but now she was talking about herself. And weirdly, instead of excusing herself, she just dug deeper. "I get paranoid, to the point where I can't enjoy myself. I'm afraid of doing something stupid, or someone doing something to me. And I'm afraid of others thinking I'm a lush." Huh. Maybe there was a bit of repressed guilt about drinking in there.

"I can't imagine you paranoid."

She smiled. "I guess I don't like losing control unless I can trust the people with me."

He smiled. "That's my girl . . . it's about control for you." He stretched his shoulders backwards before sinking deeper in the chair. "If you still want to celebrate, I'm free to be your stand-in drinking buddy. You can always trust a knight of the round table."

Continue this ill-advised chat? Drink with Duncan? Sounded like a terrible idea. "Where're the rest of the guys?"

"Sam and Travis went to a bar with that friend of theirs. And"—his nose wrinkled—"I think Barrington has finally figured out phone sex. I'm predicting I'll be sleeping on the couch from now on."

Amira snort-laughed for a second before biting her lip. Barrington was a big guy with a deep rumble of a voice, and she shared a wall with him. She'd never had a roommate downstairs and wasn't sure how soundproof the walls were. But then again . . . she shared a wall with Sameer and Travis, too, and she hadn't heard their nighttime entertainment. Yet. Maybe the quartet *did* know how to be quiet.

It was kind of depressing how much sex was happening in her basement, while she was involved in none of it. And why the hell was she thinking about the sex lives of the quartet? She shook her head to clear the images.

"Is that a no?" Duncan suddenly grinned at her. "Actually, Princess, I've been meaning to make an offer to you."

Amira's eyes widened.

"Want some guitar lessons? It was great of you to lend me your instrument, and you should come out of this arrangement with at least something after the web of nonsense we've caught you in."

She cringed. "You want to teach me to play my guitar?"

"Sure. I'm a music teacher, remember? We can start tonight." He stood, grabbing the guitar case from where it lay in the corner of the room.

She wasn't sure about this. Duncan teaching her to play the guitar? They would definitely kill each other. Or not. Maybe.

He sat next to her on the couch, oblivious to the fact that her heart rate had sped up and her palms were getting sweaty. She grabbed at the couch cushion. She might need that drink to get through this. She stood. "Bourbon?"

He grinned again, his eyes crinkling with pleasure. "That'd be great."

Amira headed to the fridge to fetch her tote bag and grabbed two glasses of ice. After pouring the bourbon, she placed his on the coffee table, then took a large gulp of hers. The amber liquid burned as it went down her throat, but she immediately felt less tense as she watched Duncan tune the guitar. Finally he placed it in her arms, moving her hands to where he wanted them, and began showing her the finger positions for the E-major chord. He sat close to her. He even used his large calloused hand to position her fingers on the frets.

She was finding it hard to breathe with Duncan so close.

He smelled like laundry detergent, wood chips, and man. Clean, all consuming, and frighteningly tempting.

Fuck. Amira realized that right now she was attracted to him. Very attracted. Damn him and his sympathetic "my niece is my princess and her mother is a drug addict" story.

"Here," he said, taking her hand again. "Curl your fingers, like this. Like a claw." His voice was hushed because he was so close, and his strong fingers on hers were sending electric sparks right up her arm.

Her face heated.

A tiny smile passed over his face. Had he realized her body was being a traitor and was jumping with joy to be near a man again? He continued the lesson, though, and she managed to learn two chords before her heart rate was too fast to ignore.

She put the guitar down. "I need another drink." Fumbling with the bottle, she refilled her glass before indicating towards his empty one. He nodded and she filled his glass, too.

Amira's hand hovered over her bag. What they needed was a snack. She bet Duncan had never had Indian street food before.

"You ever have papri chaat?" she asked.

He looked up. "No. Something Indian?"

"Yeah. Interested in trying it?"

"Sure." He grinned. "I'm game for anything you want."

She took her bag to the kitchen and assembled the papri chaat. First she put the little, fried cracker-like papri on the bottom of two wide bowls and topped them with boiled potatoes, onions, chickpeas, yogourt, tamarind chutney, coriander chutney, diced tomatoes, sev, dried spices, and cilantro leaves. After grabbing a stack of napkins and two spoons, she brought it all to the coffee table.

She showed Duncan how to eat the traditional Indian street food by crushing the papri with his spoon and mixing the mess together. They did their best to get the bites into their mouths and not on their clothes.

"This is awesome," he said. "Like spicy, sweet, and sour nachos . . . I should give this recipe to my buddy James, who has a bar back home. This is great drinking food."

Amira had to agree, and she enjoyed herself thoroughly as they polished off their bowls and their glasses of bourbon. They chatted aimlessly about grad school, her family, his hometown, and the quartet, and she almost forgot who she was talking to. Duncan was personable, funny, and easygoing. And that weird wave of attraction when he was teaching her guitar chords had passed, too. Good.

Duncan ran his finger through the puddle of tamarind chutney in his bowl and licked it clean. "So, you're glad to be going back to work, then?"

"Yeah. I'm just . . . I wonder . . ." Amira squeezed her lips together a moment before meeting Duncan's gaze. "I have a new boss. He said some things when I met him, so I don't think I'll like working with him as much."

"What'd he say?"

Amira absently picked up her empty glass. "Among other things, he called me a pretty little thing."

Duncan stared at her for about three seconds before the corners of his mouth began to upturn. "Well, I can't say I disagree with him, but it's not something you should say when you meet an employee."

Amira raised a brow. "I'm not little." She paused, swirling her drink in her hand. "Ever notice how some people always assume Asian women are tiny, even when we're not? I'm five feet, four inches tall. Exactly average for a Canadian woman. And I'm hardly waifish. But white men like to call me a *pretty little thing.*" She drained her glass.

"Maybe. Yeah, I guess Asian women are infantilized a bit. I'd never call you a pretty little thing, though. I'd be afraid you'd bite off my tongue if I did."

She laughed. "You called me a prickly porcupine the day we met. I think I prefer that."

"Sounds like your new boss is a tad sexist."

"Yeah, who isn't? I work in a male-dominated field."

"Well, for your sake, Princess, I hope you have some women you trust at work that you can bitch to when the sausage party gets out of hand."

Amira laughed so hard she nearly fell over in her seat. His solemn, serious expression while he said *sausage party* was too much for her bourbon-altered condition. They continued chatting and refilled their bowls instead of continuing the guitar lesson. He told animated tales of the eccentric musicians he worked with, his favourite students, and his parents' insane chickens. When he got up to get more ice for their third (fourth?) drinks, she wondered why she ever disliked the guy in the first place. He was loyal to his friends and family, he was educated, smart, hilarious, and a musician to boot. A musician with a sexy singing voice.

"Why'd you start singing in the first place?" she asked as she took the new drink from him.

"I always wanted to be a singer. A singer-songwriter. I worshipped Neil Young for years, since I'm from Omemee."

"Why?"

"Neil Young is from Omemee. You've heard his song 'Helpless'? That's home."

"Hey, that's cool!" She frowned. "What kind of name is Omemee, anyway? Silly. Omemee."

"It means pigeon."

"Of course it does." She took a gulp of her bourbon, dribbling a bit on her chin. After wiping it with her sleeve, she giggled. "I think I'm drunk, after all."

"You feeling paranoid?" He smirked into his glass.

"Nah, I must trust you. Weird, right? Pretty sure I don't like you."

He laughed.

They kept drinking.

Eventually the conversation drifted to his facial hair and why he had so much of it.

"The colour is so epic," he explained solemnly, "had to grow it long."

She wrinkled her nose. "Yeah, but how do you live with that scratchy thing hanging off your face? Doesn't it itch?"

"Hey." He looked genuinely offended. "It's not scratchy. Don't knock it till you feel it. I use conditioner and beard oil daily."

"Beard oil?" She laughed.

One side of his lip upturned as his eyes wrinkled with mischief. "C'mere, Princess. Touch it. Feel how soft it is."

Amira had had a lot to drink, and Duncan sat less than two feet away. And that red beard had been a target she had wanted to get her hands on since she first saw it on the train. For a split second, Amira froze in terror as she sobered enough to know she might regret this tomorrow. The two feet between them felt like two miles, and moving towards him seemed as impossible as climbing Kilimanjaro in a sari. But then he smiled and winked at her. And nothing in the world could stop her from getting her hands in that big red beacon on his face.

And it *was* soft. She let her fingers roam free, and they teased and raked through the soft yet strong, silky yet sturdy strands. That beard was so Duncan.

She smiled. "Like spun silk. I should use beard oil in my hair."

His expression darkened as he plunged his hands into her hair, loose around her shoulders. "But then your hair wouldn't smell like coconuts."

They stared at each other for several seconds, her hands on his face, his hands in her hair gently teasing the strands on the back of her neck. Each wordlessly daring the other to make a move. Finally, he lowered his hands and snaked them around her waist as he pulled her in. "Come closer, Princess," he whispered.

She could regret this later, but tonight all she could do was climb atop him, knees spread wide, straddling his strong thighs, while her hands held on to his face. He ran his hands up her sides and back into her hair. "Plenty soft enough," he whispered into her neck, inhaling deeply.

She let her thumb graze along his cheek to swipe his full lower lip, leaning in closer to his face. "You know," she murmured, "I've never kissed a man with a beard."

A tiny smile emerged. "We can fix that."

He kissed her. Gentle little bites from his lips, his soft beard tickling her face. Mere nibbles. Chaste pecks. Like a conversation, this kiss was for getting to know this side of Duncan. This sweet, softer side of him.

He lifted his face from hers and whispered into her lips, "This okay, Amira?"

Was what okay? Him kissing her like this?

No. Definitely not okay. This was not the way she wanted Duncan Galahad.

"No," she murmured. "I suspect you can do better than that."

She pressed herself closer to his hard body and curled her arms around the back of his head, scraping her fingernails through his hair.

He got the hint and grinned widely before devouring her lips. This kiss was deeper, harder, and so much hotter. His tongue stole inside for long pulls as his hands travelled to encircle her waist. He tasted like bourbon and chutney, mingled with the scent of wood chips and . . . Duncan. She groaned as her searching hands found bare skin under the hem of his flannel shirt. She'd wanted this. And she was only now understanding how much.

This time the beard didn't just tickle her but scratched and scraped along her sensitive skin. Her jaw ached. Her legs were numbing from being stretched over his thighs. She relished the feeling.

What the hell was she doing?

Doesn't matter, she told herself. Right now, she didn't care, she was just going to do it.

They ended up in a tangled mess on the couch, kissing for minutes or hours, she had no idea. Her hands had discovered that his delicious chest had hair as soft as his beard, as his hands kneaded and squeezed through her tight yoga pants.

He pulled away again, breathing heavily, green eyes dark. He rested his forehead on hers, lips only centimetres from devouring her again.

"We shouldn't be doing this," he said.

"I know. I don't even like you. You don't like me."

He chuckled, his warm breath tempting her all over again. "Believe me, I like you fine. You're drunk."

"So are you." She felt tired all of a sudden. Too tired to keep her head up. She rested it on his shoulder, her face burrowing into his neck as the room spun around her. She inhaled deeply as he began to run his hands over her back.

"That feels nice. You smell like wood chips," she said.

He laughed softly, the deep rumble vibrating through her. "That's the beard oil. It's cedar scented."

"It's nice." She hummed with contentment. "Too bad I don't like you," she whispered before closing her eyes.

He breathed a sigh. "You're going to like me even less tomorrow, Princess." He lifted her and shifted, repositioning the two of them, with their legs intertwined and her head on his chest. He kissed her cheek before tossing a blanket over them.

She fell asleep.

CHAPTER FOURTEEN

AMIRA'S PHONE RANG louder than usual the next morning, waking her. She found it next to her head, which was resting on the edge of her bed, inches away from falling off, instead of where it should have been on her pillow. She answered the phone without looking at the caller's name.

"Amira?" Sounded like Raymond.

"Yes, hi, Raymond."

"You okay?"

"Yeah, just—" She sat up, instinctively smoothing her hair with her free hand. "Just had a late night. What's up?"

"Still sleeping? Ah, must be nice to be young. But you should start getting back into your working routine, you know."

"I know, I was celebrating getting my draft done yesterday."

"Yes, that's why I'm calling you. I got your email with the attached report. I skimmed the first page, there are a few grammar issues—"

"I know. I'm going to review it again for grammar and all that, I just wanted you to look at it for content."

"Okay, I can ignore those problems, then. Your topic, though . . . wasn't your project about computer-integrated manufacturing?"

"I told you I changed it to noise control, didn't I?" She rubbed her eyes and swung her legs out of bed. The socks and sweatshirt she'd worn last night were on the floor. What the hell had happened?

"Right. Yes. Well, I'll do my best to look at this in a timely manner," Raymond said.

"Thanks. I really appreciate this."

"No problem, Amira. Speak to you soon." He disconnected before she could say anything else.

Amira sat on the edge of the bed, disoriented by the abrupt wake-up. The air felt different, and not because of the headache pounding between her temples. She looked around. Her room looked the same. She was still wearing the clothes she wore yesterday, save the socks and sweatshirt. Why hadn't she changed into her pyjamas? What had she done last night? She remembered drinking, a lot. But something else happened . . .

Holy shit . . . It all came back to her like a crash of a tsunami. *Duncan*. She squeezed her eyes closed. Amira remembered everything. The part when he tried to give her a guitar lesson. The part when they all but polished off her bottle of bourbon. The part when they shared papri chaat. When she attacked his beard to see if it really was as soft as he said it would be. When he kissed her . . .

She even remembered the part when they were making out on the basement couch like teenagers in heat.

And then she fell asleep in his arms.

She remembered it all.

She fell back on her bed.

She'd kissed the garden gnome. Not just kissed, but full-on writhing and grinding, her hands stealing under his shirt, his hands all over her. A wave of nausea overcame her.

What was she thinking? How the hell was she going to live here with him now?

Clearly, her logical brain had gone completely AWOL. She hadn't had a drunken make-out session since high school. This was why she hated drinking in public. She was always terrified she would let loose exactly like this. That she would say goodbye to the inhibitions she normally kept under lock and key. She pressed her fingers to her temples and rubbed, hoping to stave off a nasty hangover headache.

She looked at the clock on her wall. It was almost ten o'clock. To make matters worse, she was sleeping through her silent study time. She wasn't in the home stretch yet, as Raymond had reminded her—her paper needed proofreading and an ending. Coffee. She needed coffee to function.

Pulling her hair into a ponytail, she got up and quietly opened her door an inch. Coast was clear. Silence.

She snuck out towards the kitchen, keeping her head down as she passed the entrance to the family room.

"Amira! There you are," Travis said from the direction of the sofa.

Biting her lip, she looked into the room. All the boys were there. The whole blasted quartet.

"Come." Travis patted the seat next to him. "I want to ask you something."

Had Duncan told the others what happened? Sameer and Barrington smiled warmly at her in greeting, but, of course, her focus was drawn immediately to the big red gnome in the room.

Duncan didn't look at her. He was focusing on a glossy magazine in his hands, turning the pages with flourish, conspicuously ignoring her.

Fine. If he wanted to ignore her, she could to that, too. Easily.

"What's up, Travis?" She sat next to him and smiled.

"Sameer and I met up with a friend last night. He works in the costume department for the National Ballet, and he had a bunch of extra tickets for tomorrow's matinee. I thought you might like to take your little sister? She's into dance, isn't she? They're doing *Sleeping Beauty*."

"Wow. That would be amazing. Zahra loves ballet. I'll have to ask my mum if she can miss school, but I'm sure it'll be fine with her. Thank you so much."

He smiled. "It's no problem at all. Glad they'll get used."

A twinge of guilt pinched her gut. She still felt terrible Travis had been upset a few days go about her and Sameer's "relationship." They hadn't talked about it, but she was in awe that Travis could still be so generous with her.

"Bring Zahra down before you go tomorrow and I'll do her hair. You can give her a fancy afternoon out!" Travis's eyes narrowed. "Hey, you okay? Your face is all red, you have a rough night?"

"Beard burn," muttered Duncan, not lifting his head from his magazine.

She glared at the garden gnome.

"What?" Sameer asked.

"Oh, nothing." Duncan smiled at his magazine. "The stress of finishing school must be finally getting to her."

"I'm . . ." She closed her eyes a second, then glared at Duncan again. "I'm going." She stormed out and into the kitchen.

Stupid lumberjack . . . Why was he making sly comments? What must the rest of the boys think?

A wave of dizziness overcame her. She held on to the counter for support. How red was her face, anyway? Lifting up her stainless-steel coffee pot, she tried to look at herself through it.

"Don't worry, Princess, you're still the fairest of them all."

She squeezed the pot handle and spun on her heels to see Duncan grinning from the kitchen doorway.

"You need to stop calling me that. And you better not have told them what happened last night. I'd prefer to wallow in regret alone." She shot him a scowl.

His eyes narrowed. "Look, *Amira*, I came in here to offer to make your coffee for you. You slept in, and I figured you'd want to get started on your paper, since you only have two more hours of silent time left. But never mind. I forgot you're only civil to me when you want something. Or when you're drunk, apparently." He turned. "You know, Princess, you'd make more friends with honey than with that venom you like to spew around." He left.

Amira stared angrily at the doorway before slamming her coffee pot down and storming out of the kitchen and straight to her room. She could deal with no coffee. It wasn't worth it.

Once in her room, she found some painkillers and turned on her computer. But the lingering fury at Duncan and a killer hangover were not conducive to focus. She paced the room a bit before falling heavily on her bed. A nap would be nice.

She must have dozed because the next thing she was aware of was a sharp knock on her door. Ugh. Why wouldn't the boys leave her alone? At least she knew it wouldn't be

Duncan this time. He would be back to ignoring her after he told her off in the kitchen.

"Come in," she said, not bothering to lift herself up from the bed. She turned her head, expecting to see Sameer or Travis.

It *was* Duncan. Standing in her doorway, a large mug in his hand.

"You like half a sugar, right?" he asked.

She buried her face in her pillow, cursing him in her head before sitting up and looking at him. Surprisingly, that scowl from the kitchen was missing from his face.

She blinked repeatedly, trying to imagine why he was here.

"We need to talk," he said.

No. They didn't. Couldn't they just go back to hating each other? Couldn't they forget they knew exactly how it felt to be pressed up against each other, breathing heavily, skin raw with friction burns, trying to stop time and space so they could stay in that moment forever?

Should be easy to forget, right?

"Why do we need to talk?" she asked.

"You know why. Can I come in?"

She said nothing, crossing her arms over her chest.

"Amira . . ."

"You want to talk in here?" she asked, looking around her room.

He snorted. "Not like I've never been in here before."

Her mouth opened.

"Don't worry, Princess. I was a gentleman. All I did last night was guide you to your bed and watch you fall on it. Now, can we talk in here, or do you want to discuss this where everyone can hear?"

Frowning, she stood and took the mug from his hands before sitting back on the edge of her bed. He closed the door behind him.

She clutched the warm mug and inhaled deeply, surprised by the scent hitting her nose. She raised her eyebrows. "Masala chai?"

"I was going to make coffee, but . . ." He shrugged. "My stomach can't handle coffee when I'm hungover. I thought you might be the same."

She took a sip. It was a touch heavy-handed with the spices, but totally drinkable. Actually, quite delicious. Amira's stomach could usually handle coffee fine, but nothing was as soothing as good chai. "Who made it?" she asked.

"I did." He sat on the desk chair. "So, here's the thing. We're going to have to learn to be civil to each other because we still have to live together for a week. If you're pissed because you think I told the guys about your wandering hands last night, don't worry. I can keep my trap shut."

"*My* wandering hands?"

"All right. Both our wandering hands. We got a little drunk, and we got a little carried away. We can be adults about it."

"I have no problem being a mature adult. You, on the other hand, with your snide remarks and—"

He stood, nostrils flaring. "I'm out of here. I don't know why I ever expected to have a civil conversation with you."

His hand was holding the doorknob when he paused. Amira's heart rate sped as the air in the room seemed to want to leave with him.

Finally, he turned and looked at her, expression dark. "You know what I don't get? I don't get why you are such a witch to me. I helped you with that creep on the train, you hate me. I make you tea, you hate me. I take you to the library, you hate me—"

"You stranded me at the library."

"I took you first. Everything I do gets met with nastiness. You're as sweet as pie to the other guys, but I only get your poison."

"And what about you? You keep calling me Princess, even though I told you not to. I'm not some helpless princess that needs to be rescued!"

"What the hell, Amira! I call you *Princess Jasmine*. She was hardly helpless! Jasmine's the one who saved Aladdin's ass by pretending to be Jafar's slave!"

Amira sat frozen, mouth agape. Duncan Galahad was an odd man.

"Plus," she finally continued, ignoring his unnecessary princess education, "you smirk and scowl at me whenever I enter a room, and you make snide comments about me every chance you get. You obviously dislike me, so I don't see why we have to get along."

"We seemed to get along fine yesterday, and I'm not talking about our wandering hands. And lips. And . . ." He stopped, staring at her face, pupils widening.

She felt herself blush, then shot him a nasty glare.

Heat seemed to turn back to anger as he crossed his arms over his chest. "We're going to have to get along tomorrow, too, so better find some manners behind that pretty face of yours."

"What? Why do we have to get along tomorrow?"

"We're going to the ballet together."

"No, we're not."

"Yes, we are. Travis's friend gave them four tickets. I'm borrowing Sameer's car to go pick up Maddie from Omemee first. She's into dance, too. She's really excited."

Ugh. A whole day with Duncan. "But don't you have to rehearse?"

"I can miss a day. I'll catch up. They're just going to be finalizing choreography, anyway. I can work on my twerking and twisting later."

She closed her eyes. Going to the ballet would be a disaster. She would be forced to put up with his jabs all day; she couldn't exactly lose it on him in front of Zahra and his niece.

She should just skip it, but . . . she couldn't do that to Zahra. Her sister would be ecstatic about getting to go to a real ballet. Amira didn't have it in her to say no. She groaned and fell backwards on her bed, legs dangling off the edge.

Out of the corner of her eye, she saw Duncan smile.

"I'm not cancelling," he said. "I can't do that to Maddie."

"I know. I wouldn't ask you to." She blinked, staring above her. "I guess we're going to the ballet."

"Yeah." He was quiet. "You know, what happened yesterday doesn't have to mean anything. Just two kinda lonely, kinda horny drunk people killing time. It doesn't have to happen again, and it doesn't have to mean something if it does."

She sat up again, looking at him. "It doesn't?" she asked.

He shook his head. "I'm not looking for a relationship right now, and I gather you're not either. And I think we can be honest, we're not exactly each other's types. But we can be civil. Hell, we can be more than civil, we can be friends.

We've done it before. We didn't seem to have a problem interacting last night."

She raised her eyebrows.

"I meant conversation, Princess. We had good conversations."

They did. Even before the copious amounts of bourbon, she had been amazed at how easy it had been to talk to Duncan last night. But could they do it again? It was worth a shot. Peace would be better than the war zone her basement had become.

"Don't call me Princess," she said with a small smile. She smelled the chai again. "You make a decent cup of chai."

He chuckled. "Decent?"

"Yeah, if the music thing doesn't work out, you have a promising future as a chai wallah. Who taught you to make it?"

"You. I've been watching. So, friends?" He held out his hand for her to shake.

She was willing to try if he was. She took it. "Friends."

CHAPTER FIFTEEN

AS EXPECTED, MUM had no issue with Zahra missing school for free tickets to the ballet, and Zahra was beyond thrilled to go. She was even more thrilled to have a real hairstylist do her hair first. Travis pinned up her wild curls in a complicated arrangement of braids and twists and finished with a tiny tiara. She was still preening for the others when Duncan finally showed up with Maddie minutes before they had planned to leave.

Maddie Galahad was a quiet girl with large, blue eyes and hair as fiery red as her uncle's beard. She shyly greeted Amira and Zahra, but only after Duncan told her to.

"Give me five to get my duds on, then we'll go," Duncan said, heading to his room.

They took the subway downtown. Zahra, with her usual no-holding-back extroversion, used the train ride to break past Maddie's shy persona.

"Amira told me you dance, too? I'm in modern and classical Indian. I want to do ballet, too, but Mum says there has to be a limit . . . what kind of dance do you do?"

Maddie said nothing.

"She's in ballet," Duncan said. "Five years now, right, Mads? Tell them about when you guys did *The Nutcracker* at Christmas. Their costumes were something else."

Maddie looked up at Duncan, unsure, and still quiet. Zahra was unfazed, though, and kept talking.

"*The Nutcracker*? Lucky. My friend Olivia saw *The Nutcracker* downtown. Oh, it's the same place we're going now, right, Amira? This is my first time at a real ballet. These dancers came to my school once, but it was, like, a kids' thing. They didn't even wear tutus. Did you wear a tutu in *The Nutcracker*? That's a cool dress you're wearing. You could do ballet in that. Mum says I don't know how to sit still long enough to wear a long dress. She wanted me to wear a salwar kameez today, but, seriously, how embarrassing would that be? You know what a salwar kameez is? It's an Indian outfit with pants and a long top thing."

"I've seen those." Maddie nodded.

Duncan leaned in close, whispering in Amira's ear, "Your sister's a spitfire."

She smiled. "I know. Let me know if you think she's too much for Maddie. I can tell her to tone it down."

"Nah, it's good. Maddie's already warming to her."

Amira wasn't so sure. Three words in response to Zahra's speech hardly seemed like warming. But true to Duncan's word, Maddie did seem at least lukewarm by the time they reached their subway stop. Even speaking in full sentences.

They ate lunch at an Italian place, one of those massive family restaurants that catered more to tourists than locals. Zahra had finally succeeded at breaking past the last vestige of Maddie's timidity, so the girls were in an animated discussion about recent dance competitions and performances. Maddie looked to be struggling a bit to keep up with Zahra, but that was nothing new. Most people struggled to keep up with Amira's sister, even on her quiet days. But Maddie looked at Zahra with total awe, obviously desperate to impress her charismatic new friend. Duncan was amazing with her—encouraging his niece when she grew tongue-tied, while guiding the conversation towards topics Maddie was comfortable with.

"What about you, Amira? You dance like your sister?" Duncan asked.

Amira laughed. "No. Mum tried, but I'm terrible. I'm more about algorithms than natural rhythm."

He shrugged. "Eh. People can have many talents. Look at me. I can play the guitar and apparently make a *decent* cup of chai tea."

Zahra giggled. "*Chai tea* means tea tea. Amira's going to let you have it for saying that."

He winked at Zahra. "I can only hope. Why do you think I said it?"

Amira raised a brow. Was he provoking her intentionally? It wouldn't work—she was determined to be nothing but pleasant today. The conversation stayed on the topic of dance for a while longer, and since Amira could add no valuable insight, she toyed with her pasta. While swirling her agnolotti in the pink cream sauce, she tried to resist the urge to lift her head up, since her field of vision was completely dominated by Duncan.

She couldn't help noticing her garden gnome cleaned up well. Really well. Slim-fitting black dress pants, a royal blue shirt with a tight weave, and a slim black sweater vest. His beard had been neatly trimmed, and his mouth faintly turned up with amusement when he met her stare.

Crap. He noticed her checking him out.

"You clean up nice, too," he said quietly, eyes running up and down her dark teal cocktail dress appreciatively. He waggled his eyebrows.

She swallowed a laugh, kicking him under the table. He grinned and sipped his beer.

"Uncle Duncan was going to be a famous singer," Maddie announced. "He was interviewed on TV once."

"He can still be famous!" Zahra said. "I heard his group sing in the basement, they are so good! They're like those college kids from that movie, you know, the one with that blonde girl . . ."

"Sorry, sweetheart," Duncan said, smiling at Zahra, "but I don't see fame and fortune in my future anymore. I anchored that ship a long time ago." He reached his hand out to pat Maddie's gently.

His niece looked up at him and smiled.

Amira raised a brow in query at Duncan. He nodded. "Superstars tour too much. I like to be closer to home."

Maddie was still looking up at her uncle, and he still had his hand on hers. It wasn't said outright, but clearly Maddie and Duncan had discussed this before. Amira's heart swelled at the palpable affection between them. It was so touching, but also surprising. Had Duncan put his music career on hold for the sake of this child? Really? True, fame and fortune were rare occurrences, even with Duncan's talent, but even without fame, working musicians usually needed to travel. To play on tour. Duncan had said he only played in local bands around his town. Why give up his dream to stay put near his brother's daughter?

Amira adored her sister, but even she couldn't imagine putting her life on hold for her sister. She watched him, realizing that she knew so little about this man and his motivations. He smiled self-consciously as he took his hand from Maddie's to sip his drink.

"That's cool you were on TV," Amira said.

"Just a morning show out of Peterborough. Local talent showcase. Hardly big leagues."

Zahra grinned proudly. "Amira was on the news a lot last year."

Amira shot her sister a look. "Zahra, please."

"She was angry about what happened and they kept coming to interview her. She was famous. But she doesn't like to talk about it now," Zahra said.

It was Duncan's turn to raise a brow in query. Amira shook her head and looked at her sister. "I don't like to talk about it, Zahra. And that means you are not supposed to bring it up." She tried to smile. "So, anyone know anything about the principal dancer today?"

Later, when the girls giggled their way to the bathroom together, Duncan took the opportunity to butt in where he wasn't wanted. "What was that about? Why were you on the news?"

She glanced up, studying the ornate Tiffany-style chandelier above the table. "It's nothing. I barely think about it anymore. Something happened and I was a convenient target for the media to latch on to. It's not a reason anyone would want to be famous."

Amira hated anyone bringing up the airport incident, but she specifically dreaded the thought of Duncan knowing what happened that day. She knew what he would say—that she got herself into trouble because of her big mouth, that she should have held in her temper, and that he knew perfectly well how nasty Amira could be while travelling. Duncan's reaction wouldn't be different from so many other people's.

One pointed look from her would probably shut him up about the topic, but she couldn't form her face into its familiar shape of disdain. Is that all he saw in her? Fury and rage?

Was that all she had become?

She didn't know what she wanted from Duncan Galahad, but she couldn't bear the thought of him only seeing that one thing in her. Only the prickly porcupine that he excelled at provoking. Not after she'd seen his softer, nurturing side with his niece. But she wasn't sure she knew how to be anything else.

"Suit yourself," he said. "I know I've been the victim of the over-sharing of young girls. Maddie once told a date I sleep in a red plaid onesie."

That made her smile. She couldn't help but want to see that one day.

The ballet was wonderful. Amira had never been into dance, certainly not to the extent her little sister and mother loved it, but even she was awed by the graceful leaps and twirls. The athleticism and artistry on display were like nothing she had ever seen before. Still, the performance would have been even more enjoyable if she hadn't spent most of it trying to figure Duncan out.

She couldn't quite wrap her head around the revelation that he had avoided fame and fortune because of a promise to Maddie. Clearly this wasn't a normal niece-uncle relationship. Seeing as the girl barely had a mother, it was no wonder Duncan was more of a parent figure, but where did the girl's father fit in to all this? Duncan hadn't spoken of his brother much, and Amira had no idea how close they were. But they had to be close—they lived together. It seemed they co-parented this child together. Duncan was clearly more than he seemed.

She glanced at him sitting three seats over, with Zahra and Maddie between them. He appeared to be enjoying the show. Easygoing. Relaxed. Attentive to Maddie. Doting, even, but firm. He hadn't succumbed to her big eye-pouts when she asked for an ice cream cone from one of the trucks outside City Hall. He had helped draw her out of her shell so well that it was like she and Zahra had been friends forever.

And he was unusually kind to Amira today, too. Holding doors open, being polite, even thanking her for accompanying him. Not a single smirk or snarky comment. They had agreed on a truce yesterday, but Amira felt positive that this difference in his behaviour had more to do with setting an example for his niece than anything else.

She turned back towards the show. Amira had been grateful at first that the girls were between her and Duncan, but now she was hit with a disconcerting wave of longing to be closer to him. She wanted to whisper comments in his ear about the performance, maybe get his opinion about the orchestra, even make a crack about the gold butterflies in the hair of the woman in front of her. She wished she could smell his cedar and laundry soap scent, and that desire was not something she wanted to deal with right now.

She tried to be cheerful and not let on how disturbed she felt on the way home, but apparently she wasn't successful. Duncan leaned close on the train, his warm breath sending a shiver up her spine.

"You okay? You're not still upset about your sister sharing dirt about you, are you?"

"No. I'm fine. I'm over that. I'm just . . ." She fiddled with the clasp of her purse, head down.

"You're what?"

"I'm a little out of sorts on account of how nice you're being. I figured for sure we'd get kicked out for bloodshed in the audience."

"Hey"—he laughed—"I resent that! I *am* nice!"

Amira snorted. Duncan Galahad was many things . . . but she wouldn't list anything as mundane as *nice* among his attributes.

"That place was too pretty for death matches, anyway," he continued. "The acoustics were incredible, but next time, I'll take you to the kind of place where the sound is just as good *and* you can scratch your ass without your pinky raised."

Her eyebrows shot up higher than the principal dancer's leap. "Next time?"

"Sure, next time. We need to take this friendship to new levels, if you ask me. The girls seem to get along. We should take them to more shows together. Maddie could use a bit of city culture."

"This isn't quite a *friendship* . . ." she mumbled, but she made the mistake of looking at him. His eyes were warm yet slightly crinkled at the edges. His skin golden beneath his beard. And his lips, slightly curled in the corners. She bit her own lip. He watched her, with just as much interest. She shivered as his gaze swept over her face like a warm breeze.

Fuck. *Distance.* Distance between her and Duncan was what she needed.

"Uncle Duncan," Maddie said, looking up at him, blue eyes pleading. "Can I sleep over at Zahra's tonight? She has a bunk bed."

"Sorry, it's a school night. And your dad's already on his way from Omemee to get you. Maybe another time?"

"She's always welcome. Zahra lives for sleepovers," Amira said.

"Hey, you know what might work, Mads? Your dad's coming up to watch my singing competition on Sunday. Maybe if Sameer will loan me his car again, I'll come get you the night before so you can have your sleepover. Oh, sorry, Amira, I guess we should have asked you first, or your mom."

"Please, Amira, can she?" Zahra asked. "I want to teach her the Bollywood dance I'm working on."

Amira smiled. "I'm sure Mum won't mind. But he'll have to check with Maddie's dad and Sameer first."

Duncan's brother, Ryan, was already there when they got home, chatting with Barrington in the family room. He was a tall, clean-cut man who looked exactly like a narrower, less burly Duncan. It was odd—it looked like someone forgot to add the finishing touches when he was made. Like biryani without cilantro or fried onions.

"There's my girl," he said, bending to hug Maddie. "How was the fancy ballet?"

"Really good! It was better than when you and Grandma took me. Zahra said I can come to her dance recital in July. Can we? She does Indian dance, like in the movies. And Uncle Duncan said I could come sleep over before his singing competition on Sunday. I want to bring my new split-sole ballet slippers for Zahra to try. She's never worn real ballet shoes before."

"Hey now, slow down, baby girl, don't get ahead of yourself. Indian dancing, eh? That's something. Did you say thank you to the nice people for taking you out today?"

Amira stepped forward. "It was our pleasure. Zahra and Maddie got along so well, she's welcome here any time." She held out a hand for him to shake.

She looked carefully at Duncan's brother when he shook her hand. The similarity between them was so strong that she was treated to a glimpse of what Duncan would look like without a beard. Even Ryan's eyes were the same clear green—that colour bright enough to inspire ballads and prose in her mind. But on longer scrutiny, something was missing in Ryan's eyes. They were just . . . less. Duncan's eyes always seemed to flash with emotion. She had seen anger, annoyance, amusement, warmth, even arousal in Duncan's gaze. Ryan's eyes seemed almost blank. Cold?

She was imagining it. He was Duncan's brother— he wasn't cold. He was probably just an introvert, like

Maddie. Still, he looked away immediately after shaking her hand.

Amira decided to extract herself from the conversation after Barrington asked Ryan if he'd like to stay for a coffee before heading back on the road. She wasn't keen on making small talk to impress this man. Her "friendship" with Duncan was odd enough without adding a "meet the family" situation into it.

"Let's go tell Mum about the show, Zahra. It was great meeting you, Maddie. I hope we'll see you on the weekend." She waved to the men and climbed the stairs with her sister.

She was relieved to get out of there. Today had been weird.

CHAPTER SIXTEEN

THEY FOUND NANIMA cooking in the kitchen, but Mum was nowhere to be seen.

"Ah, you girls are home. How was the ballet?" Nanima asked, turning away from whatever smelled amazing on the stove.

"So good, Nanima," Zahra said. "You should have seen the jumps the ballerina did. Maddie told me what they were called, but I don't remember. She's going to teach me the five basic positions on the weekend."

Amira peeked over Nanima's shoulder to see what she was making. Looked like a chicken curry.

"Zahra, go take off that dress," Nanima said. "You'll make a mess. Olivia was here with some homework from your teacher. It's on the dining table."

"Where's Mum?" Zahra asked. "I brought her a program from the show."

"She's gone out tonight. But she told me to tell you to phone her when you get home."

Zahra picked up Nanima's phone from the kitchen counter and started to dial.

"Nah!" Nanima took the phone back. "Change out of that dress first! Don't get stains on it before Eid!"

"Can I go show Olivia—"

"Zahra, c'mon," Amira interrupted. "No arguments. Change, then homework."

Zahra groaned before heading to her room. Amira peeked into the other pot on the stove. Peas and potatoes. Too bad she was still full from lunch.

Nanima shook her head. "That girl is turning into you. She's getting so saucy these days."

Amira snorted. "Saucy?"

Nanima frowned. "Maybe sassy? Smart-mouthed. You were like that when you were her age." She smiled as she patted Amira's cheek. "You're a sweet girl now, though."

Amira tried not to snort again at being called sweet. "Where did Mum go?"

"An art show, I think. With her work friends. You eating with us tonight?"

"Probably not. We had a huge lunch. And I've got work to do. I'm hoping Raymond emailed me today with his comments on my report. And if he didn't, I still need a conclusion. I lost a whole day."

"Okay. I was going to take Zahra to Jamatkhana tonight, but she must be tired, and she has homework, too. I'll stay home with her."

"I can watch Zahra tonight."

"No, you have to focus on your school work. Can I make you a sandwich later? Your mum bought that good bread. I can make you grilled cheese and chutney like you used to like."

Amira smiled at her grandmother. Nanima was a sweetheart, no question, but she suddenly wondered if her grandmother had any regrets for all the work she did for them. While she hadn't exactly given up the chance for a lucrative career in music like Duncan did, she had sacrificed a lot to help raise children who were not her own. She even took an early retirement from her part-time job in administration after the divorce so someone could be home for Zahra. Of course, as a sixty-plus-year-old woman at the end of her working life, her situation was night and day from Duncan's, who'd been in his twenties and just starting his career when he made a commitment to Maddie. But in both cases, one thing was clear— Duncan Galahad and her grandmother were amazing people.

And wasn't that a complete one-eighty from how she had previously felt about Duncan? Just yesterday, she was both cursing the man and cursing waking up with beard burn from kissing him senseless the night before.

She shook her head, unable to comprehend the turns her life had taken in the short time since she left university.

"A sandwich would be amazing, thank you. In fact, thank you for everything you do for us. I hope you know how much we appreciate you."

Nanima waved her hand as she walked over to the dining room sideboard. She pulled out a platter. "I don't want appreciation. What else can I do? When family needs me, I'm there. Always."

Amira stepped towards her grandmother from behind and wrapped her arms around her. "Well, I consider myself very lucky to have someone like you in my family. I appreciate you."

"Yes, yes, beta. Now listen to your own advice. Change. Homework."

After changing into pyjama pants and a T-shirt, Amira booted up her computer and checked her email. Nothing from Raymond. It was fine; she couldn't really expect him to be done so soon—even if the paper was due in a few days. Raymond had a full-time job and two kids, after all. He'd get it to her on time. He had to. She pulled up her report and started working on those grammatical errors he mentioned yesterday.

She managed to get a few hours of work in before there was a knock on her door. It was, surprisingly, her mother, holding the grilled cheese and chutney sandwich Nanima had promised.

"Thanks, Mum."

"Thank your nanima. I'm just the waitress, she's the chef."

Amira grinned as she took the sandwich to her desk and sat. "You got a minute to chat?"

"Of course. What's up?" Mum sat on Amira's bed.

Amira bit her lip. "I don't know." She didn't even know why she wanted to talk to Mum. Or what she wanted to talk about. Amira's mind was a mess lately. She forced a smile. "You were at an art show?"

Mum nodded, smiling happily. "Yes, with a few of the nurses from work. One of them has a sister who's an artist. A hobbyist, at least; she's also a dentist. This was her first gallery showing. Fantastic stuff. Multimedia canvases."

Amira chuckled. "Look at us. Ballet and an art gallery on the same day. We're so . . . sophisticated."

"Change is in the air, sweetie. I just thanked Travis again for getting you girls those tickets. Zahra wouldn't stop talking about the show when I got home. And about the young girl you went with."

"Maddie. Duncan's niece." Amira paused. "Change *is* in the air. It's just . . ." She couldn't put words to what she was feeling. Things just felt different since she'd come back, and not just because of her crowded basement. She shook her head. It was probably just stress. School. And there was no question she was growing emotionally attached to those boys out there, whether she wanted to or not. Things would be back to normal next week after her report was in and the quartet left. Maybe. Hopefully.

"Amira, sweetheart, what's bugging you?"

"Nothing. I'm fine. Sounds like you had a great evening. I'm glad you're getting out with these work friends."

"Yes, it's time I had a social life again. I even agreed to go to an anniversary party on the weekend with your grand-mother. Although I think she has some unsaid motive there."

"Yup, she wants to set you up with a divorced man from Winnipeg. He's apparently in high demand, though. Reena's mum is scouting the man for her."

Mum groaned. "Of course. I should have known. Why she won't just tell me these things . . ." She stood up. "Anyway, I promised Zahra we'd read more Harry Potter before bed. 'Night, Amira."

Despite seeming uninterested in Nanima's set-up, Mum still didn't mention anything about dating anyone, and she'd had ample opportunity there. Maybe there was no one. Maybe it was only a new friend group from the hospital. Still, Amira needed to get together with her mother more often. Alone, and when they had more than five minutes to chat.

She couldn't make herself get back to her report after her mother went upstairs, so she did what she should have done immediately when she'd started to feel off-kilter this afternoon. She called her best friend.

After getting a short update on Saira's health (seemingly fine, but defensive and angry), Amira told Reena about the trip to the ballet and her weird mood there. And, like she always did after talking it out with her best friend, Amira felt better. Loads better. At least until Reena started ribbing her about Duncan.

"So, it was seeing him with his niece that made you realize his humanity, not sticking your tongue down his throat. Interesting."

"I shouldn't have told you," Amira groaned, regretting the phone call she'd made to her the night before.

"As if hiding something from me is ever an option."

Amira tried to change the subject. "Speaking of hiding, remember I thought my mum was hiding a new man? Now I'm not so sure." She told Reena about her mum's art show date.

"No, this is proof that she *is* dating someone," Reena said. "An art gallery is such a date spot. She said she went with a group of nurses, right? Nurses can be men."

"Yeah, I guess it's possible. But if she doesn't want to tell me, I don't want to pry right now."

"Agreed. With the drama with the merry minstrels, you have enough on your plate. I'm still shaken that you hooked up with Duncan. You need me to move in and act as chaperone for the next couple of days?"

"That will *not* be necessary." Amira groaned again. This topic was apparently unavoidable. "I'll lay off the bourbon, and let's hope his interest in me has waned since discovering I can't tell a croisé from a plié."

"And he could tell the difference?"

"Apparently the garden gnome is a man of many talents."

"If you ask me," Reena said, "I think you should see what other talents he's hiding. I mean, you couldn't have predicted that the man could make chai, right? Imagine what else he can do. I think a quick fling with a guy who's already living there couldn't be more convenient."

"It's a good thing I didn't ask you, then, isn't it?"

There was a soft knock on her door.

"Hang on, Ree. Seems it's drop-in hour in Amira's room again."

She opened the door to see Duncan. He was also in his pyjamas—flannel pants and a blue T-shirt. No plaid onesie.

"Hey." She smiled.

"Can I come in?"

Why? She got that they were friends now, sort of, but was he going to make a habit of coming to see her in her room every day? After the drunken make-out session, late-night room calls didn't seem like the best idea. Not if they wanted to stay vertical, at least. Did he want to stay vertical? Did she? She eyed him suspiciously.

Duncan looked tense, like he was barely holding back another angry outburst. What had she done to piss him off this time? She raised an eyebrow.

"Don't be mad, Amira," he growled, "but . . . I googled you."

Shoulders slumping, she looked away.

"Let me come in, I want to talk to you about it," he said.

"Got to go, Reena. I'll call you tomorrow." She disconnected the call.

She didn't want to talk about it. She had nothing more to say on this topic, and she'd told him as much at lunch. But one thing Amira had learned about this man was that he wouldn't let something like this go. She put her phone on her desk and motioned him in, closing the door behind him. Perching cross-legged on the bed, she waited for him to sit. He didn't take the desk chair this time, but sat on the bed next to her. She stilled. Why did he have to sit so close?

"So . . ." she started. "What did you read?"

"A bunch of articles. What happened?"

"You read them, you know."

"I want to hear it from you."

She shrugged but didn't look at him. "It was stupid. I overreacted and got burned for it. You know my temper." She played with the edge of her duvet on her unmade bed.

"Doesn't sound like overreacting to me. What happened, Amira? What did they do to you?"

She didn't answer him right away. She let her fingers lightly trail on the crumpled blanket. "It was two Decembers ago. I was flying to Philadelphia to see my dad for the holidays. He works there. Things were not going well for me at school. I didn't have many friends there, and a couple of classmates were openly hostile because I snapped at a TA after he made a sexist comment. I was thinking of throwing in the towel and quitting everything, and Dad bought me the plane ticket when I told him that. He's an engineer, too, and he's the calmest person I know. Nothing gets to him, except Mum, but that's a whole other story. My dad is so good about letting this shit roll off him. I knew he was the person to talk me off the ledge."

"You were going alone?"

"Yeah. Mum was taking Zahra to a dance showcase in Montreal, otherwise Zahra would've been with me. In the border security line, I got pulled aside. Random extra check, they said. Random, my ass . . . anyway, the guy started asking me all these questions and made me open my phone. There were a few pictures of Arabic calligraphy and illuminated Arabic manuscripts. I took them at a museum here in Toronto the week before. When he asked me who I was going to see, I told them my father, Mohammad Khan. He didn't seem to care that Dad's an executive at an engineering firm. I told them I wasn't religious. They asked about my family, what sect of Islam I belonged to, where my family lived. They gave me a *thorough* pat-down." She shuddered at the memory. "Several times."

"Bastards."

"I was born in Canada. I'm not from any countries on the travel-ban list. My mum came from India when she was fifteen, and my dad from Kenya at twenty." She paused, smoothing the balled-up duvet cover with her hand. "Yes, my parents are both immigrants, and it hasn't always been easy, but things weren't like this before. This . . . endemic . . . *sanctioned* racism. It's getting so much worse. It's heartbreaking. The world is such a trash fire, and at that moment, I just couldn't deal with it anymore. I kind of lost it on them. You've seen my temper . . . and I was already so stressed about school, and everything. They said I was being difficult. They almost arrested me, but in the end, I was let go after *questioning*."

"They didn't let you board?"

She shook her head. "Technically, I could have. They had no proof I'd done anything wrong. But they kept me so long I missed my flight. And I was so freaked out, I didn't even want to go to Philadelphia anymore. Believe it or not, one of the guys told me he didn't actually suspect I was dangerous, but he wanted to teach me a lesson. I almost spat at him."

Duncan said nothing for a while, just sat near her, staring into space. She couldn't read his expression. Had she said too much? He hadn't signed up for terrorist accusations and Islamophobia when he said he wanted a friendship with her.

But Amira long ago accepted she didn't have the luxury of simple relationships.

Finally, he spoke. "And then you went to the media?"

She nodded. "I wanted to scream to the whole country about how they treated me. The media loved the story because I'm not a hijab-wearing, conservative, religious immigrant." She shrugged, looking away from him, and spoke quietly. "I'm not very religious, but I do believe in God. And although I don't agree with all the rituals, at its core, I think Islam is a beautiful religion. I'm too much of a scientist for dogma and blind faith—but I respect those who practise faithfully." She looked at him. His expression was still hard to read, but his crystal-clear focus kept her talking. "But the media put their own spin on it. They implied it was worse that this happened to someone less religious, someone who doesn't wear a head scarf and who grew up here. As if it was okay to mistreat devout Muslims." She paused again. "I'm a Canadian citizen by birth, so I'm sheltered in ways others can't be. I can afford to lose my temper and fight back. I fought for those who couldn't." She stilled, looking at her knees. "No one should be made to feel like less of a human being because of their religion or the colour of their skin. No one. Not in my country. In my home . . ." Her voice cracked. Wavered a bit.

"Anyway . . ." She took a long breath and tried to rein in her runaway emotions. "Anyway, it was all fine. I got a lot of support. And, eventually, everyone forgot about it when the next horrible thing happened to a marginalized group."

"Was it really fine, Amira?" His gaze was direct.

God, those eyes on him. One of these days, she was going to lose herself in them.

"Yes, fine."

"So why don't you talk about it anymore?"

She shrugged. "Because it's done. I've talked about it to death, and people don't get how emotionally exhausting it is to rehash it over and over. Most have been supportive, but I made the mistake of reading the comments on some of those newspaper articles."

His hand found her knee. "Oh, Amira . . ."

Keeping her focus squarely on her own hands in her lap, she continued softly. "They said I should have been more obedient. I shouldn't have flaunted my culture or religion. I needed to assimilate here. Crossing the border is a privilege, I shouldn't take it as a right. I was a bitch. I was just another angry terrorist. My husband or father was going to beat me for speaking out when I got home. Someone said my *existence* is incompatible with Canadian values. And those were the nice ones. The Twitter comments were much, much worse."

He winced, squeezing her knee. "I'm sorry."

Her voice was barely a whisper. "I used to be very vocal on social media, but some right-wing nut sent up a call to arms to his minions, or something. The trolls pounced on me. It was vile. I got hundreds of messages. Vulgar, noxious comments. And they sent pictures. Graphic, violent images . . . Muslims being hurt, tortured . . . and then threats against me started." She looked up at him. "Honestly, Duncan, I was scared. I deleted all my social media."

"That's totally understandable." He still had his hand on her knee. He didn't seem to want to let her go, and she was glad for it.

She shrugged. "Others have gone through so much worse. Refugees are being beaten, starved, bombed. Kids separated from their families. People were shot in their mosque, here, while praying . . . all . . ." Amira squeezed her eyes shut, trying to halt her tears. "All I got were ugly words and pictures."

"I'm so sorry, Amira. Really."

She blinked, seemingly unable to stop talking to this man. "I always had trolls commenting on feeds . . . but it feels different these days. Nothing I can write or say will change anyone's mind. These people hate me. I'm not human to them. I saw their profiles on social media, and these are regular people. Not villains or monsters, but people who look just like the people I grew up with. Some of them looked like old boyfriends."

"They probably looked like me."

She looked at him. Beautiful, warm eyes. Soft, golden skin. "Yeah, a lot of them did."

He said nothing for a while, his hand on her knee the only thing she could feel. "Is that why you hated me when we met?" he finally asked softly.

"No. I didn't hate you, not really. But honestly, I . . ." Her voice trailed off. How to explain this to him? "Do you know what that creep said to me at the train station before you pretended to be my boyfriend?"

"He asked if you were from India."

"Yes. He also said he heard Canadian girls don't wear underwear."

Duncan's nostrils flared. "I knew I should've hit him."

"Guys have said they want an Indian girlfriend because we're more submissive. Others call me exotic."

"So, you've given up on all men?"

She laughed sadly. "I haven't given up on men. I like men just fine. I'd love to be in a relationship, I just don't trust easily. And I especially don't trust my own judgment. Too many people have been drawn to me because of what I am instead of who I am, and I hate that I have to be the one to figure out the difference. Navigating life is such a shit show these days."

He said nothing, staring at her for a while. It was intense. Amira was sure she said way too much and was mortified when a tear finally escaped. She tried to look away but he caught her chin. His calloused fingers wiped her tear, then rested on her cheek. He was warm, and gentle. His hand was like an anchor holding her down, stopping her from being swept away.

A small smile emerged behind the beard. "I can't force you to trust me, but I can promise to be honest with you," he said. "And . . . I wasn't honest yesterday. I lied to you." He removed his hand from her face but continued to stare at her. "I said you weren't my type, but honestly, Amira, that's not true. You are exactly my type. And not because of some exotic fetish or anything like that. Just because you're you."

"What?"

"It doesn't hurt that you're smoking hot." His voice was like lightly sanded stone, smooth between rough edges. "But I knew I wanted you the second you told me off when we met. Self-assured, confident women who fight for themselves are my catnip."

She looked back down at her hands. She wasn't a fighter. She used to be, but she didn't have it in her anymore. "I don't fight anymore. I wasn't strong enough," she whispered.

"You're still a fighter, Amira. They didn't take that from you. I saw it in you that day. Now that I know you better, I see you're not only a fighter, but brilliant, generous, funny. You are exactly my type."

This conversation seemed impossible. But here they were. Having it. "Why didn't you show me? I was sure you despised me," she whispered.

"Yeah, well"—he ran his hand over his beard—"the type of woman I'm drawn to hasn't worked out so well for me in the past. I've been burned by a couple of bad experiences myself. I'm not stable enough. My income is not predictable. I won't move out of my brother's house. I was trying to convince myself that I didn't like you, and I was an ass. I'm sorry. I'm a bit . . . argumentative."

That was an understatement. She laughed, feeling light-headed all of a sudden. Duncan was attracted to her? Not just when he was drunk? Not just as eye candy?

Was this because of her pity party?

She looked at him. His eyes still sparkled with the usual amusement, but the way he was looking at her so clearly, she believed him. She realized she trusted Duncan. It's why she had been comfortable drinking with him the other night. It's why she agreed to take Zahra to the ballet with him. It was probably why she sat down across from him on the train in the first place. He was telling the truth, and it was amazing to have someone be completely honest with her.

May as well go for broke and tell him the truth, too, she told herself. In for a penny, in for a pound, right?

"I liked you, too," she said quietly.

"No, you didn't." He smiled.

"Yeah, I did. I just didn't admit it to anyone. Or myself. Reena told you I used to have a thing for musicians, but I've also always liked . . . country boys. You're both."

"Country boys?" He laughed.

"Yes." Her face reddened. "Reena used to say I had a farm-boy fetish. You know *The Princess Bride*? She said I was looking for my own Westley to boss around. In high school, I'd narrow in on any small-town boy who moved to the city."

His eyes glazed over. "Oh, fuck, Amira. I'd love for you to boss me around."

She stared at him and felt a shiver down her back. He waggled his eyebrows at her. Damn . . .

She grabbed her pillow from behind her and hit him in the face with it. Laughing, he took it from her, threw it to the end of the bed, and rolled on top of her, easily holding her down with his large hands on her wrists. His grin faded as his eyes darkened. Amira could hear her heart beating in her own ears.

He was going to kiss her again. Duncan Galahad was going to kiss her again—except this time, they had both admitted they were attracted to each other, and maybe even inexplicably compatible. This time, they were stone-cold sober and already lying on a bed. This was no drunken hookup. This was infinitely more terrifying.

But he didn't kiss her. They stared at each other, mere inches between them, the edge of the cliff falling into eternity.

"What happens now?" she whispered.

"You tell me," he whispered back.

"This is going to complicate . . . things . . ."

"Immensely."

The way her life was going now, the last thing Amira needed was complication. But this . . . this was tempting.

She licked her lip. Terrifyingly tempting.

Duncan didn't move, his arms caging her in. The smell of cedar and soap consumed her senses. His soft beard just barely grazed her chin. He licked his lips. She knew how soft and mobile they could be. She knew what those lips tasted like. She could lift her head closer. It would take a fraction of a movement and she could have him. All that delicious skin, all those strong muscles. He wanted her. His strong heartbeat against her chest gave him away. She could forget everything, and she could lose herself with him.

But could she?

With monumental effort, she said one word. "Duncan . . ."

He sighed and released her, rolling away to lie next to her. She put her hands back down and rubbed absentmindedly at her wrists. "It's not that I'm against a no-strings-attached hookup . . ." she said.

He swallowed. "But that's not what this is."

"No."

He looked at her. "The competition is in four days."

"My project is due in five."

"I would say we can pick this back up then, but . . ."

Pick up what in five days? Even if they ignored the fact they had been at each other's throats since they met just over a week (!) ago, she'd sworn off closed-minded country boys years ago. She wanted to find someone who understood her, and a substitute music teacher from a town of fewer than two thousand people didn't really fit that bill, no matter how easy he was to talk to. Or how empathetic he had been about her truckload of baggage. Not to mention the fact that the whole quartet was planning on leaving immediately after the competition, and, true, Omemee wasn't that far (in a moment of weakness, she'd googled the distance yesterday) but far enough to make the whole getting to know each other part of the relationship tricky.

Wait, relationship? Was that what she wanted? With Duncan? She stilled . . . a few days ago, she would have been happy to never have laid eyes on him or the rest of his merry men, and now she was cataloguing the possibility of a relationship with him?

"Easy there, Princess. I can hear your gears turning from here." He leaned up on his elbow, his gaze sweeping her face. "This doesn't have to be profound. We don't have to overthink it. We can work all day and have fun"—one side of his lip upturned—"lots of fun, at night. Or . . . not. I didn't come in here for a booty call."

"Why did you come in here?"

His head fell back onto the pillow. "I was pissed off after reading about you, and maybe . . . maybe I wanted to rescue you again."

"I don't need to be rescued."

He turned his head and smiled at her again. "I know. That's why you're my type. But"—he rolled off the bed and sat on the edge, his broad back tense—"I guess it's time for me to hit the couch. You know where to find me. Not if you need me, mind you, but if you want me." He stood and nodded. "'Night, Princess."

He left, closing the door softly behind him.

Amira groaned and rolled onto her stomach, burying her face in the crook of her elbow. How the hell was she supposed to get any sleep after that?

She knew, almost from the moment she saw him, that the garden gnome would be the death of her. She willed her body's reaction to return to normal.

She hadn't imagined that it would be death by sexual frustration.

The room was silent. The whole house breathed a level of peace that hadn't been present here in a week. No singing. No arguing. She got up and glanced at the decorative clock ticking on her wall. Almost ten o'clock.

She reopened her computer and checked her email. Still no response from Raymond. Her stomach tightened. He'd get back to her soon. She opened her report and tried to pick up where she'd left off. She was far further along in her work than she'd expected to be with five days left. The tension that normally sat between her shoulder blades had eased over the last few days, and her thoughts had been able to flow freely when working. Because she was at home? Maybe.

But now that tension had snuck back in. Why hadn't Raymond responded? Her thoughts wandered back to Duncan. She still couldn't believe it. He wanted her. He liked her . . . for her. Not because of some exotic fetish or some desire to be the big, strong white man to save the princess. He wanted her, not in spite of her outspokenness, drive, and even prickly nature, but because of it. She bit her lip. They could have a very, very fun time. What was the problem?

Maybe it was fine to have one last, futureless fling before her life became nothing but work and ambition. One final dip into her secret penchant for hot musicians. Despite the constant butting heads, she had a feeling Duncan was the type to stay friendly with women he had been physical with. And the more she thought about it, the more she could see a friendship with Duncan Galahad in her future. Even play dates and high tea.

The clock ticked loudly in her room. Loud enough to drown out the rational reasons why she shouldn't do this.

She picked up her phone and opened her texting app, but stilled. Years of maternal and grandmotherly advice, years of social and cultural programming had told her the woman didn't make the first move. It was a struggle to overcome her sexist upbringing, but she was always up for a challenge.

Hands shaking, she forced herself to text two words.

Amira

Farm boy.

Duncan

On my way.

CHAPTER SEVENTEEN

AMIRA TURNED OFF her overhead light, leaving on the dim lamp on her nightstand, and stood at her door, open a crack to let Duncan in. Still wearing his pyjamas, he arrived with a wide smile and a shaving kit in one hand.

"Just so we're on the same page," he said as she softly shut the door behind him, "this time I am here for a booty call."

Suddenly nervous, Amira felt her heart rate speed up. "What's that?" She nodded to the shaving kit. "You expecting me to shave you?"

"Hell no. There are condoms in there."

She tensed even more, feeling a flutter in her gut.

He must have sensed her nerves, because his face softened. He took one step forward and watched her intently as he ran one finger from her cheek, grazing slowly down her neck and over her chest, stopping in the deep hollow between her breasts. She shivered at the touch.

With a sinful gaze, he whispered into her ear, "Give me orders, Buttercup."

That was it. Instant arousal. The tension between her shoulders got up and walked right out of the room. She smiled. "Shirt off. On the bed."

He purred, sucking her earlobe into his mouth for a second before releasing and stepping away.

Eyes on her, he slowly lowered his arms to grasp the hem of his T-shirt. He lifted it at a snail's pace, strong hips, a flat stomach, and a sprinkling of red curls. Yum.

"It *is* red," she mused as he lifted his shirt to obscure his face.

"What?" He tossed his shirt to the floor.

"Your chest hair. It's red like your beard, not auburn like your head."

"I'm red from the ears down."

"All the way down?"

He smiled as he sat in the middle of the bed. "What next, Princess?"

Amira stood in place. Exhaling slowly, she climbed on the bed, kneeling next to his thighs. "Arms behind your head."

He complied immediately, fingers interlaced behind his head resting against the headboard.

She tapped her fingers on his thigh. "What will I do with you next?"

"Anything you want," he rasped.

It was like someone had dug deep into the furthest corners of her mind to find her deepest fantasies and presented them on a silver platter. She lowered her head and kissed him, going deep from the start. He tilted to get even closer, opening wide for her, but he didn't release his hands.

It was so hot.

"So, what are you going to do next?" he asked after she broke free, his voice trembling.

"I haven't decided yet. You enjoying this?"

He swallowed. "You have no idea."

She smiled. "You're not what I expected."

"Well, you, Princess, are exactly what I expected. Or, well . . . fantasized. I'm all yours," he growled.

He looked so beautiful. That red beard was almost glowing in the dim room. His chest heaving, his hands locked in place behind him. She got up to grab a condom from his kit, stripping her clothes off along the way.

Having him here, offering himself to her, was a gift she wasn't about to refuse. And he not only let her lead, but his murmurs of appreciation told her that he was enjoying it as much as she was.

It was breathtaking.

Afterwards, she lay on his chest, basking in his warm embrace.

Duncan kissed the top of her head. "Jesus, Amira . . . you . . ."

Amazing. She'd rendered him speechless. She lifted her head up, looking into those clear green eyes. They reflected back more tenderness, and more vulnerability, than she'd expected.

She rested her head back on his shoulder, needing to break the pull of that look.

"Two questions, Princess," he whispered.

"Hmm?"

"One, can I stay here with you tonight? The couch is getting a little . . . tight. I'm a big guy."

"That you are," she said, running her hand over his chest.

"And two, are you planning to boss me around again? Because I would like that. Very much."

She laughed, burying herself in his chest as he squeezed her into him. She agreed. She would very much like to do that again, too.

· · · ·

AMIRA WOKE THE following morning curled on her side with Duncan wrapped around her, his arm warm across her chest and his hand clutching her left boob. She tried to extract the hand.

"Stop it. It's mine," he growled.

"You're awake."

"Of course I'm awake. I'm naked, wrapped around a beautiful, also naked woman . . . I don't want to miss this by sleeping."

She laughed as she turned in his arms to face him.

"Hi," he said, grinning widely.

"Hi."

He ran his fingers through her hair, loose and messy on the pillow. "So . . . this is a strange new development on our so-called friendship."

"I know." She wrinkled her nose. "Do we have to talk about it?"

"I don't know." He kissed her neck. "I can think of other things I'd rather do . . ." He kissed her chin. "But if you insist on talking . . ." He kissed her mouth, and she forgot about talking for a while.

For a long while. Long enough that he needed to get up and grab another condom from his shaving kit. "Last one," he said, returning. "Wasn't expecting any action on this trip, but I think a visit to the drugstore is in order today."

Amira tensed. A drugstore. A box of condoms. Meaning more . . . this? For how long? Was this a relationship? Did she have to spend every night with him? Was that what she wanted?

"Amira, you okay? You want this?"

She closed her eyes. He was surrounding her. The lights weren't dim this time; the daylight sun was seeping in through the crack in the shades in her high window. He obviously had no morning-after regrets. In fact, he was ready for round three. A wave of terror passed over her. How could she trust him this much?

"Amira, look at me."

She did. Those fathomless green eyes, so often crinkled in the corners with mischief, were wide, honest, and serious. "Nothing happens you don't want," he said softly.

She smiled. This man was a treasure. She wrapped her bare leg around his thigh. "I want you, now. But I can't promise more than just . . . this, okay?"

"This, right now, is everything." He kissed her gently.

This time, it was different. No one took the lead, but rather, they moved together, knowing exactly what the other needed, their gazes locked, faces inches apart.

Damn. When she had decided to sleep with him last night, she hadn't in a million years expected . . . this. Amira was no virgin, but the hookups had been few and far between the last few years, and none in over eight months. Maybe it was just the post-orgasmic haze, or maybe it had just been way too long, but she couldn't remember sex being this good. She didn't think she'd ever been with anyone she connected with so well. Someone who could relinquish control as easily as he shared it. Someone who could laugh in bed one moment, and stare intensely at her the next. And to think she found an unparalleled lover in the likes of Duncan Galahad, the bearded garden gnome.

"I should probably leave you alone," he said, grinning at her and ending their post-coital snuggles. "Not that I wouldn't love to spend the whole day in bed with you, but we had a deal. Mornings are yours."

And thoughtful to boot. Ugh . . .

She got up and grabbed her robe. Raymond had sent some literature a couple of days ago about the project she'd be working on with him when she returned to Hyde, so she figured she could get a start on reading it while she waited for him to finish with her report. "I'll come have breakfast with you first."

. . . .

SHE FOUND HIM in the kitchen after her shower, already adding milk to her coffee.

"Thanks," she said, taking it.

"Barrington made a mess of pancakes." He winked before he took his own coffee to the dining table to sit. Sameer and Travis were just coming out of their room as she walked by.

"Hey, guys," Travis said, looking at his phone. "A friend of mine sent me these new vocal exercises." He started singing scales with his face contorted into a series of bizarre pretzel formations. Sameer looked at Travis with a pinched expression for a few seconds before bursting out laughing.

"There is no chance in hell I am going to do that with this face," Barrington said. "Hey, Amira! Someone's unusually social this morning. You joining us for breakfast, too?"

Amira frowned. What did that mean? She stood at the table, a wave of panic freezing her in place. Had the boys already seen it on her face that she'd had sex, repeatedly, with their baritone?

Sameer and Travis sat, clearly clueless. Travis smiled at Amira.

She sat. Who the hell cared if they figured it out anyway? There had been nothing normal about the interpersonal dynamics in this apartment for the last week; may as well add another layer of crazy to their little family.

After all five were seated and eating, Barrington smirked again. "So, Duncan, sleep well? I think the air mattress and the couch may be missing you."

Amira reddened.

"What?" Travis asked. "Isn't he sleeping on the floor in your room?"

"Nah," Barrington said. "He's been on the couch for a few days. I think my good-night calls to Marcia were finally getting to him. But I woke up early to make you guys pancakes and our baritone wasn't on the couch. I thought maybe he went out late and got lucky, but here he is . . . in his pyjamas, hair a mess." He chuckled.

"So, where . . ." Sameer asked, looking suspiciously at Duncan.

"I'm thinking the beard slept with the beard," Barrington said, laughing.

"Shut up, Barry," Duncan said, but he was smiling.

Sameer's already wide eyes grew wider in shock, but Travis smiled proudly at Amira, nodding with appreciation. "That's awesome, guys. I knew there had to be a good reason for you to hate each other so much. You guys were doing enemies-to-lovers the whole time and we never noticed it."

By this point, Amira felt sure her face was as red as Duncan's beard.

Sameer's brows were still sky-high. "This is weird," he said.

Barrington was still chuckling. "It's hilarious. Y'all sure we're not living in some sort of *Big Brother* house? I keep expecting to trip over a cameraman." He winked as he turned his head to the right. "Tell them this is my good side."

Sameer put down his coffee mug. "Still . . . what are—"

"Consenting adults can do what they want." Travis shot a glare at his boyfriend. "I'm sure Duncan and Amira aren't going to announce an engagement and shoot an arrow through your arrangement with her . . ."

Duncan spit coffee out of his mouth.

Amira tried to get smaller, thinking about how nice it would be if the universe could open a little portal in her thrift-store chair, so she could sink into the seat and disappear.

"You know what, guys?" Duncan finally said. "Drop it. Our personal lives are ours, and don't worry, we're not going to scream it from the rafters. The only thing we should be concerned about now is the contest, and Amira's school work. You guys should maybe focus on what's important here, instead of all this henpecking."

Henpecking?

"That's sexist," Amira said. "The implication is that gossiping is not a worthwhile pursuit because women do it, hens being female chickens and all."

He stared at her with one eyebrow raised. Amira held her ground, a small smile on her face, waiting for him to make a snarky comeback. But he didn't. His gaze held hers as his eyes narrowed, turning that now familiar darker shade of green. Amira's throat went dry. She took a sip of her coffee, shifting in her seat.

Shit. It was getting hot in there.

"They really are perfect for each other," Travis informed the table.

"And on that note"—Barrington stood up, tearing Duncan's attention away from her—"I'm feeling like a fifth wheel in your game here. I'll go clean up before we do the run-through of our numbers."

"Wait, Barrington," Sameer said. "Sit. I need to talk to all of you."

Barrington sat back down.

Sameer cleared his throat, clearly apprehensive about whatever it was he needed to say. Amira glanced at Travis; he didn't seem pleased about it either.

There was no way this could end well.

"Tomorrow is my aunt's twenty-fifth wedding anniversary," Sameer announced.

"Congratulations?" Duncan said, unsure.

Sameer ran his hand through his hair. "Thanks. So, well, they're having this big party, in a hall. Biryani, sharbat, and jalebi, you know. Anyway, I have to go, I have no choice, but now my grandmother's bugging me to bring Amira with me."

This was the party Nanima and Mum were talking about. But Amira couldn't go, too. A meet-Sameer's-whole-extended-family thing? As his pretend girlfriend? No.

"I told her we only went on a couple of dates," he continued, "but she's being so insistent, and since your family is going—"

"Sameer," she interrupted. "I can't."

"She's not giving up," Sameer pleaded. "I told her I'd ask you, but so it doesn't seem like we're serious or anything, I asked if I could bring the quartet, too. So, we'd all go. Five of us. As friends."

Duncan shook his head. "Jesus Christ, Sameer."

"C'mon guys. It'll be fun. Ask Amira, the food at these things is always amazing, and with all of you there, my family won't be too . . . you know . . . intense. I hope."

Going to a big family gathering as Sameer's girlfriend was bad enough, but to bring the whole gang of merry men? With her mother, grandmother, and presumably Zahra there, too?

"Shouldn't we be rehearsing?" Barrington asked. "It's only three days before the competition."

"We don't have to stay long . . . and . . ." His voice trailed off. Sameer looked so torn up about this. Obviously he was under a lot of pressure from his family. But it was *his* family, and to subject all of them to the drama . . .

She glanced at Travis, who was uncharacteristically silent through this exchange. Sameer looked hurt, but Travis looked positively dejected. And no wonder. He would be introduced as a singing partner instead of life partner. As a nobody in Sameer's life.

"You okay with this?" she asked Travis.

Travis smiled. "Yeah, I am. I'm curious to meet his family. And . . . if this will get them off his back. Sameer's really stressed about this. Maybe it will help him."

Travis was too good. Sameer was too good. Amira's heart broke for their difficult situation.

"If it's important to you all," Duncan said, "fine. And I got to say, I'm curious about the food. What's sharbat?"

CHAPTER EIGHTEEN

"MUM, YOU STILL planning to go to that anniversary party tomorrow? I was invited, too." It was later that day, and after a hurried family dinner, Nanima rushed Zahra to dance class while Amira and Mum washed dishes.

"I was planning on it." Mum handed Amira a casserole dish to dry. "I could use a fancy night out, divorcee from Winnipeg notwithstanding. You could use a night out, too. You were so keyed up when we spoke yesterday. You seem better now, though."

Amira stifled a snort as she finished drying the dish and put it in the cupboard. It was amazing what a bit of sexual satisfaction could do for her tension levels. Even after reading about the Regent plant project while worrying about this anniversary party all day, she felt lighter and more at ease than she had in a long time.

The Regent project seemed straightforward enough and quite similar to other projects she had worked on before grad school. Regent was a large company that manufactured plastic cups and dishes, and they were significantly modernizing their large plant in the north end of the city. Raymond had already been working the job for a month, and it was expected to continue for several more.

Amira wished she could say she was excited about joining Raymond on the project, but after starting in on the literature, she couldn't help but think it sounded a bit . . . mundane. Kind of boring, to be honest. She wasn't sure what she'd expected; after all, she was heading right back to the same job she left, and she had loved that job before. Why would it seem dull now?

Mum was right about one thing, though—it had been a while since Amira had had the chance to get all decked out. These giant Indian parties were usually a lot of fun, but Amira had her reasons for worrying about going to this particular one. Namely, Sam I Am What I Am and the weird state of her relationships with the singing group.

"You don't want to go?" Mum asked, eyeing Amira.

"I don't know."

"Because of Sameer?"

Amira stilled. Although she hadn't outright said to her mother she was dating him, she'd allowed her family to think it. "It's complicated."

Her mother broke eye contact. "It's always complicated, isn't it?"

That was an understatement. Amira was pretending to date one singer while sleeping with the other. Well, maybe not *sleeping* with—as in currently in a relationship with—but rather *slept* with. Fuck buddies? Probably not, they weren't really buddies. Maybe?

"You okay, Amira? I think that spoon is probably dry by now."

Amira looked down at her grandmother's serving spoon in her hand and laughed. "Yeah, I'm fine. I think I almost dried a hole in this."

Despite the carnal satisfaction, this "thing" with Duncan had Amira twisted in knots. Relationships were weird in the beginning anyway, and since they both seemed to agree they didn't want to over-analyze this one, she wasn't sure how to categorize it. The timing was terrible—but this was no casual fling. Something else was brewing. Something stronger. She wished she could talk it out with her mother, but she had to keep up with this guise of her emerging romance with Sameer instead.

But then again, maybe her mother was hiding a new romance, too? No one else was around, and Amira had a bit of time—it was time to get to the bottom of this.

"Hey, Mum, you seeing someone new? Zahra thought maybe you were, but you haven't said anything."

The strangest expression flitted over her mother's face. A smile in her eyes that didn't quite match with the tight line of her mouth.

"Mum, you okay?"

Handing Amira the next dish to dry, her mother seemed to force a smile. "Yes, I'm fine. I can't get anything past you girls, can I? *Complicated* doesn't begin to describe this right now, but it's really early. Can we revisit this conversation later?"

So, Mum *did* have a secret . . . thing . . . starting just like Amira did. Someone who took her to the theatre and to art shows. Amira grinned and bumped her hip with her mother's as they stood side by side at the sink. "I don't know what you mean by *complicated*, but I hope it's good."

"Yes"—Mum had a real smile this time—"complicated, but yes, good, too. I'm sorry I've been moody lately, but I'm just not sure how certain family members will take this relationship. Anyway, there's no point telling anyone anything now. It's early."

Amira took a pot from Mum to dry. "You don't think Nanima will approve?"

"No, I know she won't."

Amira frowned. Sounded like her mother was dating a non-Muslim and was worried about her mother's approval, and she was probably right. Nanima was amazing, but she was traditional, and just a touch judgmental about those outside their faith. Her offhanded comments when Amira dated a steady stream of non-Muslim guys a few years ago made that point obvious, and Amira had no doubt her grandmother's passive-aggression would be worse for her daughter than for her granddaughter. Amira loved and respected her grandmother, but she could do without her judgments. Amira's own parents didn't care if she dated Muslims or not. And true, she had told Reena she was hoping her next relationship would be with a man similar to her, but that had everything to do with how well someone could understand her in an intolerant world, and nothing to do with gaining family acceptance.

Duncan Galahad was nothing like her. What the hell was she doing?

Mum turned and smiled. "I need to be more like you, sweetie. You've never let what others think stop you from doing what you want."

"You shouldn't have to compromise your relationships because of someone else's values, Mum. Hell, our own values get in the way enough, and we have to find room for others', too?"

It seemed kind of silly—Mum was a grown adult, complete with a grown adult child. To think she was afraid of taking a relationship to the next level because of her mother's approval? Was this the lesson she wanted Zahra to learn? But maybe being forty-nine years old and living with your mother created a different dynamic than most grown daughters and mothers.

And Amira, at thirty, still lived with both her mother and her grandmother.

"Mum, don't take this the wrong way, but do you think we're stuck?"

Mum picked up the large salad bowl and put it in the sink. "What do you mean, stuck?"

Amira shrugged. "I don't know. You living here with Nanima. Me living with both of you. You two are great and all, but I sometimes wonder if I'd have made different choices with my life if I'd moved out when I was twenty."

Mum shook her head. "Different choices doesn't necessarily mean better choices. Remember, Amira, I was married when I was barely nineteen and had you soon after. Of course, I don't regret that—you girls are my biggest gifts. I can't regret how you came into my life, but . . ." Mum stared out the window over the sink, her train of thought lost.

"But what?"

"I grew up fast. I had to grow up before I knew who I was."

"You don't think separating from your family so young helped you be more, I don't know, *you*?"

Mum turned and looked sharply at Amira. "You can't ever separate from your family, sweetie. Don't ever forget that; they are always there. They are you and you are them." Mum looked back into the sink.

Clearly, her mother was also having a bit of an existential crisis, and clearly, she wasn't ready to talk about it. Change was most definitely in the air. Amira wasn't much for cryptic heart-to-hearts, so she decided to steer the topic of the conversation towards herself, and away from her mother.

"I mean, it's great that I can live here," Amira said. "Lord knows affording anything decent in the city would be an utter nightmare on my finances, but I wonder if my . . . I don't know . . . view of the world is skewed because I have it so easy with you guys. It's just, I always have my family to fall back on, so why advance in life?"

"Amira, you are about to finish your master's in engineering! That is advancing! You have family support to fall back on, which has helped you succeed and overcome so many of the disadvantages in your academic and professional careers. Being a woman of colour in this world hasn't been easy, and you may not have had the strength to fight through the obstacles without the support from your father and me. And Nanima, too. You're not stuck, you're privileged."

Amira smiled reassuringly as she put away a frying pan. "I know, Mum. I was thinking more in my personal life, not professional." She kissed her mother's cheek. "I'm very grateful you guys are so awesome. Seeing the crap that Reena's parents put her through . . . ugh, I can't even imagine. Anyway, it's just such a weird time now, with graduating soon and coming back home, I can't help overthinking everything.

Raymond finally emailed today saying he'll be sending my report back tomorrow. It will be good to dig into it so I won't have all this free time for navel-gazing. What are you thinking of wearing to the party?"

Mum grinned. "I don't know. Should we coordinate colours? Like we used to when you were a girl. Maybe we can get a nice photo taken of the three of us. You and Zahra can wear your blue suits, and I can wear my gold sari."

They finished the dishes, and then Amira headed downstairs, where she found the quartet—minus Duncan—crowded around a magazine on the couch. They seemed to be arguing about something—no surprise there. Weren't they always arguing? And where was Duncan? Would asking about him now sound desperate?

"Hey, guys," she said during a lull in their heated discussion.

"Hi," Sameer said. "Duncan's in his room on the phone."

Good lord, she was becoming as transparent as a baby jellyfish. Amira sat heavily in the armchair. "What's that?" She indicated to the magazine in Barrington's hand.

Barrington tossed it on the table and slid to the other end of the couch. "Eddie Bauer catalogue. We were at the mall all day. We can't decide what to wear for the contest."

Travis glared at Barrington. "We did decide, but now someone thinks he's too cool to go along with what we'd planned."

Barrington rolled his eyes. "Seriously, Travis? You have to see the optics don't look good for me. My name is Barry. I'm a singer . . ."

Amira raised a brow, perplexed. "What are you talking about?"

Sameer chuckled. "Our costume designer friend got us outfits for the show, but Barrington didn't like them."

"What does your name have to do with it?" she asked Barrington.

"A sequined jumpsuit? I get called the black Barry Manilow or Barry Gibb often enough, I don't need to cosplay as them. Can't we lean more towards Barry White than the white Barrys?"

"He's a *ballet* costume designer," Travis said. "I'm not sure what you expected . . ."

Amira stifled a giggle. Had they all planned to wear these sequined jumpsuits? Amira had an image of Duncan's buff physique clad in sequined spandex and practically fell off her chair, laughing. "Please tell me you still have the jumpsuits . . ."

"I'm not wearing it either." That deep, slightly raspy voice behind her made her shiver. Duncan.

She turned. He was standing near the door of the room he shared with Barrington, a casual expression on his face. He wasn't looking directly at her, but not really avoiding her either. Amira's chest tightened as her hands gripped her knee. He looked so . . . normal. Unaffected. Not all wound up like she was. She turned away as he sat on the couch.

"What's up, Duncan? You were on the phone awhile," Barrington asked.

"Yeah, I was catching up with my old buddy Dale. He's a bass player. I used to play guitar in his band in high school. He had a thing up on Facebook about a gig in Toronto tonight, so I called him. By a crazy fluke, it's not far from here. Anyone up for a night out?"

Travis groaned. "God, no. I'm wiped. I'm not moving more than six inches from this very spot all night." He fell dramatically sideways on the couch, his head landing on Sameer's lap. That made Sameer squeal, then redden and giggle like a prairie schoolgirl. Amira laughed; her fake boyfriend and his real boyfriend really were precious.

"I'm not touching that comment with a ten-foot pole," Duncan said. "What about you, Barry? It sounds like a bit of a dive bar, but Dale's cool. Apparently, this new group of his plays mostly folk rock."

"Sure, I'm game. It might be a good idea to steer clear of these lovebirds tonight. Is your friend's band doing covers or original stuff?"

Barrington and Duncan talked for a while about this Dale guy's band while Amira sat, lightly fiddling with the hole forming on the knee of her jeans. Pulling on the tiny strands, watching the hole increase a millimetre at a time.

"Amira?" Duncan finally said, startling her.

"Hmm?" She looked at him.

"You coming, too?" he asked.

Amira sat up straighter. "I'm invited?"

"'Course you're invited. If you're interested." He didn't smile but held her gaze for a few moments. The temperature rose in the basement. Duncan wanted her to come with him tonight. And she wasn't even going to try to fight the urge to spend more time with him.

"Okay, I'll come," she said, not breaking eye contact with him. She watched, fascinated, as his eyes crinkled in the corners and his lips curved ever so slightly. They continued to stare at each other, long past what was probably socially acceptable.

"I'll go change," Barrington said, standing and walking towards his room. "You know, you'd think it'd be annoying to be a fifth wheel in this place, but I'm feeling inspired. The world needs more love. I may just write a song about you guys." He went into his room, loudly singing "Love Is in the Air" with his deep, bass voice. Amira snickered as she went to change.

CHAPTER NINETEEN

THE BAR WHERE Duncan's friend was playing was so close that the three of them decided to walk instead of calling a cab. It was a cloudy night, and the air was heavy with humidity. Amira walked silently for the most part, listening to Duncan and Barrington talk music along the way.

The bar wasn't really a dive bar, but rather a hipster bar masquerading as a dive bar. Exposed wood ceiling beams wound with Christmas lights lit up a narrow space dotted with beer caps nailed to the wall and neon bar signs in the shapes of palm trees and skulls. It was the kind of place with a menu ranging from quinoa salad to mac and cheese to burgers and ribs, and she could bet a cocktail list including old-fashioneds and many tequila-based concoctions. Yup. May as well post a sign out front broadcasting *Millennial Hipsters Welcome*. The existence of this place told her that her area was starting the shift towards gentrification. No shock, really, this East York neighbourhood was one of the last on the subway line that held on to its old personality. Amira skimmed the beer list. At least gentrification meant better draft beer close to home.

After ordering their drinks, they settled in to watch the band's set.

They were decent enough. Amira had been warming up to the alt-folk stuff that had become popular lately, and these guys had an interesting sound. Their singer wasn't half as good as any of the quartet, though.

Duncan barely spoke during the show, but Amira figured, since they'd come specifically to see his friend, she shouldn't expect his attention.

When the set finished and the speakers started blaring nineties house music about two decibels louder than Amira would have preferred, Duncan texted the guy to join them for a drink. He showed up about five minutes later, a beer in his hand.

Duncan's friend was a small man with mousy features, dark hair, and pale eyes. He gave Duncan one of those manly sideways bro hugs before sitting in the empty seat between Amira and Barrington, across from Duncan.

"This is Amira and Barrington," Duncan said. "Guys, this is my old jamming buddy Dale Evans. Dale and I go back to high-school days."

After a few minutes of discussion and appreciation for Dale's current band, Barrington asked, "You from the same tiny town as Duncan?"

"Nah," Dale said. "Compared to Duncan here, I was a city boy. I'm from Lindsay, about twenty minutes from Omemee. We played in a garage band there when we were kids."

"Not a lot of opportunities for me to play music in Omemee back then. Lindsay's not far. That's where kids go for anything these days. Maddie's dance school is there," Duncan added.

"We took a risk on this runt. He was only fourteen, while we were all seventeen or eighteen. His daddy used to drive him into Lindsay for practices and wait in his car. But man, Duncan's finger work was amazing, even then. We were sure he'd be the next Dave Navarro. We'd have been huge if he stuck around."

Amira wrinkled her nose. "Did you call him a runt?"

Dale laughed. "Yeah, he was scrawny back then. People thought our lead guitarist was some sort of child prodigy. He looked about twelve."

Amira looked at Duncan with one eyebrow raised, trying to imagine her lumberjack as a runt.

"I was really short until I was eighteen," Duncan said, grinning.

She squinted at him. He would have had a lot less facial hair, too. She couldn't imagine it.

Barrington laughed. "That's amazing. I'd love to see a picture."

"My website has some pictures of old Hollow Flesh gigs," Dale said.

"*Hollow Flesh?*" Amira laughed.

Duncan chuckled, rubbing his beard. "Never let teenagers pick names for rock bands. It's better than the original name, though. My mom's a nurse, she wouldn't let me play in a band called After Birth."

Amira exploded in laughter, eyeing Dale. "You guys were called *afterbirth?* That's a terrible name!"

Dale smiled, but the tight line of his mouth betrayed annoyance. "It was a cool name. It's symbolic . . . the entirety of your existence after birth. No one knows the other meaning."

"Women would know," Amira said.

"We were a metal band."

Amira frowned. "Women like metal."

"So," Barrington chimed in, always one to try to keep the peace before an argument started, "you play in any other bands, Dale?"

The guys chatted a bit about music projects, and Dale and Duncan reminisced some more before Dale reclined slightly in his chair. "So, you both in this singing group with Duncan? Is it some sort of social justice thing?"

"What? No, it's me, Barrington, and two other guys," Duncan said. "Amira's my—"

"Roommate," Amira interrupted before he could finish the sentence.

Duncan smiled. "We live in her grandmother's basement with her. With the two other guys."

"Sounds cozy," Dale said.

"You don't know the half of it." Barrington laughed.

Duncan took a long sip of his beer.

"So, Amira," Dale said, "you look like a girl who likes to party. Want to dump these sad sacks and come hang with my band? We're heading—"

"She's with me tonight," Duncan interjected. Amira turned to him, eyes wide.

"Ah. So, it's like that, is it?" Dale sipped his beer, eyes narrowing at Duncan before giving Amira a slow once-over. Gross. "Offer still stands, though, if you'd like to hang with some real musicians. Love your exotic look. What are you, anyway?"

Good lord. She had heard that one way too many times.

"What am I?" Amira asked.

"Yeah, where you from?"

"Toronto."

"No, like *really* from?" he said with a leer.

Amira groaned, turning to see Duncan's reaction to this douche canoe. Did Dale Evans not follow any bro code? Going after a girl his old buddy just laid claim to was cold. And Duncan looked pissed. Christ. How had she once again found herself in the middle of a chest-puffing display of masculinity between Duncan Galahad and a degenerate pig?

It would almost be humorous, if it weren't so annoying. She decided to put a stop to this once and for all.

"Well, Dale," Amira said with her sweetest smile. "I lived in Kingston until recently, but now I'm back in Toronto. But I'm sure that's not what you're really asking, so I'll tell you the truth." She put her pint glass down and leaned close to Dale conspiratorially. "I was actually born in . . . Markham, Ontario."

Barrington erupted in laughter.

Dale laughed as well, looking at Duncan. "This one's a pistol, ain't she?"

Duncan frowned. He still looked pissed. She forced a smile to show Duncan she could handle the likes of Dale Evans.

"I think I understand you, Dale," Amira said. "My parents are both Indian. Is that what you were looking for?"

"I knew it!" Dale grinned as if he'd won something. He hadn't. "So, you're a Hindu?" he asked.

Amira frowned. "That's kind of a personal question, isn't it?"

"Your religion isn't a personal question," Dale said.

Amira smiled her sweet smile again. "I don't know, Dale, I don't usually ask every white guy I meet if he's Catholic or Protestant."

"Yeah, but we're, like, normal here."

"Oh, hell no." Barrington straightened. She had to hand it to Dale; pissing off Barrington was no easy feat.

Duncan shot another annoyed stare at his friend. "Did you just say Amira's not normal?"

"Nah, man, she's a babe. But you know what I mean, right? She's, like, not white. When I saw you come in with these two, I knew the city changed you. Then again, you were always a bleeding lib."

Duncan was clearly furious now, and she didn't blame him. Someone was going to get hit soon.

"So," Amira said evenly, "you assume because he's friends with a black man and a brown woman, he must be nothing more than a liberal social justice warrior? Like seeing us as, I don't know, *people*, is only thanks to his politics?"

"I didn't say that," Dale snapped back.

Duncan spoke up. "Look, Dale—"

Amira put her hand out to stop him. She wanted to fight this one herself. "I'm a Muslim."

"What?" Dale asked.

"You asked if I was Hindu. I'm not. I'm Muslim."

"Really?" He snorted. "Like ISIS?"

"Are you for real?" Barrington asked.

Amira was wondering the same thing. Dale would be almost comically evil if she hadn't met people just like him before. Thankfully, they usually kept their filth online, but every once in a while, she encountered one in the wild.

Dale laughed at Duncan. "Actually, makes sense. You know the old joke: What do lead guitarists and terrorists have in common? You can't negotiate with either of them. Turns out the joke's about you and your piece here."

"What the fuck is your problem, Dale?" Duncan said.

Dale shook his head. "No problem at all, my man. Anyway, if she's a Muslim, where's her head scarf?" He nodded at Amira. "Don't you people have to cover your hair around men? Or is it okay if you're sleeping with them?"

"Seriously, shut up. Now," Duncan said, teeth clenched. Someone was definitely going to get hit very soon, and Amira would put money on *her* being the one throwing the punch.

Dale smirked at Amira. "Just asking questions."

This needed to end. She turned to see Duncan fuming with anger. He put his hand possessively on Amira's shoulder, squeezing tightly. "Have you always been such a dick, Dale, and I haven't noticed? Or is this something new you're trying out?"

Dale lifted his hands up defensively. "Jesus, Duncan, settle down. It was a joke, no offence meant. You used to be cool."

Amira lifted her pint glass, and it took every molecule of resolve in her body not to dump the beer over Dale Evans's head. But that would be a waste of a perfectly good pint. She drained it in one sip and stood. Duncan and Barrington were both already done their drinks, and she had a feeling they wouldn't object to leaving.

"Shall we go, gentlemen?" She picked up her purse. "I'd like to say it was a pleasure, but it wasn't. Get bent, Dale Evans." She smiled as she walked away, followed closely by Duncan and Barrington.

. . . .

"I'M SO SORRY, Amira," Duncan said once they were outside. His arm found her shoulder. "I had no idea Dale would be so . . . rude. I'm sorry I brought you to see him."

"You didn't know your friend was a bit racist?" Amira asked.

"I'd say a lot racist," Barrington added.

"No. I'm not really friends with him anymore, and I guess . . . it never came up before." Duncan's arm snaked around Amira's waist as they started the short walk home. He inched closer and said into her hair, "I'm sorry." Amira shivered.

"Guy was definitely an ass," Barrington said, "but I got to say, Amira, you handled that well. I hate it when someone asks me what I am. I've been known to tell people 'Vulcan' when I get that question."

Amira sighed. "I get crap like that all the time. Little too used to it."

Duncan squeezed her tighter. "I honestly don't know Dale that well anymore. I can see now he hasn't grown up at all. He's still pissed about me leaving them all those years ago."

Amira leaned into Duncan briefly, smiling. "It's fine. Wasn't your fault." She wriggled free of his grip. "We don't know who's going to see us on the way home, though. I'm with Sameer, remember?"

He nodded briefly, taking two steps away from her. She felt the loss of his warmth immediately.

The moment they were in the basement, Barrington disappeared into his room to call Marcia, and Duncan pressed Amira up against the wall near the kitchen. He nuzzled into her neck, pulling all the air from the room as his lips grazed her skin.

"I'm sorry," he whispered again.

She circled her arms around his broad back and rubbed. "It's okay, I mean it. You're not that guy."

"I know, but . . ."

"Duncan, look at me."

He lifted his head. The room was dim, so Amira couldn't quite make out the green in his eyes, but she couldn't miss the need in them. She smiled, raising her hands to the back of his neck, fingers teasing the soft skin she found there.

He sighed as relief seemed to spread through his body, and he pressed even closer. "I've been thinking about you all day," he said, lifting his finger to trail down her cheek. "This morning you said you couldn't promise anything beyond that moment, and I get that, but I've been trying to figure out how to make you want me again. I thought taking you out tonight would work, but then—"

"Not your fault, Duncan." She pulled his head down by the neck and kissed him. Kissed him hard and deep, hopefully making it clear that he was not only off the hook for the terrible night, but he was wanted, too.

His lips travelled down her neck and under her ear. "I bought more condoms," he whispered.

She grinned, slipping out from his grip and taking his hand. "C'mon then. I have some ideas of how you can make it up to me." She led him into her room.

After another mind-blowing romp in the hay with her real-life farm boy, they lay in each other's arms, warm and comfortable. She nuzzled in closer, burrowing herself in a cocoon of contentment. It had been weeks, maybe months since she'd felt so relaxed. Not a bad way to spend the night. Maybe more nights? How many?

"So, what happens now?" Amira asked, running her fingers lightly over his chest.

"What do you mean?"

"I don't know."

Duncan cushioned his head on his arm and looked at her. "If you're wondering about the future, I don't know either. I'm here for a few more days, for now at least."

She liked that answer. She smiled. "I can commit to that."

He kissed her. "Me too."

. . . .

WAKING UP IN the morning with a large, affectionate man was getting addictive, and Amira was all over the idea of a rehash of their late-night exertions, but Raymond had said he would have her report back to her today. Work first, fabulous rewards later.

"Mmmm . . ." she murmured against the top of Duncan's head as he feasted on her neck. "Have to get to work . . . it's late . . ."

He looked at her with a smile. "Yes, yes you do. And I'm not going to be the one to deprive you of your silent time." He got out of bed and picked up his clothes. "I'll make your coffee, babe." Once dressed, he left the room, humming contently to himself.

Amira turned on her computer and opened her email right away. A message from Raymond was waiting for her. She grinned. Thank god. Opening it, she skimmed it quickly before her heart absolutely sank. He *hated* it.

CHAPTER TWENTY

HANDS SHAKING, AMIRA read over Raymond's comments for a third time, shocked at what she was seeing. Raymond didn't like her report. In fact, if she read between the lines, it was clear. He thought it was a piece of crap.

She couldn't believe it. All that work. All that research and analysis. All wrong. Raymond thought that her analysis of the algorithm outcome did not match the real world in practice. He suggested she take a second look at the data and how it was processed, and at the practicality of the conclusions she drew. He advised perhaps finding solutions that were easier and cheaper to implement. He even suggested reworking her algorithms.

It amounted to redoing the whole project.

She slammed her head down on her keyboard. How the hell had this happened? Her algorithm was solid. She may not have had the time to get to know her project supervisor that well, but he hadn't had any issues with the quality or content of her work while in the lab. And the research she'd done since leaving school wasn't half-assed either—she used the most prestigious journals and drew on years of education and experience in her field. She had sunk endless hours into this project. She may never have been at the top of her class, but she put the work in.

Was it possible this wasn't a case of not working hard enough? Maybe it was a simple case of ability. She rubbed her forehead, feeling a prickle behind her eyes. That familiar uncertainty crept in, unwelcome as snow falling in the spring. This master's program had been a monumental challenge for her. Watching other students breeze by seemingly without effort. Seeing them sail through the kinds of problems that sent her searching through infinite journals and piecing together algorithms. Watching them bro-down with the professors while picking her last to work with on group projects, knowing she couldn't think on her feet as fast as them. It all stung. She knew she wasn't the smartest one there, but she thought with hard work, she could overcome her less-than-stellar natural abilities.

Apparently, she was wrong. She wasn't good enough. And if there were so many issues with her findings and the impracticalities of them, how was she going to manage a senior real-world position in the firm? How could she lead a team towards practical and durable solutions if she couldn't do it in a lab? She wouldn't be able to hack it.

She was a fraud.

There was a knock on the door. "Come in," she called from her desk.

"Hey, gorgeous. Got your coffee." Duncan placed a mug on her desk. "The guys and I are thinking we should get matching shoes, so we're going back to the mall. You need anything before we go?"

She looked up and blinked several times.

"Amira, what's wrong," he said, catching the expression on her face.

"It's Raymond. He says my report's no good."

"What? That can't be!"

"He said my sources weren't strong enough to support my lab work, and my analysis seemed rushed." Amira stood, pulling her hair into a ponytail. "Can you drive me to the library on the way to the mall? I can use . . . actually, I'd be better off at the lab." She paused in her steps. She had a few days; she *could* go back to Kingston if she needed to. There was a ten o'clock bus, if she remembered correctly. She pulled her backpack out of her closet.

"Whatever you need," he said, coming up behind her and placing his hands on her shoulders. Amira leaned into him. God, it felt good to have someone prop her up when life threw landslides in her path. This. This was what she needed.

He rubbed her shoulders. "Are you sure he didn't like it? Seems weird he would say this right before your due date."

She lowered her head to give Duncan more access to rub her neck. "I know, but he was busy. He couldn't get back to me any sooner." After a long sigh, she eased away from him and started pulling sweatpants and T-shirts out of her drawers. Would she need anything nicer? She dug out some dark-wash jeans. Taking the ten o'clock would get her to the lab by one at the latest. If she worked through the night, she had just enough time to run a new algorithm and write up the report. Maybe.

"Wait, are you leaving?" Duncan asked.

She nodded. "I need to rerun the algorithm."

"Who is this Raymond guy, anyway? One of your professors?"

"No, my mentor. He works at the firm I'm going back to." She stepped into the bathroom to pack up her makeup.

"A colleague? And you're just going to leave town because of his comment? How could he know what your professor is looking for?"

Amira walked back into the bedroom and looked at Duncan. Was he arguing with her about this? "Of course he knows. He was in the same master's program years ago. Raymond wrote me the recommendation to get into grad school."

"Well, what happens if your professor doesn't like the paper? You don't get your degree?"

"No. She'll send it back with suggested revisions."

"So, what's the problem? Send it in and see what she thinks."

"Duncan, I can't send a crappy project! I need my professor to give me a good recommendation so my boss will realize I know what the fuck I'm doing."

"Ah. So, it's to impress your dickhead boss." He paused. "Let me see the email . . ."

Gritting her teeth, Amira went back to her desk and opened the email. She stepped aside to let him read it. She didn't know what he expected to find. It was just like a man to not trust her ability to understand a goddamn email.

"Okay, I don't know much about engineering," he said, "so I can't say whether he has a valid point about your references or the practicality of this analysis he's rambling on about, but this part sounds mighty condescending to me. I detect a whiff of jealousy."

"What? He's not jealous. He's my mentor!"

"Yeah? Well, you seem blinded by hero worship. A mentor shouldn't say things like 'It is an ambitious effort, but maybe you need to narrow your scope to your ability.' And he shouldn't be so impressed that your writing is articulate. You're a thirty-year-old grad student. I should hope you'd be articulate by now."

Amira frowned, but considered the possibility. *Raymond? Jealous?* "A mentor is supposed to give constructive feedback."

"But this isn't constructive! Your report is due in three days! Can't you see that he's not acting in your best interests here, Amira? It's so clear!" Duncan stood, looming over her.

Amira took a step away from him, her jaw clenched so tight she heard it pop. It was unbelievable that after everything they'd gone through in the last few days, Duncan turned out to be yet another in the long list of men who thought they knew more about her career than she did. She silently counted to five in her head before speaking. She needed to figure out what to do about her project, and arguing with the garden gnome wasn't helping.

"You're right about one thing, Duncan; you know nothing about how things work in graduate school. You're the one butting into something outside your scope. Go buy shoes with your little singing group and keep your uninformed opinions to yourself. I have to pack."

Duncan's face clouded in anger. "I'm sorry, Your Royal Highness. I forgot, I am just a *mere musician*." He paused. "I may not know about engineering, but I'm a teacher, remember? I *went* to graduate school, and I know my way around education. There is no need to call everyone around you stupid just to convince yourself that you're smart."

He paused, staring at her for several long seconds. Finally, through gritted teeth, he spoke. "Deal with your issues without tearing down the people who care about you. You're better than that." He left, slamming the door behind him.

Amira swore loudly as she threw the open textbook on her desk against the wall. It landed on the floor with a loud thump, leaving a grey smudge on her white walls. She was so angry, she was shaking.

And she was so completely done with men who assumed they knew everything better than she did just because of that extra appendage dangling between their legs. Not half an hour ago, she had been thinking about how great it was to have someone to share the next few days with. A special gift the universe had granted her to help her right when she needed it. But no. Duncan wasn't some magical gnome that fate sent her way, he was just another man who couldn't see anything past the end of his damn beard. Fuck him.

She sat on her bed, rubbing her temples as her fury eased. What had he meant by tearing people down?

Did she do that? Amira accepted that she had a nasty temper and a tendency to judge others, especially when she felt cornered. The names she'd called Duncan since the day they met were evidence enough that she'd been tearing him down since the moment he boarded her train. But doing it to boost her own worth? That was . . . *mean*, even for her.

She bristled. But why shouldn't she prejudge people? She'd been judged almost daily since the day she decided to study engineering. Actually, long before that. Can't possibly

be as good at advanced math as a guy. Can't be taken seriously in STEM since she wears makeup and loves her hair.
Canadian girls don't wear underwear. Muslim girls are
chaste and modest.

Arabic art on her phone means she's a terrorist.

Another knock on her door. Jesus, why couldn't these
Y chromosomes leave her alone? It might just be easier at
this point to replace her goddamn door with a revolving one.

Sameer this time, eyes wide with concern, hair dishevelled.

"You okay? We heard a crash," he said.

Amira cringed as she fetched the fallen corpse of her
physics textbook from its resting place near the wall.

"Sorry. Had a fight with my textbook."

He walked into the room. "Looks like you won."

"I always win." She sat on the edge of her bed. "I thought
you guys were going shoe shopping."

"Duncan just said, 'Screw shoes,' and left, so I'm thinking,
no." He smirked and fell onto the desk chair heavily. Sameer
looked exhausted. Red eyes and slumped shoulders.

"What's your issue, Sameer? You look like shit," she said.

He chuckled. "It's taken some work to get used to your
bluntness, Amira. Just didn't sleep much last night."

It didn't look like his lack of sleep was due to the same
enjoyable distractions as hers. Amira's stomach knotted
when she remembered what she had said to Duncan. Had
she really implied he was unintelligent?

"You and Travis fighting?"

He smiled sadly. "You'd think I'd be used to it. He slept
on the couch last night. Again. We made up this morning,
but I'm wiped."

"What happened?"

"I told him he didn't have to come to my aunt's party if he didn't want to. I thought he'd be happy to get out of it. But the suggestion didn't go well."

Amira slid down the bed until she faced him and put her hand on his knee. He had to understand this. He had to get why suggesting that Travis skip the party would only make things worse, not better.

"Sameer, Travis is your partner, not a casual fling. You have to include him in your life."

"I know. I thought it would be easier, for both of us, but—"

"Travis doesn't want easy. Good relationships are never easy."

After a few moments of painful silence, he raised his chin. "So, the honeymoon's already over for you guys, too? You and Duncan want to kill each other again?"

It seemed so trivial compared to what Sameer was going through; she didn't feel right bringing it up. "Yeah. He was being a little . . . paternalistic."

Sameer laughed again, still looking at his fingers. Finally, he looked up at Amira. "I know the most serious relationship I've ever been in is a complete mess right now, so maybe I'm not the best one to give you advice, but I'm going to anyway. Forgive little things, Amira. Some things are so big you can't compromise, but little things? Love is worth compromising the little things."

Amira swallowed. Love? Already? "Duncan and I just got together a few days ago . . . we're nowhere near . . . there, yet."

"I know. But you won't have the chance to be more if you can't compromise now." He paused. "You two remind me of Travis and me when we met, except we didn't have the near bloodshed. We were so different, from different worlds, really, and not just because of religion and culture. I was a science student, he was an artist. He was out; I was . . . not. I barely accepted myself as a gay man then, and Travis was the exact opposite of who I thought I should be with."

"I think our expectations are our worst enemies."

"Yeah. Maybe it's the Indian in me, but I thought I wanted an educated professional. I imagined my family wouldn't care if I was gay if I came home with a surgeon or something . . . but that's not really what I wanted. All I wanted was Travis. From the moment I saw him, I only wanted him."

Amira straightened. "So, fight for him, Sameer! Make sure he, and the rest of the world, knows how important he is to you!"

"I know." He shrugged sadly. "I'm . . . I just don't think I'm strong enough for him. He'll realize it soon enough. But, you and Duncan . . . you two are different. I know he's crazy about you. You guys could have something."

"We're from different worlds, too."

"What do you mean? Because he's not Ismaili?"

That wasn't really the issue. Maybe. Amira had dated men belonging to pretty much every major religion, but never anyone serious. "I don't know. Sometimes I feel like no one really gets me, and maybe if I found someone culturally more like me, they'd understand me better. I wouldn't have to explain myself. Maybe not fight so much."

Sameer nodded. Of course he understood her. "I get that. Religion's just one part of you, though." He paused. "What did you guys fight about?"

"My project. My mentor, Raymond, pretty much said it was crap. Duncan said the guy sounded jealous."

Sameer smiled. "Typical Duncan."

"What do you mean?"

"He is the most loyal guy I know. Of course he wouldn't believe your mentor's assessment. Duncan will always be on your side."

"He should have stayed out of it. I didn't get this far in my field without a shitload of men giving me unwanted career advice. When it comes to knowing what's best for me, I can only trust two men."

"Who?"

"My dad and Raymond. Raymond is on my side. And Duncan didn't listen to me when I tried to tell him that."

"He cares about you and didn't like what the guy was saying about your work."

Amira bit her lip. Duncan did care about her—she didn't need anyone to convince her of that fact. And he did have a protective, white-knighting issue. Was it possible Duncan's outburst wasn't mansplaining but another case of Sir Galahad leaping to her rescue? And of course, Amira always became defensive when challenged, which only aggravated the situation.

But Duncan had been right about one thing at least—she *had* torn him down to make herself feel smart enough for grad school. He *saw* her—straight through her nastiness to the insecurities she hid below. Damn.

"I got angry at him. I yelled at him," she said.

Sameer said nothing, but one side of his mouth upturned.

"I know, typical Amira. I scream before I think. But I may have implied he was unintelligent," she said.

"He's really smart. Honestly."

"I know. He touched a nerve, and I lashed out. We are both really good at that, it seems."

This time Sameer couldn't hold in his smile. "There's something about you two. You seem patient with other people . . ."

"I'm not," Amira said, leaning back and wrapping her arms around her legs. "I wonder if it's worth all this trouble," she whispered, resting her head on her knees. She glanced at Sameer. He really looked terrible. She would bet all the chai in the house that he had cried himself to sleep last night. Sameer was a sensitive soul, and seeing him in pain broke Amira's heart. She had never had a relationship anywhere as long or as serious as Sameer and Travis's, but she'd seen enough to know that heartbreak was inevitable.

When her parents divorced years ago, both her mum and dad had been furious with each other but also sad they hadn't been able to make it work, combined with a heavy dose of guilt for hurting their daughters plus the shame of a whole community judging them and seeing them as failures for divorcing. Could all that pain be avoided?

"It would never be easy with me and Duncan. We are so different, and completely terrible at dealing with each other. My parents couldn't make it work. I don't want that to happen to me."

Sameer scoffed. "That's ridiculous. Give up on happiness because one day it might end? Take the chance, Amira! Travis and I are in a rough spot, but it doesn't mean I regret starting the relationship. It is so worth it. Duncan may be different from you, but he'll never understand you if you don't let him try. Don't drive him away expecting the worst. Fight for the best instead."

Fight for the best? Amira knew a thing or two about fighting for what she wanted. She just needed to determine if this fight was worth it.

CHAPTER TWENTY-ONE

AMIRA DIDN'T CATCH that ten o'clock bus to Kingston. Instead, she showered, changed, and sat back at her desk to reread both her report and Raymond's email, trying her best to look at them objectively. To her, the work looked fine. Good, even. True, the journal articles were not an exact match to her project, but that was the point. Science was about extrapolating specifics from broad data. Her analysis seemed sound. Her applications relevant. Was it possible Duncan was onto something?

Raymond was her superior at work, a senior engineer. But after she returned next month with her master's degree, they would both have the same level of education. Amira transitioning from subordinate to peer couldn't be the problem— the point of their mentorship had been for him to guide her towards a senior role. He encouraged her to go to grad school. How could he be jealous that she was now finishing?

Asking him for help in the first place so many years ago had been outside her comfort zone, but Raymond was different than any other man she'd worked with. Never any off-colour remarks about her gender. Never subtly discounting what she said and then taking her ideas for himself. He had always been her fiercest cheerleader. She doubted anyone would have taken notice of her at Hyde without Raymond's championing.

But there was no question that things at Hyde had changed since she left two years ago. When they'd had lunch together, Raymond said that Jim was nothing like Jennifer, but was still a great, supportive boss.

But then he discounted Jim's obvious sexism and told her she was imagining it. Minimizing Amira's experiences was not something Raymond had done before. That was gas-lighting. And she *had* been too caught up in hero worship to notice it.

She should talk to Duncan. Years with a temper worse than Hades's meant she knew when to grovel, and being born and raised in Canada meant she knew how to apologize. But issues with her lumberjack could wait, for now. What she needed first was a second opinion on her report.

And there was only one person she could think of who would give her honest feedback on short notice. Her father. She had been reluctant to show him her school work before, but she was out of options at this point.

Once she had her dad on the phone, she explained the situation with Raymond's assessment.

"Of course I'll look at it. I have back-to-back meetings for the next few days, but I'll find time."

"I was thinking I should just head back to Kingston and rework the algorithm."

"I doubt that will be necessary. You know what you're doing. Plus, at this point, you don't really have the time to start over. Don't run away, Amira. We can fix this together. I'll get back to you as soon as I can."

Amira exhaled. With his steady voice, her father had a way of calming her like no one else, but at the same time, she recognized a flutter in her stomach over the thought of him reading her crap paper. But he was right—there wasn't really enough time to rework the whole algorithm.

"Okay, thanks, Dad. I'm sending it now. Love you."

"Love you, too. I'll be in touch."

Now what? If she didn't go back to Kingston, she could go to the reference library or even search journals online for better supporting documentation. She could rewrite the analysis and try to explain the rationalization behind it better.

Or she could wait for her father. She could trust him. Hell, she could learn to trust her own abilities. And trust Duncan.

Amira stood. What she needed was to see him. She needed to know exactly how badly she had screwed up. But Sameer said Duncan went out. She didn't know where, or how long he'd be gone. Should she text him an apology? Send him a cute emoji? Or was that too couple-y? This was supposed to be casual, but just waiting for him to reappear was risky, too—all the terrible things she'd said to him would play repeatedly through his mind the longer he was alone.

Ugh. Uncertainty seemed to make her blood vibrate in her veins. She didn't know how to fix this. She decided strong chai would help her think.

But surprisingly, when she walked by the family room, she saw Duncan. Sitting alone, alternately plucking aimlessly on her guitar and writing something in a spiral notebook. He didn't look angry anymore.

She sat on the armchair across from him. He looked up and nodded before writing something else in his notebook.

"Went for a walk and the guys left to get shoes without me. Writing a song . . ." he said, looking down at the strings.

"Am I bothering you? I can leave."

A tiny smile appeared on one side of his lips, but he didn't lift his head to make eye contact. "No. When the muse wanders in and sits before you, the last thing you do is ask it to leave."

Amira raised one eyebrow. "I'm the muse?"

He grinned briefly, finally looking at her. "I find inspiration in unexpected places. You okay now?"

Amira nodded. She had no idea how to start this apology. "Yeah, I was upset about Raymond's email. I'm really sorry I took it out on you. I don't know if you've noticed, but sometimes I'm a bit of a bitch."

His snort this time easily progressed to a full-on chuckle. "Yeah, I've noticed. And it wasn't completely your fault. I stuck my nose where it wasn't wanted."

"You were trying to help, and I implied you were less than me because of my education. You're right. I was feeling a little . . . insecure. I don't think I'm better than you, Duncan. I was just rattled from Raymond's email."

He smiled warmly. "I know you don't. And I know I need to learn to keep my opinions to myself sometimes. I'm honestly sorry, Amira."

Her head tilted as she looked at the man in front of her. Only a few days of arguing, and two nights of mouth-wateringly delicious sex, and she felt like she knew him better than anyone she had ever been in a relationship with. Duncan was hotheaded and way too protective, but his humble apology was no surprise. He was a good man, with a deep sense of what was right.

She had tried to resist, but she had been drawn to his clear green eyes from the moment she saw him, even when coupled with ridiculous suspenders and copious amounts of plaid flannel. But now that she knew the man behind the face, it wasn't his broad shoulders, his tempting smile, or that breathtaking singing voice that she wanted. It was the man below all that.

She was in deep. For some reason, the realization that she was already falling for this man washed her with a wave of loneliness. This would end. If she was smart, she would put a stop to it before she fell even harder. But cutting the charged wires that connected them seemed impossible. She needed him right now. So much.

"Are you nervous about going to an Indian party tonight?" she asked.

He plucked a quiet melody on the guitar. "Not really. Sameer said the food would be good, and I'm always up for trying new things. You still going?"

She nodded. "Yup. I'm not going back to Kingston."

He looked at her, a smile in his eyes that gradually spread to his lips. "Good. That's good."

They stared at each other for a few more seconds before she spoke again. "I've sent my report to my father for his opinion on it. If he also thinks it needs work, I can speak to my professor and see if I can buy some more time."

He put the guitar down, propping it against the couch. "I'm sure it's okay, Amira. You're the smartest engineer I know."

She raised her brow. "Really? The smartest?"

"I don't cross paths with engineers much," he admitted. "What does your dad do again? Will he be able to tell you how good it is?"

They talked for a bit longer, about Amira's father, about unconditional parental support, and about the anniversary party later that evening. They sat at opposite sides of the room, and talked only about families and parties, but that lonely sensation Amira felt earlier passed. She didn't know what would happen when he left. Her degree and her job were in turmoil, but this quiet moment with Duncan was everything.

Amira smiled, feeling so much gratitude for that broken train, before moving to the seat next to him on the sofa. She reached over and kissed him gently on the cheek.

"What was that for?" he asked.

She shrugged. Grinning, she took a deliberate look around the room. "That party is not for hours and hours, and your band seems to have deserted you. Up for spending the day with me?"

He waggled his eyebrows. "Depends. What do you have in mind?"

Oh, she had lots and lots in mind. But she didn't need to tell him. Showing him would be much more fun.

After scrounging up some food, they spent hours in her room together. The rest of the quartet came home, but Duncan stayed right where she wanted him—by her side. He even joined Amira when she went for coffee with Reena in the late afternoon. It was an almost perfect day. All the uncertainty and insecurity from earlier was forgotten. Amira had rarely felt better.

Once they were back from the coffee shop, Amira headed upstairs to get ready for the party with Mum and Zahra. She had decided to play along with Mum's idea of coordinated outfits with her family and chose her favourite royal blue salwar kameez, embellished with gold beading and embroidery. She accessorized with a blue dupatta scarf and paired the whole outfit with lots of gold costume jewellery. Mum looked stunning in her gold sari with blue trim, and Zahra was dressed to the nines in a blue and gold lehenga, with shimmering bangles reaching halfway up her arms. Amira laughed as the three of them stood preening in the mirror, Zahra with a pouty-lipped pose and Mum jutting her hip out. Mum grabbed her phone to take a selfie. They looked amazing. Some would think overdressed, but there is no such thing as overdressed at an Indian party. So long as they didn't wear bridal saris, they were usually good.

Zahra grabbed her phone and handed it to Mum. "Can you take one of Amira and me with my phone? I want to send it to Maddie."

"Maddie? Like, Duncan's Maddie?" Amira hadn't realized the girls had exchanged contact information.

Zahra nodded. "She sent me a picture yesterday of her costume for *The Nutcracker*. It was so cool, she was a toy soldier."

Amira posed for the picture, feeling her heart warm to the idea of a friendship between the girls. But while watching her sister text Maddie the picture, it occurred to her that, as the threads knitting her and Duncan together strengthened, not just by their own bond but by the bond of the two girls they loved, she was risking more shattered hearts than her own if it ended.

On her way back downstairs to meet the guys, Sameer cornered Amira. He told her that other than meeting his grandmother, he didn't expect anything else of her at the party and wouldn't be upset if she didn't even hang out with him there. That was a relief. She couldn't let on she was seeing Duncan, of course, but she wasn't really one for PDAs, anyway.

There was a genuine spring in her step as she walked down the stairs with Sameer to find Travis, Duncan, and Barrington standing there, discussing shoes.

"Wow, Amira," Travis said. "You're stunning. I love that colour on you. You'll turn all the heads tonight."

Amira thanked him. She knew she looked good. She loved Indian clothes, and this particular salwar kameez was her favourite because the colour complemented her complexion, and the fit hugged her curves. Amira's gaze travelled to Duncan. He was in that royal blue dress shirt again. She laughed, making her way towards him and wrapping her arms around his neck. He leaned close but didn't kiss her.

"We match," she said.

"No, not even close. You are far, far superior. You look spectacular, babe. I want to kiss you, but then I'd be wearing that lipstick, right?"

She laughed again as she patted his cheek and went in search of her gold stiletto sandals.

The five of them drove together in Sameer's car. Surprisingly, all seemed in good spirits. She would have thought Sameer and Travis would be more like rabbits entering a den of predators, but they seemed to be putting on a brave front. Knowing that Sameer didn't have high expectations of her allowed Amira to luxuriate in the warm anticipation of the night ahead. She hoped to spend time with her mother and sister, and maybe even reconnect with some old friends. She'd even promised to dance Bollywood-style with Zahra. And she was looking forward to showing Duncan a bit more of her culture.

The perfection of her day solidified one thing for Amira— her budding thing with Duncan was far from casual. She was falling for him, and as terrifying as that was, she didn't want to fight against it. But before even entertaining the idea of a future, she needed to see if he could accept, or better embrace, the Indian part of her. Her family, her food, her music, and her religion. They weren't from the same culture, but maybe Sameer was right. Duncan deserved the chance to understand her. And he would only understand her if she was willing to show all of herself to him.

CHAPTER TWENTY-TWO

DESPITE THE PLEASANT car ride, palpable nerves hit the moment Sameer parked his car in the community centre lot. The place was huge, and the lot was full. The centre was one of those newer community hubs north of the city, complete with a library, ice arena, swimming pool, and rooms to rent for functions of various sizes. But since hockey season was over, and Amira doubted there were too many people at the library at 8:30 on a Friday night, it was likely that most of these cars were here for the anniversary party. This was a bigger deal than she expected.

The massive hall was decorated with party-store streamers in silver and navy and twenty-fifth wedding anniversary banners, and the festive atmosphere was permeated with the scent of fried food, rich spices, and perfume. Amira walked in with a nervous smile, her trepidation matched by three of the men who followed her. Sameer and Travis finally looked like fodder for wolves, and Barrington looked like he wasn't sure what to expect as a large black man walking into an Indian party. Amira glanced back at Duncan. He cheerfully crossed the threshold, handsome and confident. Nothing phased her garden gnome.

She scanned for her mother in the crowd but didn't find her.

"We need to say hello to my grandmother," Sameer whispered to her, "then I'll leave you alone."

"Amira!" Zahra appeared.

"Hey, Squish."

"Can I hang out with you guys? There's no one good here tonight."

Duncan laughed, looking down at Zahra's wide eyes. "Hey, I'm here, I'm good, aren't I? Stay close to me, Zahra. I need you to be my cultural translator tonight. How do you say congratulations in Gujarati?"

Zahra beamed, delighted to have an adult's undivided attention.

"All right, Sameer, let's go see your grandmother." Amira stood tall and applied her best fake smile. She glanced at Travis.

Travis nodded and lowered himself into a chair at a big, empty table, his expression resigned. Amira gave him a sympathetic smile. She didn't want to do this, but what choice did she have?

Amira followed Sameer towards the crowd to find Shirin. But Shirin beat them to the punch and found them before they'd moved even five feet from the table.

"Sameer!" Shirin was a small woman wearing a beige sari and a warm smile. She hugged her grandson and kissed both his cheeks before turning to Amira. "Amira, look at you! You've grown so big. I remember you when you were such a little thing!" She hugged and kissed Amira, then clutched both of Amira's hands in her own.

"Did you eat yet? We had the samosas made special. They're chicken!" She smiled before pulling Amira closer by the arm. "We're all so happy you and Sameer have found each other again, beta. You knew each other when you were babies, do you remember?"

"No, Aunty. It was a long time ago." She peeked at Sameer out of the corner of her eye, not surprised to see him blushing.

Shirin leaned closer. "You know, Sameer and his mother lived here before they moved to Ottawa. They should have stayed. Sameer needed family and friends near him. Anyway, he's here now, maybe you can convince him to stay in Toronto."

"I can't, Maa. I'm only here for the competition," Sameer said.

"And what about this singing competition? Singing Western songs with those boys . . . you should be singing Indian music! Did you know Amira's sister does Kathak dancing? We should have asked her to perform today. She's so sweet. Just like Amira. Such a sweet family." Shirin patted the top of Amira's hand as she spoke.

Amira did her best to keep her fake smile on her lips. Good thing Duncan wasn't around to hear this. He would have a choice comment about anyone labelling Amira as sweet. She looked up and saw Duncan and Zahra about a dozen feet away, looking at some blown-up photos of the couple celebrating their anniversary.

Shirin was still holding her hand, but Amira recognized the need to get away from this woman before her expression betrayed her annoyance. And after one more peek at Sameer, she thought it best to get her friend away, too. "My nanima's here, we should say hello."

"Wait," Shirin interrupted, squeezing Amira's hand tighter. "You have to meet Sameer's *masis* first. I have three daughters, you know. Neelam is my youngest." She pointed to the front of the room. "Tazim and Anar are there, they should meet anyone important to Sameer."

Amira didn't want to meet Sameer's aunties. Aunties who would look her up and down as if assessing a lamb before slaughter. Aunties who'd ask leading questions to determine her suitability to join their family. Aunties who had no idea who Sameer really was. She glanced at Travis and Barrington sitting at the table. It was the quartet that mattered to Sameer, not her.

She stood tall and squared her shoulders. "His *friends* are important to him. Sameer, what do you say we *all* go meet your aunties."

He smiled a little too tightly, but seemed to agree. He motioned to Travis and Barrington to join them as Amira motioned Duncan and her sister over.

Led by Shirin, Sameer, Amira, Travis, Barrington, Duncan, and Zahra started making the rounds of the room, taking a scenic route towards the aunties at the front. They stopped to look at the family pictures, the elaborate centrepieces of white and blue roses, and the impressive sweets table piled high with jalebi and mithai in an array of pastel colours. All while Shirin shared the full itinerary of the speeches and special entertainment that would be happening later in the night. Shirin had them stop at what felt like every little grouping of guests dotting the hall, where, speaking in Gujarati, every sari-clad Indian woman between the age of sixty and eighty was introduced as Shirin's "dearest friend." Amira was proudly presented to each of them as Sameer's special companion, while Travis, Duncan, and Barrington were lucky to get a disinterested wave and a mention as "other friends." The quartet followed somewhat stoically as Sameer and Amira were paraded around ceremoniously.

No introductions were necessary in the eighth grouping of people since Nanima was in that group. She stepped towards them and kissed Amira's cheek, then smiled at Sameer and spoke in English.

"I am so happy you have brought Amira. Do you know how hard it is to get her to come to these parties? It seems you have more influence with her than any of us do." Nanima laughed at herself before taking Sameer's hand and pressing it over Amira's. "See?" she said, looking at Shirin. "I told you they were close."

Amira extracted her hand and took a step backwards to stand next to Travis. "They're all my friends. Hey, Nanima, remember I was telling you that it was Travis who did Zahra's hair before the ballet? You said she looked like an angel."

Nanima smiled at Travis. "She looked lovely, thank you. Zahra was so happy that day."

Shirin waved her hand at Zahra. "Zahra always looks like an angel. Such a beautiful girl. Just like you, Amira. I am so happy Sameer came here and found something so meaningful." Shirin wedged herself beside Amira, effectively pushing Travis aside in the process.

Fuck. Amira turned and saw a blank expression on Travis's face. Duncan looked pissed off and moved in to stand on one side of Travis while Barrington took the other side. Travis's friends had him. But Sameer did nothing. And said nothing.

At least Sameer looked miserable. That furrowed brow and deep tension that had been his constant expression when she first met him had retuned. No doubt, he hated the way Shirin and Nanima were treating his boyfriend, but he did nothing to stop it. Amira glared at him, motioning towards Travis. *Do something!* she tried to tell him with her eyes. She hoped he understood.

Thankfully, he seemed to. It wasn't near enough, but the deliberate step he took away from Amira and his grand-mother and towards the quartet put him in a line with the other members of his group. The quartet looked complete. A united front, Amira hoped. Sameer closed his eyes a few seconds before speaking. "Maa, I'm here for the contest. My singing and my friends are meaningful for me."

Maybe it would have been enough if Sameer had looked at Travis when he said it. Or if he had stood near his boy-friend instead of next to Duncan. But Amira saw it in Travis's face. He was done. She wasn't surprised when he took a step backwards, away from the group. "I'll be at the table."

And Sameer let him go.

Amira and Sameer ended up meeting the aunties alone, as the rest of the quartet and Zahra scattered after Travis left. And it was pretty anticlimactic. The aunties seemed like lovely women with kind eyes, but they were clearly too busy with the party to pay much attention to their nephew and his "girlfriend." Finally, Amira and Sameer were able to extract themselves from Shirin's grasp, so to speak, and head to the table towards the others.

Travis and Barrington seemed deep in conversation at the table, and Zahra and Duncan weren't there. "Your sister took Duncan to get food," Barrington said, standing. "And I'm going to step out and call Marcia." He looked at Sameer, then Travis, clearly hoping that leaving them alone would mean they'd talk about what just happened. Amira extracted herself as well and went in search of her sister and Duncan.

Instead, she found her mother and grandmother just past the food line, critiquing a plate of biryani in Mum's hand.

"Amira!" her mother exclaimed. "Did you eat? The biryani has a lot of meat in it, but it's a little oily."

"It's goat," Nanima added.

Amira looked at Nanima, still annoyed at that little interaction with Shirin a few moments ago. But technically, Nanima hadn't done anything wrong—Amira had let her believe this budding romance with Sameer was real, so how could she be mad that her grandmother acted on it? Besides, it was Shirin who had been rude to Travis there, not Nanima.

"Yes, I'm going to eat, I'm just looking for . . . oh, there. Zahra." Zahra and Duncan were in the front of the line. Zahra was, of course, talking, and Duncan was leaning down, listening to her with his complete attention. Amira's chest tightened. Her little sister tended to talk a lot and hadn't quite learned the social cues of when an adult was no longer interested in her earnest monologues. Most people would have tuned her out long ago, but Duncan appeared genuinely engrossed. He cared about what Zahra was telling him.

"Why is that man alone with Zahra?" Nanima asked.

"You mean Duncan? She's explaining the food to him."

"I don't know, Amira," Nanima said. "I don't think those kinds of people should be around children. We have to look out for our little girl."

"What do you mean, *those kinds*?" Mum asked.

"Oh, you know. Men like them . . ."

Amira stared at her grandmother. She got it, and she didn't like it at all. She hadn't forgotten that the rumour mill hadn't been all too accurate when the guys first moved in, and Nanima had thought the entire quartet were all "poofs" as she called them, except for Sameer. Amira didn't want to cause a scene, but this time, she couldn't let it go. "Nanima, if you mean that Duncan shouldn't be around children because you think he's gay, that's a horrific thing to say. Gay people aren't criminals! Zahra is in no danger with Duncan. He's a teacher, for god's sake! He is a guest in your home, and I would think you would treat him like a human being. And it shouldn't make a difference, but Duncan isn't even gay."

"Lower your voice, beta. I'm glad he's not that way. At least we don't have to worry about people like that here."

Amira grimaced, frustrated beyond belief. She wasn't surprised at her grandmother's comments; after all, Nanima had been making the odd disparaging remark about homosexuals for years, but this seemed a bit extreme, even for her. Not every Muslim was homophobic, but it killed her that these sorts of prejudices existed at all in her community, especially at a time when discrimination against Muslims was so high. They should be coming together in understanding now, not building bigger walls.

Amira came close to saying exactly that to Nanima, but then she bit her lip. She didn't really think it would do much good at this point, especially here, at a party. She looked at her mother. Why wasn't Mum saying anything?

Disappointed, she shook her head at her mother. "I don't even know what to say, but clearly now is not the right time for this. I'll see you guys later." She weaved through the crowd towards Duncan and Zahra, who were just leaving the buffet table.

"Amira!" Duncan grinned when she approached. "I made you a plate. Your sister tells me this is goat biryani, cabbage sambharo, and chicken samosas." He looked down at Zahra. "Did I get that right?"

Her sister giggled. "Your pronunciation could use some work, but not bad."

He chuckled at Zahra, his hand on her shoulder as they walked back to the table. "This Indian stuff is new to me. I just need practise." They sat at the table. Duncan immediately whispered to Amira, "And a determined teacher to help me."

CHAPTER TWENTY-THREE

AMIRA'S MOOD HAD taken a deeper dive downwards after that little interaction with her grandmother. She picked at her food, moving the rice and meat through the pools of oil soaking through the thick paper plate. Even the rare and coveted goat biryani couldn't tempt her now. She understood Nanima was from another generation, but what her grandmother had said about gay people went beyond intolerance: it was hateful. More hateful than she would have expected from such a loving woman.

She wasn't the only one having a difficult night. Sameer and Travis were barely speaking, both sitting rigidly, avoiding eye contact with anyone. From the look on Travis's face, it was clear that whatever Sameer had said to him while they were alone at the table wasn't close to being enough. She'd never seen Travis's normally animated features so closed off. And Sameer looked minutes away from either bursting into tears or exploding into a fiery rage worthy of Amira's own temper.

In contrast, Duncan was happy as a lark to spend the meal listening to Zahra explain the difference between classical and modern Indian dance. At least someone was enjoying this bloody party.

Dropping her orange-stained fork, Amira pushed her plate aside. Duncan looked across Zahra and asked, "Not hungry? You didn't eat your cabbage . . . stuff. It's delicious."

"Yeah. Lost my appetite. Take it if you want."

He eagerly reached for her plate and wolfed down her leftovers.

"You know?" Sameer said, looking at his uneaten meal. "I think we should just go."

"Wait." Duncan smiled. "I still need to try that rose milk stuff Zahra told me about."

Amira smiled. He really was being adorable tonight. "Sharbat. Here"—she stood up—"I'll take you to get some."

Standing in line, Duncan leaned close. "You okay, babe?"

She huffed a sigh. "Yeah, just remembering why I don't normally come to these things."

He bent a touch closer, voice lowered. "Can I tell you again how gorgeous you look tonight? I can't stop looking at you in that outfit."

She flushed, looking around to make sure no one was watching them. "Careful," she warned. "I'm not your date tonight."

"*I know*," he purred close to her ear. Low, he fingered the soft fabric of her dupatta, the long scarf worn as part of her outfit. "This silk? Maybe you can tie me up with it later."

Oh god . . . she swallowed, trying her best to keep her composure.

"Amira, I was looking for you. Do you have a second?" Her mother's voice startled her.

"Hi, Mum."

Duncan smiled as he took three glasses of sharbat from the woman handing them out, balancing them easily in his large hands. "I'll just take these to the table. I'm sure your sister wants her milk. Catch up with you later, Amira." He left, leaving her alone with her mother. They wandered to the side of the room for a bit of privacy.

"Nice guy, that one. Different."

"Mum, he's a good guy. He's great with Zahra."

"I know. That's what I wanted to talk to you about." Mum smiled before looking out into the crowd of people. "I'm sorry about what Nanima said earlier."

Now Mum found her voice, when Nanima wasn't even there to hear it.

"I'm tired of closed-minded thinking. We're talking about human rights here," Amira said.

"I know, sweetie. You're always so good about fighting for others. Thank you for that." She looked back at Amira. "My mother is of another generation, and it's hard to unlearn what she was taught as a child. She doesn't understand the world has changed."

"That's not an excuse. She's fine being modern when it comes to iPads and KitchenAids, but she won't accept gay people? It's not like homosexuality is some new Western phenomenon; there are LGBTQ people all over the world. There have been forever. Even Muslim ones."

"*I know*." Mum nodded. "It doesn't help that she spends so much time with those women in that cooking committee. They're like a feedback loop, amplifying misconceptions." She paused. "Amira, have you forgotten that I used to be good friends with Neelam before she moved away?"

Shit . . . that was Sameer's mom. The only one in his family who knew he was gay.

"She called me after he moved downstairs. He's very lucky to have found *a friend* in you."

Amira lowered her voice. "Mum, don't say anything."

"Of course not. But be careful, honey. I understand that you want to help your friend, but you need to ask yourself, Who is this ploy benefitting? Is it helping Sameer, or helping the people who won't let him be himself?" She frowned, glancing towards Sameer's table. "He is so young. He has the luxury of a full life ahead of him. It would be wonderful for him to be able to live that life on his own terms."

"Mum, this is hardly a long-term arrangement."

"I know, but humour me while I give you some maternal advice." She looked towards Duncan, sitting with Zahra. "Be careful with that one, too. I'm wondering how long term that arrangement is . . ."

Amira stilled. There was no hiding anything from her mother. It was crazy of her to even try.

"Mum—"

"Just hear me, Amira." Mum smiled. "I saw the way he looked at you."

"It's not serious. We're just having fun." That was a lie.

"But is this the right time in your life for just fun? You'll be back at work soon. And he'll go back to his family. You have a demanding career, and I want you to think about the future. You need stability. Also, Nanima wouldn't be happy to have you bring home that one."

That was rich coming from her mother, since she was also dating someone Nanima wouldn't approve of. "Because he's white?"

"No, because he's not Muslim. And not a professional. He's a singer, isn't he? It's no problem for me, but understand that there would be opposition, and you would have to deal with that conflict."

"I just told you guys he's a teacher!" Probably wise to leave out the "substitute" identifier from his job title. Mum was easygoing, but still Indian. The academic and professional competitiveness ran deep in their culture. "And anyway . . . why should I care what Nanima or anyone else would approve of? You said you admired that I don't let what others think get in my way."

"No, you're right. I do admire that about you. I just . . . I don't know." Mum smiled sadly. "I want to make sure you're not caught up in a fantasy. That you know what to expect." She reached out and hugged her, but Amira stiffened in her mother's arms.

"I just want you to be happy, sweetie," her mother said after releasing her. "Life is hard. If you have the opportunity to make it easier for yourself, maybe take it?"

"I'll see you at home, Mum."

Amira pressed her fingers to her temples, rubbing as she walked back to the table. Since when was her family made up of small-minded cave people? They were giving her a nasty headache. As she reached the table, she saw Shirin approaching behind Sameer's seat. Crap. Sameer was leaning close talking to Travis, no doubt trying to ease the hurt in Travis's posture, and hadn't noticed the shark circling again.

"Sameer, did you eat?" Shirin asked.

Sameer stood up quickly. "Oh, yes, Maa, we all ate. Everything was delicious. We all loved . . ." His voice trailed off as his eyes closed a moment.

Ugh. This was painful to watch. Sameer couldn't keep doing this. Pleasing everyone was killing him.

"Amira, I had to see you before you left." She pulled Amira in and hugged her. They were still standing behind Travis's chair. "Now, beta, I want you to come see us at home any time. Even after Sameer's gone. You are one of the family now. You are always welcome with us." She hugged her again. Amira couldn't see Travis's face from her position, but Sameer could. And the look of mingling fear and despair on Sameer's face as he watched his boyfriend listen to his grandmother told Amira everything she needed to know. Ugh.

"I will, Aunty," she said. "Anyway, we really have to go. I have to study tonight."

"I know, your nanima told me you are an engineer! So smart! You know, one of Sameer's cousins is a chemist. And Sameer's a pharmacist! This family has been blessed. We will see you again soon."

Travis stood suddenly. The sound of his chair scraping against the floor made Amira and Shirin jump. He looked right at Sameer. "I'm not waiting for you anymore." He left the hall.

And Amira's heart shattered for her friends.

They found Travis standing near Sameer's car, typing on his phone. He said nothing as they all got in. The ride home was unnervingly silent. Amira had no idea what to say, sure that whatever she tried would be the wrong thing. Sameer and Travis sat in the front, the tension between them thick enough to seep into the back, and probably out the trunk, too. Duncan was also silent, but he held Amira's hand the whole way home, lightly tickling her palm with his fingers.

She should never have agreed to go to this party. Even if Travis said he was fine meeting Sameer's family under false pretenses, part of her knew it was wrong from the beginning. Mum was right, she shouldn't have offered this ridiculous bearding scheme at all. This was real life. Real people were hurt, and Amira felt terrible she was a part of this farce.

It was no surprise when she heard Sameer and Travis start arguing as soon as the door to their room shut behind them. Amira took off her salwar kameez, trying not to listen to their hushed, anguished voices. Duncan sat on her bed, watching her.

"This sounds worse than normal, right?" he asked.

She frowned, pulling on her plaid pyjama pants. "Sounds that way. I don't blame Travis for being upset. I know I would be."

"I know I *was*. You and I have been sleeping together for only two days, and I felt like a green-eyed monster when his grandmother welcomed you into her family. Travis must have felt like a rifle shot through his heart."

Amira laughed softly, approaching Duncan on the bed. "First of all"—she kissed him firmly—"you have a way with words. And second, you *are* a green-eyed monster, jealous or not." She went looking for a T-shirt to sleep in. "I hate that this is my fault. I wish I could do something."

A door opened and slammed. "I guess Travis is taking off again," she said, pulling on her shirt.

But they didn't hear the side door to the house open. Whoever left the bedroom hadn't left the house. "I'll go talk to him," Amira said.

Wandering into the dark family room, she found Travis sitting alone on the couch, head down.

"Hey," she said, sitting next to him.

Eyes glassy, he looked at her. "*You*. I hate you right now. You know that?"

"I know." She put her hand on his knee. "I'm sorry, Travis. Really, really sorry. I should never have suggested this ridiculous plan."

He blinked a few times and sighed. "I need to be doing something with my hands right now. Can I do your hair?"

She turned in her seat as he started raking his hands through her hair, silently working out the knots and tangles from the evening. It was strangely comforting. His hands were warm and gentle in the quiet room. Starting at a spot right above her left ear, he began braiding. He worked quietly for a while, pulling snuggly as the braid snaked over her crown. It felt so much like when her mother used to braid her hair as a child. Amira was shocked to find herself tearing up. She wished she could go back to those days sometimes.

"Ever fall in love with the wrong man, Amira?"

"No. I . . . I don't know. Sameer *does* love you."

"I know he does. That's the worst part of it. He's treating himself worse than he's treating me." He paused, still working through her hair. "He's just not ready for all this. Sameer can tell a patient the easiest way to insert yeast infection medication, but he can't say 'I'm gay' to a brown person."

She thought about her grandmother's remarks at the party. "There are people in our culture who would not accept him."

"Yes, but there are a lot who would, too, if he gave them the chance." He paused, hands stilling in her hair, before resuming her braid. "When I first met Sameer, I kept my distance for so long before giving in to that smile. Never fall for a closeted man, it's a no-brainer. But god . . . he was so adorable. I couldn't resist. You should have heard him when he first asked me out . . . he was terrified, it was the cutest thing. I had to put him out of his misery." He continued braiding. "He's come a long way. We've come a long way together. I was so proud of him when he came out to his mom. He's a different person in Ottawa now than when we met. A free and unburdened Sameer is the most beautiful thing I have ever seen, and I really thought he would go through with telling his family here. He could be such an example to them . . . it was supposed to be me his grandmother welcomed into the family."

"Not everyone is cut out for activism, Travis."

"I know. I get it, all of it. It's hard enough to be a Muslim these days, but a gay Muslim? He didn't choose this. It absolutely sucks he has to fight to just be himself, because fighting isn't who Sameer is. And I love him for it. But being somebody's secret, being on the sidelines, isn't who I am."

The braid curved around her head like a crown, ending near her left ear. He secured it with an elastic she found in her pocket and tucked in the end.

She turned to look at him once he was done. "What are you going to do?"

"I can't keep going this way. I . . . I've ended it." His voice cracking, he looked at his empty hands as he spoke.

Amira winced. "For real? Like, forever?"

Travis nodded. "I don't see how we can get over this."

"I'm so sorry. I feel terrible."

He looked at Amira. "You were trying to help. It's no one's fault, really. We're just . . . stuck. Maybe we're not meant to be together."

"Are you going back to Ottawa now?"

He shook his head. "No. Not until after the competition. I can't do that to Barrington and Duncan. We'll stick it out. Going to be an interesting couple of days . . ." He smiled. "I am glad you've hooked up with Duncan, though, and not just because him leaving the couch gives me a place to sleep. I'm glad someone can be happy during all this."

She leaned over and kissed Travis's forehead. "You're amazing. I don't think I've said this to any of you, yet, but I'm so glad the four of you turned up in my basement. I wish things could be different for you."

He smiled. "Thanks, Amira. I'd better get some sleep, though. Go do your lumberjack."

CHAPTER TWENTY-FOUR

"THEY BROKE UP," she said as she opened the door to her bedroom, glad Duncan was there. This news was worse for him. She couldn't see how they could possibly win the competition now. She sat at the desk chair, looking at the floor.

"Shit," he said. "Is Travis leaving?"

"No, he'll stay for the competition. Your rehearsals may be tense tomorrow."

"They've been tense all week. This isn't going to help us win this thing."

"No. If it's any help, it doesn't sound like a particularly fiery breakup. Travis seems more sad than angry." It wasn't much of a consolation. Her chest tightened at the memory of the wretched, dejected look on his face when she found him on the sofa. Amira picked at a loose thread on her pants, feeling completely helpless. She wished she could go back in time and prevent the quartet from coming here. She should have insisted Nanima ask them to leave when she got home from Kingston that day. The fact of it was, if the boys hadn't been here for that damn barbershop quartet competition, she wouldn't have come up with that terrible beard idea, and

Sameer and Travis would still be happy and together, like they belonged. She'd gladly give up her friendship with them for that.

But then again, this barbershop quartet competition was the only reason Duncan was here, too. It was a confusing paradox, and Amira was glad she couldn't go back in time, because she didn't really want to change the past. Four days ago, she would've been happy never to set eyes on the garden gnome again, but now . . . she looked at him . . .

And Amira noticed for the first time that he was topless. In her bed. The sheet covering his lower half was riding low enough that she wondered exactly what, if anything, he was wearing underneath it. He slowly raised his hands to rest on his chest, and she saw that they were tied together. She swallowed.

"Are you naked?"

He laughed. "Maybe. Why don't you come take a look? Why do you have Lady Guinevere hair all of a sudden?"

"Travis did it. How did you tie up your own hands?"

"They aren't really tied up, see?" He freed one hand out by stretching the elastic that was binding them.

She pointed at it. "What is that?"

"I wanted to use your pretty blue scarf but didn't want to wrinkle it. These are my suspenders."

She stared at him, blinking as he slipped his hand back into the knotted suspenders.

"So . . ." She wasn't sure what to say. She wasn't sure what they had been talking about in the first place. Who turned the heat up?

"You too upset to play?" Duncan asked, shifting a bit and

causing the sheet to slip an inch lower. "I understand that. But I'm leaving in two days. We don't have much more time together."

"I know."

"And having sex isn't going to make things worse for Sameer and Travis."

"I know. I just feel helpless." She got up and moved to sit on the edge of the bed. "Obviously, Sameer and Travis's problems run deeper than just what happened here in Toronto, but those two belong together. I wish Sameer could be honest. He doesn't even live here, who cares if his family here disowns him? His mother accepts him, shouldn't that be enough?"

"I know. But it's not so easy to give up your family. They're *family*, Amira. Means more than geography. Growing up, it was just him and his mom. He told me he always loved that he had a big, crazy family to fall back on. I know I'd think twice before doing something that would disappoint mine."

She absently stroked the skin on his wrist where the suspenders bound him, wondering about the strength of the restraint. Amira had the usual family conflicts, but nothing like this. It was hard to put herself in Sameer's place. But just like Sameer, her own mother was hiding a relationship because she was worried about her family's censure. Amira couldn't imagine doing that. Even though Mum said Nanima wouldn't be thrilled if she found out about her and Duncan, she would never let that stop her from doing what she thought was best for herself. She would never allow other people's outdated prejudices to influence any part of her own life. But there was a world of difference between Nanima not being thrilled about her relationship with Duncan, and Shirin disowning Sameer because he's gay.

And it was probably a moot point—she wasn't ready to tell Nanima about this thing with Duncan anyway.

"It's probably more than just disappointing his family," Amira said. "I'll bet there's a small dose of shame in there, too. He's probably not one hundred percent okay with being gay yet."

Duncan nodded sadly. "Yeah, I figured the same thing. One thing I've learned is it's a lot of work to escape your upbringing. I can try to be so many things, but the small-town gentleman I was raised to be is still in there. Speaking of which"—he wiggled his bound arms—"you going to keep talking when you got a farm boy tied up in your bed? I am sure Sameer and Travis won't mind."

She bit her lip. Slowly, she pulled the sheet down another half inch. Definitely naked under there. "Travis just told me to go do my lumberjack."

He laughed. "So, what are you waiting for? Do me." He raised his bound hands over his head, stretching his tight abs and firm pectorals. The stretch caused the inevitable to happen—the sheet was no longer covering anything interesting.

Damn . . . how is it possible that she found a man who saw right into her innermost desires on a broken-down train in the middle of nowhere?

He was right, of course. Whatever she did with Duncan now wouldn't change anything in the future. Wouldn't solve Sameer and Travis's problems, wouldn't win the competition, or help with her project. It wouldn't even prevent Duncan from leaving Toronto in two days.

Everything was still uncertain. Everything still hard.

But she could at least forget all that for a few more nights. She could take the pleasure offered to her, for the time being.

She smiled. "Yeah." She leaned down to gently bite his chest as he hummed with appreciation. "Should we have a safe word or something if you're going to be tied up?" she asked.

He laughed. "I'm not really tied up, though; it's an illusion."

"Still . . ." She ducked her head to nibble some more.

"Biryani," he said.

Her head jerked up. "What?"

"That's the safe word. Biryani."

"You've got to be kidding me."

"Why?" He looked hurt.

"You do realize we serve biryani at every gathering and celebration ever, and if we use it as a safe word, then every time someone offers me some, I will turn the colour of . . . well, biryani."

He laughed. "Okay. Bad choice, then."

She giggled, letting her forehead drop onto his chest.

"How about Port Hope? Remind us of where we met."

Sentimentality overcame her. That was barely two weeks ago. She hadn't felt safe that day, nervous about travelling and worried about her final report, and that creep had been harassing her at the train station. But Duncan had swept in and made things safe for her. In two days, he would be gone. And she would be alone again.

"Hey, Amira, you sad?"

"No." She sat up, blinking. "I'm fine." She smiled. "Now that I have you tied up in my bed, what will I do with you?"

"Whatever you want. I'm your farm boy, Princess Buttercup."

Later, after Amira had untied him, he turned on his side, facing her. He threw the blanket over them before wrapping his arms around her, holding her close.

"How the hell am I ever going to leave you?" he whispered into her cheek.

She had just been wondering the same thing.

. . . .

AMIRA SLEPT IN the next morning, the sunbeams seeping through the high basement window and stroking her face like warm silk. She felt a heavy weight on her bed and stirred.

"Morning, Princess." Duncan was sitting on the edge of the bed, showered and dressed, a large mug in his hand. "For you." He placed the mug on her nightstand and bent for a kiss.

She could get used to this. "Thanks," she said, propping herself up and inhaling deeply. Chai again. She could get *really* used to this.

"You were so out, I let you sleep. We're just taking a break. We started rehearsals early this morning. No practising at all tomorrow to save our voices."

Amira sat up and lifted the mug. "How are things going out there? The guys are . . . okay?"

He nodded. "Yeah, they are. Everyone's being a mature adult, but"—he rubbed his neck—"the tension is there. Hope it doesn't affect our performance tomorrow. Time will tell."

Amira sipped the chai. It was perfect, of course. "You know what I've never asked you? Why'd you join up with these guys you'd never met for this barbershop quartet, anyway? Why is this competition so important to you?"

He rubbed his hand on the back of his neck. "They don't feel like strangers; they've become great friends since we started singing together online." He paused, thinking. "I've been making music for years, I know how rare it is to find a group you connect with that well. We have magic together. But honestly, I need this win for personal reasons."

"Why? What reasons?"

"My resumé." He swung his legs onto the bed next to her. "I live in a small town. We don't even have a school in Omemee anymore, but I substitute teach for the board in neighbouring towns. Lindsay, Port Perry, even Haliburton sometimes. But none of those towns is all too big either. Anyway, there is a school in Peterborough; it's a different school board, so I don't work there, but there's this amazing music teacher. He does band and vocals, but he also brought in a top-tier guitar program and even musical theatre. He's retiring this year, and I've applied for his position."

"And winning this competition will get you that job?"

He shrugged. "I don't know. These opportunities don't come up often in the sticks. It's close by, so I wouldn't have to move out of Ryan's place. I know some of the other teachers applying, and I've been teaching longer than most of them, so you'd think I'd have it in the bag. I have tons of experience: local bands, music camps, private lessons. But some of these other teachers? One woman was in a major musical production here in Toronto. Another guy had a successful touring band. I even heard someone from one of the big performing arts schools here in the city was applying. I wanted something more unique and prestigious on my resumé. Something other than I sang in a Tragically Hip cover band at the Red Dog."

"Where?"

"A pub in Peterborough." He smiled sadly. "Not much I can do now that I haven't already done. I always tell my students: the feeling you get when making music is the reward, not the fame. Not the recognition, not the contest wins, not even album sales. That's not why we should be doing this. But"—he shrugged—"sometimes you need some prestige in order to get a leg up."

While Amira had become intimately familiar with every square inch of his body, this was a side of him she wasn't familiar with. Duncan had insecurities? Felt less than his peers? Since the day they met, he had been nothing but cocky, confident, and sure of himself, but it turned out Duncan Galahad was human, with human uncertainty, just like her. It was humbling he let her see this. Especially since . . . tomorrow was the competition. And then, he would leave. And they would have to figure out what the hell they were going to do next.

Every moment she spent with Duncan, things felt more real. Stronger. Right now, she couldn't imagine walking away from him. She wanted more. But . . .

But . . . all the concerns her mother had expressed yesterday came crashing in. Her demanding job. His unstable one. Where he lived. Their commitments to helping their families. Plus, they were from different worlds. Religion, culture, family, everything. Was she caught in a fantasy?

She looked at him, knowing he could see all the warmth, uncertainty, and confusion about the future in her eyes. The emotions were reflected in his gaze. He kissed her, so softly, with so much affection.

He pulled closer, gathering her in his arms as she twisted to close the gap between them. She wanted it all. She wanted to zip open this man and climb inside him forever. She pulled away. The want was terrifying.

"You have to rehearse," she said, leaning against his forehead.

He smiled as he pulled away. "I came here to ask you something. I know your paper is due Monday, and you're probably busy, but Sameer wanted me to check if you're coming to watch the competition tomorrow."

Amira frowned. "Why does he want me to come?"

"His grandmother is coming."

She groaned. "Are we going to do all this again?"

Duncan took her hand. "I know it's weird, but . . . I want you to come too, for me. We can't let his grandmother know about . . . us, but, be there as my friend?"

Amira thought about it. "Who else will be there?"

"Barrington's fiancée, Marcia, is driving down from Waterloo. Sameer's grandmother and one aunt are coming. My brother and Maddie. Plus, Travis's sister decided at the last minute to drive in from Ottawa. I'm thinking Travis told her about the breakup, and she's coming so he'll at least have someone on his side."

"Sounds like an awesome sister."

"Yup."

She would love to go. To see the guys perform, to support Travis, to root for Duncan, and to be there for Sameer when his family inevitably overwhelmed him with expectations he couldn't come close to meeting.

But . . .

Did she want to be there to see those expectations? Did she want to pretend to be there as Sameer's girlfriend, or did she want to announce to the world she was really Duncan's . . .

Duncan's what, exactly?

She closed her eyes.

"I'll think about it," she finally said. "Let's see what's going on with my report. It's due Monday, and I haven't heard from my dad yet." She got up and put on her furry bathrobe.

He headed to the door. "Okay. I'll be heading to Omemee in a few hours to bring Maddie for her sleepover. She's about to explode with anticipation. Hopefully the girls aren't too noisy tonight, and we'll all be productive."

He smiled again before leaving the room.

Amira fell back in bed and lay on her pillow. She stared at her ceiling.

Just like Travis, she had always loved the unusual ceilings in her home. The plaster swirls were arranged in concentric circles spiralling towards the centre, focusing her thoughts. The ceiling had personality. It was exactly what she needed.

The world wanted flat; Amira needed texture. When her friends took dance classes, she wanted a guitar. She loved old rock and new alternative music, while her friends were into pop or Bollywood. She liked the swirled ceiling instead of the flat. But over the years, her tastes had changed. Conformed. Maybe normalized?

And floating just below the surface of her consciousness, she knew why she had changed. As the world became more intolerant of people like her, part of her found ways not to be so different, not to stand out. The parts of her she couldn't change would always be in the minority, so she may as well conform with the things she could change.

She wasn't ashamed of her culture, her religion, or her skin—far from it. Amira loved being Indian. Loved her brown skin and her rich culture. Loved that she rarely got a sunburn and her everyday food was a hell of a lot more interesting than meatloaf and mashed potatoes. But she'd grown weary of dealing with the preconceptions people had about her when they saw her or learned her religion. She was tired of hearing, *Wow, I didn't know Indian girls played guitars!* Or, *Why don't you like Bollywood?* Or, *A Muslim woman who likes to be dominant? Cute.* Until the world woke the fuck up and realized that her culture and religion did not define her, but rather were just part of what made her the person she was, it would be easier to just conform to what everyone expected her to be. Just like her mother had advised her, she had taken the opportunity to make life easier for herself.

But the honest truth was she *wanted* unconventional. The burly singer, instead of the clean-cut, stable professional. The kind of man who played Black Sabbath on his ukulele and watched princess movies with his niece. She wanted the man with the red beard and suspenders, and she wanted him with her for a long time.

A Sufi saint *had* helped her that day on the train and presented her with her deepest fantasy on a platter, with the challenge to accept herself enough to accept him.

Maybe they would have a future, maybe they wouldn't. But Amira was done fighting against it. He didn't experience the world in the same way she did. He couldn't feel what it was like to fight for rights that others took for granted. To fight to merely exist. But he empathized. And given the chance, he could understand. He already understood her better than anyone else had—even despite their differences.

After the competition tomorrow, she was going to have a long talk with Duncan Galahad. She was going to tell him she wanted to keep seeing him. Omemee was only an hour-and-a-half drive from Toronto. And after the look he just gave her, Duncan would agree. It was worth it to try to make this work.

CHAPTER TWENTY-FIVE

AMIRA'S PLANNED LUNCH with Shelley from Hyde Industrial was that afternoon, and after ordering at the hot new Italian small-plates restaurant Shelley picked out, Amira discovered she was still afflicted by that little transparency problem.

Shelley flashed a knowing smirk. "What, or should I say *who*, put that grin on your face?"

Amira scoffed. "I don't know what you're talking about."

Shelley laughed. "Girl, I doubt that. I know you, Amira. Spill."

"Fine. I *may* be seeing someone. But it's too soon to tell the world yet, so subject change, please. You still committing to never committing?"

Shelley laughed. "The dating pool of acceptable people in this city is getting smaller by the minute. Practically a dating kiddie pool at this point. And I never get out of the office long enough to actually meet non-Hyde men anyway."

"What about Hyde men, then?"

"I'm HR—the only department not allowed to dip into the office talent. Ooh, speaking of dipping into office talent, here's some juicy dirt. Apparently Trevor Crane had a little fling with Mandeep in accounting. Her husband found out when she sent raunchy texts to him, thinking he was Trevor. I guess her husband didn't know her deviant side."

"Holy crap. Should you be telling me this?"

"Yeah, it's all good. I didn't find this out until they'd both left the company. Word is, they've both left their spouses, too."

"They're both gone?" Amira had liked Trevor. He was a consultant in her division and she'd worked with him on plenty of assignments. She also knew his wife was a piece of work, and the end of his marriage didn't surprise Amira. Still, his method of moving on left a lot to be desired. She didn't know this Mandeep—must have been hired after she left.

Shelley nodded. "No surprise they jumped ship. A black man and a brown woman? Still, getting involved with a co-worker seems like a disaster waiting to happen. I always warned Tori when she was checking out the new hires. Tori's working at the airport now and drooling openly outside the pilots' lounge. She always had a thing for men in uniform." Tori was hired not long before Amira left. Lovely girl, and a very good engineer. Amira had been looking forward to working with her again.

"Tori's gone, too? Is there a bit of a mass exodus going on?"

Shelley snorted. "Yeah, you could say that. Lots of new people, though. You'll have to meet Kristianne. I call her my new work wife, since you're not there. We'll all do lunch all together when you're back."

The food arrived, and as they dug in, Amira took a second to think about what Shelley had said. She'd known things at Hyde were different. Hell, she'd seen it when she met with Jim Prescott, and then Raymond. But it was still surprising to hear so many people had left. There had been little turnover among the engineers at Hyde while she was there. The culture was clearly different now. Maybe this new company culture had something to do with Raymond's less-than-complimentary assessment of her paper?

"Shelley, what did you mean, it was no surprise that a black man and a brown woman would jump ship?"

Shelley plucked a grilled octopus tentacle from the shared plate in the middle of the table and popped it in her mouth. She seemed to hesitate for moment. Finally, she smiled. "I hate to badmouth the company, but it's hard not to see what's right in front of my nose, right?"

Amira nodded.

"Jim Prescott has made a lot of changes in his divisions. Magically, senior and team-lead roles have been found for all the white men under him. Tori and Trevor left when they realized they wouldn't get promotions."

Jesus Christ. Racist as well as sexist?

"I'm in HR," Shelley continued, "so I know the guys who got promotions *were* qualified. But they weren't the only ones qualified, you know? We're talking *six* roles—the optics don't look good. And I'll bet in the new sound-reduction division, the senior roles will go to good old boys like Jim, too. While the women do the grunt work."

This was worse than she'd thought. Raymond hadn't mentioned Jim had a preference for white men.

Wait . . . Amira hesitated. *What sound-reduction division?*

"Shelley, what are you talking about?"

Shelley frowned. "You don't know about that? They're launching a big new division under Jim's umbrella. Sound and vibration reduction. There'll be a few senior consultants and a bunch of juniors. Job postings go up next week."

Amira felt a churning in her stomach. Her project was in the area of vibration and noise control. The report that Raymond trashed was on that topic. "Does Raymond Chu know about this new division?"

"Everyone knows. Raymond Chu has been angling to get the team-lead role for a while now. He didn't tell you? I figured he'd want you to move divisions with him."

Amira felt the café spin around her. Prior to her lab project, she hadn't thought twice about working in sound reduction, but after all the work she'd just done, she knew a fair bit about the field, certainly enough to apply for a senior position in the division. And Raymond knew that, since he had read her project report. But he hadn't told her about it. Because he wanted the position for himself?

Was this why he had trashed her paper?

It couldn't be a coincidence. If it was, he would have said something about the division when he sent the paper back to her. Maybe he thought that if Jim saw a letter of recommendation for Amira from Professor Kennedy, an engineer he respected, about a project on noise control, she would have a leg up on the position. And maybe he didn't want competition for the role.

The worst part was, she liked the division she was already in. She didn't want to move. And since she was the furthest thing from a white man, she didn't think Jim would give her a senior role there anyway.

Amira swallowed the bitterness rising in her throat. It was possible that Raymond had tried to sabotage both her advancement at work and her final paper for his own self-interest, at the expense of her career, her degree, and their friendship.

"You okay, Amira?"

"Yeah, Shelley, I'm fine. Lost my appetite, though." She pushed the plate of octopus towards her friend. There was no way she could stomach this now.

. . . .

ON THE LONG subway ride home, Amira replayed the conversation with Shelley in her mind, trying to make sense of it all. She wasn't sure what was worse, that the company she loved so much had turned into a petty, toxic work environment, or that Raymond, her friend and mentor, had betrayed her. She hadn't heard back from Dad yet, but she was starting to feel even more confident that there was nothing significantly wrong with her project. And everything wrong with her choice of workplace mentor.

How could she have been so blind to Raymond's true nature? She remembered Duncan's comment when they'd fought. That she was too caught up in hero worship to see that Raymond was no real supporter. Amira closed her eyes, but even the gentle sway of the subway train failed to calm her frayed nerves. She considered calling Reena to meet for drinks. Maybe with strong whiskey and Reena's steady support, she could make sense of all this crap. She was due for a check-in with Reena, anyway—she hadn't told her about the events of the engagement party yet.

But Amira knew it wasn't Reena she wanted to comfort her now. Amira wanted Duncan.

Even though this conversation with Shelley had proven he'd been right when they fought, it was him she wanted to console her, to discuss the situation with, and to reassure her that everything would end up okay. And damn, wasn't that a monumental shift in Amira's entire world view. She'd had boyfriends before, but she had never felt the urge to lay herself open to a man when she needed comfort. This was new ground for her, but Amira was in no state to analyze it. She picked up her pace on the walk home from the subway station, knowing that everything would feel easier once she was in his arms.

But Duncan wasn't there when Amira walked into the basement family room. She found only Sameer, sitting alone on the sofa.

"Where is everyone?" Amira said, joining him.

"Travis is in the bathroom, trimming Barrington's hair for tomorrow. Duncan went to pick up his niece in Omemee."

Right. Amira had forgotten about the sleepover. "How are you doing?" Amira asked.

"Fine," Sameer said, not lifting his face from the phone in his hands.

"Liar."

He dropped his phone and ran his hand through his hair. "Okay. Terrible. I feel like my world has exploded around me and is still smouldering while I'm expected to carry on as normal. Better?"

Amira shook her head. "I can't believe Travis dumped you."

He winced. "I can. It was a long time coming. I knew he'd grow tired of being with a coward."

Amira looked at him. "No," she said. "You don't get to call my friend a coward. I get it, Sameer. Family gossip, and pressure, and expectations, and fuck it all to hell. But you *are* strong. This isn't your fault. It's just a bad situation."

He rubbed the back of his neck. Amira was already in a terrible mood, but seeing Sameer so heartbroken was even more devastating. She wanted to steal him away from there, where his family wanted one thing from him and Travis wanted another. Plus, the damn competition, and the pressure to win the thing. It was too much.

"I don't get how you can still do the competition," she said.

He stared vacantly at the empty wall. "It's not fair to the others to pull out now. We'll get through it. At least with Justine coming, I don't have to suffer through four and a half hours alone with him on the drive home. I'm moving back in with my mom. Travis never has to see me again, if that's what he wants."

Amira's gut twisted. "That's not what he wants, but what do you want, Sameer?"

He didn't say anything for a while, just kept staring at the empty wall. Finally, he turned and looked at her, eyes wide and glistening. "Same thing I've always wanted. Him. But . . ." He looked down at his hands folded in his lap. "I can't be who he wants me to be."

She didn't say anything. There was no point, really. Amira was terrible at supportive pep talks because she refused to express any trite platitudes. She could say, *He'll come around* or *Maybe he'll wait for when you're ready*, but Sameer knew the truth. He was the one who needed to act if there was going to be any happily-ever-after for him and Travis. Doing nothing and hoping Travis would change his mind wasn't going to fix a damn thing. And even then, there was no guarantee for the future. It would be cruel to promise otherwise.

Amira slouched back on the couch, her head resting heavily on the cushion behind her.

"You seem like you're having a shitty day, too," Sameer said.

Amira snorted. "That's an understatement. I just had lunch with a work friend, and it looks like Duncan was right. My mentor *is* apparently trying to sabotage me. Probably because he thinks I want a job that he wants. Why is everyone an asshole lately?"

"Damn. I'm sorry, Amira."

"Yeah. You know, Sameer, I wish someone had told us back when we were little that adulting sucks. That there would always be piles of crap in our way that we cannot control."

Sameer was silent for a while, probably thinking about the steaming piles of crap that had recently gotten in the way of his happy life.

He finally turned to her. "What are you going to do?"

"What do you mean?"

"About your job, you going to confront your mentor?"

"Don't know." She stood. "But first, I am going to go over my paper again. Do some more research to confirm that I am right about this stuff before confronting anyone." She exhaled. "It's going to be a long night." She started walking towards her room.

"I'll tell the guys to leave you alone," Sameer said as she walked away.

CHAPTER TWENTY-SIX

AMIRA WAS DIGGING through obscure engineering journals online when there was a knock at the door. Jesus Christ, they were already bugging her? Unless, maybe Duncan was back?

She opened the door. It wasn't Duncan, but Barrington.

"Sorry to bother you, but we're having a bit of a situation out there. I think you need to come . . ."

What now? She followed Barrington out to the family room where she found Sameer and Travis on either side of a teary-faced Zahra.

Amira rushed to her sister and knelt on the floor in front of her. "Zahra, Squish, what's wrong?" She took her sisters hands.

Her sister sniffled and choked back another sob before speaking. "Maddie's not coming to sleep over."

"Oh no. Sweetie, I'm sorry. But that's okay, you guys can plan a sleepover another time, right? Is she not feeling well?"

"That's not it, Amira," Sameer said. He had his arm around Zahra's shoulder, but she couldn't miss the fury in his eyes.

"Why, then?" Amira asked Zahra.

"She texted me. She said her dad didn't want her sleeping at a Muslim's house."

Amira stared blankly at her baby sister.

"He said people like us are what's wrong with Canada," Zahra continued. "He told her Maddie wasn't allowed to be friends with terrorists."

Her heart was pounding and her knees gave out as her bottom hit the floor. "She really wrote that?"

Travis was holding Zahra's phone and handed it to Amira. She read the series of texts. In the terrible grammar of a ten-year-old, Maddie Galahad relayed everything her father had told her, calling Zahra a terrorist and much worse. It was vile. How could a child say this to another child?

Amira squeezed her eyes shut. *They were just words*. She could feel her heart racing, but she needed to collect herself. Mind spinning, she screen-captured the messages and forwarded the images to herself before deleting them from her sister's account. She didn't want Zahra to ever see those disgusting messages again. She put the phone on the floor. Once she could be sure she wouldn't completely lose it, Amira took Zahra's hands again and looked at the sad face belonging to the person she loved more than anyone in the world.

"I'm sorry, Zahra. I guess Maddie and her father aren't as nice as we thought they were. But they don't know the truth about us, right? Remember, we talked about this before. Some people just don't understand Muslims because they don't know any of us. But it's *their* loss. Maddie's giving up the chance to have the most awesome friend in the world because she can't look past her prejudices."

Zahra sniffled. "I know, Amira. But it was just a sleepover. Mum bought popcorn and purple nail polish. We were going to watch that ballet movie."

"Tell you what, the boys here have to practise tonight for their competition, so how about I come sleep over in your room tonight. I can do your nails, and I'll watch the movie with you. Maybe we'll even make some cookies. Does that sound good?"

Zahra's forehead wrinkled, then she nodded. Amira relaxed. "Okay. Let me get some work done on my paper, then I'll come up for dinner and we'll start our sleepover. Okay?"

"Okay," Zahra said before taking her phone and slowly walking up the stairs.

"Shit." Amira fell backwards on the floor as soon as her sister was gone and lay there with her hands over her face. It was just words. Images flitted through her mind, and she shoved them away with the crumb of strength she was able to muster.

"Poor Zahra," Barrington said from the armchair behind her.

She ran her hand over her hair. "Where's Duncan?"

"He should be home soon," Travis said. "I guess he'll be here empty-handed."

Amira sat up. "Maddie Galahad is ten years old. Where the hell would she get crap like that anyway? She was out with Zahra and me all day when we went to the ballet, and now suddenly she's Islamophobic?"

"Obviously her father," Sameer said. "And maybe Ryan didn't know you were Muslim when he agreed to the ballet."

But Duncan knew. Did he also know his brother was a bigot? That little Maddie would parrot everything Daddy said?

Another wave of nausea took hold. She gritted her teeth. "I need to speak to Duncan."

"Duncan doesn't think that way," Travis said. "His brother might, but you have to understand they're from a really tiny town. There's not a lot of diversity out there."

"No." Amira stood up. "No. I am so done with giving excuses to people who treat us like shit. If they can't get their heads out of their own asses long enough to realize we are *real people*, with *real feelings*, then I don't have to waste any more of my emotional effort to try to understand them."

The side door opened, and heavy footsteps came down the stairs. Duncan was back.

"Amira, good. We need to talk."

She looked at him. "Yeah? Go ahead, I'd love to hear what you have to say for yourself."

"Um"—he looked around at the rest of his quartet sitting in the family room—"can we go to your room?"

"No. I want your friends to hear this. After all, they were kind enough to comfort my crying sister after your niece called her a terrorist."

"What?!" he said.

Amira stepped closer to Duncan. "Your *niece* called my sister a *terrorist*. Here, look." She cued up the screen-shots on her phone and handed it to Duncan. His face whitened as he read them.

He lowered his hand and took a step backwards, hitting the wall behind him. "Shit . . . I'm sorry, Amira." He paused. "What the hell . . . I'm going to have more words with Ryan about this. It's what I wanted to talk to you about. When I got to Omemee, Ryan said he didn't want Maddie to go, and it didn't take long to figure out why."

She took her phone back from him. "And . . ."

He looked at his friends again, who were still watching silently. "Can't we talk about this alone?"

"No. I think we all need to hear this. After all, your group is quite multicultural—you have blacks, browns, and . . ." She turned to Travis.

"Just white. Half English, half French-Canadian," he replied.

"I'm not racist, Amira. You of all people should know that," Duncan said, voice rising.

She threw her right hand in the air. "Why me of all people? Because you were willing to have sex with me? People like you are never racist when it means getting some hot Indian ass! We wrote the Kama Sutra, you know. Tantric sex, that's all Indian. I don't blame you for wanting some of that action. You must have been over the moon when you discovered I'm not exactly vanilla in the bedroom." She stepped even closer to him, fists tight, boiling with rage. "But when it comes to letting your kids associate with us, on the other hand . . ."

"Amira, it was my *brother* who didn't want Maddie to come! Not me. I had nothing to do with it! I just got into a big row with him over this. I was furious. I'm not like him."

Amira closed her eyes and tried to calm herself. "I know you're not," she said finally, between clenched teeth. "But I don't really know who you *are* either. I've only known you for a few weeks, and I didn't know your family felt this way."

Duncan was silent a few breaths. "I've always been the black sheep in my family. One of the only liberals. I've tried to get them to see things my way, and I try to be a better influence for Maddie." He paused. "I've performed with all types of people, and so many of my students are from different cultures. Even refugees. I'm not like my family, I promise, please . . ."

"But you knew they felt this way?"

He looked down at his feet. "Yes, I knew. It's a small town, most of my family drank that right-wing Kool-Aid years ago. Ryan's not fond of all my gay friends either. But he doesn't say that stuff in front of Maddie."

"He obviously does! I can't believe you would let me take Zahra to spend the day with Maddie without warning me she may say something like this! Zahra's just a kid! And Ryan was here, in my house!" Her voice started to crack. She paused to collect herself. "You know I've been trying to shelter her from this crap. And you let me invite her to sleep over! After everything I told you . . . the harassment I went through, the trolls, the pictures. I can't believe—"

"I didn't know Maddie would say this stuff to Zahra." His voice rose again. "So many people have misconceptions because they don't know people like you. I thought maybe if they met you—"

"It's not my fucking job to be some Muslim ambassador!"

He said nothing. Duncan was finally speechless. He stared at her, those beautiful green eyes wide.

"It shouldn't take knowing me to understand that I'm a human being," she said.

They stared at each other for several seconds. Amira's mind flashed to the memories of the night before, how amazing it had been to sleep in his arms. How amazing it had been when he was in complete contact with her body as they made love.

Because that's what they did—they made love. It had never been just sex. She hadn't understood how complex a physical act could be until Duncan. Devastatingly real and completely present. She'd never felt so connected in her life. She'd felt *seen*. But he hadn't seen her. Not really. If he had, he wouldn't have exposed her to this.

It was impossible to accept, but the truth was that Duncan wasn't different from any of them out there. He was compassionate, but not enough. He was empathetic, but only to a point.

She met his eyes. He had never looked like this before. Not his usual argumentative self. No trace of snark on his face. He looked wrecked, and completely devastated. She had won this fight and had never felt worse.

She sat down between Sameer and Travis. "You may not think like them, but you excuse them," she said quietly. "You live with them. You put me and my family in their line of fire. You prefer to surround yourself with intolerance because it's an easier life, and you just tell yourself, *Well, at least I don't think like them. At least I'm more enlightened than my family*." Amira wiped a rogue tear that escaped as Sameer put his hand on her knee.

The room was silent. All noise in this basement for the last week and a half wasn't nearly as deafening as this silence.

"Complacency isn't enough for me," she said. "To you, it's just a liberal/conservative issue. Right wing versus left wing. But we are *real people*, and our mere existence has become political. Your family and their so-called conservative values hurt my little sister. She's eleven years old, struggling for acceptance, and discovering her self-worth. And Maddie told her she's worth less because of her race and religion. This isn't some ideology to Zahra, it's just who she is. And all she wanted was a sleepover with a new friend. But life can't be that simple for her, not because of her identity, but because of people like your brother." Amira swallowed. "And that's why there's no future for us. Not a friendship, not more. I don't blame you for your family, I know you don't feel that way. But you don't fight it either. And I can't be around that. I don't want me, or my family, to be reminded of the hate. It's destroying us, Duncan."

He looked at her, expression absolutely broken. "I don't know what to say . . ."

Amira stood, not meeting his eyes. "I have to work on my project. I won't be here later because I have a sleepover to go to. You guys rehearse as long as you want tonight, it won't bother me."

She left the room without turning around.

CHAPTER TWENTY-SEVEN

SHAKING, AMIRA SAT on the edge of her bed.

Her mind was spinning. Her report—she should work on her project. After wiping away another tear, she sat at her desk and stared at her computer. She couldn't concentrate.

She stood up again, pushing her heavy limbs that wanted to hold her in place, and stopped in the middle of her room. The house was so quiet. No one talking. No cheerful singing. Not even any arguing. Only the loud ticking of the damn clock on her wall. Amira pulled it down and yanked the batteries out of it.

She placed the clock heavily in the corner of her room, next to Duncan's bag. The dark green duffel bag was open, showing her a peek of his worn blue jeans and one of his many flannel shirts. Duncan had moved his things into her room only yesterday, and already his stuff was strewn about as if it had always been here. His shaving kit in the bathroom, complete with cedar-scented beard oil. His plaid pyjama pants tossed on the chair. Even the guitar she loaned him was leaning up against the corner of the room. He had fiddled with it every day, sometimes singing softly while playing simple chords, other times letting his fingers glide effortlessly over the frets into complicated arrangements. Duncan was talented. She loved watching him play.

Amira packed his things into his bag and left them in the hallway, along with the guitar. She didn't think it was necessary to tell him she didn't want him sleeping in her room anymore.

Once her space was tidy, she stood in the middle of the room again. She needed something else to do. Something else to distract her from her thoughts. Her mind was racing in circles, a sharp stab of pain in her chest muddling everything.

Betrayed. That's how she felt. Betrayed by the fucked-up world that had normalized bigotry. Her logic hadn't left her— she understood that it wasn't really Duncan's fault that his brother and niece had hurt Zahra, but she still felt betrayed by him. She knew they came from different worlds, but it hadn't occurred to her that Duncan's world actively hated hers. He should have told her that. He should have told her that involving herself with him would mean constantly fighting against hate.

But one image wouldn't leave her mind: the anguished look on Duncan's face when she walked away from him. It was in sharp contrast to the man she had grown so close to. It wasn't much of a consolation to know that he was probably hurting right now, too, but at least it confirmed that her feelings for him weren't one-sided.

Another image popped into her head: the priceless look on his face when he'd tied himself up with his own suspenders last night. It was a mixture of pride, arousal, and mischief that was so quintessentially Duncan. No man had ever been willing to be so vulnerable with her. No one had ever understood what Amira wanted. Or needed. She had finally found someone who got her.

But no. He didn't get her. He didn't get why it hurt so much that her existence was nothing but a political issue to some people. And he didn't get how important it was for her to shield her family, her little sister, from the realities of this world for as long as possible.

Sameer said to fight for the good—the best—relationship. Well, this was not something she could fight for. This was the big thing she couldn't compromise on.

Amira's text tone rang, startling her. It was Reena.

> **Reena**
> Can you take a break from your new man and meet me at the Sparrow? I want to hear about the fancy party.

> **Amira**
> There is no more new man. His family thinks we're terrorists and made Zahra cry. I promised her a sleepover, I have to stay in.

> **Reena**
> Oh crap. You need me to bring my sleeping bag and join you?

Amira almost wrote back that, no, she was fine, she didn't need her best friend's comfort after the combustion of a relationship that was only days old, but her fingers stilled over her phone. The truth was, she was not fine. About Duncan, about her conversation earlier with Shelley, and about Sameer and Travis. And maybe there was nothing wrong with leaning on her friend when the universe seemed to be conspiring to shatter everything she cared about.

Amira

Yes. Please. I need you.

Finally, it was time to go upstairs for dinner. Amira packed a small bag of things since she had no intention of coming back downstairs until the barbershop quartet left her home. She couldn't face any of them right now.

Duncan's bag had been removed from the hallway, and she didn't see anyone around. Good.

Dinner with her family felt strange. Zahra seemed to have snapped back from her earlier disappointment reasonably well. She didn't mention Maddie at all and seemed excited that Amira was going to sleep in her room, but it was an act. Zahra's enthusiasm was muted. Forced. It broke Amira's heart all over again. Every time Zahra had to face these small fights, these little injustices, Amira's spitfire sister would become just a little bit more muted, a little less herself. It was a tough pill to swallow. Amira hoped that the likes of Ryan Galahad wouldn't dim her sister's light any more than this.

CHAPTER TWENTY-EIGHT

REENA SHOWED UP halfway through the meal, a platter of sticky buns in one hand and a sleeping bag in the other.

"These were waiting in my freezer for the call of an emergency slumber party," she said solemnly to Zahra.

Zahra smiled. Reena, clearly understanding Amira's subtle cues, didn't ask any questions or even mention Duncan or his family while she joined them for some of Nanima's delectable curries. After eating, they changed into their pyjamas, popped popcorn, and settled in the living room to watch the ballet movie.

Amira whispered to Reena once the movie was on. "Thanks for coming."

"No problem at all. I was glad to get out of the house." Reena put a handful of popcorn in her mouth.

"Is Saira still reeling? You said you thought the battle was coming to a head."

Reena smiled with a swell of pride as she finished chewing. "Oh yeah, she's reeling. She's even more pissed now because she's *moving out*."

Amira's hand shot to her mouth. "What?"

"I asked her to leave last night. And, shockingly, she agreed. She's moving back in with our parents."

"Oh my god, Ree, that's amazing! Way to go! You stood up to her!"

Reena's grin widened. "I did. You should have seen me. Although—"

A knock at the front door startled them. Nanima and Mum had gone to Jamatkhana, so Amira paused the movie and answered the door.

Surprisingly, it was Travis, holding a tray of cupcakes and a tote bag.

"Cupcakes!" Zahra squealed.

He grinned. "Hi, Zahra. I thought you might want a special hairdo for your slumber party?"

"Yes! Amira, can he stay? I want him to braid my hair again . . ."

"Sure." Amira smiled, letting Travis in.

"I hope I'm not out of line here," he said, removing his shoes and walking into the living room, "but I went to the drugstore and picked up some hair dye. How would you like some pink streaks in your hair, Zahra?"

Amira's eyes bugged out.

"Permanent pink streaks?" Reena asked.

"I bought temporary dye," Travis assured. "It washes right out. But I also bought the permanent stuff. I'll have to bleach her hair first for that, but the colour will be much brighter."

Amira shook her head. "You are not bleaching my sister's hair without getting my mother's permission."

"Can you ask her?" he asked.

Zahra's phone was in her hand immediately. "I'm texting

Mum. I know she'll say yes . . . Olivia dyed her hair purple and Mum said it looked cute."

After a few texts back and forth, Mum texted Amira for more information. Eventually they had the approval. Mum was happy a real stylist was doing it, unlike Olivia's botched job. She also probably wanted to cheer Zahra up a bit. Hopefully Zahra wouldn't discover she could get whatever she wanted from any of them tonight.

An hour and a half later, Zahra was as happy as a frolicking unicorn in a meadow, with wide pink streaks in hair that Travis had blow-dried straight.

"I love it!" she said, hugging him. "Thank you, thank you, thank you! It's better than Olivia's. I look amazing!"

"You look gorgeous, Zahra," Reena said. "You have to do mine one day, Travis."

Zahra did look amazing. It brought tears to Amira's eyes to see how happy her sister was. She looked towards the kitchen, blinking. "How about we get those cupcakes and sticky buns now, Zahra. Can you put them on plates while Travis and I clean up here?"

Zahra bounded towards the kitchen, grinning ear to ear.

"Thank you," Amira said to Travis as soon as her sister was gone. "You don't know how happy you've made her. Thank you so much."

He grinned, putting his hair dryer in his tote bag. "I was happy to do it. I needed the distraction. And you should thank all of us. The four of us came up with this idea together. We wanted to put a smile on her face again."

"Well, it worked. And I'm sure the cupcakes will work, too," Amira said.

"Those were all Duncan. He left right after you went into your room earlier and came back an hour later with those."

Amira looked away.

"He's really sorry, Amira," Travis said.

"I'm still not exactly sure what happened," Reena said, confused.

"I'll tell you in a bit." She turned to Travis. "You want to stick around and watch a ballet movie with us, or are you guys still rehearsing?"

He shook his head. "No, we're done. I'll stay. It's awkward as all hell down there. Sameer and I are barely speaking, and Duncan's moping around like a sad puppy. A movie might be just the ticket." He smiled sadly as he reached back into his tote bag. "I have this, too." He pulled out a green bottle with a gold-foil-capped cork. "Prosecco. I bought this bottle to celebrate Sameer finally telling his grandmother about me. Tonight we'll both celebrate our miserable new status as single instead."

Reena looked back and forth between Travis and Amira. "Single? You and Sameer broke up? Jesus, Amira, it's only been a day since we spoke! What the hell is going on?"

The ballet movie was terrible. Zahra sat on the floor, close to the TV, away from Amira, Reena, and Travis on the couch, since she'd declared her big sister and her friends had no taste in movies. It was convenient, as it gave Travis and Amira the opportunity to get Reena up to speed on the basement barbershop drama—all over elegant flutes of sparkling wine, sticky buns, popcorn, and cupcakes. Reena's eyes widened when Amira got to the part about the terrorist accusations, but Amira shook her head slightly, wordlessly letting her friend know she didn't want to go deeper on this, yet.

"So," Amira said, turning to Travis with a hushed voice, "things can't be that bad if you and Sameer are talking today."

Travis frowned. "We're trying. We still want to win the competition, but . . . *ugh*. We'll be together all day tomorrow, too. Can I recommend *not* spending two days non-stop with a man you just broke up with?" He paused, watching the film for a few seconds. "But who knows, maybe this'll make it easier to stay friends after. It will be a slow and painful torture, but I can't imagine cutting him out completely. I want Sameer in my life, as a friend."

"But not more than friends?" Reena asked.

He squeezed his lips together. "No. Not more. I can't budge on this." He paused to sip his wine. "I guess it's a lot like you and Duncan, isn't it? Sameer and Duncan are not willing to stand up to their families, and we both know we're too good for that."

"Maybe, but you and Sameer were together for a year and a half, me and Duncan had three days," Amira said.

"The past doesn't matter. We both lost the potential for a future."

Reena took another cupcake from the tray on the coffee table. They looked delicious, but Amira wouldn't eat something bought with Duncan's guilt. The sticky buns were enough.

"There must be a way, Travis," Reena said. "You two are so perfect together."

"It's a lost cause," he said. "Sameer doesn't understand why I can't wait anymore. Don't get me wrong, I totally understand his struggle, and I'm honestly not forcing him to be out if he's not ready. I just . . . it feels like he's ashamed of me, sometimes." His eyes closed momentarily before he faced Amira, shoulders squaring. "It's like you said to Duncan, complacency isn't enough for *me*. It may be fine for others to live with secrecy, but it's not right for me. He won't even post a picture of us together on social media. He's always preoccupied with what others will say." Travis looked towards the door leading to the basement. "He says it should be enough that he loves me, but it's not. I want more. I *deserve* more. And he deserves it even more than I do."

Amira leaned back in her seat and raised her half-empty flute glass. "Here's to not being anyone's family secret." She drained the glass, the cool bubbles tingling on the way down her throat. "I wish there was a way to make it okay for you, though."

"Yeah," Reena said. "I can't believe Sameer's family would be so rude about this. No one in my family gave two shits when my cousin Marley told us she's bi. Except my mother. But then, my mother thinks bare shoulders are an affront to humanity, so . . ." Reena drained her glass. "Poor quartet. Is Barrington happy at least?"

Amira giggled, feeling light-headed. "He looked terrified to see Zahra crying. I think he wanted to buy her a kitten."

Travis took another bite of his sticky bun and chewed while looking appreciatively at Amira. "You were fierce earlier. I wanted to stand and applaud after you tore into Duncan. Never seen anyone shrink so small. But I think a standing ovation wouldn't have been appropriate. He is our baritone, after all. I think I'm supposed to be on his side." His eyes narrowed conspiratorially. "What did you mean by *not exactly vanilla in the bedroom*?"

Amira laughed silently and slapped him lightly on the shoulder. "We'll talk later. Not in front of Zahra."

They watched the movie for a bit, before they wrinkled their noses and turned to each other again. Terrible.

"Oh, I wanted to ask you, are you still coming tomorrow?" Travis asked.

"I wasn't planning on it."

"No. You have to come. It would mean a lot to us. All of us. And . . . you don't have to worry about Sameer's family. You dumped him earlier today."

"I did?" Amira laughed.

"Yeah, but you've decided to stay friends. Sameer called his grandmother and told her not to make a fuss over you at the show. He thought she may listen if you dumped him first."

"That was the easiest breakup I've ever had. Way easier than . . ." She paused, thinking about Duncan. She bit her lip. "He's going to be there, isn't he? Duncan's brother."

"Yup. And that's why you should come. Let's normalize this shit. Gays and Muslims all singing and being happy together. Let's show him what we're really like."

"I'll come, too, Meer," Reena said. "Let's fill that hall up with so much brown love that maybe the bigots will get scared and leave."

She wished Ryan wasn't going, but this ridiculous barbershop quartet had come to mean a lot to her, and this could be one of the last times she saw them. She wanted to see the performance they had been working on so hard. She wanted to celebrate their accomplishment with them.

Amira sat up straighter. "Okay. I may regret it, but I want to go. For you."

Later, after Travis left and Zahra was snoring softly on the top bunk above them, Amira and Reena huddled together in the bottom bunk so they could finally really talk about what had happened to Amira and Zahra.

"I can't even believe it. Poor Zahra. You think she'll be okay?" Reena asked.

"Yeah, the pink hair helped. She won't ever forget what her friend called her, but I'm sure it won't be the only time she'll be called a terrorist." Amira squeezed the pillow on her lap. "I can't believe Duncan's brother would spew that nonsense to his child."

"What's his name? I'm googling him." Reena pulled her phone out of her bag.

"Ryan Galahad."

"If he says it in front of his child, I'm sure he's vocal to others online. And . . . yup. You do *not* want to see his Twitter." She scrolled through silently, wisely not showing the Twitter feed to Amira. "Jesus, he really believes this stuff? Whatever happened to common sense? Ugh. I can't believe your lumberjack is related to this . . . *thing*."

"I know. And he's not my lumberjack anymore."

"So, his family is a complete deal breaker? You guys were so hot for each other."

"I can't work through this. He lives with his brother. They're close."

"Such a shame. Duncan is your manic pixie dream . . . man."

What the hell was Reena talking about this time? "What?"

"Manic pixie dream girl is a plot device, a trope in rom-coms. A girl, or in your case, a man, whose quirky personality and love of life teaches the stodgy hero how to enjoy life," Reena said.

"I'm stodgy?"

"Sometimes."

Amira shook her head. "Pixie or gnome, or whatever, I can't look at him without thinking his family hates me for no real reason. I just can't."

"If you're going to rule out anyone who has Islamophobic family members, you won't have many men left in North America," Reena said sadly.

"I know. Remember, I wanted to find a boyfriend from inside our culture for that reason." She frowned, squeezing her pillow tighter. "And it's more than just that with Duncan." Amira turned to face the bright-purple door in her sister's bedroom, feeling her chest tighten. "If he'd only told me about them. I don't know, I feel like he hid this from me intentionally."

"If you'd known about his family, would you have started anything with him?"

"I don't know. Probably. Would've been nice to have that dialogue, you know? He had plenty of opportunities to tell me; we had a lot of conversations about this stuff. At least I would have known what I was getting into. And I would have kept Zahra away from his family."

Reena was silent for a bit, then frowned. "The Galahad brothers are not brave knights, after all. Bunch of man-boys."

"Yeah. And we're going to see them both tomorrow."

"You sure you want to go? You don't owe them anything."

"Yeah, I do want to. For Travis and Sameer, mostly. Travis is right. We need to normalize this shit. I'm done letting bigots prevent me from doing what I want."

"It sucks, though. I still can't believe he let you call him farm boy. You'd think someone willing to role-play *The Princess Bride* would be an automatic keeper. Not to mention he learned to make your chai."

"Yeah, but that was just because he discovered his own love of masala chai." She paused, thinking. "Anyone ever examine the power dynamics in that movie? The farm boy has no choice but to do whatever Buttercup wants. He's her bloody servant. And it's all made out to be this great act of love."

Reena smiled. "It *is* an act of love. He still obeys when he's a pirate. It's not the words, Amira, it's the way he looks at her. He sees more than just the spoiled princess. He always did. He sees what she needs."

Amira blinked, hearing the melancholy in Reena's voice. Reena really deserved to find her own happily-ever-after. Soon. They both deserved it. She rested on her friend's shoulder and sighed. "Well, I guess we see the truth now. Duncan Galahad was no farm boy."

CHAPTER TWENTY-NINE

AMIRA'S PHONE RANG early the next morning, waking her. Her father.

"Oh my god, what time is it?" Reena mumbled as Amira answered the call.

"Morning, Dad," Amira grumbled.

"Daddy!" Zahra yelped from the top bunk.

Her father chuckled. "Zahra's with you?"

"Yeah, I slept in her room. Here, you'd better talk to her first."

After Zahra told their father all about their sleepover and her new pink hair, she dangled her arm over the edge of her bed to hand Amira her phone, then hopped down the ladder and pulled Reena out of bed to find Mum and breakfast.

"Pink hair, Amira?" Dad asked.

"Mum said yes."

"I'm sure she did, but"—he paused—"that's a fight for another day. I woke up early today to go over your paper with you. I've finished my review of it."

Amira's chest tightened with nerves. "Well, what did you think?"

"Honestly? I was a proud papa reading it. It is very good, Amira."

"Really?"

"Yes, really. I made some notes, little things you can fix. I've emailed them to you. Overall, I can't see why your professor wouldn't accept this. You've done an excellent job."

Amira fell back onto her pillow, body going slack. "Oh, I am so relieved. Did you see Raymond's notes?"

"I didn't agree with his assessment. I'm sure if you reworked your algorithms to address his concerns, it would be good, too, but that doesn't mean the report isn't excellent as is. I disagree with his opinion that you are beyond your scope. You've clearly demonstrated comprehension of your topic. You took a direct but novel approach to solve the problem. Maybe Raymond expected a more conventional solution, but that's not why you're doing this master's degree. I'm not convinced your applications are impractical."

She listened to him speak more about her algorithms and suggestions for some extra real-world applications to add, all while a warmth radiated from her core. There was nothing like praise from her father. A huge part of why she'd decided to do this master's program was her hope to be more like him. Always so smart, so capable. But then she struggled in the program and avoided sending him any of her school work or grades because she knew she wasn't living up to his high standards.

But this time, she was. He was proud of her.

"Thank you, Dad. Seriously, I'm so glad you like it."

"It's not a matter of like, Amira. You know what you're talking about, and it shows. In fact, I'd seriously consider hiring you for a position in noise control. I know the president of a firm in Toronto that specializes in that area. Would you like me to see if he has a place for you there?"

"No, it's fine. I . . ." Amira paused. "I don't really want to specialize in acoustics. Hyde is actually starting up a new sound-reduction division, but I think I'm caught in some office politics there."

"It's a booming field. And if you're having problems at Hyde, now is a good time to move on. Let me ask my friend Robert, he may at least know of—"

"No, Dad, it's fine. Thank you." She valued her father's opinion but she needed to solve this herself. She still wasn't sure if it was time yet to leave the company she had loved.

"Is something else wrong?" he asked. "You sound down."

Amira paused. Should she tell Dad what happened with Duncan? "Yeah, I had a terrible day yesterday, not just because of this work crap. Can I ask you something?"

"Of course."

"Since you've been in the US, are the people there, you know, friendly to you?"

"Honestly, yes. Everyone here has been so kind. I have more workplace friends in Philadelphia than I ever had in Toronto."

"Are there a lot of, you know, conservatives there? Do they accept you?"

"If you're asking if I've had any problems because I'm a Muslim, no, not personally. Philadelphia is primarily liberal, and quite multicultural. I have found that most who have a problem with Muslims haven't had the chance to get to know any."

"Yeah, I guess that's true here, too."

Dad was quiet a moment before speaking. "Amira, what you went through last year was traumatic. It's no wonder you're still affected by it. It's wrong for people to distrust us, but they're being told by people who look like them that *we* are the enemy. It's a dangerous time for Muslims, but I have to believe that even if humanity as a whole is bad right now, individual people are not. I fully believe we are seeing a shift—and that the value of increased diversity, starting in the workplace, is finally being recognized. Variety is the spice of life! Can you imagine curry made with only one spice?"

Typical Dad. Profound, intelligent, caring. Amira missed him so much. "I know, Dad, but I'm tired of excusing this. I don't care anymore *why* someone is intolerant. I just . . ." She sighed. "Anyway, I'll take a look at your email. Thanks for doing this for me. Love you, Dad."

"I love you too, Amira. We need to discuss plans for the summer, but get your paper in first. And once again, well done."

Amira lay in the bottom bunk of her sister's bed for some time. Her mind was swirling with contrasting feelings of relief that her father liked her paper and anger at Raymond for wasting so much of her time. And, of course, disappointment with Duncan and his family. Dad said some people just needed to get to know a Muslim. Well, Duncan *knew* her. At least, she thought he did.

Finally, she forced herself to get up. She found Zahra and Reena kneading dough in the kitchen.

"She's teaching me to make those sticky cinnamon buns we had last night," Zahra said.

Amira smiled. "Sounds delicious. I'm just going to get some chai, then can I use your desk to work, Zahra?"

Zahra nodded as Amira poured a cup from the pot simmering on the stove.

"You work. I'll stay with Zahra until it's time for us to go," Reena said, waving Amira out of the room.

Amira set up her computer in her sister's bedroom and started going over her dad's notes. His points were valid. There were things she could have included but didn't, and a few arguments that were redundant. He thought her research was sound and the rationale for her approach was appropriate. And Dad knew his stuff. He had more education, and more experience in the field, than Raymond. She added one more quick analysis as the finishing touch to the report.

While working, her mind stayed fixated on Raymond. She still didn't know what the hell had happened there. Dad said that he agreed with many of Raymond's points about her work, and he thought the paper would work as well if she redid it according to Raymond's suggestions. Maybe he wasn't trying to sabotage her after all. Perhaps just the opposite—he wanted to challenge her to lift her work to a higher standard and maybe prove she could implement practical solutions at Hyde. Maybe he did want her to move to the new division with him, and he knew a great project would impress Jim enough to allow her transfer.

But if that were the case, why hadn't he told her about the division? What would be the point of hiding it from her? Her return-to-work date was after the internal job postings would be taken down. She would have missed this opportunity altogether if Shelley hadn't told her. Would she have come back to see Raymond leading the new division? What would he have said to her?

She pushed these thoughts out of her head. Her only priority right now was to get the damn report ready to submit tomorrow, then worry what the hell she was going to do about her job.

Amira stayed upstairs and worked until she heard the boys leave for the competition, then she went down to her room to change. Reena would be back soon to pick her up. Amira needed to mentally prepare herself to face Duncan again.

· · · ·

THE ONTARIO REGION Barbershop Quartet Competition was held in a theatre north of the city, one of those medium-sized concert halls that local schools and amateur theatre groups rented. The crowd was bigger than expected, and Amira was glad she saw no one she knew as they walked in.

"Hi, you're Amira and Reena, right?" an unfamiliar voice behind her said.

Amira turned to see a small woman with tightly curled bobbed hair and a yellow sundress. She had one of those faces that could be anywhere between sixteen and twenty-nine years old.

"I'm Marcia, Barrington's girlfriend," she continued. "Well, I guess, fiancée. I'm still getting used to that. He showed me a picture of you two, at a brewpub."

Marcia was cute, but she looked about the size of Barrington's left femur. "Hi, Marcia. Yeah, I'm Amira, this is Reena."

"Can I sit with you? I don't know anyone else here."

"Of course. Let's go find seats."

As they made their way down the aisle, someone else called Amira's name, motioning them over to their row. It was Shirin and one of Sameer's aunties.

Damn.

Amira smiled, knowing she really didn't have a choice but to join them. Nanima would hear about it if she didn't, and she wouldn't be thrilled if Amira snubbed her best friend. Thankfully, after squeezing down to the empty seats, Amira found herself sitting next to the aunty, not Shirin. Reena, then Marcia, were on her other side. She scanned the crowd. No sign of Ryan or Maddie. Good. Maybe they'd pulled a no-show. Duncan would be disappointed at that, though, despite everything.

"Amira," Shirin said, leaning over the aunty, "I'm happy you came for Sameer. He told me you're not dating anymore but are still friends."

"I'm friends with all of them. They're good guys." She tried to smile.

"Sameer is such a good boy. Did you know he is a pharmacist? He works so hard, he needs a nice girl like you to take care of him. Maybe . . ."

"Maa, please. Don't embarrass her," Sameer's aunty said. She turned to Amira and smiled. "I'm Tazim. Sameer's mother is my youngest sister. I think we met at the anniversary party? It was great of all Sameer's friends to come."

"It was a lovely party."

"Looks like they're starting," Marcia interrupted.

Amira looked towards the darkened stage. The curtains were open, and the house lights were dimming. Out of the corner of her eye, she saw him. Ryan *was* here, sitting in the same row as her, but on the opposite side of the theatre. And it looked like he was alone. Maddie wasn't with him.

Ryan Galahad. Unassuming and clean-cut. Good-looking, too. Just sitting, waiting for the show to start. Not worrying about anything. Comfortable in the knowledge that he could do or say whatever the hell he wanted to.

Why had she agreed to come to this thing? Her heart rate sped up.

Finally, the master of ceremonies stepped onstage. Or, Amira corrected herself, *masters* of ceremonies. Should she be surprised it was a quartet?

Three older men—two with white hair, one with no hair—and a middle-aged woman. All wearing identical red-and-white-striped blazers, white pants, and red bow ties and holding straw hats. And instead of talking, they were singing.

Because of course they were. This was absurd. Amira looked around. People of all ages filled the crowd, likely friends and family of the competitors. There was also a sizable contingent of millennials, clad in copious amounts of floral prints and plaid, jewel-toned glasses perched on their faces, who were cheering wildly for the quartet on the stage. Weirdly, all that earnest joy had an unexpected effect on Amira—she felt her own heart swell.

"Welcome to the fourteenth annual Ontario Region Barbershop Quartet Competition. Today we have the privilege of showcasing the best of the best in barbershop singing from across Ontario."

A month ago, if someone had told her she would choose to spend the day before her final report was due at a barbershop quartet competition, she would have told them to please share the amazing, psychedelic marijuana they'd been smoking. This was unreal.

The striped crooners took turns singing the rules of the competition. The online process of elimination had narrowed the enormous pool of video applicants down to ten finalists, who would compete today. Each would be given ten minutes onstage, and they could sing as many songs as they wanted to during their time. All group members were required to vocalize in each song.

Amira looked at the program in her hand, noticing right away that Sam I Am What I Am was not listed. But, of course, the guys had told her it was a temporary name. She had no idea what final name they chose. She skimmed the member names listed beneath each group name.

There it was. Her heart skipped a beat to see Duncan's name in print. But the group name . . . her guys were the . . . A-Team? Odd choice. They were on second to last. Oh well. She settled in, making herself comfortable for the long show.

By the fourth group (Tony and The Four-Tones), Amira decided that, although she liked *her* barbershop quartet, she didn't care much for barbershop as a musical genre. It wasn't that the groups up there weren't any good; she just found them all dull. Vanilla. Most of the groups were all men, although some groups had a woman or two. Most sang the same type of songs: old Motown, adult contemporary, or the odd country song. The groups were all identically dressed: the men in suits; the women in either colourful fifties-style dresses or simple all black. All in all, Amira wasn't impressed.

"These guys are all great!" Reena said beside her, foot tapping to the beat. Amira rolled her eyes at her friend.

"Sorry, Miss Too Cool for A Cappella. I'm enjoying it," Reena said.

"Me too!" Marcia added. "I'm so nervous for Barrington. This is the biggest audience he's sung for."

The performances continued to underwhelm until the sixth group took the stage. It was Fourth Fret, the quartet they had gone to see at the brewpub beer festival.

And just like that night, they were good. Really good.

How these four people managed to engage, entertain, and feed off each other as if they were one entity was a mystery. It was magical to watch. Even the songs they chose were unique. They started with "Purple Rain," seamlessly transitioning to a newer song, "Starboy" by the Weeknd, then finishing with a Celine Dion song, of all things. They had the audience on their feet during the finale of "Heart Will Go On," belting out the drawn-out notes with them. Amira thought she saw tears in the audience.

Ugh.

How the hell was the A-Team (she still couldn't get over that ridiculous name) supposed to beat them?

The next group (Rock Me Down Low) were good, too. Maybe not as good as Fourth Fret, but the all-women group's heavy-metal arrangements were surprisingly well done. Metallica's "One" sung a cappella by a barbershop quartet dressed as pin-up models? Sure, why not. Amira was quickly changing her mind about disliking barbershop, realizing all it needed was a little variety. As her father said, what's a curry with only one spice?

Finally, it was time for the A-Team, and the knot in Amira's stomach wouldn't have been tighter if she had been up there on the stage herself. She squeezed her leg tightly as they walked onstage, led by the garden gnome himself.

She swallowed. He looked good. It had only been a day since she'd seen him, but somehow it felt like so much longer. Had Duncan always been so tall? His hair was stylishly trimmed and mussed, and his beard groomed, looking like red flames in the bright stage lighting. No doubt Travis gussied up the boys himself; they all looked neater. A little more polished.

They were dressed identically, like most of the performers, but there was no sequined spandex or even polyester in sight. They all wore the same red plaid shirt (miraculously not flannel), dark jeans, and red sneakers, but Barrington wore an open vest atop his shirt, Travis a black skinny tie, Sameer a black bow tie, and Duncan wore his black suspenders.

Amira clutched her armrest. The last time she'd seen those suspenders, Duncan had been tied up with them. Naked. In her bed.

They walked to the centre of the stage, smiling, and started singing.

They started with "Stand by Me," as expected. And they sounded good. She knew she was biased, but Amira thought their voices sounded stronger than the other groups. Her skin erupted in the usual goosebumps during Duncan's chorus. Their stage presence was on point, too. They looked at each other, they smiled, they fed off each other. There was no indication to the audience that two members of the A-Team had just ended their long, loving relationship. Or that a third member had just been dumped—albeit after only a three-day fling. But she was still shaken up over it, so she figured Duncan might be as well.

But Amira could tell. Sameer and Travis's wide smiles didn't quite reach their eyes. And maybe it was just wistful hoping, but Duncan seemed a tiny bit less *Duncan* than normal. The guys were pros, though—they sounded incredible, and in Amira's completely subjective opinion, they were still one of the better groups, despite the events of the last few days. Apparently "The Show Must Go On" would have been an appropriate song had they decided to sing it today. Her heart shattered a little bit more for her friends.

As they reached the end of "Stand by Me," they all quieted, except Barrington, who was humming a bass note. His voice quieted a bit, and Travis's clear alto voice sang the first lines of "Jolene," successfully getting the name right instead of substituting his sister's name. Amira smiled to herself as the others joined in, singing the Dolly Parton song better than she had heard them practise it. Finally, they slowed again before transitioning to their last song.

The song was "Always Something There to Remind Me," a song that Amira had always thought was an eighties new-wave track. But Duncan had schooled her otherwise on Friday afternoon, informing her it was written in the sixties and recorded by many artists, including Dionne Warwick. Amira hadn't believed him, and it had provoked an exasperating, hilarious argument (and even pillow fight) where neither of them backed down until Duncan hollered for all the guys to come into her room (thankfully at a point when she had clothes on) to set her straight. The memory tightened her chest.

But now, she was struck with the irony of this being their last song, an uptempo track about a lover who is constantly reminded of a lost love, and thus cannot move on. She shivered. The guys sang together, looking out into the audience. And Duncan's gaze was squarely on her. His smooth, deep voice sent their usual jolts right to her core. It felt like he was singing to *her*.

Ridiculous. Of course he wasn't singing it to her. Amira was disgusted at how sentimental she had become. Mere days with Sir Garden Gnome and she was Snow White pining for her prince to come. That he was singing to her was something Reena would assume.

"He's singing to you . . ." Reena said, leaning into Amira's ear, as if on cue.

Amira scoffed and sank lower in her seat.

She peeked over to watch Ryan. He was smiling as his brother sang on the stage. There was visible brotherly affection there. Ryan clapped and sang along like the rest of the audience, tapping his feet, face swelled with pride.

Amira tore her gaze away, looking back at the stage in time to see the A-Team bow.

Duncan smiled, tipped an imaginary hat in her direction, and the guys walked off the stage.

CHAPTER THIRTY

THE FINAL PERFORMANCE was similar to the earlier ones. Four older men dressed in identical blue suits singing fifties classics while snapping and twisting on their toes. Not Amira's cup of tea. In her opinion, this contest was really between Fourth Fret, Rock Me Down Low, and the A-Team. But Amira was well aware that, as an engineer who knew absolutely nothing about barbershop quartets, she wasn't exactly qualified to judge the merit of the contestants.

Reena, apparently, did feel qualified. "I think they have a chance," she whispered in Amira's ear as the final group left the stage.

"Who, these guys? I thought they were dull," Amira said.

"No, the A-Team. I think they'll at least get in the top three."

Amira shrugged. She did hope they would win. But after a split-second reanalysis of her current life choices, Amira didn't want to let on that she was so invested in the plight of a barbershop quartet called the A-Team at the Ontario Region Barbershop Quartet Competition.

She needed to detach herself from this insanity. She needed to examine how these four oddball singers had wedged themselves so completely in her psyche that she was all tied up in knots waiting to find out if they had won their damn singing competition. Maybe it was because this was a strange time in her life, a time of transition: finishing grad school, moving back to Toronto, going back to work. She was just overly emotional because of change. It was stress—that's why she had grown so attached to them. Everything would be fine after the report was submitted. Everything would go back to normal once the guys left.

A sharp stab of pain pierced behind her eyes. God, now she was crying? She needed to get a grip. She rubbed her temples. Soon, the red-striped, straw-hatted woman took the stage alone, without her accompanying group, and spoke instead of sang.

"Thank you to the amazing teams! Let's give another huge round of applause for all the talent and hard work we saw on the stage today! Weren't they all spectacular?" She paused, allowing the audience time to clap. "Now, our esteemed judges are going off-stage to do their scoring magic, and in the meantime, we have a surprise for you—one of the groups you saw today has offered to entertain the audience with one more number while the judges are considering the performances. And . . . in opposition to everything barbershop stands for, they're using an instrument! Now, before we get any angry comments on our live-stream—all nine of the other groups *and* the judges were informed, and they gave their blessings to our bravest of contestants. In fact, most of the other contestants agreed to accompany them onstage. So, it's going to get a bit crowded up here! A big round of applause for the *A-Team*!"

Holy shit. What were the guys up to?

The stage did get crowded. About thirty singers, aged eighteen through eighty, walked onstage, standing on the edges to make room for the A-Team. As earlier, Duncan walked on first, but this time, instead of walking empty-handed, he was holding Amira's Fender acoustic/electric guitar. Barrington followed carrying a rather large amplifier, then Sameer with a wooden stool, and finally Travis, holding nothing. Sameer put the stool in the middle of the stage. Duncan plugged the guitar into the amplifier and turned it on. After adjusting the volume, he sat on the stool, a sombre expression on his face. The other three guys stood behind him.

What was going on?

Barrington started humming quietly, a simple repeating melody, and motioned the other singers on the stage to join in. Duncan began to strum simple chords on the guitar. The melody sounded familiar but she couldn't place it. Was Duncan going to sing something . . . alone . . . why?

But just at the moment when she expected him to start singing, Sameer walked around to the front of the stage and began to sing a slow, haunting tune—in Hindi.

Tanha chandni mein gaate gaate
parbat se tumhari awaz chali, Kiranon me dhuli
Tumhare geet bina, meri tanhai bhi meri na rahi

Amira heard Shirin gasp two seats away from her. "This is an Indian song," Shirin said in Gujarati. "This is who Sameer is."

Amira watched the boys on the stage. Duncan was still strumming with a serious expression, Barrington was still humming low, Sameer was singing alone, his expressive face bursting with emotion, and Travis stood frozen, mouth agape. He had no idea what was going on.

"It's a love song, Amira," Shirin whispered loud, leaning over Tazim. "He's singing for you."

No, he wasn't. Amira watched in awe as Sameer, still singing, took Travis's hand and pulled him forward. As the song slowed, Sameer slowly lowered to one knee.

Holy shit.

Sameer was proposing to Travis.

On a live-streamed performance.

In front of an audience of hundreds.

In front of his grandmother.

Oh. My. God.

"Oh no," Amira heard Tazim say under her breath. Tazim's hand covered her mouth, but she didn't seem so much shocked as worried. Amira guessed more people in Sameer's family knew about his orientation than he realized. Shirin's face, on the other hand, held only complete shock. She turned to Amira . . . and Amira couldn't help but smile. She felt too much joy for her friends to hold it in.

Shirin watched Amira's expression for a few seconds, saying nothing as the realization that Amira knew about this relationship washed over her face. She finally turned away, her nose wrinkled. Shirin was disappointed. Maybe even disgusted by both her and her grandson.

But on the stage, Sameer had the widest smile Amira had

ever seen, and Travis had tears in his eyes. Travis finally nodded and laughed.

"Of course. Yes." He hauled Sameer up by the arm and kissed him. Right there, in front of hundreds, Sameer and Travis kissed like their love was the most beautiful thing in the world.

Because it was.

The crowd went wild. Barrington and Duncan grabbed their friends to congratulate and hug them, and all the other barbershop singers on the stage joined, hugging and congratulating the happy couple. Amira's face ached from smiling so big, and her cheeks were wet with tears. Reena next to her was hooting and hollering and hugging Marcia. It was amazing. A stage full of barbershop singers supporting, accepting, and welcoming Sameer and Travis. That up there, that was their family, and it was the only one that mattered right now. Not the scowling woman sitting two seats over from Amira, not judgments from people like Ryan Galahad, who Amira couldn't see but she assumed wasn't impressed. But all that was just noise. And you didn't have to listen to the noise.

You could ignore it and find your own harmony.

After it seemed like every singer on the stage had hugged either Travis, Sameer, or both, the red-striped crooners returned to the stage.

"We're not sure if anyone can top that amazing performance," one of them said, "so it's a good thing we're ending with it. On behalf of the International Barbershop Quartet Association, we would like to congratulate the happy couple. We hope for many, many years of blissful harmony for you. But now it's time to award our winners. It was a tough competition this year, and it was a challenge for the judges to choose only three groups among these spectacular performances. But we have narrowed it down. Our third-place group is . . . the A-Team!"

Amira's shoulders fell. Third place was good, but the boys wanted a win. But as her guys stepped forward to accept their trophies, the wide grins on their faces hadn't faded one bit since Sameer's proposal. No trophy could top what Sameer and Travis found. Third place hadn't soured this moment one bit.

Second place was one of the cookie-cutter traditional groups, and unsurprisingly, Fourth Fret came in first. But Amira didn't care.

A grand finale where all forty-odd singers sang "Happy Together" followed by more bows and applause, and the Ontario Region Barbershop Quartet Competition was over.

CHAPTER THIRTY-ONE

WOW. WHAT A rush.

"That was easily the most romantic thing I've ever seen, and I've mainlined John Hughes movies," Reena said.

"I can't stop smiling," Marcia agreed. "I haven't even met them all, but I feel like pinching their cheeks. That is one adorable barbershop quartet."

Amira grinned. They really were adorable. All of them. "Let's go find them."

Reena, Marcia, and Amira fought through the crowd rushing the stage. They reached the stairs when Amira looked back to see Shirin and Tazim leaving. They weren't even planning to say anything to Sameer. Amira pushed her disappointment aside—she only wanted to focus on Sameer and Travis's happiness right now. She couldn't let anything taint that. She rushed straight to Sameer and hugged him tighter than she had ever hugged anyone, and then she stepped back to look at him. He still had a goofy smile on his face, and there was a new ease in his posture, a visible weight removed from his shoulders. Travis was right—Sameer unburdened was a beautiful thing.

"You did it," Amira said.

"I did." He smiled. "No more secrets."

Someone tackled her from behind and wrapped his arms around her. She turned her head to see Travis, and beside him was a striking woman with hair in shades of blue, purple, and green. His sister, Justine, Amira assumed.

"Sorry I stole your boyfriend, Amira." Travis laughed, squeezing her.

"I'll get over it. One day." She grinned.

Justine suddenly giggled at her brother. "Now you're Jolene."

Travis let go of Amira and introduced Justine to everyone. Then Barrington introduced Marcia around. Travis stood behind Sameer, arms wrapped around his waist. He affectionately rested his chin on Sameer's shoulder. Sameer held on to Travis hands and smiled.

"I can't believe he did that. You must have been shocked," Amira said to Travis, shaking her head.

"Well, sort of." He laughed. "He kind of warned me. He took me aside right after our main numbers and asked if I would take him back if he told his grandmother and his entire family about me today. I said yeah, I probably would. But I didn't think he'd actually do it."

"But you didn't know about the song?"

"No, I thought Duncan was going to sing something, not Sameer. I can't believe he did that in front of the audience." He kissed Sameer's cheek. "The three of them planned it last night while we were watching the terrible ballet movie."

"That awful movie ended up being good for something," Amira said. "My Hindi's not great, what did that song mean?" She was used to subtitles in her Bollywood movies.

Sameer's cheeks tinged with pink while he translated. "While singing alone in the moonlight, your voice came from the mountains, washed in sunlight. Without your song, even my loneliness is no longer my own." He giggled nervously. "Or something like that . . . it's from a Bollywood movie."

"*Mere Dil Ki Awaaz*," Reena added. "I love that movie. Super romantic."

"Ooh, let's watch it when we get home. And sing the whole thing to me later, okay, babe?" Travis said as Sameer blushed. "I'm still in shock. *Sameer?* Planning a spectacle like that?" He kissed Sameer's cheek again.

"Why the spectacle?" Justine asked. "Good thing I was here to see it. No one back home will believe this. It's so completely unlike you."

Sameer looked at Travis's face affectionately. "Travis deserves it. After what I've put him through, he deserved to hear me say I love him and want to spend the rest of my life with him sung from the top of the CN Tower. I'm taking control of my own gossip. Let them try to beat this." His smile waned just a bit. "Did you see my grandmother?"

"I'm sorry, Sameer. I think she left," Amira said.

Travis squeezed a bit tighter. "It's okay, babe."

"I know," Sameer said. "It'll be fine. If they can't accept me, then . . . it's fine. Travis has enough family to go around. And I have these guys . . ." He turned and smiled at Barrington, whose arm was around Marcia's waist. Barrington grinned and gave Sameer a thumbs-up.

Someone was missing from this little family. The person Sameer had called the glue that held them together. Amira bit her lip, saying nothing about their missing baritone.

"Where did you get your ridiculous new name? The A-Team?" Reena asked.

"It's for you." Sameer smiled at Amira.

"For me?"

Travis laughed. "Yeah, *Amira's Team*. We were trying to think of a name a few days ago and got stuck on trying to think of something with our first initials."

Barrington chimed in. "And with the rest of the guys' names spelling out STD . . . well, we needed to add you."

Travis grinned. "You've been there since we first came together, and we felt like you were really a member of our group."

"We were almost going with Amira's Boys, but Barry thought of the A-Team," Sameer added.

"I'm going to get some gold chains for our next show. Beats spandex and sequins," Barrington said matter-of-factly.

Amira laughed as her chest swelled with pride. These were her guys. It was humbling to be considered one of their team.

A firm hand tapping her shoulder startled her. She stilled. She knew it was Duncan. Her heart started racing.

"Hi," he said when she turned around. There was that unfamiliar expression again. Uneasy. Hurt. She hated it on him.

"Congratulations," Amira said.

"Thanks. Third place isn't so bad . . ." He ran his hand over his beard. "Um, can we talk? My brother wants to apologize to you. He's waiting by my truck."

Amira looked at Duncan. Really looked at him. He looked almost the same as the day she first saw him. Plaid shirt. Suspenders. Bright-red beard and the greenest eyes she had ever seen. The confident swagger had lessened, but he was still the same man she'd dismissed when he walked down that train aisle. Two weeks wasn't enough time to develop such strong feelings, either positive or negative, for anyone, but Amira wasn't one to bullshit herself. She had developed strong feelings for him. She might just be in love with him.

Ryan wanted to apologize to her. No doubt Duncan gave him an earful about what Maddie had done to Zahra. He didn't believe the same things as his brother, and he was trying hard with his niece. She looked at Duncan's face. He was a good man, she had to believe that.

She would listen to him, and to his brother. She owed him that much. She wasn't about to do this alone, though. "Okay. Reena comes, too."

Duncan looked like he was going to object, but Amira raised one eyebrow, daring him to. "Fine."

The blue skies and bright sun outside bathed Amira in a warmth that should have relaxed her muscles as they walked. But in reality, she had never felt more knots in her shoulders as she followed Duncan across the parking lot towards an enormous black pickup truck. Her heart was beating too fast, her hands were sweaty, and all she wanted to do was scream *fuck you* to the man she could see leaning against the truck, looking at his phone. But for the sake of the larger man with the tense back who she was following, she wouldn't. She would hear Ryan's apology.

"Ryan, you remember Amira Khan. And this is Amira's friend, Reena."

"Pleasure to see you again," Ryan drawled. Even his voice sounded like Duncan's. It was disconcerting. He was like the anti–Duncan Galahad. The evil one.

Amira nodded.

"I owe you an apology," Ryan started. "I heard about the texts Maddie sent your sister. I'm sorry it upset her."

"You didn't know your daughter texted that stuff to her?" Amira asked.

"Nah, I didn't even know they were texting each other. But kids, you know how it is. The things they pick up at school. Maddie didn't mean any offence."

"She called my sister a terrorist. I'm thinking she *did* mean offence," Amira said.

Ryan's posture stiffened. "She's just a kid. You have to remember, we live in a small town. There's not a lot of different kinds of people at Maddie's school, and you know how kids talk."

"I also know how adults talk," Amira said.

"And I've seen your Twitter account," Reena added. "All your 'Canadian values,' and 'immigrants are destroying the country' bullshit. You're an online troll. Actually, a white supremacist."

Ryan's nostrils flared at Reena before turning back to Amira. "Well, I didn't mean *you* specifically. Anyway, Duncan here told me how he's gotten to know you and your family, and you're not like the others . . . so, I'm sorry we offended you. I think if we take the time to get to know each other, maybe I'll see things different." He looked at his brother before turning back to Amira. "Forgive me?"

That was a terrible apology, but at least he looked sincere. Like his brother, there was something honest about Ryan Galahad. The kind of man who told his own truths, no-holds-barred. Not hiding behind masks or false manners. Not altering his behaviour to suit the others around him, ever.

Because he never really had to.

Amira looked him right in the eye. "I'm going to be straight with you, Ryan. I'm glad you apologized, even though that wasn't the best apology. I'm not sure you've figured out what a raging asshole you are, but at least you tried. It took your brother getting close to a Muslim for you to realize *we are people*, and for your daughter's sake, I'm glad you figured that out. But no, I don't forgive you. You said I'm not like the others? Well, you couldn't be more wrong. I am exactly like the others. My parents are immigrants. I am a Muslim. I may not be very devout, but I'm a believer. I am exactly who you say is destroying the country. And now you want to get to know me? Sorry, but I don't have any intention of wasting my time with someone so he can learn *not* to be a racist dick. Read a fucking book for your education, bud."

Ryan's teeth clenched. He looked to Duncan, whose expression was harder to read. "I said I was sorry," Ryan finally said. "I feel bad, and I'm trying to make amends, and now you're calling me an asshole? What is it you want from me, lady?"

Amira stood taller. "I don't want anything from you. You're the one who wants something from me. You want for-giveness, so you can feel better about yourself. And now I'm the villain because I won't grant it to you? *You wronged us.* You and your irrational hatred hurt my sister in a way she'll never forget. She felt betrayed beyond belief when her new friend abandoned her and called her horrific names. You have a daughter that age, you know how fragile their self-worth is. How hard they want to fit in. You taught my sister that, no matter how sweet she is, no matter how many late-night texts she sends her friends gushing about ballet movies, there will always be people who won't respect her because of her religion, her skin, or her culture, and who won't see the awesome kid she is. And by the way, Zahra's awesomeness is partly *because* of her religion, her culture, and her skin. Not in spite of it. I don't want your apology. It's going to take a hell of a lot more than words to make amends for what you are doing to us." She turned and started to walk away.

"Amira, wait," Duncan called after her.

Pausing, Amira turned back to them. As they stood next to each other, all Amira could see was how similar Duncan and Ryan looked. Similar eyes. Similar facial shape. Similar posture. Cut from the same cloth? She had thought Duncan different from his family, but as he himself told her once, the small-town gentleman he was raised to be would always be in there.

A relationship with Duncan would mean connections and family contact. Birthday parties and weddings. Friday dinners and holidays. What would Duncan say if his family made towel-head jokes at the dinner table? Or if they started spewing nonsense against immigration or the country's welcoming of refugees? What would he say to his family if they hurt Zahra again? Would he be loyal to his family, or to her? Or both?

Duncan would support her. He would stand up for her, and insist they apologize to her, like he probably insisted Ryan apologize today. He would smooth everything out, hoping everyone would be civil to each other. And it would happen again. And there would be tension, and family fights, and avoidance. And she could never be herself around them.

She would always be censuring herself, worried about confirming their preconceptions about her. And she would resent Duncan for it.

"And you know what the worst part is?" she said before either of the brothers could speak. "I believe you. I believe you both feel bad about upsetting Zahra. Even though you are terrible at apologizing, Ryan, you're not lying; you meant that apology. You know how I know that? Because I know Duncan, and what you see is what you get. I don't know you, Ryan, but I suspect you're the same way. You're both unapologetically yourselves. And that is a privilege people like me don't have. We're always hiding behind masks, trying to fit ourselves to what people like you think we should be. I don't have the luxury to be outraged. Because if I act like the outspoken bitch that Duncan knows I am, I'm the one in the wrong. I'm the villain. The angry Muslim, disenfranchised enough to join a terror cell. I'm done with this shit. I'm not what's wrong with this country, Ryan, you are. Let's go, Reena." This time she really walked away, and neither Galahad brother tried to stop her. Good.

CHAPTER THIRTY-TWO

AMIRA'S EXIT WOULD have been a hell of a lot more dramatic if she and Reena didn't have to walk the length of the parking lot to get to Reena's car, while two sets of Galahad eyes watched. It probably would have been better, too, if she hadn't dropped her purse while only about three cars away from the enormous truck, her hands shaking too much for her to keep a grip on it.

"You okay?" Reena asked, holding Amira's elbow.

"I will be," Amira said between clenched teeth. "I just need to get out of here."

The second she closed the door of Reena's car, her text tone rang. That had better not be Duncan-fucking-Galahad, begging her to come back and let him speak. No. She was going to be the one to get the last word with the Galahad brothers.

Thankfully, it was Sameer instead.

Sameer

We're going out for dinner and drinks to celebrate. You coming?

Amira

Who's going?

Sameer

Whole A-Team plus Marcia and Justine.
Third place is worthy of celebration.

Amira dropped her head to rest on the window, heart still beating too fast, and hands still shaking too much.

Amira

I don't think so. Would love to see you and Travis before you go, though. When you leaving?

Sameer

Not till tomorrow. Barry and Duncan are packed and leaving straight after dinner. Travis and I will leave late tomorrow morning. Can we do breakfast first?

Amira

Sure. No problem. See you in the morning.

Amira turned her phone off and tossed it in her purse. "Take me home, Reena."

When she got home, Amira found her mother alone in the dining room, setting the table. The house smelled strongly of Nanima's cooking, but Amira couldn't see her grandmother. Mum immediately turned to Amira, face washed with concern and curiosity. "Good, Amira, you're here. What happened today?" she asked.

How did Mum know something had happened at the competition? "Why?" Amira asked.

Mum spread out three plates on the table. "Nanima got a call from Shirin. Something to do with Sameer's show. She immediately went into her room to speak privately."

Gossip spreads fast . . . Shirin was likely telling Nanima all about Sameer's marriage proposal. Amira bit her tongue so she wouldn't swear in front of Zahra. Wait, Zahra wasn't here. "Where's Zahra? Why isn't she setting the table?"

Mum walked into the kitchen and started pouring water into glasses. "She's having dinner and spending the night across the street at Olivia's. I'm working at four in the morning. I know your paper's due and I don't want her bothering you. Olivia's mother offered to take Zahra to school."

Amira joined her mother in the kitchen to get spoons. "What about Nanima?" Nanima watched Zahra and took her to school in the morning regularly—several times a week when Mum worked early.

"I just . . . I wanted to give my mother some quiet time. What happened at the show?"

"You don't know what Shirin told Nanima?" she asked.

"No clue," Mum said. "I was—"

"Amira!" Nanima appeared in the kitchen doorway. "Oh, my poor beta. I am so sorry. I heard about what happened today." She approached Amira, arms outstretched.

Amira stiffened as her grandmother hugged her. This was not good.

"Shirin told me what Sameer did at his show. I am going to bring them dinner. She can't cook in her condition. Your mum can stay here with you, if you are upset, too."

Mum looked confused. "What did Sameer do? Are you upset, Amira?"

Amira's teeth clenched. "Yes, I had a terrible day. But Sameer had nothing to do with it. I'm very happy about what Sameer did today."

"What did he do?" Mum asked again.

Nanima pulled out a few large glass bowls from a low cupboard. "He sang a song to that boy, the one he came here with. The one that cuts hair. I knew I shouldn't have rented to those men, look what they did to little Sameer! I'm so sorry, Amira. You were going out with him." She started spooning rice from a pot on the stove into one of the bowls.

"He did what?" Mum asked.

Amira turned to her mother. "It was sweet, Mum. Sameer proposed to Travis onstage today." She forced a smile at her grandmother. "They've been together for over a year. I was never really dating Sameer. I'm sorry for misleading you."

Mum's hand went to her mouth. "Oh my," she said.

Nanima's jaw tightened. "A year? You told me he was going out with *you*." She shook the wooden spoon in her hand at Amira's face, causing small grains of rice to fly about the room. "Shirin said you knew about them, but I told her you wouldn't lie to me. And those two are not getting married. They can't, two boys *cannot* get married."

"Yes, they *can*," Mum said, her voice rising to match her mother's. "Same-sex marriage has been legal for well over a decade."

Nanima turned to look at Mum, face flashing with an expression Amira hadn't seen on her usually loving grandmother. Fury? Disappointment?

The stare-off between Mum and Nanima went on for several long seconds. And then even longer. There was a silent conversation moving between their eyes that Amira couldn't begin to understand. What the hell was going on?

"It is wrong. It's against Islam. Perversion doesn't belong in our culture," Nanima hissed. They'd clearly had this conversation before. She'd never seen Mum and Nanima so angry with each other. For the second time this week, Amira wondered if there was more to her mother's relationship with her mother than she knew.

Finally, Nanima turned away from Mum and resumed spooning dal from a pot with sharp movements. "All of you lied to us," she spat out, voice shaking with anger. "After everything I've done for you, you would disappoint your family like this? I expected more from you, Amira."

Mum stepped forward, in front of Amira. "What would compel any of us to be honest with you when this is what you give us for it? You, and everyone like you, can't play God forever. Eventually, you have to let people live their own lives, even if it's against your backwards beliefs." She spun, grabbing the rest of the pot of dal in one hand and the rice in the other, walked to the dining room, and thumped them down on the table.

Amira picked up a third pot containing eggplant and slowly made her way over to sit with her mother. There was definitely more to this conversation than Sameer and Travis.

Nanima left the house without another word. Mum didn't turn around, just continued quietly spooning yogourt onto her plate.

"Mum?" Amira said.

"Yes?"

"What the hell is going on?"

"Nothing. You tell me, Amira." She put a fresh chapatti on her plate, then held one out for Amira, still not looking up. "You said you were upset, but not about Sameer. What were you upset about?"

"Mum."

"Yes?"

"Don't do this. Tell me what you two were really talking about."

"Amira, please . . ."

"Does this have anything to do with that new man you're dating? Nanima found out he's not Muslim?"

Mum put down her spoon. She finally looked at Amira's face. "No. She still doesn't know I'm seeing anyone. But . . . Amira, I'm not dating a man. I'm dating a woman."

Amira blinked repeatedly.

What?

Mum picked up her spoon and ran it through her rice. "I know you're surprised, honey."

Surprised? Shocked? Bewildered? Maybe. *Upset?* Most definitely.

"Oh, Mum." Amira looked at her mother, whose eyes were wet with tears, and it broke Amira's heart. She walked around the table, lowered her knees to the hardwood floor in front of her, and hugged her mother's shoulders tightly.

"How could you have listened to your own mother say those things? Today . . . and before, too. I'm so, so sorry, Mum," Amira whispered.

Mother and daughter hugged silently for a long time. Mum's heart had to be full of pain and hurt after that argument with Nanima, and Amira wished she could take it all away from her. Nanima had been spewing her bigotry about the possibility of the quartet being gay for two weeks, and Mum had to listen to it, all while she was in a relationship with a woman.

But why hadn't she said anything to Amira? Amira wouldn't have been like Nanima; she would've accepted anything that made Mum happy. Mum had to know that.

Finally, she gently pushed Amira away. "Go, eat, before the dal gets cold. We can talk and eat."

Amira reluctantly returned to her seat and stared at her mother. How well did she know the woman in front of her? Mum had always been around, in the background, but Amira had never considered her mother to be a driving force in her life. She thought herself closer to her father. More similar. She had followed in his career footsteps, and she always admired his strength and integrity.

But Mum . . . Mum was the predictable one. She worked hard, went to Jamatkhana, avoided arguments, and pleased everyone. Had she been hiding a secret identity all this time? How could she have lived that way?

"Who knows this?" Amira asked.

"Not many people. A few at work. Laura, the woman I'm seeing, is a nurse at the hospital. Surgical." She took a sip of water. "Your father knows."

"You told him?"

"I had to. We were married for over twenty years, he had a right to know. Your father is a remarkable man. He was quite understanding."

"Was this the real reason for your divorce?"

"No. Amira, please don't think I didn't love your father. I did. Very much." She looked down at her plate. "In every way."

Amira's eyes widened.

"I'm attracted to both men and women," Mum said quietly. "I always have been. Laura isn't the first. I had a . . . dramatic love affair with a girl when I was sixteen. My parents found out about it. That's what Nanima and I were talking about."

"But you only moved to Canada when you were fifteen!"

"I know. I met her in school here."

"What happened to her?"

Mum shrugged. "After my parents found out, they came very close to sending me back to India. They forbid me from seeing her. I wasn't allowed to leave the house, I wasn't allowed anything at all."

Amira tried to imagine it. Her mother, a teenage Indian immigrant in the eighties, in an intense, secret love affair with a Canadian teenage girl. Add a beach scene and some lens flares, and Amira could imagine it as a great indie coming-of-age movie.

But this wasn't a movie—this was her mother's life, and Amira wished she had known about it, wished she had taken enough interest to know Mum was much more than she seemed. How could she have been so self-absorbed that she hadn't noticed who her own mother was?

"They forced you apart?" Amira asked.

Mum nodded. "Her family, too. My parents told the school, who told her parents. They pulled her out and transferred her to the Catholic high school, and I never saw her again." She smiled sadly. "I was miserable. I was practically under house arrest. Only allowed to go to Jamatkhana and school."

"Ugh. That sounds horrible." Amira had a sudden thought. "Wait . . . did others know about it? At Jamatkhana, I mean." It would explain so much about how people like Reena's mother treated Mum.

Mum nodded. "My parents tried to hide everything, but gossip spread. My parents found Mohammad for me to try to alleviate the gossip."

"What!?! Jesus, Mum! Your and Dad's marriage was *arranged*? They forced you to marry him? Why didn't you ever tell me?" This was huge.

Mum shrugged again. "I don't know if they would have forced me to marry him, but it didn't matter. I *wanted* to marry him. I fell in love with him. He was so kind and accepting. He understood me. I was furious with my parents for trying to run my life, and I saw the marriage as a way out of the house."

"So, he knew you were bisexual?"

"Yes. I told him everything. But truly, Amira, that wasn't why we divorced." She stilled. "He was just never around. One contract or business trip after another. I didn't want to be sitting home the rest of my life, waiting for my husband to come back. You were almost grown, and I saw all the loneliness I felt when I raised you starting over again with Zahra. That wasn't the future I wanted."

"And Laura is your future?"

"I meant it when I said it was early, we've barely started dating." She smiled. "I'm enjoying myself. I'm just living in the present now."

Amira smiled. "And you're not letting your family get in your way anymore."

"No, I'm not. My future is mine only."

Amira's heart swelled. Sameer was happy—she remembered his face after the show, when he had Travis wrapped around him. He looked like a different person, released from the burdens that had entangled him for so long. He and Travis stood taller, walked prouder, both with an unmistakable rhythm and harmony that connected them. Forever. And Mum was happy. Amira now understood that spark, that lightness in Mum's mannerisms that she'd noticed when she first came home. She loved Mum's new attitude of not caring a bit what others would say. Everyone around her was taking control of their own future, haters be damned.

She couldn't understand how anyone could look at Sameer's and Travis's faces and not be moved by their joy. She was so disappointed that people like Nanima and Shirin still would not embrace it.

"But, Mum, one question. After everything that happened back then, how could you have moved in with Nanima again? Why did you even speak to your parents at all after you got married? You guys even bought a house around the corner from them. Why wouldn't you take the opportunity to go far, far away?"

Mum finished chewing her bite, and then took another sip of water, before speaking. "You needed grandparents, Amira. We didn't have any other family in Canada, and you needed a connection to your culture and your religion. And then I moved back here only a few years after your grandfather died, when I was newly divorced. Zahra was still little,

341

and you were starting university soon. I needed help, and Nanima needed company. She's my mother, Amira. I forgave her. They were new to the country. Everything was so foreign to them. And a daughter who was prone to histrionics proclaiming undying love to a girl wasn't what they expected out of Canada."

Amira wrinkled her nose. Mum wasn't prone to histrionics, was she? "But what about now? Nanima has lived in Canada for thirty-five years. Are you going to tell her about Laura now?"

"Yes, if the relationship continues. And we'll see what happens then. I've been saving for a down payment on a place of my own for a while. I'd hoped to convince her to sell this house and get a condo in one of those seniors' buildings in a year or two. But now I think I may want to move sooner rather than later. I'm not hiding this from her again, and I will live on my own terms. That's why I've been trying to depend on Nanima less for help with Zahra."

Amira grinned. "You're amazing. And, of course, I'm here to help with Zahra whenever I can."

"I hope she will have an open mind if I tell her, but we'll see." She smiled. "What about you, Amira. Are you planning to stay here? Have you thought at all about *your* future?"

Amira looked down at her nearly empty plate of food. Her future . . . a future where she was going back to a job with a boss who didn't respect her because she wasn't a white male, and where her mentor didn't believe her when she said her boss was sexist and may have trashed her report right before it was due so she wouldn't get a job he wanted. A future where she lived with an intolerant

grandmother and a mother who had to hide her relationship. A future where Amira was alone. What future did she
have, really?

Words Travis had said to her yesterday crashed through
her mind. *The past doesn't matter. We both lost the potential
for a future.*

A future with Duncan? *Bullshit.* Three nights and . . . she
counted in her head . . . seven rolls in the hay did not equal
a future.

Amira excused herself from the dining table, bringing
her plate and the leftover rice to the kitchen while blinking
repeatedly to prevent the tears from forming. What was supposed to happen now? Could she confront Raymond? Go
back to her job after everything she knew? Could she continue to live in this house, with a grandmother she loved but
who believed people like Mum and Sameer didn't deserve to
be happy? Amira would never respect Nanima's views, but
did that mean she had to leave Nanima's house?

It all made her feel lost. And whenever Amira felt lost,
she became angry. Looking out the window over the kitchen
sink, she remembered the day last December when she had
been escorted out of the airport. She had been furious, and
she had not let go of that anger when the dust settled on
the event and its aftermath. True, she stopped fighting once
it all became too much. She'd stuck her head underground
and stopped engaging with others on social media, stopped
writing articles on the Muslim perspective, and learned to
avoid the news when it became too painful. But she hadn't
stopped being angry.

Angry at everyone. Everything. The damn rent-a-cops who

walked her out of the airport terminal. The mouth-breathing trolls targeting and harassing her. The people telling her to go back to her own country and sending her vile pictures of violence she couldn't scrub from her mind. People like Ryan Galahad teaching their children to assign value according to a person's race.

People like Duncan forgiving them.

And now, just to live her life as she knew it, she had to forgive, too. Forgive her grandmother for her intolerance. Forgive her mother for excusing it. Forgive Raymond for his dishonesty. Amira's head spun in circles. She held on to the counter in her grandmother's kitchen, the warm, setting sun blinding her through the west-facing windows. She wanted to scream. She wanted to cry.

"Sweetheart?" She turned to see Mum behind her. Amira couldn't help it. Her tears flowed freely as she fell into her mother's arms.

Her mother held her, gently stroking her head as Amira's anger finally unfolded to expose the pain inside. She sobbed and couldn't even be bothered to feel embarrassed for this breakdown—if you couldn't lose it in your mother's arms, who could you count on?

Her mother released her when she had calmed, but held on to her arms. "Amira, I know you care about your friends, but this is not about Sameer and his boyfriend, right?"

She shook her head.

"You're upset about Duncan. It was more serious with him than you let on."

Amira turned her focus to the window, peeking at the setting sun. "It's so stupid, Mum. This is not like me, it was less than a week. I should be stronger." She wiped her wet cheeks.

"You fell in love after a week?" Mum smiled. "I'm not surprised. This is exactly like you."

"What?"

Her mother touched Amira's cheek. "You have the biggest heart, Amira. You love so quickly, and fiercely. Loyal, protective, and unwavering. And when you finally met your match, you fell in love fast. You have the biggest heart in the world. It might be too big for you, sometimes."

"No, Mum." Amira sniffled. "I'm always angry."

"You're angry because of your big heart. You're angry because you won't sit back and let people get hurt."

Amira looked down. Why was this so hard? She was so tired of outrage. Of anger. But how could she get past this with Duncan? How could she not be furious with him? "I just . . . I don't know what to do."

Her mother squeezed Amira's arms. "I don't know what you should do either. I understand why you're angry at him. What happened to Zahra is unforgivable. He should have told you his brother's beliefs. He *should* have told you what you were getting into." Mum walked to the other side of the kitchen and silently took out a pot and filled it with water for chai.

She put the pot on the stove to heat as Amira pulled the tea tin out of the cupboard and added three teaspoons to the pot. She gently crushed some cardamom pods, cinnamon, peppercorns, and ginger in a mortar and pestle, letting the warm aromas calm her. It was a familiar ritual, one carried out countless times with her mother or grandmother, but in Amira's emotional state, all she could think about was how much she missed this.

She missed these tiny rituals, these small moments with her family that were becoming rarer—and would soon end, it seemed. Her family was changing. Zahra wasn't a baby anymore, and her mother was moving on with her life in new ways. Amira wished she could hold on to the past and keep everything the way it was, but she didn't really want that either.

As the chai started to boil, her mother looked up. Amira couldn't be sure, but she thought she saw tears in Mum's eyes, too. "I used to wonder what I would have been like . . . who I would have been if I had been allowed to be myself back then. Seeing you, my beautiful daughter all grown up, I realize, at least I hope, I would have been just like you. Give yourself permission to be that, sweetie. Just you is more than enough for anyone who matters."

CHAPTER THIRTY-THREE

THE NEXT DAY was the project due date. And despite the truck-load of drama in her life, Amira was ready. After breakfast with Travis and Sameer, and after waving them off as they left for Ottawa, she went back to her now empty basement and gave a final spit-shine to her report. She hovered over the submit button for several long seconds before taking the plunge. There was nothing she could do now but wait for Professor Kennedy's response.

After submitting, she saw an email from Raymond asking if she had time for a meeting this week.

Why? Why did Raymond choose *now* to meet? After her due date, after he knew she submitted the report that he had deemed worthless. She stared at her computer for a while, not sure what to do. Finally, she agreed, and arranged to meet him in the Hyde office the next day.

Her project was done. The barbershop quartet was gone. It was time to deal with her work problems now.

. . . .

RAYMOND WAS ALONE in his cubicle the following morning when she approached. Alone, and looking rather pleased with himself.

"Amira, I'm glad you could make it." He stood. "Let's go to a meeting room."

She followed her mentor to one of the small meeting rooms that lined the wide-open space with its grid of cubicles, nodding and smiling at some of her former co-workers as she passed. She had a bad feeling about this, but her racing heart and sweaty hands were masked by her professional smile that at least looked the part.

"Here, sit," Raymond said, pulling out a chair for her before taking the one on the other side of the table. That was new. Pausing a second to take inventory of all her dealings with this man over the last six years, she didn't remember him ever pulling out a chair for her. And watching his face carefully, she detected a slight furrow in his brow. He seemed jumpy. Maybe he felt bad about what he had done? Was he going to mention the sound-reduction division? She considered the merits of showing her hand and mentioning that she'd had lunch with Shelley.

Amira hung her bag on the back of the chair. "So, Raymond, how are Alice and the boys? Is Jacob still playing with that Lego robot I got him for his birthday?"

He smiled tightly. He was definitely feeling guilty. Good. "Yes," he said. "He's obsessed with it. And now Andrew wants one, too. Did you get your report in on time?"

"Just barely. Thank you for your insight on it, by the way. It was very eye-opening."

Raymond shifted. There was no missing his discomfort now. Even someone who didn't know him as well as Amira did would see it.

Of course, Amira had realized she really didn't know this man at all.

"I wanted to give you the heads-up about some changes here at Hyde," he said. "So you're not blindsided when you return."

"Oh?"

"There is a new division opening, and a new consultant role will be available. I know you said you were interested in moving up, so I wanted to let you know before the posting closes on Thursday."

"A *senior* consultant role?"

Raymond nodded. "I will warn you, though, there will be a lot of competition. I know many consultants who are interested. Not just at the Toronto office either."

"Who's the hiring manager?"

"Jim Prescott. The division will be under him."

Amira blinked repeatedly. Was he going to tell her the name of the new division? Or mention the fact that he apparently would give his left arm to move into the role himself? Had he brought her here today just to ease his conscience?

Amira looked at Raymond. Why was he doing this? Getting caught in this sort of corporate back-stabbing seemed so unlike the Raymond who'd helped her find her feet at Hyde all those years ago. But Shelley confirmed that Hyde had changed since Amira left. Jim had a clear preference for old boys' club–type managers, and a small but brilliant middle-aged Chinese man would not have attracted his interest. Maybe Raymond had to learn to play dirty to catch Jim's notice. Amira felt a wash of pity for her old friend.

But even straining to understand Raymond's motivations didn't change the fact that he misled her. Worse, there was little she could do about it. Even if she never set foot in the Hyde office again, industrial engineering wasn't exactly a huge community. She couldn't burn any bridges at Hyde. She was vibrating with the urge to confront him when a knock on the glass door startled her.

Damn. Jim Prescott.

He walked in without waiting for a response and grinned at Raymond.

"There you are, Ray. I've been looking for you. I'm meeting with the CEO of Alumicore Industries. We'll need to wine and dine to get the acoustics contract with them. I'd like you to join us, see how these things are done." He turned to Amira. "Oh, I'm sorry, miss. Aren't you the consultant on leave? What was it . . . Amelia?"

Raymond smiled. "I was just telling her about the new division and roles. Amira was with Hyde for four years and is returning after she's done her degree. She's been out of the loop for a while, but she might be ready to move up in the company. I've been mentoring her—it's important to guide those walking in the path behind us."

What?! *Walking in the path behind him?* Amira smiled tightly but considered using her bag to whack Raymond Chu in the face.

Jim Prescott frowned. "You were here that long? I'm impressed. Hyde is a very fast-paced, challenging workplace. It's quite an accomplishment to last as a consultant. The new division will be technically complex, not all smiling and chatting." He slapped Raymond on his back. "Lucky girl to have someone like Ray looking out for you, though. He really impressed me with his knowledge in the field of noise control. You should think about applying for the junior role there when the job postings go up next week."

That's it. Amira had had just about enough of this. She stood, swinging her bag over her shoulder.

"My *name* is *Amira*, not Amelia or Almira. And you're right, Mr. Prescott, it *is* an accomplishment that a pretty little thing like me lasted this long at the big-boy table at Hyde. I am quite proud of myself. So maybe it's best I leave on a high note. This company is not what it used to be. I took the job here to consult on engineering projects, not wine and dine, or drink scotch at steak houses. I am obviously not a good fit for this place anymore."

She put her hand on the door handle and looked at Raymond. Working for the likes of Jim Prescott had changed her friend. Amira wondered if she would have changed, too, if she'd been here for the last two years. And would it change her now if she came back? "Consider this notice of my resignation. I will not be returning after my leave of absence." She smiled directly at Raymond before leaving the room. "And give my best to Alice, Raymond. I will be sure to send a robot for Andrew on his birthday next month. Goodbye."

She walked out the door and straight out the building without a glance backwards.

. . . .

AMIRA SHOULD HAVE been upset on the long streetcar and subway ride home. She should have felt unsure about her future, maybe even felt some nausea or crippling regret about what she had done. And she should definitely have felt anger. After all, she had quit her job on the spot. And although she had tried not to burn any bridges on the way out, she wasn't so sure she was successful at that. She couldn't count on Jim Prescott, or Raymond for that matter, for any help finding a new job. She had no other prospects, no other income coming in, and now had to work from the bottom up all over again.

She *should* have been devastated.

But Amira had never felt better. True, it was a rash, on-the-spot decision. True, she'd once again given in to her emotions and done something irreversible on impulse. But Amira knew . . . *knew* with every molecule in every cell of her being that she'd done the right thing. There was no place at Hyde Industries for her anymore. Raymond wasn't her hero, her mentor, her friend, or the man who was going to guide her career to success anymore.

No one was going to guide her career . . . but her.

Amira was done with letting people get away with this. Raymond was weak, and if he wanted a pretty little thing in the office to fawn over him and make him look good in the old boys' club? Well, he picked the wrong engineer for that.

Just like Duncan's family. They weren't going to get a quiet Muslim to be nice face to face with, all while bitching about immigrants behind her back, convinced that Sharia law was going to enslave them all. Amira had a reputation for being strong-willed? Angry? A witch?

Well, it was time for the witch to polish up her broom, because she was going to fly away from all this nonsense. She couldn't fight the injustices, but she could walk away for her own sanity.

Getting home, she found the house empty, save for Nanima in the kitchen. The air was heady with the scent of spices and hot oil. It smelled like Nanima was making her famous veggie pakoras. Amira wandered in and snatched a crispy morsel from the paper-towel-lined tray.

Nanima grinned, watching Amira devour the pakora. "Amira, beta. You look happy. What put that smile on your face?"

Amira looked at her grandmother and stilled, her smile dissolving. This was the first time she had seen Nanima since she'd said that awful stuff about Sameer, Travis, and, really, Mum. She still couldn't wrap her head around the fact that Nanima could call her own daughter *wrong* and *perverted*.

She swallowed the now-bitter-tasting pakora. She'd always been close to her grandmother, but now that she knew the history between her mother and grandmother, she realized that this was a bit of a miracle. Her mother had selflessly maintained a relationship with her parents after getting married despite the emotional abuse she'd put up with as a teenager, just so Amira could have grandparents.

Clearly Mum was a better person than any of them. Amira would never have forgiven Nanima had she been in her mum's place back then. And looking at her grandmother at this moment, the woman who'd been the steady, loving, nurturing fixture in Amira's life since birth, she wasn't sure she could forgive her now.

"Where's Mum?" Amira asked. She was on early shift all week, so she should have been home by now.

"She went out with a friend after work. A museum," Nanima said, dipping some red peppers in the pakora batter before dropping them into the hot oil.

Good. Hopefully Mum was getting support from Laura, or someone else she could talk to. Mum had to be hurting hard. Amira should have called her to check in today, but she'd been too wrapped up in her work.

"Did you apologize to her?" Amira asked.

"Why?"

"For what you said after the barbershop competition."

"I didn't say anything bad."

"You said homosexuality was wrong."

Nanima turned away from the hot oil, annoyance brewing in her gaze. "I wasn't talking about her, I was talking about Sameer. And it *is* wrong. Islam says—"

"You *were* talking about her, and we both know it. Mum told me what happened when she was young."

Nanima's expression darkened as she turned off the stove and wiped her hands. "She shouldn't have told you about the past. She was young, she's put that behind her."

Amira's jaw tightened. There was no way she was going to tell Nanima that Mum hadn't exactly put that life behind her—that was Mum's discussion to have with her mother. But she also wasn't going to end this without speaking her mind either.

"She may have been young then, but she is the same person she has always been. And whoever she decides to love, I will never hold it against her. There is enough hate in the world, Nanima. I can't believe you chose to reject your daughter because of who she loved."

"I didn't reject her. She lives with me, doesn't she? You grew up here in the West, you can't understand—"

"No, Nanima. You don't understand. You, and Shirin, and everyone like you is choosing to dismiss a huge part of who Sameer and Mum are. Sameer and Mum! Two of the best people I know! Whether they live here, in India, or in Timbuktu, for all I care, it wouldn't change who they are. Only difference is, here their love has been legal a long time. They aren't hurting a soul! And your bigotry is hurting people like them so much!" Amira closed her eyes, feeling tears well. "You are hurting someone who loves you."

Nanima took a step forward, putting a hand on Amira's arm. "Amira, please. You are getting too worked up . . . calm down."

Amira shook her arm free. "No. Nanima, I'm not going to budge on this. Remember what you told me after I was kicked out of the airport last year? You said we will always be discriminated against for what we are: Indian Muslims. You told me that all we can do is live well, live ethically, and respect others. Maybe it's time you took your own advice, and maybe—"

"Amira, enough. This has nothing to do with you."

"You're wrong, Nanima. It has everything to do with me. I make it my business. She is my mother. And your daughter. And neither of us deserves her, but I'm going to love her unconditionally. That's what family is supposed to do." Amira picked up her purse from where she'd left it on the kitchen floor and walked away from her grandmother's bewildered expression.

She went straight down to the basement family room, dropped her bag, and sat on the sofa. The house was silent.

After how crowded it had been, Amira had grown used to having someone around to talk to when shit hit the fan, and Amira couldn't believe the sheer volume of crap flying around her life right now.

She didn't have a job anymore.

She could no longer respect her grandmother.

Her sister had been called a terrorist.

She had finally found a man she thought understood her, who she could see a future with, but that relationship self-destructed before it even got off the ground.

It had been a monumentally, extraordinarily craptastic couple of weeks.

She leaned back on the sofa, thinking about how optimistic she had been on the train ride home, at least until the train broke down.

But . . .

Life was a steaming turd-ball, yes. But maybe there was a lot to be happy about, too?

She had stood up to Raymond and Jim Prescott and wasn't going to let them walk all over her anymore.

She had defended her sister and told Ryan Galahad how big of a dick he really was.

She had stood up to her grandmother and told her she should love Mum unconditionally.

She had helped Sameer see that accepting his family's prejudices was killing him.

She had found out about her mother's past, and possible future, and felt closer to her for it.

She had finished her project report, and if all went well when it was evaluated, she would soon have her master's degree.

And even if things had gone belly up with Duncan, she was happy to have met him and couldn't regret a thing, at least not when the sex was *that* good.

Amira smiled to herself. It was going to take a lot of work to put the pieces of her life back together, but she was up for it. Hadn't she always craved control? Well, now she had lots of control over her future.

CHAPTER THIRTY-FOUR

THREE WEEKS LATER.

There were few people in the world Amira would brave a Toronto cocktail bar on a Friday night for, but when she got an unexpected text that her favourite recently engaged couple would be at one, she happily took the subway downtown after Friday night dinner with her family. Arriving at the dim, painfully trendy place a little after eight, she weaved through the crowd and found Sameer and Travis cozied up on one side of a booth near the back. She hadn't seen them since the day after the barbershop quartet competition, and she missed them more than she would have thought.

"Amira! There you are! Come sit!" Travis beamed, getting up to hug her before sitting back down beside Sameer with a grin. They both had complicated-looking drinks in front of them. She assumed each had way too many ingredients and was described with words like *infused with* or *derived from*. She ordered a microbrew instead, happy the beer list was as impressive as the cocktail list.

"What are you guys doing in Toronto?" Amira asked after ordering.

Sameer smiled. "Long story. Short version is, remember Fourth Fret?"

"Yeah, the group who won the competition."

"Yup. They had a gig booked at the busker festival downtown on Sunday, but two of them got bronchitis. They asked us to help fill in."

"Oh wow! I'll bring Zahra to see you, she'd love it. But you came all the way from Ottawa for just this one gig?"

"I needed to make a trip here anyway," Sameer said. "It's time I talked to my grandmother."

"Shit. Really?"

Travis smiled. "Most of his family have been really supportive."

"I had some long-distance heart-to-heart chats," Sameer added, "and, yeah, they've been good. We're staying at my Tazim aunty's place this weekend."

"But you haven't spoken to your grandmother?"

"No, not since the barbershop competition," Sameer said. "The family has tried, but she's a stubborn old bird. She's blaming my mother, the fact that I didn't have a father, and all sorts of crap. My mum begged her to see me; we're going over there tomorrow." He took Travis's hand.

Amira blew out a puff of air. In contrast, things had been quiet on the homophobe front at her home for the last few weeks. Nanima hadn't mentioned the argument with Mum and Amira, no doubt learning that fighting that fight would go nowhere. And Mum still hadn't told anyone else about Laura. Everyone was carrying on like normal.

It wouldn't last. Mum would tell Nanima soon. To prepare for that, Amira had taken over a lot of the child-care duties that Nanima normally did—easy since she had no job. And Mum had requested a more stable work schedule, so she wouldn't have to rely on others as much. Amira had actually spent a lot of time with Zahra and Mum lately, and she felt closer to her mother than she'd ever been. Mum had even introduced her to Laura.

But she'd seen little of her grandmother. She wasn't sure who was avoiding whom, but Amira was sad about the change. She still held out hope that Nanima would take it well when Mum told her about Laura, but Amira was also mourning the loss of a relationship that had meant so much to her for so long.

Her family was teetering on the edge of a sharp chasm and things were about to change drastically. No one knew which way the wind would blow, but Mum and Amira were preparing their parachutes in case they had to jump.

As if Sameer could see what Amira was thinking about, he nodded to her. "How are things holding up in your house?"

"Same." She smiled.

"You know," Sameer continued, "my mum has rekindled her friendship with your mother. They had a long talk on the phone the other day."

Amira tilted her head. How much did Sameer know about her recent family drama?

"She told me some things . . . some gossip about when they were young. Apparently, your mother was a good friend to my mum when she got pregnant . . . unwed. And my mother helped yours through some drama when they were teenagers."

Maybe Sameer did know about her mother's past, and maybe even her present. It didn't matter. Of all people, he would be discreet. "Crazy. I didn't realize they were that close. Funny to think of our families having full, interesting lives before we came along."

Sameer laughed. "I know. I can't even imagine my mum in the eighties. Anyway, she told me to tell you that you, your mother, and your sister have an open invitation to visit her in Ottawa anytime. She even dug up a picture of you and me together when I was a baby." He pulled out his phone and fiddled with it a bit. Amira's text tone rang and she saw that Sameer had texted her the photo.

It was a shot of Amira at about five years old, holding a bundled baby in her arms. This was obviously the picture Nanima had told her about, but what surprised Amira was that seeing it now brought a torrential wave of memories to the surface. She remembered the moment in vivid detail. Her mother had taken her to a friend's house to see a new baby who had been born, and they had let Amira hold him. It was the first time Amira had ever held a baby, and it was love at first sight. His skinny little legs and tiny fingers and frowning mouth. She remembered being overcome with feelings of protectiveness for the baby.

Her mother had made some comments about Amira one day having a brother or sister of her own, but Amira hadn't wanted that. She told her mother she wanted to love and take care of this baby, not any other. She was clearly an overly dramatic child.

Amira also remembered something else. There was secrecy around the visit. They weren't living with Nanima then, but Mum told her not to tell Nanima they were going to see the baby. And there were hushed voices behind Amira as she snuggled baby Sameer, staring at his scrunched-up face and humming gently to soothe him. Maybe she had sensed the drama surrounding Sameer's birth and wanted to shelter him from it. She knew that, not long after, Sameer's mother left Toronto with her son, starting a new life away from the judgments of her family and community.

Amira looked up at adult Sameer, eyes stinging as she put her phone down. "I remember this. I was so in love with you then. I begged my mother to let me keep you."

Travis beamed as he kissed the side of Sameer's head. "He is rather lovable. But *I'm* keeping him. Sorry."

Amira smiled as she sipped her beer. "Do you think your grandmother will ever come around?"

Sameer shrugged. "Maybe she will. I don't know, but I have to try. I hate that there's this great rift in the family because of me. I can't start a married life with Travis without trying to smooth it out."

"Family is important," Travis added. "We have to show them love is better than hiding."

"Yes," Sameer said with a grin. "And even if my grandmother doesn't accept this relationship, I'm not going to let that stand in my way anymore. They'll only learn to accept our love if we show them love. Right, Amira?"

Amira wasn't too dense to get what the guys were implying. They were talking about Duncan, of course, and the implosion of their relationship because of his family. She couldn't expect to have drinks with these two without someone bringing the garden gnome to the front of her mind. To tell the annoying truth, she hadn't been able to do much lately without their maddening baritone occupying most of the space in her brain. He was aggravating her more out of sight than he ever had when he'd been around. And that said a lot, because for a time, no one aggravated her as much as Duncan Galahad.

"Have you spoken to him?" she asked, not needing to reveal who she meant.

"Yeah," Travis said. "Lots. He feels terrible about what happened."

Amira dug her fingernail into the cardboard coaster under her drink. She didn't want to talk about Duncan. She bit her lip.

Travis smiled sympathetically, understanding this was a topic Amira wasn't ready for. "When are you going back to work?" he asked, not realizing that was another topic Amira wasn't keen on discussing.

She paused, then smiled sadly. "I'm not. I resigned."

Sameer looked at her. "Crap. Really? Because of your mentor?"

"Yes, in part. Let's just say I'm not interested in ass-kissing to try and weasel my way into a club that wouldn't let me in anyway. Hyde is more toxic than it used to be."

Travis wrinkled his nose. "So, you just up and quit?"

She nodded. "Maybe it's time for a fresh start. A new Amira."

"That's big, though," Sameer said. "What will you do now?"

Amira smiled. "I'll be okay. I have an amazing letter of recommendation from my professor and she had some job leads for me. I have an interview next week with a friend of my dad's who owns a small consulting firm that specializes in noise control. And I've applied to a lot of jobs at manufacturing plants outside Toronto."

"You'd leave the city?" Travis asked.

Amira shrugged. "I'm thinking about it. It's a good time for a change. Things are kind of unsettled at home, maybe it's time to move out. But I can't afford to live alone in Toronto." She cringed. "I'm not sure roommates are a great idea. I've applied for positions in Waterloo, Windsor, and Peterborough."

Sameer raised his eyebrows. "Peterborough?"

Amira reddened. "I know Duncan lives near there, but that's not why I applied. It's a good job . . ."

"Still, though," Sameer said, glancing at Travis.

Travis only smiled. "He'll be here Sunday," he added.

That wasn't a surprise. Why wouldn't Duncan drive an hour and a half into the city to see his friends sing? Loyalty . . . that was his thing.

Amira poked another hole in the cardboard coaster. She wasn't sure she was ready to see him again. Eventually, their paths would have to cross if she was going to stay friends with Sameer and Travis, but she wished she could have more time to figure out her life first. Things had already been so emotionally intense lately with the work and family crap going on, but even through all that, Duncan-fucking-Galahad was never far from the front of her conscious mind. It shouldn't have been that way. Duncan should have been nothing but a memory.

Amira had met with Professor Kennedy on schedule a week after she submitted the report and quite literally dropped to her knees with relief when her professor said it was accepted and granted her the credits. She still had bruises after that less-than-intelligent reaction. She chatted briefly with her professor about having quit her job and why. And while Professor Kennedy didn't flat-out tell Amira that she had done the right thing, she did give sage advice about watching your own back as a woman in the industry and avoiding situations where you didn't have someone on your side. Professor Kennedy said she would be happy to look out for appropriate opportunities for Amira and give her any references she needed. "Women in STEM need to stick together," Professor Kennedy had said with a smile.

Her convocation ceremony was next week, when she would proudly accept her master's degree in front of both her parents, her sister, and her grandmother. Amira had done it. She'd finished graduate school and she was so proud of herself. But predictably, Amira wasn't happy. Also predictably, she was utterly furious about that.

How the hell had someone like Duncan Galahad—a garden gnome, a snarky, overprotective, white-knighting bearded wonder—wormed his way so deep under her skin that she couldn't enjoy reaching a milestone she had worked so hard for? He and his xenophobic family had stolen her joy.

Xenophobic was the worst name she allowed herself to call Ryan in her inner dialogue since the competition, and that had been a challenge. Her choice thoughts about him on the days immediately after seeing him would have made a longshoreman blush.

No. She was bigger than him. Better. She wouldn't resort to name-calling, even in her head. She had no doubt that Ryan called her every name in that blushing longshoreman's dictionary, though, and she didn't care one dime about that.

But wondering what Duncan thought of her stole too many of the hours when she should have been sleeping each night, leaving her groggy in the morning and short-tempered during the day. Did he think she was out of line for yelling at his brother? Did he see her point of view at all? Had she explained why she was upset clearly enough to make him get it?

And now she would have to see him again in two days while she was still spinning from their last encounter. She'd have liked to have waited until she could get through a day without thinking about him. Screw a day, she would be happy with an hour.

"The whole A-Team will be singing together again. In person," Travis said.

"I thought you said only two members of Fourth Fret were sick?"

"Yeah, but they asked all four of us to join them. We will be the rare barbershop sextet."

Amira wrinkled her nose. "Sextet? That's terrible. Sounds kinky."

Travis laughed. "Yeah, I can see why they normally keep to four in a barbershop group. Still going to come?"

Amira looked down at the mutilated remains of the cardboard coaster. She raked the mound of shredded paper over the wood of the table, making a small pile of red and white while thinking about what to do. It wasn't just herself she had to consider, but Zahra, too. She hadn't mentioned Maddie or Duncan once since the guys left, but Amira knew her sister. Zahra also hadn't said anything about ballet and she even shot down her mother's offer of signing her up for a ballet class next year. Zahra wasn't over her new friend's betrayal.

"You two won't be able to avoid each other forever," Travis said. "We're going to have a huge wedding and we want both of you in the wedding party."

"What? But I've only known you for, like, what, a month? I can't be in your wedding party!"

Sameer laughed. "We used to hang out when I was a baby, remember? And anyway, we wouldn't be engaged if it wasn't for you. That day before the competition, when you told off Duncan . . . you inspired me. By not coming out and living the life I wanted to live, I was excusing all of them. That night, I thought to myself, *What would Amira do?* And I came up with the song idea. You don't know how much you helped me." He grinned.

Amira frowned. "I wouldn't have done that. I have a terrible singing voice! And stage fright."

He laughed. "Fine. Will you be my grooms-maid anyway?"

"Is that a thing? Grooms-maid?"

"Travis gets to have one: Justine. So I get one, too. Right now we're fighting over who gets Barry and who gets Duncan."

"I'm thinking we'll play musical attendants. They can switch sides for every picture," Travis said.

Amira gave them a pointed look. "Also, *musical* because you're making the wedding party sing, right?"

Travis nodded. "You'd better believe it."

She frowned. "You guys really want to have a big wedding?"

"Yup. Huge." Travis smiled. "We know *everyone* in Ottawa, and we both have enormous extended families. We're going to invite all of them. Let them decide if they want to show up, but we're not hiding anything. Like I said to you earlier, we're going to normalize this shit."

Amira smiled. "Well, I'd be honoured to be included. Even if I have to march down the aisle with the garden gnome himself." She paused. "I'll need vocal lessons."

Travis smiled. "I know a music teacher. Will you come Sunday?"

"You really want me to come that much?"

"Yes, of course!" Travis groaned. "We're Amira's team, remember?"

"We didn't have to tell you Duncan was coming," Sameer added. "We could have lied to get you to see him."

"But you didn't," Amira said.

"No," Sameer said. "He wants to see you, Amira. He wants to talk to you about what happened. I'm not excusing him, but I think you need to hear what he has to say. There's more to this than you know."

She sighed. She couldn't avoid him forever. And maybe this was the best place to get the damn meeting over with—in public and with her friends. If she wanted to avoid Zahra hearing the conversation, she could get one of the guys to hang out with her for a bit.

"Ugh. Fine. I'll come. Tell your garden gnome I'll see him at the busker festival."

CHAPTER THIRTY-FIVE

ON SUNDAY, WITH two hours left before she and Zahra planned to head downtown to see the A-Team at the festival, Amira sat on her bed in her underwear, trying to decide what to wear.

A sundress? It was warm enough . . . but . . . would Duncan think she was dressing up just for him?

Jeans? Maybe . . . but Duncan saw her in jeans all the time when he was here. Jeans wouldn't make much of an impression.

This was ridiculous. She was overthinking this. Tied up in knots at the thought of seeing him again. She had second-guessed going to this festival so many times she practically had whiplash. But both Sameer and Travis texted her several times to make sure she would show up, so she didn't think she could get out of it at this point. Plus, Zahra was looking forward to it.

She finally decided to get her sister's wardrobe advice. Zahra was young, but no one in the house could match her fashion sense. Amira threw on her furry purple bathrobe and headed out of her room to find her sister. But strangely, she found Zahra standing in the basement kitchen.

With Duncan.

Duncan Galahad was in her house. Breathing her air. Taking up so much space, just like he always had.

"Amira!" Zahra said. "Look, Duncan brought me a ukulele!"

Amira tore her gaze from the red beard in the room to see her sister was, indeed, holding a ukulele. A pink, shiny ukulele.

"You didn't have to do that," Amira said to him, barely hearing her own voice over her loudly beating heart.

He looked at Amira, those wide green eyes intense, and without their usual confidence. "I was telling Zahra . . . before . . . I teach kids her age to play the uke. She seemed interested. I have some beginner books here she can learn from, or . . ." His voice trailed off as he awkwardly handed her a small stack of slim music books. Amira took them and placed them on the kitchen counter. A peace offering? Had he brought Zahra a gift to impress Amira?

He looked at Amira, gaze meeting hers. No sparkle of mischief like the day she met him.

"Can I go across the street and show this to Olivia?" Zahra asked. "She has one, too."

"Sure, Squish. Let Nanima know you're going. We're leaving in a couple of hours, okay?" Amira said as her sister was already on her way up the stairs. She looked at Duncan. "Thank you. I'm sure Zahra will enjoy the ukulele."

"It's no problem." He ran his fingers through his hair. "I just got into town. I drove down for a show later today."

"I know. Zahra and I are coming to watch you guys."

"Yeah, Sameer told me. But . . . can we talk first? I can wait while you change."

Amira was still frozen in place, mesmerized by the man in her kitchen. She had expected this conversation to happen in public, after their performance and after she had acclimated herself to being in his presence again. And after she had put some clothes on would have been nice, too.

But he was here now. And maybe it was a good idea to get this difficult talk over with before the sextet performed at the busker festival. *Sextet* . . . god, that sounded so wrong.

She peeled her focus away from his face to look at the rest of Duncan. Dressed in a simple grey T-shirt and jeans, he looked both exactly the same and completely different than the last time she saw him. He looked good. Really good. It was amazing what warmer weather could do for a Canadian's aesthetic appeal. She liked his forearms and biceps on full display. Her gaze swept back to his face and she finally put her finger on what was different.

"Your beard."

He instinctively rubbed the red hairs on his chin. "What about it?"

"It's less . . . bushy. And a lot shorter."

"It's my summer look. Travis is going to kill me for changing it before a show, but it was getting too damn hot. So, can we talk?"

Amira tensed. "Fine. Let's go sit." She walked into the family room.

Duncan followed her. "Don't you need to change?"

She looked down at the bulky floor-length robe. This monstrosity covered more of her than the sundress she was thinking of wearing. And now that he was here, retreating to her room, even just to change, would lead to overthinking.

She wanted to get this over with. "No, it's fine. Sit." Amira took the oversized armchair, watching as Duncan perched tensely on the couch.

"Okay . . ." He ran his hand over the back of his neck. "This is tough . . ."

"I won't bite your head off."

"I know. I owe you an apology. And an explanation," he said.

"Okay," Amira said, fighting to keep her expression neutral. "Go ahead."

He folded his hands in his lap. "Since I left Toronto, I've done a lot of thinking about everything you said to me and Ryan that day, and . . . you were right. All of it. Even though I don't have an issue with you being a Muslim, by not taking a stand against my family and by excusing them, I was just as bad. I'm really sorry. I should have told you about my family before I introduced you, or Zahra, to them. Before I even got involved with you. You deserved honesty from me. But"—he paused—"I never told you why I stay with Ryan and Maddie."

"To help with her, right?"

"Yes. But there is a reason Ryan needs help." He rubbed his hand over his beard. "I did teachers college here in Toronto, and I had every intention of staying in the city when I was done. Jobs are scarce at home, and there was so much more . . . life here. A couple of months before I was done school, my dad called from Omemee to tell me Ryan and Shay went on a bender. Ryan was in jail, and they didn't know where Shay or Maddie were."

Amira's hand shot to her mouth. "Oh my god."

He looked down. "I told you Maddie's mom, Shayna, was a drug addict, but what I didn't make clear is that my brother was actually worse than her back then. They'd been good since Maddie was born and we were optimistic they'd put it behind them for the sake of the baby, but something happened that night. They relapsed, hard. Ryan was arrested, high as a kite, after they destroyed some cars, but Shay disappeared with the baby. Dad thought she may have ended up in Toronto, and he was able to get Ryan to give us some names of her friends in the city when he sobered the next day."

"Oh, Duncan. I'm sorry."

He nodded. "It took me four days to find them. They were in this grimy little apartment. Really, a barely converted garage. Shay had bruises on her arms and legs and open sores on her face. The place smelled like vomit, and there were diapers and formula everywhere. Probably stolen. Shay wasn't wearing a shirt when I walked in—and she was trying to nurse Maddie."

Amira's heart sank. "How old was Maddie?"

"Maybe five months old? I took the baby from her arms and Shay didn't stop me. I think she may have thought I was Ryan. But she was too high to do anything. There was a half-naked man passed out on the bed beside her."

"Shit."

"Yeah. It was a hell of a scene. I should have called the cops, but . . . instead, I walked Maddie to the nearest hospital. She seemed fine, a little dehydrated, but luckily her responses were normal. She happily drank two bottles of formula in the emergency room. They released her into my care after I said I would take her back to Omemee to my parents, but it was the middle of the night. I took her by bus back to my bachelor apartment with the formula and diapers they gave me at the hospital. I stayed up all night with that baby. She cried a bit. I learned how to give her a bottle and change a diaper. Google was my friend. I promised her—no matter what happened—I would always be her uncle Duncan, and I would always do right by her. My parents drove down the next day to pick her up. They were eventually granted custody. They had her until she was three. Ryan got custody back after he went to rehab and had been clean two years."

"Wow." She had known Maddie's mother was a sore spot for Duncan, but Amira never imagined it had been this bad. Amira's heart clenched. Poor Maddie.

"One of the reasons Ryan was granted full custody was because I was living with him, and our parents were nearby. We all testified we intended to play an active role in her life and help Ryan with her. We've all rallied together to raise that girl. Ryan's good now, he's been clean for years, but, I don't know . . . I worry. He relapsed before. Maddie needed stability in her life, and I was determined that the crazy liberal musician uncle was going to be it."

Considering the lengths Amira was willing to go to when her sister was hurting, she now understood Duncan's devotion to Maddie. "So, you stayed there to protect her."

"Yeah. I knew my family was conservative, and a bit racist. But . . ." He looked down. "I didn't really think it was a big deal. What you said that day—that to me, it was just politics—you were right. My family had been through a lot, and yeah, maybe sometimes I didn't want to rock the boat with Ryan, but . . . it was just an abstract thing, you know? They didn't like Muslims, or immigrants, or gay people, but I wasn't like them. It was fine, a lot of families have different politics."

"But this isn't just politics, it's hatred," Amira said. "You get that being a recovering addict is not an excuse for racism, right?"

Duncan cringed. "I know. Ryan and I don't see eye to eye on a lot of things, but I had no idea he was this bad. I didn't know about his online stuff. He never says that extreme crap to me. Probably because he knows I'd rip him a new one if he did."

Amira blinked a few times, then exhaled. "I am sorry your brother has issues with addiction. And I get why you stay with him." She understood better than she did before. After all, she was still living with Nanima, and Nanima hadn't exactly changed her tune either. But Duncan should have told her about Ryan. "But I don't understand how you could have kept it from me after I told you what I went through."

Duncan was silent a moment. "I'm sorry," he said. He looked at her face briefly before looking down at his hands again. "I was afraid if I told you about my family, you'd hate me. I saw the way you reacted to my friend Dale that night, and . . . I have no excuse. I *should* have talked to you about it. But . . ." He lowered his voice. "The more time we spent together, I . . . was crazy about you, and I didn't want you to have another thing to hate about me."

Amira blinked. She hadn't exactly been subtle about her disdain for Duncan at the beginning. And that night when they met Dale, Amira had egged the guy on a bit. Duncan may not have realized how seriously she took these things.

If Duncan *had* told her about Ryan, what would she have done? She would have been pissed off at Duncan, that's what would have happened. She probably *would* have held his family's views against him.

But she would have been able to protect her sister from it better. And she would have been able to talk to him about his family's prejudice. She would have helped him see that these issues were bigger than he saw them to be. And then she would have fallen in love with him anyway. Duncan was a good man. A great man. Caring, generous, and understanding.

But at least her eyes would have been open about what their future held.

"I don't blame you at all, Amira. I was a coward," he continued. "I should have told you before getting involved with you. I never imagined Maddie would do something like that to Zahra. But . . . I hope now you understand why I live with them. I'm sorry."

"You came here looking for forgiveness?"

His eyes met hers, and they were the sincerest she had ever seen on him. "No. Like you told Ryan, you have no obligation to forgive me. I don't want you to. But I still needed to apologize."

Amira watched his face for several long seconds, unsure of what to say. "What *do* you want from me, then?"

Eyes pleading, he shrugged. "I don't know. Maybe your friendship back? Maybe your help and guidance on how to keep my promise to Maddie while not excusing Ryan anymore? I . . ." He trailed off, looking at his fingers. "I'm moving out."

"What?"

"I got that music teacher job. I'm moving to Peterborough."

Amira caught her breath. "Congratulations. But . . . you're not moving out because of this, are you? Doesn't Maddie still need you?"

"Yes, she does. But I'll only be twenty minutes away. I need to get out of that town. Put some distance between me and my family. But I'll still be in Maddie's life. Peterborough is bigger—I'll be able to expose her to so much there." He paused awhile before speaking quietly. "Plus, I want to be able to have my friends visit me. Sameer and Travis, Barrington, and even you?"

She thought for a bit before answering. "We can't exactly pick up where we left off."

"I know. And we can't start over either."

"No. There's no magical button to press that can make me forget."

"No," he said, looking down at his feet. "You're right." He stood up. "Thank you for listening to me, though. I really appreciate that, but I'll go now."

He started to walk towards the door.

"Wait, Duncan."

He turned back.

"Come here," she said softly.

He walked towards her before falling to his knees, hands folded in his lap. His eyes were fathomless, deep-green chasms swirling with regret and pain.

She blinked, feeling a sharp prick behind her eyeballs. When she looked at him again, the same glassiness was reflected in his eyes.

This was impossible. How could they both feel so much after so short a time?

"Why is this so hard?" she whispered. "We barely knew each other. Ending it should have been easier."

"Nothing's been easy since the moment I met you," he said. "You've tied me in knots since you sat across from me that day on the train."

"You tied yourself up for me—once."

A small smile snuck onto his face as his pupils widened. He chuckled lightly. "You always made me laugh. I miss that."

She reached out and touched his cheek, his soft beard tickling her hand. He leaned into her touch.

She closed her eyes. She wanted so much to bend down and rub her cheek against his. To kiss those soft lips until they could drown out all the culture and expectations, and families and prejudices. She wished all of it was just noise that they could ignore.

"I don't want to walk away from you again," she whispered. "But I don't know how to walk forward."

She lowered her head with a sigh, their foreheads meeting with a light touch. "I can't abandon them, I'm sorry," he said.

She sat up straight again, breaking all contact between them. "I haven't asked you to."

"I know. But I'm not going to let this slide anymore either. Maddie needs me more than ever. She needs someone to take her to the ballet, to let her taste goat biryani, and show her there is a whole world outside her little corner. I can't change my brother, or my parents, by cutting off contact with them. I want to *show* them what real love is."

Amira raised her head as a sharp prickle hit her sinuses. Duncan rested his hands on her knees, pressing the soft fleece of her robe against her sensitive skin.

He locked his gaze on her. "Amira, I think . . . no, I *know* I've never felt like this about anyone before. I can't forget you, and I've been doing nothing but kicking my own ass for screwing up my chances. You're right—we can't start over. We can't forget. I don't deserve another chance, but I'd like one anyway."

They were so different. There were huge barriers between them. Religion. Culture. Career choices. Geographical distance, too. Not to mention both of them knew exactly how to piss the other off. It would be an uphill battle, but maybe their perfect harmony inside would overcome all the differences.

But *hate*. That was a bigger problem. Being with Duncan would mean fighting against more hate. Did she want to do that anymore?

Amira squeezed her lips together. Maybe she just needed a new approach. She had tried fighting with anger. She had tried fighting with avoidance. None of that had worked—hate still destroyed her.

Maybe it was time to start fighting with love.

And who knows? There was always that job in Peterborough.

She pressed closer to him, nuzzling his cheek before sliding off the armchair to her knees in front of him. He sighed as his arms wrapped around her waist, locking them together.

He held her tightly, his lips finding her neck. "Are you sure?"

She inhaled deeply. That clean smell of soap, beard oil, and Duncan; she hadn't realized how much she missed a smell until she had it back.

"Yes. We're going to fight for us."

She could feel him smile against her as he nestled into her. "I really hope you aren't going to say we should take it nice and slow to start . . ." He mouthed kisses along her neck, gently nudging her bathrobe open in the process.

She giggled. "When have I ever been anything resembling nice?" she asked, stretching her neck to allow him better access.

He laughed, the deep rumble reverberating through her. "God, I've missed you." He began pawing at her robe, trying to get it out of the way.

She laughed, feeling light-headed. "Don't you have a gig soon? I'm sure you have to be there before me."

"I have an hour."

She smiled as she caught his mouth in a kiss . . . a deep, hard, long kiss. The beard was shorter, but it still tickled her face. His strong body still felt like home. She was going to stay here forever.

He finally pulled away and murmured, "Can we go to your room?"

She smiled as she stood. "Yes, we have time." Amira untied her bathrobe as she walked, and then pulled the soft fleece belt out of its loops. She held it out to him. "We're going to need this, farm boy . . ."

He smiled wryly, green eyes focused on her. Seeing her. "Lead the way, Buttercup."

ACKNOWLEDGEMENTS

I've been a story creator all my life. My daydreams were bloated with complicated plot twists and fleshed-out characters, but those tales never left the comfort of my mind. It was only three years ago that I finally started writing down the stories swirling through my head, and it's simply amazing that today I am now writing the acknowledgements for my first novel. I am so grateful for the opportunity to thank those who helped me reach this dream.

First, to my editor at HarperCollins Canada, Jennifer Lambert, who not only took a chance on my silly little book about a bunch of singers but who also saw my vision for this story better than even I could. I am endlessly grateful for her guidance and kindness. Thank you to Iris Tupholme and the entire team at HarperCollins Canada. I am so happy *The Chai Factor* has so much support behind it.

Thank you to my agent, Rachel Brooks, whose editorial advice and determination to find this book its perfect home were invaluable. I am so happy to have such a talented partner in my writing career. And thank you to Beth Phelan for the amazing #DVPit program, which allowed me to connect with literary agents who not only support but champion diversity in publishing.

ACKNOWLEDGEMENTS

Thank you to those who helped me with the little details in this book, including the beta readers and critique friends who looked at early drafts and queries. Thank you to Sonali Dev and Falguni Kothari for helping translate my words into beautiful Hindi poetry for my favourite scene. And thank you to Zoe York for coming up with my book's fabulous title over a Thai dinner. Thank you to my brilliant friend Aye Nyein San, who helped me sound like I knew what the hell I was talking about with regards to engineering and academics. And thank you to Nika Rylski, who facilitated a workshop on writing romantic comedies for Toronto Romance Writers, during which I first jotted down the premise for this book.

As an introverted South Asian Muslim, I wasn't sure there was a place for me in the romance industry. I'd like to thank the 2017 board of directors of the Romance Writers of America, and especially Tessa Dare, for not only making sure I knew I belonged, but for figuratively pulling up a chair to the table for me and welcoming me to the national conference.

To Roselle Lim, my release-day sister from another mister, and the person I turn to when publishing makes me anxious, thank you. I can't think of another person, or book, that I'd rather share this day with. And thank you to Alisa Kwitney, the absolute best conference roommate in existence, and to Laura Heffernan, for always being my biggest cheerleader.

To the fabulous writers in my Twitter chat group: Tif Marcelo, Sheryl Nantus, A.S. Fenichel, Naima Simone, Mina Beckett, Laura Brown, Juliette Cross, Robin Lovett, and Mona Shroff. You ladies are always there for me, and whether we're talking about books or butts, I know I can count on you for laughs and unconditional support.

ACKNOWLEDGEMENTS

To my amazing peers at Toronto Romance Writers, I feel so lucky to have found my local writers' clan so early. And an extra thank you to Jackie Lau, Fallon DeMornay, and Alana Delacroix, who I can always count on when I need a laugh, a hug, a sounding board, or someone to share a drink with to celebrate successes.

Thank you to the bravest and most loving people I know, my parents, Nazir and Shahida Pirani. Their steady support through whatever new endeavour I take on has been such a blessing. And thank you to the rest of my family and friends who have gifted me with so much support and encouragement, especially my sister, Alya, my mother-in-law, Judi, and my sister-in-law, Meredith.

To my inspiration and my biggest joys, my spectacularly awesome kids, Khalil and Anissa. Thank you for being my live-in brainstorming buddies, and thank you for putting up with a few too many frozen pizza dinners.

And finally, to my husband, Tony. We are not the characters in this book, but I can't deny that I was inspired by our connection. A city girl and a country boy of different races, religions, and tolerances to cold weather. We've thrived for twenty-two years thanks to unending encouragement, support, and, best of all, lots of laughter. This one's for you, babe.